IMMINENT DANGER

Dee J. Adams

ISBN-13: 978-0-9892452-3-4

Edited by Melissa Johnson
Cover Art by Croco Designs
Interior Formatting by Author E.M.S.

Published in the United States of America.

Dedication

This one is for my brother, Malcolm, and sister, Eileen. I'm glad I have you guys as backup. Thanks for being an awesome safety net.

And for Mom and Dad... I miss you both a ton.

Acknowledgments

There are a few people who need serious thanking. The first thank you goes to my medic to the stars, Dan Lora. Dan patched me up on set more than a few times and he was so patient with all my questions about first responders. He's one of my favorite people and if you stay tuned, you'll see an appearance from him in an upcoming book!

I have to thank Sara Gonzales for answering so many of my dance/dancer questions. She's amazingly talented and gave me a great picture of a dancer's life.

Thank you to the ladies who keep me sane and make sure I stay on track with my stories. I don't know where I'd be without Kate Willoughby and Lynne Marshall. You won't find smarter, funnier or more wonderful women anywhere!

Speaking of smart, funny and wonderful, those words also describe my awesome editor, Melissa Johnson. She makes my stories stronger and therefore better. I couldn't do it without her. Thank you, Melissa!

Another amazing woman who does more for me than I deserve is Julie Goldstein, my good luck charm, publicist and most importantly, friend. Thank you, Julie, for all you do. I am forever yours.

I couldn't do any of this without the support of my terrific family. Thanks to Sean and Katelyn for your never-ending love and hugs.

As usual, any mistakes are my own.

Chapter One

"Coming through," Abbey called. The farther she jogged down the large cavernous Sports Center hallway, the more it emptied out as people rushed toward the stage for the sold out concert. She'd never felt more like a salmon traveling upstream. Everyone wanted to see Seger Hughes when he made his entrance. Including her. Unfortunately, she doubted she'd get back in time.

Her boss, Julie Fraser, had accidentally left the courtside Lakers tickets she'd promised to Seger in an envelope in the car, so being the all-around gofer/get-it-done-girl, Abbey had to retrieve the tickets. Abbey never put anything off for fear it might come back to bite her in the ass later. She had *do it now, do it right* mentality and didn't expect that to change.

She really had no right to be pissy about this unexpected run, since she hadn't paid for the concert tickets anyway. A ton of perks came with the job of being an assistant to an Oscar and Emmy winning actress, but with those perks came the reality that as long as she accepted them, she was on the job, which meant unexpected things cropped up...like making runs to the car for a forgetful actress.

The credentials around Abbey's neck gave her all-access to the venue, so getting in and out wasn't the problem. Doing it as fast as humanly possible so she could see Seger open the show was the problem. She didn't want to miss her favorite song, *Always Believe*.

Of course, getting back faster also put her in Blake St. John's vicinity for that much longer, but she was willing to put up with him for the sake of seeing Seger live. She rolled her eyes at the thought as she jogged down the now almost empty hallway. A few late concert-goers—all VIPs—straggled in.

She had to be honest with herself about Blake. Putting up with him wasn't the problem. It was putting up with her pounding heart and sweaty palms every time she was around him that bothered her. Blake had admitted to falling *head over ass in love* with her the minute he met her. She seriously doubted *that*.

Now that Julie had married Blake's boss, Troy, it seemed as if they were forever in each other's company.

Perfect.

Not so much.

Abbey picked up her pace as the end of the corridor grew closer. All she had to do was get out the door, get to the car, grab the envelope and run like hell back to see the concert opening.

At the door, she threw her momentum against the heavy metal and shoved it open to the dusky evening. She nearly barreled over the guard watching the area from the outside.

"Oh my, God! I'm so sorry," she said to the tall, dark-skinned man with a tight Afro haircut, bushy beard and *event staff* stenciled on his T-shirt. She hoped her apology would take the stink eye out of his angry face. His quick once-over sent chills down her back and his lecherous smile gave her the impetus to keep moving. "Really! I'm sorry," she said jogging backward toward the car. "I'm in a hurry!"

He didn't wave or say a word, just watched her go, and Abbey turned and ran full out for the car, her VIP badge bouncing against her chest, her lungs heaving as the hot air of a Southern California summer night made her sticky.

The car wasn't parked that far away because Julie was a VIP after all, and that did afford her a good amount of luxuries in her life. But the cars that had parked on either side of Troy's black BMW—a mint green Jaguar on one side and a white convertible Mercedes on the other—had boxed in his car, so getting in the door without scratching anybody's paint job became an exercise in sucking in air and sliding sideways inside the passenger door.

Abbey took two seconds to get her breath as she leaned her head against the seat rest. God, she needed a vacation. Or a dance job. Either one would make her deliriously happy.

With her two seconds gone, Abbey looked around the seat for the envelope containing the Lakers tickets. Not in the glove compartment, not on the floor, not under the seat. She checked the center console. Bingo. Hallelujah.

She sucked in another breath to exit the car then started running back to the concert. She slowed as she neared the same door she'd come out of a few minutes ago. No security guard in sight. God, what if the door was locked? What if she had to run all the way around to a different entrance to get back inside?

So much for seeing Seger's opening song.

Glancing around for the guard, Abbey grabbed the handle. Before she had a chance to pull, it blew wide open and a man tore out moving at hyper-speed. Her heart nearly exploded as they collided. Impact knocked them both down and he cursed as he sprawled on top of her. The panic in his dark eyes registered as fast as the bloody cut on his cheek. Had that happened just now?

"Are you o—"

"Move," he finally shouted as he scrambled to his feet. That seemed excessively rude since he'd been the one to knock her down. The guy wasn't much bigger than her, mostly bald with an average face. The next second, he was up and running, and just as Abbey got to her feet, the closed door crashed open again. At least this time she had enough distance behind the door to keep from getting bowled over by the two guys who came running out.

Her pulse raced as she watched the two men tackle the man who'd knocked her down. Abbey took a step toward them, her hand against her pounding heart.

One guy threw a hard punch and the man underneath screamed. The fear and agony in the sound made her cringe.

"Run! Get help! Hurry!" he screamed.

What? Wasn't he the bad guy if he was being chased? Especially since one of the men on top of him was the same guard wearing the event-staff T-shirt?

Both men looked back and seemed to see her for the first time. The new guy had a big Fu-Manchu mustache, sunglasses, baseball cap and a giant knife glinting red and wet in the parking lot light. Seeing that—plus the deadly look on both their faces— dried up every bit of spit in Abbey's mouth.

Run! Get help! Hurry! The words flashed in her brain as the danger hit her head on.

"Get her!" the man with the knife yelled.

The black man pulled a gun from a shoulder holster as he rose to his feet.

Fear strangled her heart. *No fucking way!*

She ran to the door and yanked on the handle. Her shoulder nearly came out of its socket when the door didn't budge. Locked! *What the fuck?* Abbey glanced back as she took off running along the side of the building, with the black man on her tail and the other guy leaning over the injured man, still lying on the pavement.

Holy shit!

Abbey flew over the cement, her pulse beating hard and loud between her ears as she raced along the curve of the wall to the front of the building. The cars on her left would provide a better hiding place, but she needed people. She needed to get lost in a crowd.

But what if this guy didn't care about a crowd? What if she was leading a maniac into a crowded concert because of what she'd just witnessed? What had she witnessed? A stabbing! *Ohgodohgod!* The man had screamed because he'd been knifed, not punched. The blood on the knife had been his blood!

Sweat popped out of every pore and the overhead parking lights blurred as she continued to haul ass as fast as possible.

She dared a glance behind her. The man was catching up and Abbey was breathing too hard to find her voice. A pop-pop sounded behind her and she waited for the bullets to hit. They didn't. She would've screamed for all she was worth if she had a second to take in extra air. She checked behind her one last time as she came to the edge of the building and cut right.

A brick wall stopped her. Strong arms came around her and this time, the scream dying to get out, let loose.

"Abbey! Abbey! Jesus, it's me. What's wrong?"

Wild eyed, Abbey focused enough to make out Blake, all six foot three inches of lean muscle and dark auburn hair. His stunning blue eyes were filled with concern. She wanted to leap into his arms for protection, wanted to take a second and enjoy the relief of having help, but the more seconds that ticked by, the closer the man came. Just because she didn't see him, didn't mean he wasn't there.

"Run!" she screamed, yanking him back toward the stadium

doors. "Hurry! Run!" No other words formed on her parched tongue. Pulling air into her fried lungs hurt. "Gun! He has a gun! Inside!" There, that seemed to help because Blake was pushing her ahead of him as they sprinted into the building, flashing their badges.

"Get inside! Everyone!" Abbey yelled to the event staff and public still walking to their seats. "He has a gun! There's a man with a gun!" Her shout got everyone moving in all directions. Event staff closed the doors as security drew weapons and urged people away from the glass doors.

With armed security closing in, Abbey finally slowed as she backed up toward one of the alleyways leading into the concert. Peeking around Blake's shoulder, she kept her eyes on the door the whole time, waiting for the man chasing her to come into view.

As the seconds ticked by into minutes, as the security slowly closed in on the doors, clearly intending to venture outside, Blake disengaged Abbey's tight grip on his hand and pulled her against him.

"It's okay. You're okay. I think we're safe."

Safe. The word, the relief, triggered a release. She refused to cry and her breathing got ragged as she fought back tears and buried her face in his soft black T-shirt. There was no denying the absolute certainty that she'd barely avoided a brutal death. She just needed a minute to regroup.

"It's okay," he murmured into her hair. "I've got you. I've got you." His arms wrapped around her tight and Abbey squeezed him close, held on like her life depended on it. As the possibilities seeped in, she couldn't manage to breathe.

Blake pulled away and she needed his strength too much for that. She wanted the comfort he was so good at providing. "Abbey, look at me," he ordered.

But she didn't want to face him. She especially didn't want him to see her so weak. It seemed that's how he always saw her. When she was at her most defenseless. She hated it.

"Abbey!" He barked her name again and this time Abbey met his gaze. True concern clouded his gorgeous blue eyes as he held her face in his big hands. "Breathe," he told her. "Breathe with me. C'mon. In and out. You know the drill."

The first time they'd met, she'd had a panic attack in a broken elevator and he'd talked her through it. Her sister and parents had always been the only people capable of calming her down from an attack before then. But Blake had a way about him. A confidence. He was a couple of years younger than her, but seemed to have an old soul that talked to her.

Abbey just refused to listen.

"Abbey!" Blake said sharply. "Look at me. Concentrate."

She blinked, focused and followed his lead, taking long breaths and releasing them slowly until she had a rhythm, until the air flowed into her lungs the way it was supposed to.

"There you go. That's my girl." Blake wrapped his arms around her again and Abbey let him. She not only let him, she burrowed deep into his chest and breathed in his woodsy fresh scent. He always smelled so good and avoiding him had become harder and harder over the months since her their bosses had married.

She didn't get nearly enough time in Blake's arms before fresh chaos erupted in the form of police invading the lobby. Though it seemed the danger had passed, now they had the aftermath.

Blake let her go and pulled out his cell phone from his back pocket.

Abbey crossed her arms and forced herself to stop shaking. "Who are you texting?"

"Troy."

She bobbed her head. Good. Troy would know what to do. He was one of the best private investigators in the city and he knew dozens of officers in multiple stations. Abbey moved toward the police who swarmed the area. Two uniformed officers came her way. "Tell him to hurry," she said over her shoulder.

"I did." Blake caught up to her, put his arm around her shoulders and Abbey didn't try to pull away.

Chapter Two

The simple fact that Abbey let Blake touch her told him she was freaked out. Of course, the place was still buzzing with energy. People clustered in groups talking and pointing, and police converged nearby.

Blake hadn't seen her this anxious since the day he'd met her. He'd never forget that day. Never forget the smile on her face when she'd thanked him for holding the elevator and never forget the panic and fear a few minutes later when that same elevator had nearly dropped them.

In general, he'd never met a cooler chick than Abbey Washington. Cool in every sense of the word. She had style, grace and she was a master at giving the cold shoulder. He'd been certain they'd made a connection in the hour they were stuck in that elevator. But he'd never been more wrong. Even when he found out who she was months later and they ended up spending a serious amount of time together because of their bosses, she'd just pretended that he didn't exist.

What the hell was a guy supposed to think? Besides, he didn't want to be with someone who didn't want to be with him. He wasn't an idiot. Even if that person was as fucking beautiful as Abbey. God, every time he looked at her he found something else to drool over. He loved the smoky green of her eyes, the color of her light mocha skin, the long dark eyelashes that fluttered when she blinked and the smooth perfection of her shoulders when she wore a little strappy top. Most of all, he went bat-shit crazy for her full lips. Lips that he'd been dying to kiss for more months than was healthy.

Okay, so the world had a ton of beautiful women and he

didn't want to be like every other guy who chased after her. But watching her over the past year, seeing how much she cared for her boss, the way she went above and beyond her job to make sure Julie had everything she needed, made keeping his distance from her that much harder.

Jesus, the way she held onto him now, with her arm around his waist, clutching his shirt like she belonged to him, like she wanted him with her, sent every caveman cell in his system on *protect*.

And *mine*.

Two cops approached and Blake gave Abbey's shoulder a reassuring squeeze. One uniformed officer packed a solid beer gut and buzz cut hair. The other, a younger female with her dark hair pulled into a tight bun stood just as tall at about six feet and looked police-academy fit.

"I'm Officer Holland," the heavy-set one said. "This is my partner, Officer Brinkman." He pulled a small notepad from his back pocket. "Miss, are you the one that—"

"You have to hurry," Abbey said, pulling out of Blake's grasp and moving toward the door. "There's a man out by the parking lot. He was attacked. Stabbed. He needs help!"

"Whoa, whoa," the cop said, "Stay right there. "Where is this guy?" he asked while thumbing the walkie-talkie on his shoulder.

"Near the artist entrance. I watched him get tackled by two guys, then one stabbed him. You have to hurry!" She started moving again and the female cop reached out and snagged her arm.

"Slow down," she said. "We need to make sure it's safe out there. We've got officers who'll find the man if he's there."

The other cop gave some orders and directions over the walkie-talkie.

"*If* he's there? Where else would he be?" Abbey lifted her arms like she didn't see any other options. "Trust me, he wasn't walking away from what I witnessed. The knife was…" She swallowed and shivered, looked to him for help.

"You okay?" She nodded, but she still had that freaked out look in her eyes.

"And who are you?" the same cop asked, his brows pulling together in the middle.

Blake took a measured breath. "My name's Blake St. John. This is Abbey Washington."

The cop took notes in the small pad. "And you two are..." he gestured between them, "...together?"

Abbey took a step away from him and Blake wanted to punch the guy.

"No," she said. "Our bosses are married so I guess you could say we work together." She kept glancing toward the doors, craning her neck like the people chasing her might burst through any second.

"What exactly happened?" the second cop asked. She kept a sharp eye on Abbey.

Abbey ran her hand over her straight shoulder-length hair and took a deep breath. "I was about to enter the back door near the artist entrance and a man flew threw just before I opened it. We bumped into each other and went down. I noticed a cut on his face and I thought it happened when we hit each other. But then he got up and started running. Two guys came out a second later and started chasing him. They tackled him near the first row of cars at that entrance. One of them stabbed him."

"Stabbed him?" The first cop said, looking up from his notes. "Are you sure?"

"Yes." Abbey nodded. "I heard him scream. I saw the knife. He yelled at me to run and get help. I tried to go in the same door, but it was locked so I started running. One of the guys pulled out a gun and started chasing me. He fired at me."

"Can you tell me how many shots you heard?" Brinkman asked.

"I don't know. Two. Maybe three. I'm not sure," Abbey replied.

The cops glanced at each other and Officer Brinkman stepped away and spoke into the microphone on her shoulder.

"So they had a knife and a gun?" The older cop busily scribbled in his pad.

"Yes. Both. I didn't stick around to see what else they had hidden in their pockets. I ran like hell." She swallowed and started shaking. "I'll never forget that man's face as long as I live." She took an unsteady breath.

Blake didn't give a shit what Abbey or the cops thought and

wrapped his arm around her again. She didn't stop him and the big cop lifted a bushy eyebrow.

"Did they find him yet? He's got to be there. I don't think he could walk."

"Find who yet?"

Blake glanced over his shoulder to see Troy and Julie coming closer. Good deal. Troy would know exactly how to handle this. As usual, their appearance caused a stir with onlookers, not just because they made a hell of a striking couple, but Troy's wife was mega-famous. Though his boss could've been a model or actor with his rugged good looks, he had always been a private man. Learning to live in the public eye was the price Troy paid for being married to the woman he loved.

"What's going on?" Julie asked, landing at Abbey's side.

Abbey pulled away from him again, but Blake refused to be crushed by the abandonment.

"What happened?" Julie eyed Blake and he glanced at Troy. Abbey might be leery of saying anything since Julie was a victim of a bullet wound a year ago.

"Whoa. Everybody slow down," the first cop said as his partner returned. "And I need you two to—" He'd lifted a hand to gesture to Troy and Julie to back off then did a double take. "Are you Julie Fraser?" His gaze widened a bit in the usual reaction when people came face to face with her. Nicknamed "America's Sweetheart," Julie had become Hollywood royalty at a young age. Her honey blond hair and striking blue eyes turned heads wherever she went, but it was her down-to-earth personality and sense of humor that kept people coming back for more.

"Yes, I am. Abbey works for me. What happened?" Julie asked. "Are you all right?" She held Abbey at arms' length and gave her a thorough once over.

"If you don't mind, I need to ask her a few more questions." The officer focused on Abbey before his walkie-talkie squawked and he lifted it from his belt.

"No sign of anyone here," a voice said.

"That's impossible," Abbey insisted. "He was there a few minutes ago...at the artist entrance. I'm sure of it." She pointed in the direction she'd come from and the second cop used her walkie-talkie. As this took place, more and more black-and-white cruisers pulled up to the front entrance.

Blake hated the fear in Abbey's eyes. He liked her smiling and carefree. Not that she lived her life always smiling and carefree, especially when he was around. She guarded herself more than anyone he'd ever known. Even his twin brother. But he'd caught her smiling and laughing a few times when she didn't know he was around.

She wreaked havoc on a guy's ego.

"It's taking forever," she said. "Did they find him? Those men have to be long gone by now with all the police cars here."

The second officer's walkie squawked. "On further inspection, we've got blood, but no body."

Her eyes went wide. "What? He has to be there! I saw him. He was on the ground."

"Let's go take a look," the officer said, letting Abbey take them to the artist entrance with an escort of five officers around them, all with weapons drawn. Abbey's gaze darted across the whole area and Blake took it all in just as his boss did. Troy never missed a thing.

It took a couple of minutes to walk around the building and as they neared the exact spot, Abbey got more and more agitated.

"This is it," she said, picking up her pace. "We collided right outside that door at the end on the left." She rushed ahead, leading the way, because it was just like Abbey to want to help someone. "And they tackled him over there, by those cars." She pointed toward a row of cars that included a red Mustang, a black Mercedes convertible and two white Escalades. Parking lights overhead had turned on as the evening got darker.

The officers exchanged a glance and followed her, just as other officers wearing body armor came out from between two other dark SUVs.

"Did you get him?" Abbey asked the officers. She pushed past them.

"Nobody to get, but we found blood," one said. "Which direction were you running? We'll start searching for bullets."

"That way." Abbey pointed toward the main entrance. "I stayed along the curve of the wall." Shaking her head, she moved forward. "Oh my God. They must have taken him." She looked around, clearly searching for something. Or someone. She swallowed and Blake saw her chest to rise and fall with labored breaths. She was about to have another panic attack.

Blake moved right in front of her. "It's okay. Abbey, it's okay." He set his hands on her shoulders and searched for a reason, any reason that might justify the missing man. "Maybe someone else came and helped him. Maybe he crawled out and got help." More likely, she was right and the guys who knifed him took him and were long gone.

"We know something happened," one of the new cops said. "We've got blood."

She was already shaking her head. "They took him," she murmured. She turned to the group of cops staring at her. "They took him. He told me to run. Told me to bring help fast and I didn't."

"It was kind of hard with a man shooting at you and chasing you," Julie reminded her.

"I'm guessing he was still alive or they'd probably have left him," Troy replied. He'd been listening to the conversation, watching Abbey and scanning the scene. A man of few words, he said the one thing that everyone was thinking. "Either way, the guy is not in a good place."

Kim Jacobs picked up her luggage at the LAX baggage claim and rolled her large Gucci suitcase out to the curb among the other travelers arriving in Los Angeles. Families, couples and singles all jostled for space as they moved toward the curb or crosswalk. The stench of exhaust fumes smacked her nostrils and added a nasty layer to the uncomfortable heat as dusk fell on the City of Angels.

She'd needed a change of scenery from Indiana. She'd never planned to live there, so the last few years had been a battle to stay out of obligation to her business partner. This trip to L.A. provided not only a much needed vacation—albeit a working one—but the chance to decide if maybe she required another life change. She'd already made two in the past decade.

"Hope you didn't screw yourself with this favor," she muttered to herself as she stopped at the curb. Agreeing to help her old college roommate's husband wade through his financial issues had put her on the clock. Especially since her best friend back in Indiana was pregnant and due to have a baby in a few weeks.

It seemed everyone around her was married or pregnant and she was still single and lonely. She'd had a feeling years ago that her move to Indiana from Chicago would do her no good and she'd been right. But that's where the business had led her, so that's where she'd gone. There went another few years down the toilet. She was quickly heading down that road to thirty with no prospects in sight.

A sleek black limousine slid to a stop in front of her. A cute chauffeur with steel gray hair got out and walked around the car. His wrinkle-free suit fit over broad shoulders and his healthy tan said he did more than sit in his car all day. His body and hair color didn't match at all and made it hard to discern his age. He could've been anywhere between thirty-five and fifty-five.

"Miss Jacobs, I can take your bags," he said.

Kim held on tight. Stephanie hadn't mentioned sending a car for her. "Thanks, but I'm waiting for—" Wait. How would he know her name unless...

The back passenger door opened and a leggy brunette got out of the car, a smile from ear to ear as she laughed. Her slinky black trousers fell over four-inch black Jimmy Choos. The low-cut cream top exposed a cleavage only money could buy and the tone figure under the whole outfit indicated a woman who worked hard to keep herself in great shape. "You better lighten up, sister," she said. "You're in SoCal now."

Kim relaxed and grinned as she let the chauffeur take her bags. "I should've known it was you." She hugged her first college roommate, Stephanie Wyncott, then stepped back. "Wow. Looks like being married to a millionaire agrees with you." Kim really wasn't too jealous since Stephanie's husband was about thirty years older than her. As much as she'd wanted to be in the lap of luxury, she wasn't willing to waste the best years of her life on a guy who might not be able to get it up more than once a week.

"Life is okay," Stephanie said, pulling back. She shook her head as she assessed Kim. "But you. You haven't changed a day since college. I see you still dress for a party no matter where you are. You're gorgeous."

Kim waved away the comment and dismissed her own black skirt, high heels and silk top. Fashion was one of the reasons she and Stephanie had bonded so quickly. They both liked to look their best. "Thank you. It takes one to know one."

"You know it, girl. C'mon, get in the car. I'm dying to catch up."

Kim slid into the black leather seat as the chauffer closed her bags in the trunk. Across from her sat another seat for two and adjacent to that was a mini bar and small fridge. "This is nice. I didn't know you had a personal chauffer."

"I don't. This is Fido," she said as the man climbed back behind the wheel. "Fido, this is my old buddy, Kim Jacobs."

"Nice to officially meet you, Miss Jacobs. I hope you have a nice stay here. The weather should be perfect." His light gray-blue gaze met hers from the rearview mirror. Kim hadn't met too many limo drivers, but she doubted they had as much sex appeal as this guy.

"The weather is always perfect," Stephanie said as she slid into the limo next to Kim. "I call Fido anytime I need a ride. There is no one else I trust more. No Fido, no limo. Besides, I hate driving in the traffic."

"Must be nice," Kim murmured. Although business had certainly been better the last few years, she wasn't anywhere near the limo stage, and as time marched on, she didn't see it happening in her future either.

"The good with the bad," Stephanie said softly and Kim caught the sadness behind her smile. "Speaking of bad, I'm still upset that I missed your parents' funeral."

The usual pain that accompanied any mention of her parents stabbed Kim's heart. "You were out of the country. It's okay. I know you would've been there if you could."

"Are you doing okay?" Stephanie asked, concern evident in her tone and eyes.

"Yeah. You know what they say... Time heals." Didn't matter that Kim was an adult, it had taken her a while to deal with being an orphan. The unexpected loss of her parents three years ago had been a giant shock.

Stephanie sighed. "I know, but it still sucks. I'm so sorry. And thank you again for coming to help us with this money mess. Carl has been stressing big time not knowing what's happening. He's really hoping you can sort this out."

"I'm happy to do what I can. I guess I'm not sure why you wanted *me*," Kim said.

"Because I trust you." Stephanie's gaze said it all. "I've never trusted our accountant and only now is Carl beginning to see why."

"So he just quit returning your calls?" Kim asked.

"Pretty much. Carl has so much going on that he needs someone he can trust to go through all the books. I told him that person is you. I know I'm pulling you away from your own business, but you kind of sounded like you needed a change so…"

"It's okay. I did. Do. Need the change." She'd been restless in Indiana and with what Stephanie and Carl offered to pay her for helping them through this issue, she could afford the time away. Her partner, Chelsea Rivers, understood her need to go. Chelsea's own life had turned out perfectly. She had the adoring, gorgeous husband, with a child on the way and she wanted the same for her best friend. Kim just worried that maybe she missed the boat when it came to love. She'd dated and slept with more men than any woman should, all in the hopes of bagging Mr. Right on the Money.

She'd learned her lesson the hard way. Giving herself had only whittled away her self- esteem. When she looked in the mirror, she no longer saw the blonde bombshell she used to be. She saw a foolish idiot who needed to grow up and take charge of her life.

The drive into Holmby Hills passed by in a blur of palm trees, smog and the setting sun as Stephanie caught Kim up on life in general. Aside from emails and speaking to each other a few times a year, they'd only seen each other once, at Chelsea's wedding four years ago.

"I can't believe that girl is going to have a baby," Stephanie said, crossing her legs and shifting in the plush leather seats.

"Yeah, what happened to us? You and I used to be the first to do everything."

"That's the truth." Stephanie's smile turned melancholy. "I was the first to get married."

"Twice," They both said in unison. And laughed. Stephanie's first marriage had lasted all of forty-seven days. Viva Las Vegas.

"Speaking of marriage. How's Carl?" Kim asked. "Besides stressed."

"That pretty much covers it," Stephanie said with a humorless chuckle. "He'll be better knowing you're getting to the bottom of things."

"This sounds very intriguing," Kim admitted.

"Nothing intriguing about it. Carl just wants to know what's up with his money."

"Can't blame the man for that."

The scenery shifted from heavy freeway traffic to office buildings then to a residential neighborhood with houses bigger than her condo building in Indiana. Thirty minutes after they picked her up, the car pulled through huge white wrought iron gates. Kim's jaw nearly hit the limo floor as she surveyed the huge estate. The two level monolith stretched long and deep with park-like terraced grounds in the front, and a long paved road that led to a giant circular driveway with a massive fountain in the middle. Stephanie had sent a few pictures when they moved in a couple of years ago, but they didn't do the place justice.

Kim knew Stephanie had married into money, but she hadn't realized the amount of money.

"I see business has been good for Carl."

Stephanie nodded. "It has. And it keeps him very busy."

Kim read between the sad lines. Stephanie was lonely. It was in her eyes and in the tone of her voice. "What keeps you busy?" Kim asked. "You could go back to school and get your arts degree. I don't see anything stopping you."

"School?" Stephanie laughed. "At this point?" She shook her head. "I don't think so. I've been volunteering at the museum a few days a week. Between that, the gym and my shopping sprees, my days are full."

And lonely, but Kim didn't say it out loud.

"C'mon," Stephanie said, getting out of the car. "I've got the guest room in the east wing set up for you. I thought you might like to have some privacy while you're here. We've got an extra car for you, too, so you can get around."

Kim pretty much missed everything after the words *east wing*.

Fido grabbed her bags from the trunk and bought them inside. The front entry of the house was *Architectural Digest*-worthy: Black and white tile flooring that led to a double curved staircase and a chandelier overhead that must have cost hundreds of thousands of dollars.

"Crazy, right?" Stephanie said. "I always wonder what people think when they first walk in." Though Kim had come from a modest upbringing, Stephanie's family had been downright poor. It was Stephanie's brain that got her a full ride into college. "Fido, you can set the bags down here. We'll take them up later."

He kept the bags in his hands. "It's no trouble, Mrs. Wyncott. Only take me a minute." Fido headed upstairs like he knew where he was going. Apparently he did more than just drive Stephanie to the airport.

"Stop it. It's not what you're thinking," she said. "I've known Fido for more than five years now. He's a very good listener, but I don't think he'd touch me with a ten foot pole. The man has integrity. One of the reasons I like him so much." She headed toward the back of the house. "C'mon, let's have a drink."

Kim followed Stephanie down a wide hallway and into a step-down living room with thick white carpeting and a massive circular bar on the far end. Three sets of French doors gave a perfect view of paved pathways in the manicured back lawn that led to different sections of the estate. Kim spotted tennis court lights off to the left, a pool off to the right and a guesthouse directly in the back.

Stephanie went straight to the bar and poured herself a stiff shot.

"Soda for me," Kim said. Her days of drinking hard liquor were few and far between.

Taking a sip of her shot, Stephanie smiled sadly. "Looks like my girl has changed."

"Yeah. I had to. I didn't like what I saw in the mirror."

There was a long pause before Stephanie downed the rest of her shot. "Maybe that's why I quit looking in the mirror." Then she poured herself another.

Chapter Three

Abbey walked out of the police station nearly five hours later, after waiting and interviewing several times over. A near full moon cast light over the mostly empty parking lot. "That poor guy," she said, relieved to breathe fresh air. Julie, Troy and Blake surrounded her. "Who knows where those men have taken him? He could be dead by now." She'd never forget his scream and the panic in his voice as he'd called for help.

"The good news is that you are *not* dead," Troy said. His voice of reason always cut to the chase.

"I won't argue with that," Abbey muttered, checking her watch. Almost one in the morning. The small basketball in the center of her watch reminded her of something.

The tickets.

She froze and Blake bumped into her.

"Whoa. Sorry," he said, grabbing her shoulders to steady them both. His warmth seeped through her thin shirt, but she turned and he had to let go.

"What's wrong?" Julie asked.

"The Lakers tickets." She glanced between the three of them. "I lost the Lakers tickets. I didn't think about it until just now. What if the gunmen took them?"

"More likely someone else found them," Troy said. "I doubt the gunmen stopped to pick up what you dropped."

"But what if they did, thinking it was some sort of ID? Do you think they'd use the tickets? Maybe we could find them that way."

"They'd more likely sell them," Blake said.

Troy nodded. "Probably. We can tell the detectives and it's

something I can check out. I'll make a few phone calls and we'll see if anyone shows up in the seats."

Julie looked sympathetic as she reached for Abbey's hand and pulled her toward the car. "C'mon, let's get you home. Big day tomorrow. You need to get some sleep before meeting with the sketch artist."

"I don't think they call them that when they're working with a computer app," Abbey said.

"Whatever. The point is you have to be back in a few hours. How about you stay with us tonight?" she asked.

"That's a good idea," Blake said.

Abbey glanced over her shoulder and glowered at him. What gave him the right to an opinion on this?

"What?" He pulled his innocent face with his brows slanted and eyes wide. He moved in close and whispered in her ear. "The last thing you need is another panic attack while you're alone. C'mon, Abbey. I don't want to worry about you."

Someone could have knocked her over with a feather. How could a guy she'd ignored for the past year care about her? Moving away, she got some distance from his mouth-watering scent. "You don't have to worry about me. I'm not your responsibility." She reached for the door.

"I didn't say you were." He stopped her with a hand on her arm. "But you are my friend."

The concern in his blue eyes struck a chord and Abbey pulled out of his grip. Yes, they'd had to work together a lot this past year, but *friend?* She never would've called him a friend. It wasn't that she didn't want him as a friend, she just didn't know how to *be* around him.

Her adrenaline had crashed a while back and she was tired. She kept a few extra things at Julie's house in case of emergencies, but emergencies had never included anything like this. They usually entailed really early trips to the airport or really late events when Julie didn't want her on the road. Of course both of those loads had lightened when Julie married Troy since he was now the one taking her to late night events.

"Fine." Abbey didn't want to argue and he had a point. Besides, her car was at their house anyway because they'd all gone to the concert in Troy's BMW. "Sorry you missed the concert." Just one more thing to feel bad about. A stellar night.

Of course missing the concert was better than a bullet to her brain.

Blake opened the back door for her, but Abbey hesitated. She couldn't get the man's scream out of her mind. The fear and pain in the sound would be with her for a long time. And the man who chased her... A chill spread down her spine despite the warm night.

The three people she spent the most time with hovered around her. It was the oddest sensation to know these people had her back. She expected it from Julie. Yes, Julie was her boss, but she was also a friend. What she hadn't expected was Troy's alliance and Blake's sudden possessiveness. In one horror of a night, all three had become her support system.

She felt Blake's heat at her back as Julie and Troy got in the front seats. He didn't touch her, but he let her know he was there.

"It's going to be okay," he whispered. "The detectives will figure out what's happening. These guys are good. What's important is you're okay. You're safe."

She didn't see how they were going to find the injured man before it was too late. As far as her being safe... God, she'd lived the last nine years trying to feel safe and knowing everything could change in an instant. For the second time in her life, it all had.

Kwami paced his Culver City apartment waiting for news. The downstairs neighbor he'd hired to clean hadn't shown again and his place was a pit. Beer bottles overflowed the trash can and empty plates littered the chipped white tile counter. His dirty clothes lay in a mound in the hallway because he didn't have any fucking time for laundry. It was way past time to move out of this dump, but that wouldn't happen for another couple of years, not until Mal graduated college.

The phone rang—finally—and he snatched it off the table and checked the screen. Damon. "Talk to me." It was almost one already. Waiting had been agonizing.

"I got her," Damon said. "She just came out of the police station. She's with the same group of people from the concert and I swear one of them is Julie Fraser. Can you believe it? Julie fucking Fraser." He laughed. "Must be California. Didn't deal with shit like this in New Jersey. Anyway, I'll follow her home. It won't be long now."

"Just get her fucking name. I don't care how you do it. I want her name and I want an address." He pulled the kitchen chair back and sat down.

"You'll get it. Quit snapping at me."

"If you weren't such a douche bag, maybe I would. You put us in this position, so you better fucking fix it. I told you we were only supposed to scare him. You fucking sliced Berman in two. What the fuck?"

"Stop ragging me about it. I told you, the little shithead lifted up into my knife after I tackled him. Besides, he got what he deserved. It was going to happen sooner or later. Did you dump him?" Damon asked.

"Yeah. He's gone. You're fucking welcome."

Damon laughed. "Try doing an Internet search of Julie Fraser. Maybe you'll find a picture or article with this chick. They seem pretty tight. Hey. Gotta go."

"Don't lose them."

"Not a chance. I had to fucking shave off my 'stache because of this bitch. She's not getting away from me." Damon's Fu Manchu had been too recognizable and she'd gotten too good a look at Kwami when she'd originally come out of the door, so Damon had taken a pair of scissors then an electric razor to remove his signature look. He'd added a baseball cap and sunglasses, and Kwami had sent him to mill around the scene like all the other idiots watching the cops and, more importantly, watching their girl.

The call ended and Kwami tossed the phone onto the table. He shoved back and the chair slammed into the floor. There shouldn't have been any witnesses. He couldn't afford the attention. Shit. Once the boss found out, if the boss found out, his ass was going to be in a giant sling.

His mobile rang again. *Now what?* But when he checked the screen and saw his brother's name, his anger evaporated. "Hey, what's up? Everything okay?" The kid probably needed money.

"Dude, you won't believe this."

Kwami pictured Mal's gap-tooth grin and a shot of brotherly love warmed his cold heart. "What? You won the lottery?"

"I got a fucking ninety-four on my English test! A ninety-four! Can you believe it? Oh man, I am freaking out!"

Pride burst in Kwami's chest. "That's great. I said you could ace that test, didn't I? You just have to do the work." He looked around his pit of an apartment as Mal rambled about the essay he wrote and decided the sacrifice was worth it. "Do you need any money?" he asked when his little brother stopped for a breath.

"I think I'm good this month. I'm learning to budget a little better."

"Well, hallelujah for math class."

Mal laughed. "I'm on the home stretch," he reminded him. He paused before continuing. "Can I come home this summer?"

Kwami swallowed, his gut twisting into a ball. "We talked about this. You're better off taking some summer courses and keeping your job. You'll graduate quicker. Find a good job quicker." Besides, he didn't know how long he'd be dealing with little miss witness and he wanted Mal as far away as possible.

"You've got a good job and you didn't graduate college. Maybe when I graduate and start work, you can go back to school," Mal suggested softly.

"We'll talk about it when the time comes." Kwami sometimes wondered if he'd live to see the day that Mal graduated. He'd had a few too many close calls lately. Working for Facinetti's operation had decimated his personal code of honor, but the money paid for Mal's education so he couldn't back out now.

"You always say that and I think it's just a bunch of bullshit." The bite in his tone cut through Kwami. "I'll talk to you later." The connection went dead.

"Fuck." Kwami threw his empty beer bottle in the sink and it cracked into four chunks. The last thing he needed was to have Mal pissed at him. Maybe if he handled this situation quickly enough, Mal could come home for a week or two this summer.

Kwami paced the room, needing a plan. That chick got a look at both him and Damon, and he couldn't afford to be identified. He'd never intended to murder anybody. Douche bag Damon had screwed him big time by killing Berman.

Now he really would have to make someone disappear and he didn't see a choice. No way in hell would he let Mal end up the way he had. He'd do anything to keep his little brother in school, anything to protect him, and that meant staying out of prison.

"Bye, Mr. Frost! Have a good day," the production assistant chirped with a shy wave from behind her cluttered desk. Her straight blond hair hung down her back in shiny waves and her surgically enhanced breasts pushed out high and full against her snug white T-shirt.

"Now..." He didn't remember her name so he skipped it. "What did I tell you when I got here?" he asked, his signature smile in place.

"*Leo*," she said, flushing. "Have a good day, *Leo*." Her blush brightened. It wasn't every girl in town who got to be on a first name basis with one of America's biggest action movie heroes.

"You know it. You, too, babe."

"I'm really looking forward to seeing your new film," she added. Was she hoping for an invitation to the premiere party? Not a chance in hell of that happening. He was done with her type.

Still, he had a reputation to uphold, so he winked at her and opened the double doors as the rising sun blazed into his eyes. "Hope you like it!" He set his sunglasses in place as he strolled to Stella, his black Boxster S Porsche and the only female who understood him. His cell phone buzzed in his pocket and he checked the screen. His pulse stuttered.

The Marion Institute.

Megan.

The last thing he expected this morning was to hear from the East Coast. A wave of heat rolled beneath his skin as he quickly punched the accept button. The Institute rarely called and when they did, he panicked. It meant something had happened to Megan. He moved quicker to his car for privacy. Cameras could show up from out of nowhere.

The woman spoke so fast he barely heard her. But a few words definitely stuck out as he opened Stella's door and eased into the soft leather driver's seat, like, *checks*, *bounced* and *debt collection*.

"Wait. Slow down. That's not possible," Leo told the accounting department representative. They'd spoken last month as well. The fact that he'd been awake since O-dark hundred to promote his new movie on L.A.'s top-ranked morning show seriously limited his comprehension. "I'm sorry, what was your name again?"

"Tanya Brubaker."

"Right. Tanya. I'm sure there was a mistake. I'll make a couple of calls and get this straightened out." As soon as the rest of the West Coast woke up. It was still damn early.

"Mr. Frost, you said that last month, too, and it hasn't been straightened out. I'm afraid we'll need a cashier's check to cover the last two months' payment and that comes to forty-two thousand dollars."

"Wait a minute? Last month never got taken care of? I was told otherwise." Now the bill was doubled? Forty-two grand was a drop in the bucket, so why hadn't his accountant/business manager sent the money?

"Mr. Frost, are you there?"

"Of course. Not a problem at all. I'll get that to you ASAP. Talk to you soon. Bye now." Leo disconnected the call and ran his hand through his hair. "Time to find out what the fuck is happening."

He called Nathan and immediately got rolled over to voice mail. "Nathan, you're getting on my every last nerve. Wake up, dammit. Call me back before I take my business and money elsewhere. This isn't funny anymore. I don't care if we've been friends for twenty years, because this is bullshit. The Institute wants to know why my last two checks have bounced and frankly, so do I. Call me back. Yesterday." Leo disconnected and rested his head against the seat.

Now what? Now he had to wait for a fucking bank to open so he could get a fucking cashier's check for forty-two grand. What if the press got wind of that? Screw it. He'd think of something. He'd leak a well-disguised drug habit or something sordid to keep the public happy. It had been working for years, hadn't it? As long as they thought the worst of him, no one dug deep enough to find out what he didn't want them to know. Give the people enough dirt to discuss up front and they didn't think you were hiding something. The public was predictable. Leo knew that all too well.

The industry knew him as a shallow, egomaniac who only cared about himself and he was happy to keep them thinking that. He didn't give a shit what they said about him anyway. As long as they didn't dig into his life, they could think anything they wanted.

His phone rang. "About time, Nathan." But he checked the screen and it wasn't Nathan. "Shit." He didn't want to talk to Candace. Hell, he barely remembered her face, but she'd snagged his phone and programmed her number into it and never failed to call him at the worst possible times. She must have seen his interview and knew he was awake. He let the call go to voice mail.

He barely remembered the last time he'd had sex, but he knew it had been with Candace. He also knew he didn't want to have sex with her again. Using Candace to get Carrie Ann Loughlin off his mind had been a big mistake, but he wanted to believe he hadn't been the one to drive his co-star to insanity. It wasn't every day a guy worked with an actress who went off the deep end and committed murder. Sleeping with Candace had seemed like a good way to get back some confidence. Good news was Candace hadn't gone crazy. Bad news was that she was driving *him* crazy.

Never in a million years had he thought he'd get tired of having sex, but that had happened too. The physical relief wasn't worth the emptiness he felt afterward. Everyone wanted a chunk of him and for years he'd played the game. He took what women offered him because it made them happy. For a while it had made him happy, but now, after so long, it only made him feel like shit.

It wasn't that he wanted a relationship or marriage. Hell no. But he did want someone to talk to, someone to trust. Someone who wouldn't run to the rag mags with his real secrets, not the fabricated ones he fed to the press. He hadn't found that person. Hell, he probably wouldn't even know if he did. He'd become as jaded as he made himself out to be, all in the name of privacy.

Blake let himself into Troy and Julie's mammoth kitchen from the back patio. This wasn't the first time he'd crashed in their pool house and he doubted it would be the last. It seemed stupid to go home and sleep for three hours just to be back first thing this morning, so he'd stayed. Abbey, Troy and Julie had told him to go home, that he didn't have to go to the police station, but he wouldn't consider the idea. He wanted to be with Abbey as she built the composite sketch of the suspect. Something about the way she'd described the guard at the door made his insides buzz. The words *broad forehead* and *bushy beard* stuck in his head like an old wad of gum and brought to mind a face he'd never forget.

Abbey had sat for hours looking through mug shots last night and had come up empty, which made everyone think that the suspects didn't have a record. The man Blake had in mind also *did not* have a record and the coincidence freaked him out. Logically, there was no way this was the same man who had changed his life. His brother's life.

But what if it was? Blake couldn't shake the possibility. It's why he'd decided to go into private investigation.

Troy Mills had been instrumental in saving his family and Blake wanted to learn from him. The man had incredible instincts and had taught Blake to never ignore his gut feeling. Blake's gut was definitely talking to him now and it was telling him to keep Abbey close.

Closing the door quietly behind him, Blake stopped at the sight of Abbey at the black granite counter in front of the coffeemaker. It was way too early for her to be up. Wearing a form-fitting white top with thin straps and loose black sweats that draped over the sweet curve of her ass, she looked as if she'd already spent time in Troy's home gym.

"Good morning," he said softly.

"Morning."

He noticed the lack of *good* return.

She glanced over her shoulder and he saw why. Her red-rimmed eyes had that bruised quality of someone who had a lot on her mind. A black band held back her straight hair.

"Did you sleep at all?" He pulled a mug with a *Dangerous Race* logo from the overhead cabinet next to her.

"Thanks, Blake. I know I look like crap, but did you have to say it?"

Fuck. She always did this. Put words in his mouth and twisted what he never said. She had perfected keeping him and every other man at arm's length. He just didn't know why.

"Actually, I asked because *I* didn't sleep because the bed in the pool house is too soft. *You,* as always, look gorgeous."

She dropped her chin to her chest and Blake watched her struggle to hold it together.

"Abbey…" Frustration bubbled over the edges. It ripped him up to see her so upset. He never knew what to say to her and this was a hundred times worse because he wanted to say the right thing.

"I'm sorry," she whispered. Then she laughed, a dry sound that carried no humor at all before turning to him. "Thank you for yesterday, for being at the Sports Center. Thank you for staying at the police station all that time too."

Blake shrugged. "I had to." Her doe-eyed look gave him the opportunity to change her mood. "I had to because Troy was my ride." He grinned and she smacked his chest, but this time a real smile lifted the corners of her spectacular lips.

How long could a man go dreaming about a pair of lips before he actually got to kiss them? If he *ever* got to kiss them.

She watched him for a few seconds with those mesmerizing green eyes before focusing back on the coffeemaker.

Blake rarely, if ever, got any alone time with Abbey and when he did, she was quick to vacate the premises. "Ab, you know whatever happens, I'm here for you."

She didn't say anything at first, as if she had to measure her answer. "I know. I just hate that you always see me at my worst." She didn't even glance at him and Blake zeroed in on her, shocked at her admission. It was the most serious thing she'd ever said to him.

"Hardly. I usually see you at your best. When you're taking care of Julie or putting out fires to make her life perfect."

She snorted. "I wouldn't say I make her life perfect."

"Yeah, but you come damn close. I see all the stuff you do that goes above and beyond your job. You don't just pick her clothes up from the cleaners, but you put them away. You don't just go grocery shopping for her, but you make her favorite meals so their ready to heat up. You make sure her car is washed and gassed up. Those are only the things I see, which means there's a ton of stuff you do that I don't see. You handle all the little things that make her life easier. I think you're amazing."

She stayed quiet for a minute as she got some milk from the fridge. "Why are you being so nice to me, when I'm such a bitch to you?"

Blake nodded, stoic, but pumping a mental fist in the air with the topic. Sometimes he wondered the same thing, but if Abbey thought about their first meeting, she'd know why. Blake just didn't plan to set himself up for another fall. Not yet anyway. "That is a very good question and it deserves an answer. Why *are* you such a bitch to me?"

The look on her face was priceless. Her jaw open, her eyes wide. Blake laughed and gently used his index finger to close her mouth. Just the tiny touch zinged through him. That brief contact of her soft skin sent a bolt of heat straight to his gut.

When she didn't respond, Blake tried something else. "You're nice to Troy and I figure it's because he's not a threat to you since he's disgustingly happy being married to Julie. And of course, you love Julie, which is clear in every way imaginable since you take such good care of her. So I see you being nice on a regular basis. You're just not that nice to me. So then I ask myself, Blake—I call myself Blake since that's my name— Blake, why do you think Abbey hates you so much?"

Her hint of a smile dimmed at his question. "I don't hate y—"

"And I answer myself, Blake, she doesn't hate you. She's afraid of you." He took a second to gauge her reaction, her grin long gone. Looking at him, she blinked and swallowed, but she didn't say anything.

Shit, he hated being right.

Chapter Four

Abbey turned away from Blake and poured the milk as she struggled to find a response. He was one of the nicest guys she'd ever met. He was funny, gorgeous and had everything a girl would want. He didn't have a threatening bone in his body and he was one hundred percent right. She was scared of him.

Strike that.

She wasn't scared of *Blake* specifically. She was scared of all men. But there was no way in hell she planned on admitting that. No one but her family knew her private issues. Not even Julie knew what happened to her nine years ago, and Abbey never planned to tell her, either. That incident was in the past and needed to stay there.

Blake walked to the other side of the large kitchen. "So I'm right." He took a deep breath before he turned. "I don't know what I ever did to make you feel that way. You have to know that I would never, could never, hurt you." His eyes narrowed as he thought about something. "I scared you in the elevator that first time, didn't I?" He'd nearly kissed her that day. She'd been so freaked out with the elevator about to drop them, and he'd insisted he could take her mind off it. "I swear I only wanted you to think about something else besides dying in an elevator car. Please, Ab. I'm sorry."

"Don't," she said, returning the milk and grabbing the chai from the fridge. Coffee for Troy, chai for Julie. "You have nothing to apologize for." She turned and saw the frustration in his eyes. God, he was so gorgeous standing there with the morning sun highlighting the red in his dark hair and the stubble covering his jaw. Those mile wide shoulders belonged on a football player and his ass, in an Armani underwear ad. "You didn't scare me in the elevator. You probably saved my life." She poured the chai into Julie's mug. "I'm the one who needs to apologize. I'm sorry I've been so horrible." He deserved it to his face, so she met his gaze. "I'm sorry I've been a bitch. You don't deserve to be treated that way by anybody."

"You haven't been a bitch. Just a puzzle." He studied her now. Troy had done a great job of teaching him how to read people. Abbey kept her posture straight the way she always did and didn't blink. "Why are you scared, Abbey?"

Damn it, why'd he have to be so astute? So sweet? Why did he sound so concerned and gentle? That time she blinked. God, did he think all he had to do was ask...that he had a right to know just because he softened his tone?

Footsteps in the hallway preceded Troy and Julie's voices, and Abbey turned back to the counter to finish making the chai. "I made your coffee and chai," she said as they entered.

Julie stepped up behind her and set her hands on her shoulders. "You didn't have to do this. I was hoping you'd sleep in until we had to go. I wanted to bring *you* some coffee."

"You know me. I'm always up early. If I don't work out first thing in the morning, I won't get it done." Abbey turned and gave her a quick hug. She didn't like people behind her. "You guys really don't have to go with me," she said again. She hated upending everyone's busy lives.

Julie glared at her. "I'm not letting you go back to the police station by yourself and I won't say it again. Deal with it."

A grin lit Abbey up from the inside. She really did love her boss. "Yes, ma'—"

"Don't you dare ma'am me," Julie said. "I'm not even thirty."

"Yes, sir," Abbey said obediently.

Troy chuckled. "Looks like Abbey is learning from the master." Then he bumped his wife's shoulder with his own.

"Comedy is all in the timing," Julie said and the bell for the microwave dinged. "See. Just like that. Timing." She lifted an eyebrow and snagged her chai.

Abbey glanced at Blake, but her smile faded when she saw the serious look in his eyes. He wasn't done with their conversation. He was like Troy when it came to wanting answers.

Just like yesterday, Julie, Troy and Blake took her back to the police station. She barely noticed the hot summer sun and didn't like the way they constantly looked around as if she might be a target. Wouldn't the shooters be long gone by now? Troy and Blake were paranoid because they were PIs. Looking around was second nature to them. Maybe if she said it in three languages she'd believe it. Too bad she didn't know that many languages.

A buff police officer showed them to a private room with gray walls, nothing but a barebones desk, a couple of chairs and a computer. "Officer Rivera will be right with you." The small room lacked windows and already Abbey's claustrophobia made her skin prickle. Didn't matter that the people supporting her were in sight.

An officer walked in and put his hand out. "Hi, I'm Officer Rivera. Miss Washington?" Older than she expected, the man had to be in his late fifties. His short gray hair, brown eyes and weathered face struck her as retired cop, not active duty.

"Yes. Hi. Nice to meet you." She shook his hand, caught the once over he gave her and stood a little taller. She introduced Julie, Troy and Blake.

"I usually like to do this without anyone else but the witness," he said, with a sympathetic look. "There can be too much distraction with too many people in the room."

Troy read his message loud and clear. "Julie and I will wait out front. Blake, maybe you should stay. You were there longer than we were. You might have seen something and you don't even realize it. Maybe something Abbey says might spark a memory." He glanced at the officer. "You okay if he stays?"

"Yeah. If he was there, he might be able to add something. It's fine."

Troy ushered his wife toward the door. "We'll stay close by."

Abbey never got a second to argue because the door closed behind them.

"Have a seat." The officer moved the extra chair behind the desk so they both faced the computer. Blake leaned against the wall, his expression poker-face blank.

With rattled nerves, Abbey picked at the polish on her thumbnail. The room took her back nine years, after she'd been rescued. When the authorities asked her about what happened. It closed in on her now the way it did then. She'd wanted to get away from the stares as her parents had walked through the station, but the small room had been a different hell. Four walls closing in on her... It seemed like a lifetime ago. It seemed like yesterday. Funny how it went either way. Abbey blinked back the memory and focused on the man behind the computer. "Where do we start? How do we do this?"

Officer Rivera tapped at his keyboard and never looked up. "Just describe each man you saw yesterday. One at a time. It's easy."

Easy? This seemed like the farthest thing from easy she'd ever done. Sure, she'd seen the guy, and the cops had discovered that the man at the door hadn't really been part of the event staff, but could she describe either one well enough for this man to make a composite? What if she got it completely wrong and the pictures didn't look anything like either man? How could she make him fix it?

"Relax. You'll do fine. I know it's scary, but this software is pretty good. I think you'll be surprised what you can remember. I'll help you." He gave her a supportive smile and showed off a slightly crooked front tooth. "Let's start with the first man, the one with the knife. What was the shape of his face? Round? Oval? Maybe he had a square jaw?" He pulled up a page that covered every possible jaw line and Abbey finally had to describe it and let the officer choose. As she looked at the picture, she could help define it better.

That's how it went for the next forty-five minutes. Officer Rivera asked questions and tapped on his keyboard. Blake didn't budge from his spot near the wall, but she could practically feel his tension, which did nothing for her nerves. Still he quietly urged her on when she got frustrated and didn't think she could come up with anything else specific about the man besides his thick, bushy eyebrows, fat nose and Fu Manchu, which they all knew he could shave off in a heartbeat. His dark sunglasses had hid his eyes and his cap had covered his head. Not a whole lot to work with.

Officer Rivera put a few final touches on the face then turned the monitor toward her. "What do you think? Close?"

"That's good," she said. "But we still can't really see him."

"The point is to see what you saw." With a little more prompting, he made a few adjustments and refined the picture even more. Then they took a break before starting on the next one with the same process. Another forty-five minutes later he adjusted the monitor toward her again.

Blake had come around them as she'd described the other suspect and stood behind Abbey's chair. "Holy shit," he said softly.

Abbey and the officer both glanced at him. He looked as pale as Abbey had ever seen him. "What's wrong?" she asked.

"The guy you just described." Blake ran his hand over his jaw, but never took his gaze off the computer screen. "I know him."

"How? From where?" Abbey stood as Blake swallowed hard. She'd never seen him like this. "Who is he?"

"The only name I have for him is Kwami. He's already wanted for kidnapping and assault, among other things."

"Who'd he kidnap," Officer Rivera asked, grabbing a nearby phone off the base.

Blake took a deep breath. "Me. And my whole family."

A cold chill streaked down Abbey's back. She knew Blake's history because Julie had starred in the movie written about the event. It had been national news when his family had been rescued.

"He was one of the guys who worked for Paul Facinetti two years ago. He was in the car that got away when the cops zeroed in on the house." Blake's eyes turned icy blue. "He's the one who cut off Brendan's earlobe."

Abbey knew this from the movie about the event, and she'd met Blake's twin brother, Brendan, a few times during the past year.

The officer listened carefully to Blake then called the detectives on the case. Blake took a moment to send a text. A few minutes later, the small room filled up when the detectives assigned the case and Troy and Julie all filed in.

"You're sure this is the guy from your kidnapping?" Detective O'Kelly asked as Rivera handed him the printout of the composite. O'Kelly's blond hair and blue eyes were better suited to an actor than a cop.

"I'm sure," Blake said. "I'll never forget his face. Problem is he wasn't in the system two years ago and I doubt he is now or someone would've caught the connection."

"This gives us something to work with," O'Kelly replied. "We'll dive back into Paul Facinetti's life and see if we can't find more on this guy. If I remember right, Facinetti's cousin took over his end of the business so we've got a good place to start."

"The whole reason I went into this line of work was to find the asshole who hurt my brother. I want this son of a bitch behind bars where he belongs." Every muscle seemed taut, and the intensity in Blake's eyes might've scared Abbey if she didn't know him.

Abbey had never asked Blake about the ordeal, but looking at him now, she realized it had affected him as profoundly as her own assault.

Kim took her breakfast dishes to the sink and looked out the window at the backyard. The bright sun climbed up and over the trees and made the small ripple in the aqua pool sparkle like diamonds. She looked around the opulent grounds. Not a bad life if you had it. Of course, she didn't. Her stay was only temporary. A huge drag considering she could get used to this place. A girl could dream.

"I told you the maid would do that. What are you daydreaming about over there?" Stephanie asked as she came closer, sipping her coffee.

"Life," Kim said, facing the massive kitchen with its gray granite counters, mosaic backsplash and antique cabinets. The dark porcelain flooring sparkled with a high sheen. "Just wondering when I might get one." She smiled at her friend because she didn't want to be a Debbie Downer. "So what's the plan for today? Am I going to Carl's office or am I working from here?" She had no delusions about the amount of work ahead of her if Carl wanted her to go through the books. Apparently the man had his finger in everything from entertainment to sports to finance. If he suspected a problem, Kim doubted it was going to be something glaringly obvious. If this Nathan guy had really embezzled from him, and he was halfway decent at it, he should've been able to hide it, which meant Kim had to take her time.

"I think Carl wants to go to Nathan's office first and see if he

can talk to him face-to-face. But he wants you to go with him."
Stephanie poured herself a second cup of coffee. "Carl thinks if
Nathan sees an outside source about to go through the files that
he'll come clean. Personally, I think Carl has given him way too
many chances already, but there's nothing I can do about it now.
The damage is done, whatever it is."

"Consider me one of the Avengers. I've come to save the
day."

"Well, I certainly hope so," a voice said from the doorway.
Carl hadn't come home by the time they'd gone to bed last night,
so Kim hadn't seen him yet. In fact, she'd only met him the
weekend of the wedding. After the ceremony the couple had
gone off to their month long European honeymoon. Yeah, she'd
see one of those in her dreams too.

"How are you, Kim?" Carl came into the room and hugged
her. He was close to sixty, medium height and on the skinny
side. His brown eyes seemed to sink into his head and he kept his
thin hair spiked in some attempt to look rock-star cool. Carl
swore every gray hair on his head came from years of hard work.
He'd always struck her as a bit cold and his hug didn't change
her perception. Her heart went out to Stephanie a little bit more.
Kim may have wanted to marry for money, but not at the cost of
love. She'd thought falling for a rich guy would be as easy as
falling for any man, but she'd learned the hard way when no one
fell for her. Oh, they were happy to get lucky, but when it came
to the morning after, they were more concerned with getting out
the door.

Yes. Ouch. Repeatedly.

So she'd learned. After taking multiple bats to the head,
figuratively speaking, of course.

"I'm fine, Carl. Sorry I was asleep last night when you got
in."

He waved a hand as he leaned toward Stephanie and pecked
her cheek. "Don't think twice about it."

"If you lived here, you'd know it's a common occurrence,"
Stephanie said. The undercurrent in her tone put Kim on guard.

Carl gave a deliberate look to the cup in Stephanie's hand. "Is
that your second?" He lifted gray eyebrows. "We've talked about
your caffeine intake, Stephanie."

Kim wouldn't have put up with that tone for a million bucks, but Stephanie took a measured breath and tossed the rest of her coffee down the sink.

Trouble in paradise. Damn. She hated being in the middle of it.

"Stephanie told me you want to go to Nathan's office this morning. Are we picking up files or just hoping to see him?" Kim asked.

"Both if I can manage. He won't answer his phone, so I have to stop by the office. I don't know why Bonnie, his secretary, hasn't returned my call either. It's all a big mystery."

"Who doesn't love a mystery?" Kim hadn't meant to blurt that aloud and when Carl frowned, she felt two inches tall.

"I, for one, could do without it," he snipped. "Especially when it concerns my money."

"Of course. Sorry. Didn't mean to imply otherwise." It wasn't as if Kim didn't understand the meaning of a dollar.

Stephanie gave her a small shake of her head. A gesture that said, *don't let him bother you.*

Kim crinkled her nose in return. *Not a problem.* It took a lot more than Carl to scare her. No one ever thought she was tough. She probably perpetuated that notion with her wardrobe, but just because she liked beautiful clothes and frilly girl things didn't mean she wasn't tough.

"Stephanie, I don't imagine you'd want to come with us. We'll be going from Nathan's office to my office. I'll bring Kim home tonight."

That news came as a surprise to both of them since they'd discussed Kim using their extra car…a convertible Mercedes she was dying to drive. They shared a glance. Apparently the king had spoken.

"I thought Kim and I might be able to catch up at lunch," Stephanie said.

"I'm not paying her to have lunch with you." Carl finally looked at his wife and sighed as if she'd just dropped a two-ton load of crap on his shoulders. "You can have lunch with her this weekend. It's not long off. Don't pout. You know how I hate that."

Stephanie's look could have frozen the sun. Kim bit her tongue—literally—to keep from saying something to Carl. Nothing about Stephanie indicated a pout, which probably accounted for the steam coming out of her ears. As each minute went by, Kim hated that she'd agreed to help the man.

"Okay then." Stephanie's voice was as icy as a shallow pond in a Montana winter. "I'll see you later, Kim. Don't let him work you too hard. Especially since you left your own job to come help us." That last bit was directed completely at Carl and he nodded to confirm Stephanie's message.

It was going to be an interesting stay.

Leo made a trip home to take off his makeup from the morning show and change into some more comfortable shoes. Slipping on the new Nikes he'd picked up at a recent gifting didn't help his pissy mood nearly enough. His phone call to the bank to transfer the funds didn't really go as he'd hoped, especially when the *representative* told him he didn't have enough funds for the transaction. After a fifteen minute argument, Leo gave up. Time to go to the source. A few minutes later, he was out the door and ready to confront Nathan.

As he waited for the green wrought-iron gate to slide open, he revved Stella's engine. She was the only female on the planet who didn't give him shit and he loved every sleek inch of her. "Stella, my love, you are sounding awfully sexy this morning." He revved the engine again just to let the neighbors know he was taking off. That must have caused a few eye rolls. Smiling, Leo slapped on his Maui Jim shades, pulled onto the street and headed into Beverly Hills.

He almost never went to Nathan's office. Nathan usually came to him. But Leo had already wasted too much time and if the man thought he could dodge trouble a minute longer, then he was wrong. Oh so very wrong.

Leo might've been a lot of things to a lot of people, but he was never late with a payment on anything. People often billed him as a ladies man, but just as often, an egomaniac, sleazeball or scumbag. They either loved him or hated him. He didn't run into too much middle ground. Most women liked his fast moves and others weren't fans, but he rolled with the dice and didn't really care what anyone thought about him. After years of setting up *Leo Frost*, he'd gotten what he wanted with amazing results. It didn't take away from his talent, but it occasionally made it hard to be taken seriously by people on the business side of his life.

Everybody had a breaking point though, and Leo was just about at his. Nathan had seen to that.

Leo pulled into the small parking lot of Nathan's stand-alone building where two cars were already parked. The single story building itself wasn't any great shakes, but the real estate it occupied was prime Beverly Hills. An old white Honda that desperately needed a wash took the corner spot and a gorgeous maroon Bentley Rolls Royce had the primo space by the door. He whistled as he unfolded his six feet two inches out of Stella and took a stroll around the Bentley. It must have been shipped from England because the steering wheel sat on the right. *Nice.* It was old, too, but in mint condition with a tan canvas convertible top. Must have cost a quarter of a mill' easy. He could've afforded one for himself, but Stella was more his style. Sleek, shiny and untouchable on the road if he wanted to let her out to play.

"Don't go away, Stella. I'll be fast." He hit the alarm and Stella double chirped her reply.

"Nathan, you jackass, ready or not, here I come." Leo swung open the front door and three heads turned his way. Bonnie, Nathan's assistant, stood behind her big cluttered desk on the right. With her frizzy red hair and glasses, she looked wigged out. Four large windows showed that the offices in back were currently unoccupied. The two people in front of him didn't look familiar. Although why the blonde was spending time with a guy old enough to be her father was beyond him. Stiletto heels accentuated her outstanding calves and a short black skirt clung to her perfectly curved ass. A long beaded necklace cut the divide of her full breasts beneath a turquoise silk shirt. What a waste of a gorgeous woman. Did the old guy know how good he had it? Probably.

Bonnie's eyes widened at the sight of him. The blonde cocked her head just slightly as she, too, recognized him.

Leo stepped behind them and waited his turn in line.

The old guy didn't bat an eye and just turned back to his conversation. "When was the last time you talked to him?" he asked.

Bonnie's attention zeroed back on the man. "I don't know. Yesterday morning, I think. It's been a little busy."

Was that because Nathan was dodging all his clients? Interesting. No, *disturbing* was more like it.

"I want my files," the old guy said. "Now."

Bonnie shoved her glasses farther on her nose. "Um. But...I don't think I'm supposed to."

"I don't give a flying fuck what you think you're supposed to do. I'm telling you what you're going to do. Go into Nathan's office and get my files. Carl Wyncott." He crossed his arms over his chest. "Now."

No reason not to get on this boat. "Me, too, Bonnie. I'll just take my files." Maybe the old guy had info that Leo didn't. Something was definitely fishy. Leo needed his money and he needed it now. At least a chunk of it. He needed to access his investment accounts. Nathan had handled all things financial for almost twenty years. Leo just wanted to ream out the jerk before he actually left him.

"Why don't I text Nathan and see—"

"Why don't you get your fat ass into the filing ca—"

"Hey!" The blonde faced him, hands on her hips and murder in her eyes. "I've had just about enough of the way you treat people." Her green eyes sparkled with fire. "If you don't apologize to her this instant, you can kiss my help goodbye."

Leo hid his smile. He liked this chick. Fluff on the outside and steel within. She reminded him of a stuntwoman he worked with a few times over the years. That blonde also had green eyes. Leo still felt like shit when he thought about her. Years ago, he'd misread her signals big time and made a move when he shouldn't have. He'd paid the price with a bruised rib. Laughing had hurt like a bitch for a week. Hell, taking a deep breath had hurt. He'd stayed seriously clear of her after that incident. Later he wanted to apologize to her in private, but she never gave him the chance.

The old guy, Carl, clenched his jaw as Bonnie scurried to the back office. He headed toward the door and spoke to the blonde over his shoulder. "Get the file, I'll wait for you in the car." Poof, he was gone, out the door in two seconds flat minus the apology she demanded.

The wide-eyed surprise on the blonde's face told the story. She probably felt all of two inches tall right about now. Leo checked out her ring finger, relieved to see it empty. At least she wasn't married to the asshole.

"Who peed in *his* Wheaties?" Leo asked, hoping to elicit a smile.

Her flat stare landed on him. No smile for miles. Ah...she was one of *those*. That fraction of the population who hated him because of who he was, a single, wealthy, famous actor who had the world at his feet, not a care, without a shred of commitment, or drop of conscience in any of his marrow. Times like this he wondered if he'd gone a little too far with his act.

He gave her his best smile and stuck out his hand. "Hi. I'm Leo."

She sighed, looked at his hand and considered something before shaking it in a brief hard squeeze. "Yeah, hi. I thought so." Then she turned back to the desk and waited for Bonnie.

Leo leaned his head back and stared at the ceiling for a second. Uncomfortable much?

"Usually, when someone introduces themselves, it's customary for the other person to reciprocate." He really did want to know her name. Any time he made a boner move, he thought about Ellie Morgan, the stuntwoman, and her right elbow. Now anytime he saw a green-eyed blonde in fuck-me stilettoes, he'd remember this chick.

She faced him. "Is it really necessary? We'll never see each other again." It wasn't so much her tone that irked him as the thought that she didn't even want to give him her name.

"Exactly, so I'd like to know the name of the woman who put Carl Wyncott in his place." Leo had never heard of the guy, but obviously he had importance to someone somewhere.

She looked toward the back office where she found no sign of Bonnie to save her, before facing him again. "Kim. My name is Kim. Happy?" She gave him her back. And a very nice back it was. A year ago, Leo would've been working hard to score with this woman, but now, he couldn't imagine it. Strike that. He *could* imagine it; he just didn't want to.

He had to laugh. The times had changed.

Kim turned back around. "Did I say something to amuse you?" She had not one inch of playfulness in her and if she did, she hid it well.

Leo shook his head. "Nope. Not a thing. I was just thinking you really must have disliked my last movie to hate me bad enough that you can't even look at me."

A faint blush crept up her cheeks and an equal dose of retribution filled Leo's chest. He should be used to the judgmental looks he got on a regular basis, but sometimes they hurt just like anything else. Granted, he usually received adoration from pretty women, not condemnation, so maybe that's what pricked at him.

She sighed and her eyes didn't waver. "Actually, I loved the last movie I saw you in."

This was more like it. "Yeah, which one was that?" He'd had two releases in the last eight months.

"Dangerous Race."

Huh. He shot that film years ago. He must have had five or six movies released since then. "Wow." Okay, so there had to be a reason she quit seeing his movies, even though she said she liked it. "If you liked it so much, how come you didn't see any more recent films?"

"The movie was based on true life incidents. My business partner was one of the people involved."

"No shit?" Now this was interesting. "Who's your business partner?"

"Chelsea Harding. She's Trace Bradshaw's—"

"Twin sister," he finished for her. "I know. I did my homework." Even though they'd used a different name for her in the film, he knew the players. "How is she anyway? That was a pretty rough time she had."

"She's fine. About to have a baby. She's living the dream."

Leo held back a snort. "Her dream maybe."

"But not yours, I take it?"

He shook his head. "Not in this lifetime. Some people are meant to be parents. Others are meant to make fun of those people." He raised his hand. "I'm the latter."

She glanced up at the ceiling, so he apparently said something wrong. Nothing new there, but he usually did it on purpose. For the second time, she gave him her back. "You're going to be one lonely man," she muttered under her breath.

This time he did snort. He was already a lonely man. "Was I not supposed to hear that?"

She sighed. "Does it matter?" She craned her neck, clearly looking for Bonnie.

"I guess not. I mean, it's not like I have any feelings or

anything. Why don't you go ahead and tell me something else about my future. I'm interested to hear it."

Kim turned around again, her head canted to the side. "I only know what your reputation tells me." Her eyebrows lifted. "Oh, and I know that you cornered a female crewmember while you were filming *Beyond the Realm* and held her against her will against one of the trailers."

Jesus, he'd just been thinking about that encounter. How the hell did this woman know about it? "She'd been flirting with me until that point," Leo pointed out. "If I'd known she didn't want to play, I wouldn't have touched her."

"Right. I believe you." With her arms crossed over her chest, her body language said something very different.

"How'd you find out about that?" he asked. It happened at least seven years ago, maybe eight. Talk about a skeleton in the closet. It shouldn't bother him, since he'd worked for so many years to cultivate the bad-boy-without-a-clue persona. Maybe Ellie had said something to someone after all. But this many years later and he was just finding out about it made him rethink that idea. Shit, he should've found the privacy to apologize to her.

"The production coordinator on *Dangerous Race* was a P.A. on *Beyond the Realm*. He saw the incident. Chelsea overheard him telling someone at the premiere party. She told me."

Leo shook his head. This town was too damn small. Hell, the world was too damn small, and he was getting tired of playing the sleazeball.

"For the record, I never make moves on married women and I don't tangle with anyone who doesn't want to play, but I can't help it when they make passes at me." Usually, he never asked about relationships. It was easier to not know. He also stayed clear of anything younger than twenty-two. He'd learned the hard way to check for ID.

She opened her mouth to say something, but Bonnie reappeared with a few files and a flash drive. "Sorry it took me so long," Bonnie apologized. "Here you go." She handed everything to Kim.

"This is all of it, right?" Kim asked. She clearly didn't want to face the wrath of Carl.

"Yes." Bonnie put her palms up and spread her arms wide. "I

promise that's everything." She looked at Leo. "Mr. Frost, I'll get yours next. Just give me one minute." She disappeared behind the same door.

Kim juggled the files and the drive, and Leo sprang to open the door for her. "I've got it," she grumbled, just as a loose note from inside the top file slid out. Leo caught it before it fell on the floor, but the move brought them up close and personal. She had the most amazing eyes he'd ever seen. Not sea green as he originally thought, but a bright emerald green.

"Anyone ever tell you how beautiful your eyes are?" he asked.

"Oh for God's sake." She sidestepped him and elbowed her way out the door. Leo smiled as she strutted toward the Bentley, her ass swaying with each precise step, her back straight and killer legs that he imagined would feel like perfection wrapped around his hips.

Good bye, Kim. Nice to meet you. Too bad he'd never see her again. She was worth a second look.

As she headed to the car, the trunk on the Bentley rose. At the same time, a black GTO pulled in and parked next to Stella. Leo went back into the office to wait for his files. A minute later, a man came in. He was big and black. As the door closed, a breeze blew his shirt up and the gun handle sticking from his waistband made Leo wary. His research for roles had taught him that most undercover officers or PIs used some type of holster for their weapons. The man looked around the office with hard eyes.

"Where the fuck is everybody?" he asked.

Yeah. Not an officer of the law. "Are you a client?"

"Who the fuck wants to know?" His eyes narrowed as recognition dawned. "Well, fuck me," he muttered.

"I'll pass," Leo growled back.

When Bonnie came out, her eyes widened and she froze for a second before snapping her gaze to Leo's. "There is one more thing, if you can wait just one minute and I'll get it for you. It's in the very back office." She handed Leo his stuff then turned to the new, big guy. "Can I help you?"

What the hell? Why couldn't she finish with him so he could take off? Unless she didn't want to be alone with the guy. *That* he understood.

The dude had the cool swagger that Leo had perfected on screen. "Yeah. I'm looking for Nathan," he said.

Wasn't everyone?

Bonnie swallowed. She looked extra nervous, more frazzled than before. "He's not in. Are you a new client?"

The guy looked around before he focused on Bonnie. "You know what, I'll come back later when you're not so busy." He sauntered out the same way he'd come in and Bonnie sighed when the door clicked closed behind him.

"Thanks for staying," she said, hand over her heart.

"I take it the guy isn't a client?"

She shook her head. "Never seen him before. He was kind of intimidating."

Kind of? Try, *very.* "Ah, he was nothing. I could've taken him."

Bonnie smiled, the dreamy, thankful grin of a woman who loved him. "I'll be right back. Let me get that flash drive." Her cheeks flushed as she turned. She was one of those women who thought he walked on the moon. A fan until the bitter end. Nathan had told him as much. She thought he was the man who appeared on the big screen. The action hero who could handle five adversaries a la James Bond, straighten his tie and bed the beauty all before the sun went down.

If she only knew.

Chapter Five

The hot bright sun of late morning beat down as they exited the police station. Abbey's brain hadn't caught up to everything that had happened after the detectives left with the composite. Blake had been kidnapped by the man who'd chased her? It seemed unbelievable and only reminded her how little she really knew about him. She'd never known what to say about his kidnapping or if she should ask about it. If he were anything like her, he wouldn't want to relive it. She sure wouldn't blame him for that.

Her phone rang and she checked the screen. "My agent." Her pulse raced like it always did when her agent called. It usually meant an audition. Abbey had begun to land more and more dance jobs. Most were only one or two day shoots at the max, but Julie had to make do without her. Though Abbey felt a little guilty, they both knew she never planned to stay on with Julie forever. Assistant jobs were revolving door positions. Abbey had been upfront about her desire to dance and Julie had understood. "Hi, Mallory. Whatcha got?"

"Hi, Abbey. You've got an audition in Hollywood this afternoon. Can you make it?"

Julie didn't have anything major planned for her today, just a few errands that she could manage around an audition. "You know it. What's it for?" Abbey asked.

"A new dance/reality show pilot."

That could be promising. "Sounds horrible," she deadpanned. "What time?"

Mallory laughed at her delivery as Blake watched her, his eyes narrowed and unhappy. Abbey ignored him and reached for the backseat handle of Troy's Beemer.

"How fast can you get there? They're seeing people all day," Mallory said. "This is big. They need separate teams and team captains. There'll probably be a lot of mix and match to see what works." She rattled off the address, a dance studio Abbey recognized. "Call me when you're done and let me know how it went."

Abbey slid into the back seat. "I will. Talk to you late—" But Mallory had already disconnected. Typical. Abbey mentally considered the audition clothes in her closet. For something like this, she needed to stand out more than ever.

"You're not seriously thinking of going out on an audition today, are you?" Blake asked, facing her.

Abbey resisted the eye roll, but she couldn't hold back a sigh. "Yes, I am going on this audition because it's for a pilot. If I land it and it goes, I have permanent work." She really couldn't explain it any more concisely than that. She shot her boss an apologetic look since she hadn't even asked for the time off yet.

"I don't think it's a good idea." He looked toward Troy and Julie getting settled in the front seat. "Do you?"

"No offense," Abbey said, cutting off Julie before she got started. "But this is my life and if I get an audition, then I'm going." Period. End of story, but those words came though without having to say them as she folded her arms and dared anyone to argue. "Besides, why isn't it a good idea?"

"I don't know," Blake said. "I just don't have a good feeling. I'm worried about you."

"You don't need to be." Abbey buckled her seat belt.

"It's not about what I need or want. It's about the way I feel. I don't like that these guys are out there and I don't want you to be alone. Can I at least go with you?"

Abbey's patience slipped a notch as she met his gaze. "This is ridiculous. You cannot think to babysit me for the rest of time."

"I'm not talking about the rest of time, I'm talking about today. This week. The next two weeks. Just until I feel like you're safe."

The thought that she might be a target made her skin crawl and reminded her of Blake's bomb back inside. Yes, the suspect had been an accomplice in the stabbing of a man and he'd chased her, and knowing he'd kidnapped a whole family added another layer of *bad* to the equation. There was one thing she hadn't realized before now. She had more in common with Blake St. John than she originally thought and it wasn't anything good.

Blake didn't care how much Abbey hated having a bodyguard, because until the SOB who saw her got caught, he planned to stick to her like a second skin.

Yeah, right. If only *that* were possible.

At the moment, he waited for Abbey to emerge from her bedroom. She'd disappeared a half hour ago to get ready for her audition and left Blake to loiter in her living room. Abbey's one bedroom apartment was as original as the woman who lived in it. It was twice the size of his place. Working for Julie had obviously agreed with Abbey's wallet.

The pictures lined up on a funky distressed teal bookcase told him a little more about her. A portrait showed a loving, tight-knit family; the four of them in jeans and white shirts with big smiles for each other. Almost as if this had been an outtake and not the picture they might've chosen as the one to frame. That one shot captured the love between her parents. The two of them couldn't not have been more polar opposites in appearance. Abbey's dad's dark-as-night skin contrasted sharply with her mother's pale complexion and light blond hair. Abbey clearly got her green eyes from her mother, but she had her father's wide smile...at least when she chose to smile. The other female in the photo had to be her sister.

Blake checked out a couple more pictures on the shelf... Abbey with her sister, and one with her parents in formal attire. They made a good-looking couple.

He turned back to the apartment. Man, what a mess. He nearly laughed. It wasn't at all what he expected. She kept Julie so organized, he would've sworn she was a neat freak. Not the case. Not even close.

And he liked it.

He liked that she had a flaw, because up until now—aside from her attitude toward him—she had seemed perfect. She had vulnerability, a shyness that drew him in, and when she laughed, the husky sound slid through him like the best liquor. Everything about her absolutely lit him up. The color of her eyes, the smoothness of her skin, the fullness of her lips... Hell, even her great posture gave him a woody. Her dancer's body was clean lines and pure muscle. Every move she made reeked of grace and elegance.

Yet her apartment... Clothes covered most of the white sofa and matching chair. A few empty cups and plates littered the beige tile counter and pine table. It didn't look dirty, it just looked messy. Lived in. Or not lived in. As if the time she spent here was only enough to get what she needed and run to the next event. Like now.

Blake chuckled.

"You're in a good mood," Abbey said, coming out of her bedroom.

Blake turned and nearly dropped to the ground in supplication. It took a concerted effort to keep his jaw from hitting the floor.

Abbey canted her head. "What?"

What? Was she kidding? *What* was that in thirty minutes she'd transformed herself from stunning girl to absolute Miss Universe perfection. He didn't often see her wearing makeup and the effect it had on her already smooth skin and clear green eyes nearly brought him to his knees. Her dirty blond hair hung smooth and long around her shoulders, and the form-fitting strappy neon pink top and black leggings with a matching pink stripe down the side showed off her toned dancer's body. He pegged her at five foot eight and she was all legs. The girl had legs to her neck. Legs he wanted wrapped around his waist as he pushed inside of her and sent them both—

"Hello." Abbey snapped her fingers in the air. "Blake. Yo."

He snapped out of his daydream.

"What's got you on another planet?" She headed to the sofa and left the smell of citrus in her wake. She rifled through her bag for something.

"Uh...nothing." He backed up toward the door. "You ready to go?" If he stayed in her apartment much longer, she might end up out of those clothes she wore. Man, he could imagine stripping everything off her. Slowly and surely exposing every inch of smooth, soft skin.

"I don't know." She put a hand on her hip and cocked a stance. "You ready to stop looking at me like I'm your next meal?"

His gaze flashed to hers and he smiled. "Was I doing that?"

She nodded with one eyebrow arched high.

"Sorry. I couldn't help myself. I'll work on it."

"Good. You need to." She swung a large bag over her shoulder. "C'mon. I don't want to be late," she said, passing him to open the front door.

Blake kept an eye out in the hallway as Abbey locked up. He'd never felt more itchy, and working with Troy had taught him to trust his instincts. He looked around the quiet neighborhood as he and Abbey headed toward his SUV. "See any unfamiliar cars around?" he asked as he opened the passenger door for her.

"I'm not here enough to see familiar cars much less unfamiliar ones." She tossed her bag on the passenger floor then hopped in the seat.

Blake scanned the tree-lined neighborhood before getting behind the wheel a few seconds later. He clicked his seat belt, cranked the engine and merged into traffic. "So how long will this thing take?"

"Hard to tell. Probably three hours to start. It depends on how many people they called and how much they want to see. If I make the cut, I could be there longer."

"Three *hours?*" That sounded crazy. "You do this all the time? Jumping when your agent calls, scrambling to get across town to make an audition, then scrambling back to Julie when you're done?" He slowed for the stop sign at the corner of her block.

She nodded. "Pretty much. I'm lucky she's mostly flexible."

"How long have you been dancing?" he asked, checking the intersection and moving through it.

"As long as I can remember. My mom put me in ballet when I was little and I loved it."

Blake pictured a tiny Abbey wearing a tutu and outshining all the other girls.

"Why are you smiling like that?" she asked.

"I have a vivid picture of you wearing a pink tutu with your hair in a bun and your arms over your head." He caught a rare grin as she nodded.

"That about sums it up. We had tap and gymnastics, too, but I loved ballet the most." Her smile faded as she gazed out the window.

Before he had a chance to ask her more, she gave him directions to the studio and cranked the radio. Just when he thought he might actually have a conversation with her, she pulled the plug. After arriving at their destination twenty-five minutes later, he had to drop Abbey off at the front because of a lack of street parking on his part and lack of time on hers.

Jumping out of the SUV, she glanced down the street and pointed. "Hey, there's a car leaving. Grab that meter while it's open or you'll be driving around forever. I'll text you when I'm done."

"Sounds good." Blake watched her enter the building, way too interested in the curve of her ass before remembering he needed to snag parking in the newly opened space across the next intersection. After sliding into the spot, he dumped most of his change in the two hour meter then strolled to the studio. Dozens of dancers loitered outside the building, some stretching, some texting and some talking on their phones. A few minutes later, he spotted Abbey through the glass window as she warmed up with a group of five other people. They all had numbers pinned to their clothes. Eventually, they got into two lines with someone at the front of the room showing them moves. Abbey mesmerized him. She caught on in seconds and nailed the dance with ultimate precision. She had more skill than Michael Jackson and Lady Gaga put together. Hell, every gaze in the studio followed her. It was impossible not to.

How the hell had she not bagged more dance jobs before now?

The sun warmed his shoulders as he watched her. The beat of the hip hop music vibrated through the window and it seemed as if Abbey had been born to the dance. She swiveled and jumped, turned and lunged, bumped and grinded.

A primal thumping started in Blake's chest as he continued to watch her. Her moves were like a sunset or a rainbow, where each position spoke its own color then merged into another and another. Abbey created an artistic autograph that belonged strictly to her.

Once the dancers had warmed up, a woman came in with a clipboard and started calling numbers. Blake couldn't hear her, but he read her lips. *Number five.* Looked like his girl was still in. Check that. She wasn't his girl, he just wished to hell she was.

One hour ticked by. Then two. Blake fed the meter and came back. He checked his watch for the tenth time then scanned the block. Three hours. Everything looked normal. People walked by with pets or lovers and cars zoomed past going way faster than the speed limit. Normal Los Angeles.

Right before they hit four hours, the door opened and Abbey finally came out, a smile on her face. Not just a regular smile, but an *I have a secret* smile. Blake moved toward her when a young woman cut in front of him.

"Abbey!" she squealed and hugged the stuffing out of her.

For a quick second, Abbey froze in midhug, but she pulled back and smiled. "Courtney! I haven't seen you in months. How are you?"

Uh oh. Blake knew a delay when he saw one. This might take a few minutes. He remembered all the times he and his brothers waited for their mom when she gabbed with the neighbors or ran into someone at the grocery store or gym. Her *I'll only be a minute*, usually lasted about twenty. If they were lucky. He checked his watch again then glanced at his SUV...where a parking enforcement Prius was gliding into a loading zone a couple spots in front of him.

"Oh, shit," he muttered as he took off for the car. "Abbey!" he called over his shoulder. "Feeding the meter! Be right back."

She acknowledged him with a wave and kept talking to her friend.

Blake just made the meter and shoved in a few more nickels. The only thing he had left in his pocket. It bought him nine minutes. Highway robbery. "Thank you, City of Los Angeles," he grumbled. The meter maid tapped her pencil on her pad and gave him the stink eye before walking back to her car.

An engine revved loud and Blake's pulse bumped up. He looked up the street and saw some teenagers screwing with a monster Chevy truck jacked up on high suspension. He shook off the tension and huffed out a breath. "Everything's fine, St. John. Don't get your boxers in a bunch," he told himself quietly, using his big brother's favorite line.

Blake checked his watch against the meter and looked up as the monster truck revved again. A black car with full on black tinted windows passed the Chevy. The car closed the distance, then suddenly the tires squealed, burning rubber. Blake's pulse did a full on gainer as the car shot forward.

"Abbey," he said, not nearly loud enough. The car jumped the sidewalk from an open loading zone area and barreled toward her. "Abbey!" This time Blake yelled at the top of his lungs as he sprinted toward her. He'd never make it in time. Not even close. "Watch out!"

Abbey turned and saw the car as other pedestrians scrambled out of the way. She dove at her friend and they both went flying into the natural cover of the building's inset doorway.

Breathing hard, Blake stopped short as the car whistled past where Abbey had been seconds before. It showed no signs of slowing down. The car bounced off the curb, made no effort to turn. Sunlight glinted off the dark windshield. Too late.

"Aw, fuck," Blake whispered. The motherfucker planned to run him down too.

Blake took a millisecond to notice the stucco building on his left. He dove toward the road and sailed over the hood of a compact car. Horns blared, tires screeched and Blake had a quick vision of his family standing over his casket as he caught sight of the yellow Hummer coming right at him. He was about to be road kill on this crowded street. A female scream added to the noise buzzing in his brain.

He landed on the unforgiving asphalt and rolled, his momentum taking him directly into traffic. The deafening squeal of tires pierced the air and the overpowering smell of burning rubber filled his nostrils. The whole side of his body slammed into something hot and hard, stopping him like a brick wall. Pain ripped through him and took his air with it.

Just like that, the lights went out on the sunny day.

Chapter Six

"Blake!" Abbey sprinted toward Blake, trying to get the license number of the black Mercedes that had shot like a bullet down the sidewalk, but the plate had been removed. Her heart thundered as the car sped down the street and she scrambled to get to Blake. The dark-haired driver of the Hummer that almost hit him emerged from the car yelling in a foreign language.

"Someone call 911!" she screamed through her parched mouth, looking around for help. The driver was already on the phone. On the street, Blake lay still. Abbey's chest tightened. "Blake." She barely got his name out as she crouched next to him. The tire of the giant Hummer had stopped his momentum. If he'd landed a couple seconds earlier the tire would've rolled right over him instead of stopping him. A crowd gathered near her as she scanned his face for any sign that he heard her. She'd left her bag containing her phone back at the dance studio when she'd tackled Courtney to the ground.

Abbey gently touched Blake's head. "Blake? Can you hear me?" His arm had terrible road rash and a rip in his shirt showed a bloody slice on his shoulder. Sirens wailed closer. "Blake. I'm here. It's Abbey, I'm right here. I swear I won't leave you."

His eyes fluttered open and he squinted into the blazing sun. "Ab?" he choked out.

Her relief gusted out in a massive breath. He tried to get up and Abbey kept his shoulders down. "Don't move." She blinked back the sting in her eyes and shifted to shade his face. "Ambulance is coming. You're going to be fine." *Please, God, let him be fine.*

He shut his eyes and shook his head. "Fuck, that hurt." He tried to get up again. "I'm okay."

"Would you just wait a frickin' minute until the ambulance gets here?" she argued, with maybe too much voice, but now she was pissed. Pissed at whoever did this, pissed that Blake wouldn't take a second to chill.

Blake's amazing blue eyes locked onto hers. "Abbey Washington, are you *mad* at me?" The wonder in his voice irked her more.

"No! Yes! No! Just stay here until the paramedics check you out. Please. Here, lay on this." She slid her sweatshirt under his head.

His brows quirked and he got the strangest expression on his face. As the seconds ticked by, her anger faded. He'd nearly been killed. "You have a streak of grease on your cheek," he said quietly. His gaze roamed from her mouth to her eyes and a slight grin lifted the corner of his lips.

Just that devastating half smile sent a second massive wave of relief washing through her and her own, albeit small, smile creased her lips. "Yeah, maybe so, but you've got tire tread on yours."

His grin got wider. "Is that why my face hurts?"

"Honey, it may hurt you, but it's killing me." Abbey used the old one liner she'd heard her boss use in the past. As each second ticked by, her panic edged farther away. The sun continued to beat down on them and a drop of sweat trickled between Abbey's breasts.

"Stop the fucking presses. Was that a joke? Did I just hear you make a joke?" He angled his head back and looked around. "Anyone have a pen and paper. I need to document this for the record."

Abbey held back a laugh and gently smacked his steel bicep. "Don't tease me. You scared the crap out of me."

Blake nodded, the humor gone from his eyes. "Trust me. You are not alone. When I saw that asshole coming down the street, I got pretty scared myself."

If he hadn't yelled, she'd be dead. He'd saved her life and nearly been killed at the same time. No way would she turn her back on that. Abbey reached for his hand as police, fire truck and an ambulance pulled up to the scene. Thank God. With the help came a fresh sting behind her eyes.

"Hey." He squeezed her hand. "I'm okay." Gingerly he moved his arm and leg to prove nothing was broken. "I swear, Ab, if I thought I was really hurt, I'd say something, but—"

"Miss, I need you to move back." Two EMTs crouched next to her with a giant, red tackle box of equipment and Abbey shoved over to give them room, but she didn't—wouldn't—leave Blake's side. One name badge read F. Hodge. The other read, D. Hernandez. Hodge asked Blake questions. *What was today's date? When was his birthday? Who was the President?* He took his pulse and checked his eyes with a penlight. "Your pulse is a little elevated, but that's normal," he said.

"Yeah, it's not every day a guy gets to make out with a Hummer tire. That'll get anybody's pulse rockin'."

The EMT lifted an amused eyebrow. Before either one of them said anything, Hernandez sliced Blake's shirt with a pair of scissors and peeled it off him.

"Dude!" Blake grimaced and let out a frustrated sigh. "No worries. It wasn't like it was my favorite T-shirt or anything." He pegged Abbey with a flat stare. He loved his Black Eyed Peas concert T.

Oops. She lifted her brows and shrugged her shoulders. They were just doing their job.

Hodge checked Blake's arm and shoulder. The cut on his shoulder didn't seem as bad as Abbey originally thought. It didn't require stitches. It was the rest of the picture that had Abbey stunned in silence. She knew Blake was ripped, because of their encounter in the elevator so long ago, but she had no clue just *how ripped*. A flush rose from her chest to her face as she stared at his unbelievable six-pack. "No contusions or lacerations," Hodge said, still inspecting Blake, "but I think we should take you in to be safe."

Blake groaned. "I *really* don't want to do that." He struggled to sit up and Abbey helped. He leaned against the tire that had nearly flattened him. "See?" He spread his arms wide. "All good. No hospital required." His shoulders looked even bigger as he sat there. Abbey forced herself to watch the growing crowd because it was too hard to look at a shirtless Blake. He was simply too beautiful.

Hodge held up a few fingers. "How many you see?"

"Three." Blake looked between them. "See. Good as new."

He pushed to get to his feet and wobbled a little, but Abbey wrapped an arm around his waist and got her shoulder under his armpit to steady him. *Ohgodohgod*. Holding him like this was suicide not to mention setting precedent. It gave him the opportunity to touch her back. To get up close and personal, when she rarely allowed anyone into her personal space.

The crowd had grown to several dozen people and the driver of the Hummer was talking with an officer, gesturing wildly as if the whole thing was Blake's fault.

"Look, I can't make you go to the hospital," Hodge said. "But I recommend you do. You don't want to mess around with head injuries."

"I don't have a head injury," Blake insisted. A bead of sweat eased down his cheek and Abbey wanted to get him out of the sun.

"You lost consciousness," she said, her anger making an encore appearance.

"I landed hard and got the wind knocked out of me," Blake argued. "I'm sore, but I'll be fine. If I think I need to, I'll go to the emergency room later."

"Chances are you'll wait a long time," Hernandez said, his warning clear. "You know that right?"

"I'll take the risk." Blake nodded. "Thank you, though."

Hernandez gestured to the ambulance. "Why don't you sit down for a minute and let me clean up your road rash."

"Deal." Blake let her and Hodge help him to the ambulance. He sat on the edge of the interior as Hernandez rifled in his box. Abbey took a step for a little distance, but Blake snagged her hand in his. "Where do you think you're going?" His hand was warm and strong and Abbey felt a flush heat her cheeks.

"Just giving these good men room to work," she said, scrambling for the first available excuse.

The look Blake gave her, the honest concern she saw in his eyes nailed her straight in the stomach. *Stay*. He didn't say it, but it was there in his eyes. So she squeezed his hand and stayed close.

If Blake had known that nearly getting run down would get Abbey to hold his hand or—holy hell—make a joke, he'd have considered standing in traffic months ago. He'd never felt happier than to have her soft hand snug in his. Soft was an understatement. He'd never touched smoother skin in his life. He'd been fascinated with the color and natural shine of her skin from the minute he'd laid eyes on her over a year ago. The woman practically glowed of health and natural beauty. As he looked at their clasped hands, the way her long, elegant fingers held tight, something dawned on him. The only time Abbey let him in, let him touch her, was in times of crisis. First when they were trapped in the elevator, second when she'd been running for her life at the Sports Center and now. As a budding PI he should be able to figure out what all that meant.

A couple of cops approached from the other side of the street and Blake got ready for the inevitable. The cops would separate them to take their statements. He'd have to let Abbey go. Damn cops.

"Abbey?" her friend called, walking toward them. "Are you okay?" She was the exact opposite of Abbey, with pale white skin and platinum blond hair. She had the same dancer's body; narrow, long and toned.

Abbey squeezed his hand before pulling away. "Yeah. Thanks," she said, reaching for her bag as Courtney—if he remembered right—held it out to her. "Sorry about the tackle."

"Are you kidding me? You saved us." She looked at Blake and gave him a very flirtatious smile. "Hi, I'm Courtney." Her soft brown eyes ate him up like he was sugar in a room full of salt.

Abbey's perfect brows bunched together just the slightest bit. Was she jealous? Couldn't be. She'd made it very clear that she wanted nothing to do with him…or any guy as far as he could tell. He even once considered that she might play for the other team, but he'd never seen her with another female either, so he doubted that was the case. Something had happened to her and he wanted more than anything to find out what that was.

"This is Blake," Abbey said, completing the introductions. Probably because he'd gone mute.

"Uh, hi. Nice to meet you." He didn't shake her hand, because everyone would see him flinch and he was busting his ass to make sure no one knew how much he hurt. Nothing was broken, but he'd definitely bruised a couple of ribs, not to mention the whole right side of his body. The EMT had irrigated the slice on his shoulder and now cleaned the road rash on his arm. Every nerve ending burned like a bitch.

"Thanks for giving us the warning back there." Courtney gestured over her shoulder and gave him another beautiful smile. He wouldn't mind that look coming from Abbey, but this girl just didn't do it for him. "That guy must be whacked out on something to drive down the sidewalk like that."

Or he was out to kill, but that seemed out of left field, didn't it?

The cops finally closed in on them, and Courtney and Abbey each went with a different officer while one stayed and talked to Blake.

It was another forty minutes, a signed form declining a trip to the hospital and a bandaged right arm later, before they slowly walked to Blake's Explorer. He jingled the keys. "You okay to drive? I think I need to sit and close my eyes for a few minutes."

Abbey opened the passenger door for him and he climbed aboard at the speed of a snail. "You should've gone to the hospital," she said, helping him in.

"I don't want to go to the hospital. Too much hassle. I just want to go home."

"You can't go home. Brendan's out of town. I didn't forget that. You aren't supposed to sleep for more than a couple hours at a time. You need someone to be with you." She closed his door and walked to the driver's side as Blake leaned his head against the seat rest and closed his eyes. Was she offering for the job because, idiot that he was, he'd take her up on it. She adjusted the seat and rearview mirrors then started his old Explorer. Smart girl that *she* was, she programmed her phone into his Bluetooth car system.

Who did she want to talk to? "What are you doing now?" he asked.

"I'm calling Troy and letting him know he has another house guest for a couple of days."

"Don't—" His sudden attempt to face her sent a shock of pain sizzling through his chest and a sharp gasp—and f-bomb—from his mouth. Shit. He didn't want to impose on his boss. He would stay with his folks except they were out of town on an anniversary cruise.

Abbey set an arm over the steering wheel and gave him a

sidelong glance. One arched brow and the *I told you so* on her face was all it took for Blake to cave. Plus, this way he could be closer to her.

"Fine. Whatever." Gently, he settled back in the seat as Abbey made the call to Troy then pulled into traffic. "We need to at least stop at my place so I can get a change of clothes." His were shredded and filthy. The EMT had given him an extra hospital scrub that had been tucked away in the ambulance, but his favorite Black Eyed Peas T-shirt was dust in the wind.

"Deal. That I can do," Abbey said, glancing at him, all business. What would it take to get back the girl who smiled and joked?

When they arrived at Troy and Julie's house in Beverly Hills, Abbey ran around to the passenger side to help him out and Blake took advantage of her strength, setting his arm over her shoulder as she wrapped her arm around his waist. This close, he smelled the mix of her citrus shampoo and the sweat she'd worked up between her audition and the afternoon's blazing sun. The heady scent wreaked havoc with his decision to keep her at a distance.

The door opened before they got to it and Troy and Julie both came out. Troy took Abbey's spot as they walked up the four front steps and into the house.

"Did you get a look at him?" Troy asked quietly, going straight for business. Abbey's phone call from the car had given him the basic report.

Blake shook his head. "No. The glare on the windshield was too bright and the tint on the side glass was too dark. Well, that and he was coming at me too fast to do anything but get the hell out of the way."

"Thank God you did," Julie said, leading the way toward the bedrooms. "We set you up in the office. I want you closer than the pool house. The pullout is a queen, so it's plenty big."

"It's great. Perfect. Look, I hate that I'm putting you guys out. You really don't need—"

"Don't even finish that sentence," Troy said. They reached the office where the bed had already been pulled out and made in the large room. Troy's half of the office consisted of a large mahogany desk and leather chair facing one wall. The other side, with another mahogany desk only antique, smaller and more feminine, belonged to Julie. The tan paint gave the room a cool, relaxed atmosphere and the pullout sofa at the far end of the room indicated where they might sometimes meet in the middle. "Maybe the ladies can get you some water," Troy suggested.

Blake caught the look in his eye. He wanted to talk privately. "Yeah," Blake said. "Water sounds great. A couple of ibuprofen chaser would help too." No lie there. He'd taken a couple pain relievers at his apartment, knowing the soreness was only going to get worse, but he hadn't planned on *this much* worse.

"Coming right up," Julie said. "Abbey, you get the ibuprofen in the guest bathroom and I'll get the water."

As soon as they cleared the room, Troy closed the door. "We have a serious situation. I can't see this as random, given what Abbey witnessed yesterday. I think these guys have been following her, waiting for a chance to get rid of a witness. What also concerns me, though, is the possibility that the guy from your family's kidnapping might have been the one driving, and recognized *you* from two years ago."

Blake let Troy's words settle as he kicked off his boots. "It would sure explain why he didn't bother turning on the street," Blake said as Troy helped him lean back on the bed. He'd not only helped kidnap the whole family, but he'd mutilated his twin brother by slicing off his earlobe. Unless the guy did something like that on a regular basis, Blake didn't see how he'd forget Brendan's face. A face that Blake happened to share. "Or maybe it was a random dude whacked out on crack. Who knows. I sure as hell didn't expect him to try and run me down, but your idea would explain it."

"Got torn up, did you?" Troy said, gesturing to his arm.

"Little bit. Nothing that won't heal in a few days."

"And your ribs?"

"Bruised."

Troy lifted a dark eyebrow. "You sure about that?"

"Mostly." Blake didn't like the skeptical look on Troy's face. "Look, I know a cracked rib when I have one. Trust me. It hurts, but it's not broken." At least he was pretty sure. God, he was so damn tired all of a sudden. At least with Abbey safe at Troy's place, he could close his eyes for a few minutes and rest.

Abbey and Julie came back in with water and pain relievers, which he dutifully swallowed. Abbey reached for the glass when he finished, but Blake took her hand. Her eyes widened at the contact. "Thanks for coming to my rescue earlier."

Troy, perceptive boss that he was, grabbed his wife and quietly left the room.

"What are you talking about? You saved me. I'd be flattened on the sidewalk if it weren't for you. I'm just glad you're okay." She studied him, her eyes bright with concern. "You are okay, right?"

"Would you care if I wasn't?" It was a selfish expedition on his part, but he wanted to know where he stood with her. Would they forever be work acquaintances, friends or did he have a chance for more?

"Of course I would." Her brows shot together in an irritated pucker. "What kind of question is that?"

He leaned back on the pillow, stroked his thumb across the softness of her knuckle. "Sorry." He shook his head. "I just get the feeling that you really don't like me that much." He released her hand when she pulled away and her actions said more than words.

"That's not true. It's not the case at all." She stood up, looking like a deer in the proverbial headlights. "I better see if I can help Julie with dinner. I'll be back to check on you in a little while." She zipped out of the room in seconds flat.

"Fuck," Blake muttered, easing farther down on the mattress. The move cost him, as familiar pain throbbed in his chest and out to his arm and shoulder. It sucked almost as much as his inability to communicate with Abbey.

Kwami threw his gloves across the room as he entered his apartment. He bee-lined to the fridge and snagged a much-needed cold brew. He opened the bottle and chugged half as the cold air of the open fridge wafted over his hot skin. It was a fucking million degrees outside and he'd made it even hotter by torching his ride. The dark Guinness tasted bitter on his tongue, and Kwami welcomed the bite. After another minute in front of the fridge, he sat his ass in his comfortable massage chair. After paying for two years of Mal's private high school and two years of college tuition, he'd splurged and gifted himself with this bad boy last Christmas. Wiping a hand down his face, he settled in the soft leather and turned on the controller.

The rollers in the chair went to work and Kwami forced himself to relax. The shit was going to hit the fan soon enough, so he planned to enjoy a few minutes of peace.

Kwami snatched the remote and turned on the flat screen. He flipped the station to the local news to see if his handiwork made—

A smile curved his lips as the helicopter camera showed his gift to the inner city. The black Mercedes he'd jacked was now a burned out piece of shit. It was possible the owner didn't even realize it was gone yet.

The last hour began replaying in his head. He'd been so close to taking the girl out. The dude too. The guy's face popped into his head. Again. Why the fuck did he look so familiar?

His phone rang and he reached in his pocket, checked the number. *Damon*. Kwami hit Talk. "Qué pasa, man? What's up?"

"What's up is I never heard from you? Did you get her?"

So much for his relax time. "Not yet. But I will."

"You sound pretty relaxed for a dude who's going to eat a bullet if they manage to ID you. Facinetti's going to take you out before the cops get near you. He won't want the hassle, K."

"It won't get to Facinetti if you keep your mouth shut. I'll get her." Kwami said.

"Damn bitch is going to pay for making me shave my 'stache, you can count on it," Damon said.

Kwami listened to him complain for another minute before he ended the call and tossed his phone on the table. Killing her had seemed the smartest thing because it eliminated the chance of her identifying him.

Except she'd been too fast. He'd been a second away from creaming her on the sidewalk, but the shithead down the road had warned her. Kwami hadn't so much as heard him yell as see his mouth move and because of that, he'd been the next target. But why did the shithead look so familiar?

The massage cycle ended on the chair and Kwami got up to pace. The guy, the guy... Who was that guy? He knew him. He was sure of it. Dark hair, light eyes. Dark hair, light eyes.

That was it. There were four all together, but two of them had been twins. "Well, fuck me." Kwami rubbed his jaw, thinking back two years. "What was the name? The name?" He wracked his brain. There'd been six family members all together and the mom had been one hot piece of ass...shit what was the name? It was simple. Smith, Jones...no... John! Yeah, that was it. Wait. No. St. John! That was it. He was one of the St. John twins.

Kwami wiped a hand across his jaw. "The one with two full earlobes, or the one without." Facinetti had told him to take the whole ear off, but Kwami hadn't been able to. He'd barely managed to slice off the chunk he had without puking. But he'd laughed and talked through the whole thing like it was business as usual. That had been one hell of gig. He'd barely gotten away.

But this brought up a whole new bag if issues. What if the kid saw him today? What if—between both of them—they made a positive ID and connected him to any of the Facinetti family? He'd started working for Michael not long after Paul had been sentenced.

Now he had two people to get rid of. Just what he needed.

"What were the fucking chances of this happening?" he muttered to himself.

The TV cameras cut back to the burning Benz. He hadn't left any prints because he'd been wearing gloves, but he saw no reason to take any chances. No hair or DNA to find if everything in the interior gets incinerated. As it definitely did by the looks of things.

He may not have gotten what he wanted today, but he had to admit it was a hell of a ride. Besides, he had no doubt he'd succeed. He had to. He'd take the advice he dished to his brother. Do the work and you'll get what you want. That's why he always had a job and always made top dollar.

It was only a matter of time with these two. A matter of time.

Chapter Seven

Abbey eased the door open and stepped into the dark office, now Blake's room for the immediate future. She'd never been more torn in her life. To be living under the same roof with him, even for one or two nights, was almost more than she could handle. He made her itch to do things she didn't want to do. He made her think about all the natural things she'd possibly— probably—been missing out on as an adult.

The road rash on his arm cut a livid red distinction from the sleeve of the white T-shirt he wore. He'd thrown back the comforter and only a clean beige sheet covered him from the waist down.

Gingerly Abbey sat at the edge of the bed and set her hand on his arm. "Blake? Wake up. I need you to wake up." The EMT had been very clear about not letting him sleep for more than a couple of hours at a time until they knew for certain he really didn't have a major head trauma. Abbey wished for the thousandth time that Blake had gone to the hospital to get checked out. Why was he so stubborn? She shook his arm again. "Bla—"

"I heard you. I'm up," he croaked out in a sleepy voice. He turned his head toward her, his eyes just slits of blue. "Why'd you creep in so quiet if you planned on waking me up?"

"How do you know I crept? Maybe I came in with a bullhorn."

"Liar," he mumbled, but he was smiling and that made her smile.

Don't be so cute! God, he was nearly irresistible when he grinned like that. "How do you feel?" She leaned over and felt his forehead for fever.

"I'm good as long as you keep your hand there. Feels good. Nice and cool."

"Are you hot?" she asked. He didn't feel hot.

He didn't say anything for a few seconds. He just watched her with that devil look in his eyes and made her feel self-conscious about her tank top and sleep shorts. That was when she realized he was taking her question in a completely different context and heat warmed her cheeks. "I'm feeling sore," he finally told her. "Kind of like... I don't know. Like I got hit by a car."

She smiled at him because he was so damn adorable. But her better sense shoved its way forward and slammed some reality into her. She didn't have the tools to make a relationship work. She stood to leave, but Blake grabbed her hand.

"Don't go. Stay a while. Please." He patted the space next to him on the other side of the bed. "C'mon. I promise to be good." His eyes drifted shut for a second.

Lie down next to him? She swallowed her nervous tension. This was Blake, a nice guy she'd known for over a year. He never did anything to make her uncomfortable. She managed to do that all by herself.

"C'mon, Ab. Consider this a horizontal chair. You're just gonna sit and hang out for a few minutes." He looked so sad Abbey couldn't refuse him. She crawled over his legs and settled next to him on the bed, keeping a good distance between them.

"Why are you in Siberia?" he mumbled. "Too far away."

"You're going to be asleep in less than a minute. It doesn't matter."

"Matters to me," he murmured. He fumbled for her hand and found it. Closed his fingers around hers. "Thanks."

She barely heard the word before he got it out. Then he was fast asleep. Abbey gently took her hand back and set her watch alarm for another two hours. Now she should go back to her own room. Blake was asleep and wouldn't know either way if she stayed or left. But she didn't move. Couldn't move. In fact, she did the thing she'd never thought she'd ever do. She slid her hand back into his. He didn't budge, so she eased a little closer to get a better view of their clasped hands.

He had more road rash on his knuckles and a fresh surge of sympathy oozed through her veins. His big hand engulfed hers. It was warm and strong even as he slept. He was always so strong, so competent and sure. From the first day she'd met him he'd been in control. He didn't have a shy bone in his body. His very hot, cut, gorgeous body.

God, just thinking back to the afternoon when the EMT had sliced off his shirt, she'd wanted to run her hands along the divide between his chest and abs. She'd wanted to taste his skin in those little valleys.

Who are you? It was a good question to ask herself since she'd never thought she'd have these feelings or urges. Ever. Of course it didn't mean she'd ever make good on them either.

Though they'd iced the whole side of his body where he'd slammed into the tire, the bruise on his face was already showing. His cheekbone and eye were going to be a solid purple and black tomorrow. Her lids got heavy as she watched him. Poor guy.

Abby's watch alarm went off—the sound of an old time European ambulance—and she jolted awake and shut it down. The room came into focus and it wasn't hers. A wave of heat flushed her skin. She'd fallen asleep in Blake's bed. Next to him! Her panic faded as she turned to him, his eyes closed, his breathing steady. A wave of embarrassment washed through her quickly followed by remorse for having to rouse him from sleep again. She yawned and gently touched his shoulder. "Blake?"

"I'm awake. Who could sleep through that siren of an alarm?" he asked in a sleepy croak.

Grinning, Abbey cocked her elbow and leaned her head on her hand. "My sister for one."

"No way. I don't believe you." His gorgeous blue eyes opened and stared right at her.

"Honest to God, truth. Bernie can sleep through an earthquake."

"Bernie?" he asked.

"Short for Bernadette. She's my big sis."

Blake gingerly adjusted on his side, bent his arm under his head to see her better. "How much bigger? By how many years?"

"Four."

"How come you never told me about your sister?"

"I don't know." She shrugged. "It's not important. It's just never come up."

He watched her so closely, as if he could figure out her life story if he stared long enough. "Tell me something else about you." His voice sounded sleepy and sexy and Abbey wished she were brave enough to let herself go with him.

"Like what?" At his impatient glare, she smiled. "What's to tell? Really? I work for Julie, I'm a dancer, I have one big sister and my parents moved to North Carolina to be with my Dad's parents a couple of years ago. That's my story."

"You just told me the *only* things I *already* knew about you."

She hadn't told him any of that besides Bernie. "How could you already know?"

He rolled his eyes. "Seriously, you're going to ask me that knowing I work for Troy, a private investigator?"

"Does that mean you were investigating me?" She didn't know if she should be angry or flattered.

"No," Blake replied. "It means I wanted to know more about you because you won't ever talk to me."

"That's not true," she argued. He made a wide-eyed face at her and she had to come clean. "Okay, maybe sometimes I'm not great at conversation." One dark eyebrow lifted a fraction. "Maybe more than sometimes," she admitted. But if he tried to get more out of her now, she'd be out of here faster than he could blink. In fact, it was way past time for her to leave this bed. She lifted her head and eased back.

"Don't. Please, Abbey. Just stay. I promise I won't ask you any questions. Just stay with me. I sleep better with you here."

She shook her head and fought back a tired grin. "You're sleeping because you tangled with a Hummer, you're loaded up on ibuprofen and you're wiped out."

"You take the comp out of compliment, you know that?" he asked.

She settled next to him again and they watched each other for a long minute. "Well this is fascinating," she murmured.

"I don't believe it," he said in a lazy drawl. "Two jokes in one day. I must have landed in an alternate universe." Keeping her grin under wraps wasn't possible and he smiled back at her. "Do you have any idea how fucking beautiful you are when you smile like that?" His raw whisper hit her on a cellular level.

Heat burned up her cheeks and she blinked. How was she supposed to answer that? "You make it sound like I never smile."

"If you do, it's not when I'm around. You have no idea how much I want to change that."

"Blaaake." She drew out his name, a warning to stop because she didn't know how to make it any clearer that nothing was going to happen between them.

"Abbeeeey," he replied softly. He was too sweet and she smiled from the warm fuzzies at the way he said her name.

"That's what I'm talking about." He watched her for a second and sighed. "Okay fine. You don't want to talk about you. Let's talk about me." He rolled onto his back. "What do you want to know?"

Now this she could handle. "I know you have an older sister, two older brothers and Brendan is your twin brother, but who's the older twin, you or Brendan?"

"Me, of course. Thank God. It's about the only thing I have to lord over him."

"Spoken like a true big brother." She grinned at his sidelong glance. "I met your sister."

Blake shifted on his back and tried to adjust his pillow, and Abbey leaned in to help him when he grimaced in pain. "When?" he finally asked when he was comfortable enough.

"During filming. Julie introduced us one afternoon. I only saw her a few times, but she seemed really nice." *Payback* was a true story based on Jess Bryant's life. A story that involved not only her husband, but her whole family, including Blake.

"My big sis. I'm really proud of her." The slight curve of Blake's lips hinted at a grin. "She worked herself into the ground for that film."

Abbey still didn't want to ask him about being kidnapped. The topic opened the door to sharing, and she wasn't great at talking about herself, but remembering the movie and seeing Blake so banged up now had her emotions riding a thin line.

His whole family had gone through hell and she didn't know what to say. "That whole ordeal must have been a nightmare." Without even thinking, she reached out and took his hand.

Blake could've died and gone to heaven right at that very

minute. The way Abbey said his name made every wish, dream and fantasy he'd ever had about her seem like a possibility. It was the first time Abbey had ever reached out to him while not in a crisis. He would've made a joke about it, but doing so would only push her away. He knew her well enough to guess that.

It had bothered him that in all this time she hadn't said one goddamn word in sympathy for his being kidnapped and tied up for the better part of four days. Her lack of interest had actually curbed his rampant desire to get her under the sheets.

Watching her wide green eyes shining in sympathy and concern made him feel like a total heel for being mad at her all those months ago. Time had pretty much gotten him over the anger, but he'd filed it away as ammunition whenever he got soft around her, whenever he'd catch himself staring and daydreaming about touching her or kissing her.

"You don't need to look at me like that," he said softly.

"How did you...? How are you? How did you deal with that?"

He saw her looking at his ears. "You're thinking of Brendan. My ears are fine. Intact." The names had been changed in the movie so only people really close to the family knew it was about them.

"But still. The ending of the movie. Is that what really happened?"

"You mean, did the whole family get shot?" He nodded. "All true."

That sympathy was back as Abbey's brows knit together. "And everyone recovered from it okay?" She adjusted from sitting on her shins to crossing her legs in front of her. Her mile long legs gleamed in the moonlight streaming in from the window and he fought the urge to reach out and touch all that soft skin.

Blake couldn't help but grin at her tone. "You did see the movie, right?"

She smacked his arm. "Don't make fun of me. It was still a movie and just because it was based on true events doesn't mean that's what actually happened." She glanced up to the ceiling. "Whenever I ran into Jess while doing stuff for Julie, she was so nice to me. Like we were friends or something."

"You talked to her?"

"Not a ton, but a couple of times. She was kind of busy, producing and directing."

Blake nodded. "Yeah, she worked her ass off. Tanner and she didn't go on their honeymoon until after she'd finished up in editing. Jess had actually cornered Blake midway through production when he'd visited the set and asked him point blank what the situation was with Abbey. He hadn't been able to hide his feelings from his sis. Jess had a made a point to talk to Abbey a little bit more just to see if she passed inspection. "She liked you," he said.

Abbey narrowed her eyes at him.

He laughed and regretted it instantly when a shock of pain zipped through his chest. "I'm serious. She thought you were very nice and very good at your job. She thought it was sweet how much you take care of Julie." He squeezed her hand. "You're very good at taking care of the people you care about."

She dipped her head, shy. She really didn't know how to take a compliment. He felt her slipping away.

"Did you meet my brother-in-law? The Monster."

She met his gaze, a smile growing on her lips. "You really called him that?"

"We called him a lot of things," Blake admitted. "We weren't sure about him in the beginning. Actually, after our first introduction to the guy, we wanted to kill him, but he grew on us. He's really good for Jess. They make a great team." He envied Jess her relationship with Tanner. They reminded him of his parents. He wanted something like that for himself, which was why he'd tried his damnedest to keep away from Abbey. She didn't want anything to do with him and life was too short to force a feeling that wasn't there. He wanted someone who wanted him, someone he could confide in through the good and the bad. He'd been doing really well until she'd run into his arms like a tight end headed to the end zone. And boom, he was right back in the palm of her hand, needing to comfort her, needing to keep her safe and wishing like hell that she felt the same way.

"Julie introduced me to Tanner in the very beginning, but I never really talked to him after that. He was pretty busy too. I read that this was their first project together."

"Yep. Jess jumped in with both feet and dragged Tanner with

her." He grinned at the picture. His tiny, big sis, dragging her giant of a husband anywhere always made him smile.

"The guy that kidnapped you is still in prison?" she asked.

"For a very long time," Blake confirmed.

"And the guy that nearly ran us over today... You think he remembers you too?'" she asked.

Blake nodded. "It's possible. Yeah." He hated the worry in her pretty eyes and squeezed her hand. "Hey, it's going to be all right. We're safe here. Troy made this place a fortress."

"But what happens when we're not here? I can't hide out at Julie and Troy's house until I'm old and brittle. I have a life to live." She closed her eyes and shook her head as if something else was behind the words.

"Don't we all," Blake said around a yawn. His involuntary stretch sent a fresh wave of pain across his middle.

Unfortunately, Abbey had a sharp eye on him. "You can have a couple more ibuprofen if you want, then you should go back to sleep and get a few more hours of rest." Abbey reset her watch alarm and shifted like she might leave.

"I'm okay. Will you stay?" Blake closed his eyes and squeezed her hand. He hadn't been lying. He did sleep better with her next to him. The fresh citrus scent of her seeped into his pores with every breath and relaxed him like a full body massage.

She exhaled a long-suffering sigh, but he gave her a pitiful look and she caved with a tilt of her head. "Fine. But I'm not staying all night long. Just a few more minutes." She propped up a pillow against the headboard and leaned against it, still sitting up.

"Few more minutes is good," he mumbled and passed out again.

A light sensation along his neck woke him slowly. Something was different, but he couldn't figure out what. He didn't budge as he let his senses come to life. First, his pillow was different, not as fluffy. He caught the fresh scent of Abbey and wanted to inhale all of her. He liked that she was still here with him. But wait...she was more than here. He had his arm wrapped around a different pillow. A moving pillow. A breathing pillow. And his hand wasn't wrapped around a pillow, it was cupped around...a hip. He concentrated on the soft sensation along his neck, the way the caress sent every nerve ending alert and begging for more. He took another whiff, careful to keep his breathing even, careful to make sure Abbey thought he was still asleep. Because somehow, he'd ended up laying his head on her stomach and instead of shoving him off or away, she'd let him stay. That light caress against his neck was her fingers gently weaving through his hair. He didn't want to move, could barely manage to get air into this lungs knowing it was Abbey touching him now.

Then a feeling came over him and he wanted to block it out completely. He was not feeling pressure *there*. No, no, no. Not now. But Mother Nature said, "Yes, now."

Fucknuts. He had to go to the bathroom.

Chapter Eight

Moonbeams filtered in from the window as Abbey gently stroked Blake's soft hair. It slid between her fingers like thick silk and the red streaks glistened in the pale light. She'd have to wake him up soon and end the few perfect minutes she'd stolen to touch him. To touch him. She hardly ever touched anyone, with the exception of dance partners. Usually she didn't think too much about it, but taking this time with Blake set a precedent for her.

When he'd rolled onto her and woken her out of a deep sleep, she'd nearly jumped a mile. Especially when he'd closed his hand over her hip. But in the seconds it had taken her to rear up, she'd realized he was sound asleep. That one factor changed everything. His possessive touch hadn't scared her. On the contrary, it was nice to pretend she could even consider enjoying the way his hand cupped her hip. His warm breath wafted across her stomach and tickled the bare spot below her T-shirt and above her shorts.

For the gazillionth time, she wished she were normal. Wished she wasn't so afraid of people. Of men. Of contact and connection. But making connections meant sharing stories and she could never share her story with anyone she cared about. Sure, her sister, parents and a few other professionals knew her secret, but no one else did and that suited her fine.

Blake took a deep breath and Abbey froze. Oh God, was he awake? She'd promised herself she'd only stay like this a few minutes. She didn't want him to catch her like this, fondling his hair or being caught beneath him.

"Ab," he murmured.

Shit! She removed her fingers from the softness of his hair. "What?"

"I knew you'd stop," he mumbled, then sighed again. "I have to go to the little boy's room."

Abbey shook her head and couldn't help the smile that found its way to her mouth. "The little boy's room, huh?" she repeated, easing away from Blake as he rolled over, a grimace on his face. "You need some help?"

"No." His face squinted into a pucker as he tried to sit up and finally plopped back down. "Yes."

"Mm-hmm. I thought so." She moved to his side of the bed and helped him up and over to the bathroom. "Do you need some help or are you gonna get everything handled in there?"

Blake's sidelong glance nearly melted her panties. "That's three. I'm totally making a list. Three jokes in one day. This is a new record, right?"

Why did she do this to herself? Why did she say things she knew he would pounce on? Especially when his reaction would cause a chain reaction. She loved his jokes and his devastating smiles.

She sobered immediately. That was the problem. She wouldn't be able to keep him smiling. Her true nature was a relationship killer. Her skittishness. Her inability to touch and be touched like a normal human being.

"I fucked up again," he said softly, turning to face her. "I always say the wrong thing around you. Maybe you should just slap some tape across my mouth and we'd be fine."

She shoved him gently into the bathroom. "Go do your business, boy. It's the middle of the night and I want to get back in bed. My bed," she clarified before he could make another smart remark.

He watched her for a sec then closed the door behind him.

Abbey sighed, wishing the night over already. Wishing she'd never gone to that Seger Hughes concert to begin with. Wishing she could be different.

Kim sat back in the comfortable leather of the booth and watched the club rage around her. The music blared, strobe lights flashed in the dark room, bodies undulated on the dance floor and the smell of sweat and perfume hung in the air. She hadn't been to a club in so long she'd forgotten the chaos. The way the bass rumbled in the furniture beneath her, the way the sound drowned out almost everything. Everything but her thoughts.

Stephanie came back from the bar with their drinks. "Here you go," she called, speaking over the music and handing over Kim's club soda with lime. Stephanie slid into the booth in her short black skirt and silver sequined top. "You sure you don't want anything stronger?"

"I'm sure." She hadn't quit drinking completely, but she'd quit drinking in clubs. Well, most of the time. She made bad decisions while drinking alcohol. Very bad decisions. She got too loose when she drank. She let her guard down. Life was too short to lose control like that on a regular basis, especially in a strange town.

"What do you think of the club?" Stephanie tipped her chin toward the packed dance floor.

"Carl is really one of the owners?" Kim asked. He hadn't struck her as a club owner. He struck her as a pompous asshole, but those were two separate things. The club owners she'd known in the past had been fairly decent guys. Not that she remembered very well.

"Yeah." Stephanie laughed and took a long drink of her rum and Coke. "Shocker, right?" She pointed to the blond bartender with impressive breasts busting out of her black tank top as she mixed drinks. "That's his mistress."

Kim nearly choked on her club soda. "You know this for certain?"

She nodded, a gleam in her eye. "I hired a private investigator to make sure. He's got proof. Pictures, motel receipts. The bastard thinks I don't know…but I do. I know a lot."

Kim had no idea what she'd do in the same position, but Stephanie's narrowed eyes said she didn't have the same issue. "You have a definite plan," Kim said. "What is it?"

"I'm actually still working on it. I just know I gave up my education for him. I admit marrying him for security, but I wouldn't have if I didn't honestly like him." She shook her head. "He's changed. I thought he appreciated me, respected me, but all I am to him is something pretty on his arm, something to flaunt to his friends. Do I want him to pay for that? For treating me like something he owns instead of someone he loves... yeah. I do." She took a sip of her drink. "If that makes me a bitch then so be it. He made me what I am today. I'm not sure what's happening with the money thing, so I'm waiting. I hope to God it's not as serious as he makes it out to be. Have you found anything yet?" she asked.

"Not yet, but I haven't looked at everything. Hell, I didn't even know this place existed. I didn't find it in the paperwork so far."

"Surprise," Stephanie said. She took another hefty swallow.

"Stephanie," Carl eased up to the table and moved Stephanie's drink out of her reach. "I'd like to speak with you for a minute." He indicated a door on the wall behind them, and Stephanie gave Kim a *now*-what-is-it stare.

"Fine. I'm coming. Be right back," Stephanie said to Kim, then went with Carl.

Carl kept his hand around her slim waist as the crowd swallowed them. Stephanie's heels gave her a solid two inches of height over her husband.

"Fancy meeting you here," a male voice said, a voice that sounded vaguely familiar.

Kim glanced up to see Leo Frost standing over her table. What were the chances? "Hello." She really couldn't ignore the man. Wearing a pair of dark blue jeans and a white button-up shirt with thin navy stripes, the sleeves rolled up his muscular forearms, Leo's look shouted Hollywood Royalty.

It was interesting to see the number of women who watched him — and subsequently — her.

He took the open spot next to her in the booth. "Mind if I sit down?"

She lifted a brow as she snorted. "Would it matter if I did?" She moved over to get a few more inches of personal space.

He flashed his famous smile and Kim had to admit that it packed a punch. The man was gorgeous, no doubt about it. But he was also a dickhead of major proportions. He'd lost her as a fan even before she'd learned about his altercation with Ellie Morgan. Looking back, Kim suspected it was when the high school cheerleader had pressed charges against him.

"What's a pretty lady like you doing sitting all alone in a club like this?"

"Is that the best line you've got?" She really wasn't in the mood for small talk, but she also wasn't a fan of sitting alone in a club. Too many unpleasant things had come of that in the past.

Leo pressed his lips together and nodded his head. "Tough crowd, tough crowd. Let's try again." He narrowed his outstanding blue eyes. "You couldn't have been stood up. That would be pure stupidity on someone's part."

Okay, so he didn't plan to give up. Why that should set her palms tingling, she didn't know. "No, not stood up. Here with a friend. A female friend," she stressed. "It's girls' night out so…" She made a gesture to shoo him away. "Feel free to bother someone else."

Carl picked that minute to come back to the table. "Stephanie wasn't feeling very well and she took the limo home. She didn't want to cut your night short. The driver will come back for you as soon as he drops her off. Hope it's not too much of an inconvenience." He gave her a chilly nod and turned to leave.

"Wait!" Kim called. Carl faced her and she continued. "I'll go with her."

"Too late. They've left." With that declaration, he walked away.

Kim opened her mouth, but nothing came out. Stephanie took the limo home? *Without her?* What the hell? So she was stuck here? With Leo Frost and half the eyes in the club watching them?

Leo eased back against the booth as if he planned to stay. "You look like you just lost your best friend."

Maybe because she had.

"Good thing I'm here to keep you company until the limo comes back." He shot her a smile as he adjusted to face her more.

"Unless I grab a taxi and get a ride home," she said.

"Taxis are hard to come by in this neighborhood. C'mon, hang around a few minutes. I'm harmless."

This did not make sense. "Why?"

"Why?" he repeated. "Why what?"

"Why me? You've got a club full of women who'd give their teeth to spend time with you, but you're sitting here with me. Why?"

Leo tilted his head and leaned one forearm on the table and

the other on the back of the booth as he sat forward. "I'm not sure. I guess because I liked the way you stood up for Bonnie at Nathan's office. People don't stand up anymore. I hate when bullies get away with shit."

Damn. Kim studied him and slid her finger over the rim of her glass. She actually liked that answer. More importantly, she hadn't expected it.

"I think you might've said something to Wyncott a minute ago too, but he bugged out too fast. Smart man. For a bully. If you really want to jam out of here, I'll be happy to take you home."

A nice offer, but one she doubted she'd accept. It wasn't like she couldn't wait for the limo to return and worst-case scenario had her waiting for a cab. Besides, he was kind of growing on her.

"I see your brain working." Leo took a sip of the drink in his hand. "Smoke is puffing out of your ears."

Damn. Hard to resist that one. A grin curved her lips.

"It's about time. Shit, I was going to have to pull out the big guns."

Her smile widened. "I'm afraid to ask," she said, taking a sip of her soda. "What's 'about time'?"

"Good, you should be afraid 'cause it's top secret. If I told you, I'd have to kill you."

Kim chuckled as a waitress stopped at the table and set down drinks in front of them. "Oh, I didn't order those," she said, pushing the glass away.

"Compliments of Mr. Wyncott," she said. "The tab is open for as long as you're here." She gave Leo a furtive glance before bustling off to another table.

"Well, that's nice of the man." Leo said, finishing off his old drink and lifting the fresh one. But he didn't take a sip. He just looked at it. "Mine's different than yours," he said.

Kim picked up her glass and sniffed. "Jack Daniels and water. On the rocks," she said. Her usual. Her *old* usual. It had been a long time since she'd had one in a bar. Interesting how Carl knew her drink. "What about you?"

Leo took a sip. "Seven and Seven. The man did his homework."

"Why?" Kim asked. "Weird."

"You look like you need to solve the oil crisis." His piercing blue eyes seemed to see right through her. He picked up her Jack and handed it to her. "Maybe he knows he's a prick and he's trying to make up for it."

"Do pricks do that?"

Exhaling hard, he lifted his own drink. "You're asking like I should know. I won't take offense. Yet." He clinked his glass to hers. "Here's to making new friends."

One Jack wouldn't kill her. It wasn't like she planned on having any more. She could nurse this until the limo came back. Kim took a sip and felt the cold bite as it slid down her throat. "Wow. Strong."

Leo leaned toward her and she caught a whiff of him. Pheromone heaven. The guy smelled fantastic...a combination of spice and man. "I need you to do me a favor," he said.

The old naughty side of her screamed to come out and play. There were a dozen different responses on the tip of her tongue about the kind of favor she'd love to do for him. The kind of thing her old self participated in on a regular basis, but the reincarnated Kim kept her gaze steady. "Really...and why would I do that? We don't know each other."

"We could amend that by talking tonight." He took another sip of his whiskey.

"Is that what you really want or are you looking for something else? Because I guarantee that you will not, under any circumstances, get lucky with me tonight." She sounded so sure of her statement, she even believed it herself.

He grinned and it was like getting hit with a sex stick. Her woman parts wanted to get smacked again. Repeatedly. Kim crossed her legs and took a steady breath. *Easy, easy.*

"That's what I like about you. No fucking around. No bullshit." He took another sip of his drink.

Kim didn't say anything as she took another swallow of Jack. The liquor gave her sense of power. It always did, which was why she'd learned to keep her distance. "So you don't like bullshit, but you work in a business that's full of it. How's that working for you?" She expected a smile, but instead she got a glimpse of desolate eyes before Leo turned back to his whiskey.

"You want to know the truth?" He took another long swallow. "It's kind of not."

The server came by and Leo snagged her arm. "We'll have two more."

Kim tried to protest, but Leo stopped her and gestured for the drinks. He waited for the waitress to go before he leaned toward her. "I figure we don't have to drink 'em, but we should let Carl pay for them anyway."

For the first time in a long time, Kim let loose a real smile. "I do love that way of thinking."

"See? I'm not such a bad guy," Leo offered before he tossed back the last of his drink.

"You are a very bad guy," Kim corrected, but Leo hit her with another one of his smiles and she didn't care. She took another swallow instead.

Leo quit drinking halfway through his second seven and seven, but he ordered a third round for them both anyway. It had taken a ton of coaxing to get Kim to take even a sip of her first drink, but she'd slowly polished off the whole thing. The more she drank, the more she let loose and the less he had to work at making her smile. He should've gone home an hour ago. He'd planned to. He hadn't bargained on running into the blond bombshell from Nathan's office, nor had he planned to sit down and talk to her. Usually when he encountered one of *those* that believed everything they read in the paper or the tabloids, he stayed as far away as possible. But tonight he'd been so lonely that even talking with someone who hated him seemed better than going home to his empty house.

Kim took another sip of her drink and looked around the bar. "I can't believe the limo isn't back yet." She reached for her phone. "I want to text Stephanie real fast. Sorry." With speedy fingers she typed out a message. A second later, her eyes widened. "Oh shit," she muttered. "I hope that wasn't what I think it was." She lifted her bag and picked something up. "Stephanie's purse is here." She reached inside and fished for something. "With her phone," she added, showing Leo the phone with the new text flashed on the screen. "I knew I felt it vibrate. Son of a bitch. I can't believe Stephanie left this here." She gathered both bags. "Look, sorry to bail on you, but I'm worried about her now."

Leo edged out of the booth and let her out. Her short red skirt matched the black and red patterned silk top. The outfit screamed *party girl* and showed off long toned legs. She swayed on her stilettoes when she stood up. "Whoa," he said, steadying her by her shoulders. "You okay?"

"Yeah. Sorry. I knew those drinks were strong." Her gaze flitted away. "I just need to call a cab. I haven't seen Carl and I don't want to talk to him anyway, the asshole. I'm not waiting for that limo anymore." She took another wobbly step and Leo hooked her arm with his.

"Tell you what. Let's go with my original offer. I'll drop you off. Where does Carl the Asshole live?"

Kim giggled and Leo would've bet big money that she didn't do that often. "Holmby Hills. But I don't want to impose." She looked as deadly serious as a drunk woman could.

"You're not. I offered. Besides, we're practically neighbors."

Kim looked up at him with wide, green, very untrusting eyes. "You're sure?"

"Abso-fucking-lutely. Yes."

She nodded. "Okay then. Let's hit it."

The waitress brought their third round and Leo tossed a twenty-dollar bill on her tray. "Thanks, Marly. This is for you."

"You're leaving? Don't you want your drinks?"

"Nope. We're calling it a night." Leo wrapped an arm around Kim's waist since she didn't look too steady on her four-inch heels. Once outside, he gave his ticket to the valet and they waited for his car to come around.

Photographers stood behind a red rope and a line to enter the club stretched about twenty people long. The murmur of people recognizing him whispered through the crowd. A limo pulled up to the curb just as Carl the Asshole came out of the club.

"Kim! There you are," Carl said. "I was looking all over for you." The driver of the limo got out and opened the back door. "I just got word that the limo returned so Phillip can take you back to the house."

Kim didn't make a move. "Where's Fido?" she asked.

Who the hell was Fido?

"Who?" Carl asked. Apparently Leo wasn't the only one in the dark. "It doesn't matter." He took Kim's arm and tugged her toward the car.

"Hey!" Kim snatched her arm back. "Do not touch me, Carl.

I'm not very comfortable with this." Flashes of light split the darkness as photographers caught the exchange.

Carl clenched his jaw. "You're staying at my house and I'm making sure you get there safely. It doesn't take a genius to figure it out."

Green eyes narrowed dangerously. "Is that right?" Kim said softly. She might have had one too many drinks, but the insult hadn't gotten by her. "Leo, does your offer still stand?" Her gaze never wavered from Carl the Asshole.

The valet pulled up with Stella in perfect movie timing. "You bet it does."

"Wonderful. Thank you." A second valet opened the passenger door and Kim slid into the seat, her miles of leg gleaming in the streetlight. "Goodbye, Carl. See you in the office tomorrow."

"Not likely," The Asshole muttered and, with a dismissive look to Leo, strode back into his club.

Leo slipped the valet a ten and got behind the wheel. "Let me guess," he said, pulling into traffic and happy to leave the circus behind. "I was the lesser of two evils."

Kim turned in her seat and faced him. "If we're being honest, yes. But if I were to be even more honest, I'd say that I'm not sure why you've gotten such bad press. Unless you've been on your best behavior tonight. Or maybe you've turned a new leaf and no one's caught on."

"Or maybe this is my usual MO and I become a real asshole like Carl."

She nodded. "True. Good point. But I really hope that isn't the case. Because so far, I like you a little."

Leo huffed a laugh. "A little?"

She canted her head and studied him. "I don't know you well enough to like you a lot."

He glanced over to find her watching him closely then set his eyes back on the road. "Fair enough." He had her put the address into his GPS as he drove toward the freeway. A few silent minutes went by as Leo passed downtown skyscrapers and late night traffic. "So just how much do we hate Carl the Asshole?"

She laughed and the pure delight in the sound hit him like a club. It had been so long since he'd enjoyed anything in life that he'd forgotten the feeling.

"A lot. We hate him a lot."

"Why? I should know so I can trash talk him appropriately." He slowed for a red light.

Kim exhaled a burst of air. "He treats his wife like shit. As far as I can tell he treats everyone like shit and apparently he's having an affair. I'm not a fan." That last line she directed at him and Leo didn't want to be on her wrong side.

"Hey, don't look at me like that. I'm one of the good guys."

"You do tip well. I saw that. But was it for my benefit or is that your norm?"

This time, he laughed as the light turned green and he accelerated. "I'm guilty of tossing tens and twenties at valet attendants and restaurant and bar servers. They work hard and they don't get paid nearly enough, so quit with the evil eye."

"Honey, if I was giving you the evil eye, you'd know it."

"I'll keep that in mind." Leo passed a slow moving Nissan on the right. "Tell me why you're so worried about your friend."

"I don't like that she didn't say anything before she left. I mean, I know we're both big girls, but a woman doesn't leave a restaurant or club without her purse or without saying goodbye to the person she came with. It's just not done." She shook her head. "I don't have a good feeling."

"That could be the Jack Daniels in your stomach."

She didn't argue.

"Wow, look at that." She pointed off in the distance where the giant harvest moon looked like a huge ball of fire in the sky. "Is it the smog that does that?"

"Probably," Leo said. "I've never seen it that orange before. It's like it's on fire."

"Yeah. A giant round bonfire in the sky. It's amazing."

Leo cringed at her reference. "I'm not a fan of fire unless it's contained in a fireplace."

"Why?" Kim asked, amusement in her tone. "Been burned?"

Leo nodded. "Yep. Senior year. Bonfire got a little out of control. No need to relive that experience."

"I think that's one of my biggest fears...dying by fire." She shuddered. "That and drowning."

"If you use the water to put out the fire, you can knock out both fears in one shot."

She chuckled. "If it were only that easy, right?" She faced

him again, one long leg stretched out toward the console. "What about you? What are you afraid of? Besides fire."

That was easy. His biggest fear was people finding out about Megan. He didn't want her ending up on some tabloid cover with some horrific headline about her affliction and the fact that he'd kept her a secret. He'd lived his whole life outrageously so that her privacy remained intact. He'd walked the line of making enough money to ensure she always had the care she needed without letting his fame touch Megan.

"I'm waiting," she prodded. "Fears?"

He chuckled at her curt order. Of course he had more than one fear, so he went with number two. "I'm afraid of being stuck...of losing my freedom." He instantly regretted the admission.

"You and most every other man, but at least you're admitting it." She faced forward. "I don't know if that makes you stupid or brave. Most guys don't cop to that one. They lead us along to get what they want then just bail with the first sign of emotion."

Her body language said he'd lost her. Not that he'd intended anything happening with them tonight or ever. Yes, she was very pretty, but it took more than a pretty face to get him hot and bothered these days. In fact, he wished like hell he knew what might get him hot and bothered because he needed a release of some kind. It didn't have to be sexual, he'd take a soul destroying workout right about now.

"I'll go with brave," he said. "Fits my image better. Stupid is so..."

"Stupid?" Kim supplied.

"Yeah." He glanced at her as she leaned her head on the seat rest.

"I shouldn't have had that Jack. I blame you."

"Not feeling so hot?" he asked.

"Not so much. There was a reason I quit drinking and now I remember it."

The familiar pressure of guilt crushed Leo's chest. "I didn't just push you off the wagon tonight, did I? That would make me feel like total crapshit."

She smiled with closed eyes. "No worries. I'm not in AA. I was on the verge of a drinking problem, but I recognized it and nipped it in the bud. I don't have to drink. I usually don't, which is why after one drink and two sips of a second, I'm so buzzed."

"As long as I wasn't the bad influence."

"Stephanie probably would've had me drinking with her if she'd stuck around."

"Aha, so you can't blame me." He took the freeway on-ramp and hit the gas. The car zoomed like a comet into traffic. "It's all Stephanie's fault."

Kim shot him a one-eyed glare.

The subject of Stephanie brought to mind a lot of questions. "So Stephanie is a good friend of yours and she's married to The Asshole." Kim nodded. "And she wanted to marry a guy old enough to be her father because...?"

"Because she was piss poor broke her whole life and decided early on that she didn't want to die the way she was born." Kim cracked open her eyes and shifted her head along the seat rest to watch him. "I don't blame her. It's a cruel world and people have to do things to survive."

"You don't have to sell your soul to the devil."

"Maybe you do before you figure out you shouldn't and by then it's too late."

With one sentence, she probably told him more than she realized. "You sound like someone who speaks from experience," Leo said. He eased into the left lane and passed a semi along with a dozen other cars. Stella loved to let it out.

"Not the same experience as Stephanie. Let's just say we all travel our own journey and we learn as we go." Her forlorn expression said more than her words.

"This conversation is way too deep for me." Leo cruised along the empty road, traveling way over the speed limit. The dialogue quieted until they got closer to Holmby Hills.

"Is that smoke?" Kim asked.

Leo thought she'd fallen asleep. He glanced up where she pointed. Smoke drifted against the giant harvest moon. "Someone lost something tonight." As Leo made his way closer to their destination, he realized they were headed straight for it.

"Oh my God," Kim said. "That's their neighborhood." She sat up straighter in the seat. "That is totally their neighborhood."

Leo turned down the street, expecting to see fire trucks but an empty street greeted him instead.

"Oh, shit. It's Stephanie's house!" Any alcohol high Kim had been riding seemed to vanish as she stared at the mansion. Smoke poured out of nearly every window and an orange glow lit the interior of the house. "Stephanie! She's in there! Where's the fire department? We need help!" Leo stopped the car and Kim scrambled out, teetering on her stilettos, digging through her purse. "Code, code, what's the code?"

Leo called 911 and reported the address. A couple of windows upstairs exploded and glass rained down on the front lawn.

"Stephanie!" Kim screamed. She started punching numbers in the keypad but the gate didn't open. "Stephanie!" The desperation in her voice sounded shrill. "Pull your car up against the wall," she ordered.

"What the hell for?"

She waved her hands toward the house. "I need to get her out. She's in there. I need to get her out!"

"Kim, that's crazy. You don't know that. You can't go in there. The whole fucking thing is on fire."

Flames shot out of the windows and the loud crackling sounded like a bonfire gone wild. Sirens wailed in the distance.

Kim yanked off her heels and ran for the wrought iron gate. She leaped up and caught the top of the giant W that decorated the bars. She hooked her foot into the bottom of the letter and heaved herself up. The woman had some muscle. Leo hadn't thought she'd make it, so when she got to the top of the W with no signs of slowing down, he took off to save her from herself.

"Kim! Dammit, wait for the firemen. You can't go in there!"

She jumped over the side and Leo had no choice but to follow. He got over in seconds and ran to catch up to her. Sirens blared louder as fire trucks pulled up along the gate. Leo didn't want to hurt her, but didn't see any other way to stop her. He tackled Kim just as the house exploded in a massive orange fireball, sending debris and ash into the air that rained down on them in a scalding hot shower.

Chapter Nine

The deafening sound reverberated in Kim's head and the ground shook beneath her as Leo's weight pressed her down. The smell of green grass mixed with the smoke in the air. Debris and hot embers rained down on them like a freak meteor shower.

Kim struggled to get free, but didn't have much of a chance with the bulk of Leo on top of her. "I need to help her," she screamed, clawing the lawn. Panting, she fought to get free, but Leo kept her pinned. When she finally stopped and looked up, all the blood drained from her face.

The house was practically gone, the roof blown off into nothing and the front walls collapsed to the interior. Despair crept up and strangled her chest, her throat. The Jack Daniels in her stomach swirled with vile intent.

"Stephanie." She barely got the name out. "Stephanie!" She screamed at the top of her lungs. Maybe she'd gotten out the back or... Kim scanned the expanse of the massive front lawn, but didn't see any sign of her. She dropped her head on the ground as her stomach roiled more. "No, no, no," she said, over and over.

"Fuck," Leo swore and moved off her fast.

She turned to see him scrambling to pull off his shirt, a shirt that was smoking in the back. Rushing to help, she yanked it over his head and tossed it aside. Leo stood there, clenching his fists and his jaw, his eyes closed, his back arched as he clearly fought the pain of the burn. "Here sit down," she told him, helping him to the lawn. "We need some help here!" she called to the firemen and paramedics still outside the gate. They had the jaws of life out and were attempting to cut the wrought iron. Kim ran to the walk-in gate and opened it from the inside so paramedics could enter. "My friend is in the house!" she screamed over the crackling blaze as they filed in. "Someone's in the house!" Firemen manning the hoses started dousing the house from the street, but it hardly seemed to make a dent in the flames. Kim started for the house again, but strong hands held her back.

"Get back!" A fireman yelled over the noise. "Stay out of the way!"

The weight in Kim's chest threatened to crush her lungs. She couldn't breathe. Couldn't think. The Jack in her stomach finally swirled to the point of no return. She lurched out of the fireman's hold and ran for the hedges along the front wall of the estate. Violently, she heaved the contents of her stomach onto the hibiscus plants.

Someone approached from behind her and set an arm on her back. "C'mon, come sit over here. I think your friend needs you."

Her friend was dead.

Kim looked up and realized the man wasn't talking about Stephanie.

Paramedics had Leo on his stomach as they attended to the wounds on his back. Kim sat near his head and, feeling very useless, she stroked her fingers through his hair as she divided her attention between the burning house and Leo's blistered back. God, his hair was so soft and thick.

He craned his head and looked up at her with his cobalt blue eyes.

"I'm sorry," she said before he got a word out. "I didn't know the house was going to blow up." Another explosion happened, but this one landed in her chest like a guilt grenade. She shook her head. "I'm so sorry," she said quietly. "You wouldn't have gotten hurt if you hadn't tackled me. What were you thinking doing such a stupid thing?"

One dark eyebrow lifted high. "You're shittin' me, right?"

She smiled slightly even as the sting of tears burned her eyes. "Yeah. I guess I am," she said softly. "Thanks for saving my ass."

"As long as you brought it up...I happen to think it's a pretty fine ass." Leo took her hand and linked their fingers. "Sorry." he gestured toward the house.

The tears she'd been holding back finally slipped down her cheeks. Stephanie was gone. If she was in that house, she couldn't have survived.

Oh shit. Carl. She needed to call Carl.

"I'll be back in a sec, okay," she told Leo. "I need to get my purse and call Carl." Kim picked her way through the yard in her bare feet, avoiding hot chunks of burning wood. She found her shoes outside the gate and picked them up before retrieving her purse from Leo's Porsche. She scrolled through her contacts but couldn't find his number. Frustration sizzled down her spine. She hadn't added him to her contact list yet. Dammit.

Stephanie's phone! She snagged Stephanie's purse, found the phone, and punched Carl's number.

"What?" he demanded. *What. A. Prick.*

"It's Kim. Carl, something's happened. You need to come home. Stephanie is...Stephanie is..." She didn't know what Stephanie was. Until her body was recovered, Kim chose to avoid thinking the worst. "You need to come home now."

"I'm a little busy at the moment." If there was something worse than a prick, Carl was it.

"Carl, your house just fucking exploded and it's burning to the ground. I suggest you get in your fucking car and come home." Kim disconnected the call and a fresh sting of tears blurred her eyes.

A strong arm came around her shoulders and she looked up at a shirtless Leo. She'd forgotten how ripped he was. It had been years since she'd seen him in *Dangerous Race*. The movie had an R rating because the sex scenes were so hot. His washboard abs came from hard workouts and a huge amount of discipline.

She spotted the edge of the bandages along his side. "Are you okay?"

"Nothing time and burn cream won't cure." He tipped his chin toward the phone in her hand. "The Asshole is on his way?"

"Yeah." She shook her head. "I shouldn't have lost my temper with him, but he makes it hard to be civil. Still." She gestured to the house and her bottom lip trembled. "This is...this is really..." She couldn't finish and Leo pulled her against him. She tried to hold it in, tried to keep a breakdown from happening and the effort shook her shoulders.

"I'm sorry," Leo whispered, his lips so close to her ear. "I'm so sorry."

He didn't try to downplay it. Didn't try to pretend that everything was all right. She might've lost her friend tonight. She held onto the hope that until they had proof, Stephanie wasn't dead. He held her like that for a long time. Right up until Carl pulled up in his Bentley, got out of his car and surveyed what was left of his house.

"What happened here?" he asked, his eyes wide as he took in the scene. It was the first drop of emotion she'd noticed from him.

"I have no idea. We pulled up and it was fully engulfed in flames."

"Where's Stephanie?" he asked, scanning the yard like he expected to see her with them.

Oh God, how did she break the news? "I never saw her." Maybe he'd understand what she meant. "Maybe she went to a neighbor's house after she got home. Or maybe she realized she forgot her purse and headed back to the club." All of a sudden her spirits picked up. Yes! That made perfect sense! Maybe she hadn't been in the house after all. Maybe she was at the club now, wondering where Kim was.

Kim only hoped. Until the authorities investigated the site, they wouldn't know for sure.

A police officer took their statement and Kim told them what little she knew. The first point of business was to find the limo driver and see if he'd actually taken Stephanie home or if she'd had him drop her off somewhere else. Although Kim had no idea where she might go, especially without her purse and ID, but until they found her body, she chose to think the best case scenario.

"I guess we need to find a hotel," Carl muttered, looking a little shell-shocked at his burned out house.

"A hotel," Kim repeated stupidly. Yes, she'd need a new place to stay. "Oh, damn," she murmured. All of her stuff had been in the house...all her clothes and luggage, gone. She closed her eyes at the insignificance of the personal loss. But Carl's meaning finally registered with her whacked out brain.

"We have to stay somewhere tonight." He gestured toward

his Bentley and Kim stood frozen, staring at him. "What are you waiting for? An engraved invitation? Let's go."

Not in this lifetime. Not even if he quadrupled her salary. She still had her wallet and credit cards. She didn't need Carl. "No." She didn't say it loud and having the steely hard gaze focused on her sent a wash of cold chills down her back.

"Don't be a fool." Carl's beady eyes bored right through her. "You have no place else to stay. You don't have a choice."

Prick to the tenth power.

She turned to Leo. "Can you take me to a nearby hotel. I'd really appreciate it."

He watched her for a second and considered something. "How about you come to my place? It's closer than anything in the area and it's a hell of a lot cheaper."

God, she didn't want to do that either. Staying with Leo Frost? What kind of suicide was that?

"Don't look at me like I'm him," he said, thumbing over his shoulder to Carl. "You'll have your own room, your own shower and I've got an extra car you can drive. I won't get near you, won't touch you." His solemn expression sold her. The man knew how to win an argument. No wonder he'd won so many awards. He was a master convincer. "C'mon. What do you say?"

Kim didn't even look at Carl. "I say, Thank you. You're on."

Hot water sluiced over Blake's shoulders as he stood under the shower spray in the opulent travertine tile shower. Two days had gone by. Two days of being near Abbey and at the same time, being a thousand miles *away* from Abbey. She was a pro at creating distance between them.

Blake shook his head to force the thought out of his mind. He shut down the stream, snagged the thick microfiber towel over the glass door and got out of the shower. Although his bruises looked like he'd gone ten rounds with a bull, he felt much better. At least he could move without pain ripping through his muscles. Recuperating in his boss's tricked out house was way better than his no frills apartment.

Now if he could just figure out Abbey, he'd be batting a thousand. The healthier he got, the more she drifted away from him. He closed his eyes and thought back to the other night when he'd woken up with her fingers playing in his hair. He wanted more of that. A lot more. He wanted to be able to touch her that way. To not only run his hands through her hair, but across her skin. To taste the softness of her lips, the sweetness of her body.

He opened his eyes and exhaled a hard breath. He needed a life.

He also needed to get back to his own place. Toweling off the water, he reached for his clothes on the counter. He couldn't hide out here anymore. Yeah, he'd needed the time to heal a bit, but no one was going to run him down or catch him unaware again. Not him or Abbey.

The police still hadn't found their guy and Blake knew he was out there. Waiting, watching. There was no *if* the guy planned to strike again. It was *when* and *where*.

Blake gingerly pulled on his faded jeans, a white T-shirt and headed into the kitchen.

"How you feeling?" Troy asked as he poured himself some coffee. "Want some?" He lifted the pot.

"Sure. Thanks," Blake replied. "I'm better. I look like shit, but at least I can move." He took the mug Troy offered and sipped a taste. Good stuff. "Look, I just want to thank you and Julie for letting me hang here the last couple of days. You didn't have to, and I appreciate it, but I'm good to go home. I don't want to overstay my welcome. I would appreciate if you let Abbey stay though. I'm worried about her." Blake took another swallow of his coffee.

Troy nodded. "We planned on it. Julie's worried about her too. We all are."

Footsteps sounded in the hallway and Abbey entered the kitchen. Dressed in her dance gear—the same outfit with the hot pink stripe—and her makeup and hair done to perfection, she looked like a movie star in the making. No, she looked like a goddess. Like the woman who held the key to every fantasy he'd ever had. She was the pot of gold at the end of the rainbow.

Blake blinked a couple of times and cleared the fog in his head. "You're pretty decked out." A giant understatement. She was pure unadulterated sweetness. So where the hell did she think she was going? "Hot date?" At eight thirty in the morning, he doubted it.

"Hot audition," she said. "My stupid phone never rang, but

my agent called last night and left a voice mail. I've got a callback from the audition the other day. I'm in the running for one of the show regulars. This is way bigger than I anticipated. I thought I was going for one of the dance teams."

A swell of pride for Abbey washed through Blake. It was about time she was up for something big. But no sooner had the thought appeared, another one came right on its heels. Blake glanced at Troy when reality set in. "You aren't seriously going to this? What time is the audition?"

"A couple of hours." She tilted her head and glared at him as she ignored his first question. "I have to leave here in thirty minutes. I need to get there early and warm up."

Dying to say, *no*, Blake held back that response and said, "I'm going with you then."

Abbey lifted one perfect eyebrow and Blake returned the look with narrowed eyes, daring her to argue. "Excuse me?" she said with one hand perched on her hip.

A big-ass wave of frustration crashed in on him. "I said, 'I'm going with you.'" He ran a hand through his hair and paced across the kitchen to keep from grabbing Abbey and tying her to a kitchen chair. "Did you forget what happened two days ago? Do you think because some time has passed that this guy is conveniently gone?"

Abbey clenched her jaw and stood up straighter, which actually didn't seem possible. "No," she said coolly. "I haven't forgotten." She strode over to him and faced him head on. Her citrus scent climbed into his head and made his brain cells fuzzy. "I thought maybe you or Troy could make sure no one's following me when I leave. You'd know if someone was and once we decide I'm clear, then I don't have to worry. Because if he's not sitting out front, then he's not going to know where I'm headed. For your information, I don't take what happened lightly, but I don't expect you to escort me all over town for the rest of my life or until this guy is caught."

Julie walked into the room and to the giant stainless steel fridge. "I remember having a similar conversation with you about a year ago," she said with a pointed look at her husband.

Troy acknowledged her with a shrug. "Very true. And who was right about keeping you under wraps from everyone?"

A loud exhale accompanied Julie's eye roll. "He was a girl in a past life," she told Abbey. "He never lets me forget anything."

"I can't help it if I'm right." Troy lifted his hands in an innocent gesture.

Abbey wasn't having any part of it. "Look, I get it, okay. But I can't live my whole life in your house waiting for the other shoe to drop. We have a much better chance of actually catching this guy if I'm out doing my thing. Was your plan to wait until he made a move on me here? I doubt it," she said, pacing away from them. "You'd probably rather keep me hidden here for God knows how long. Which brings to mind my job. How am I supposed to do my job if I'm stuck here?" She glanced at Julie and let them think on that for a few seconds as she picked up her bag from the counter. "I have to leave here soon and I appreciate one of you guys following me for a few miles to make sure no one else is." She looked between Troy and Blake before opening her bag and rifling through it. "I left my keys in the bedroom. I'll be right back." She left the room and Blake faced the wall and thunked his head twice.

Shit, he needed to get his boots on before she walked out the door. He couldn't go with her barefoot. He headed to the office.

Troy's voice followed him from the kitchen. "I'll follow you guys for a little while and make sure you're not tailed. Abbey had a point. Unless the guy is watching the house he has no way to know where she is or where she's going."

"He sure as hell knew she was at that audition," Blake said over his shoulder. It took him less than a minute to jam his feet into his size thirteen Timberlands and get back to the kitchen.

A few minutes later, Abbey entered and picked up her bag. "Are you going to follow me?" she asked Blake.

"Nope. I'm taking you. Troy is going to follow us."

"I guess there's no point in arguing that you could still use some down time." She didn't bother meeting his gaze.

"I guess you're right."

She huffed a sigh and headed to the front door, leaving him and Troy following behind like lap dogs. "See you later," she called.

"Bye," Julie yelled. "Break legs."

Blake shook his head. He never understood how breaking a leg meant good luck.

Outside, he opened the passenger door to his Explorer and

waited until Abbey climbed in. The garage door lifted and Troy pulled his BMW out of one of the three car bins. Easing into the driver's seat, Blake grabbed his shades from the dash and slid them on before cranking the engine. He hated the silence between them.

"You know this is only about protecting you, right? I'm not the dick you're making me out to be."

"I never said you were a dick. You just don't seem to understand that this is my life. My dream. I can't let an opportunity like this go by."

Blake grunted.

Traffic was a bitch and Blake pulled off the main road onto the surface streets to avoid it. He checked the rearview mirror to see if anyone followed. He called Troy from the Bluetooth unit. "Any sign of anything?" he asked his boss.

"Not a thing. I'll let you know if I spot anyone on your tail."

"Got it. Thanks."

They made it to the audition and Blake found a parking place along the street. He walked Abbey into the building then waited in the downstairs lobby. Dozens of dancers loitered in the area and they all looked toned and beautiful.

Blake stood at the big windows near the door and kept an eye out on the street. He watched for slow cruising vehicles or suspicious people. Most especially he looked for a man named Kwami.

"Abbey Washington," a petite redhead called, looking up from her clipboard.

"Right here." Abbey stood, tossed her pack over her shoulder and followed the casting assistant into the room. At least a half dozen people sat behind two six-foot-long tables. Most of them had their heads down as they played on their cell phones. Abbey had never done more than dance for an audition. She either danced and got the job...or didn't get the job. This interview went way past her norm. She had to do something to catch their attention and keep it.

"This is Abbey," the woman said, introducing her to the group. She handed Abbey's headshot to the person on the end and exited the room.

"Hi, Abbey," a few people said as she dropped her pack in

the corner and stood on the mark on the floor opposite six pairs of eyes now focused on her.

"Hi," she said, her smile genuine since adrenaline cruised through her veins.

The casting director adjusted the lens on the camera. "Slate please," she said. "And profiles."

"I'm Abbey Washington. I'm twenty-four." She turned and gave the camera both right and left profiles. That was a first too.

"Great," the casting director said after a few seconds of tape. "We're going to improvise things. I hope that's okay."

Abbey gave them her best smile. "Of course." Like she had an option, which she didn't.

No one knew better than her that she'd hibernated in a mental cell of her own making for the past nine years. If she didn't step out of it now and show these people she had what it took to land this show, then she didn't deserve it. She channeled her lighthearted boss with the great comic timing.

"What's your favorite hobby?" one of the producers asked.

"That's easy." She scanned the room. "Dancing."

"What's your favorite style of dance?" a woman on the far end asked.

"Oh, wow, that's like a asking a mother who her favorite child is," Abbey joked. The producers smiled. "I love hip hop, of course, but I'm also a little old fashioned and I adore ballet. Tap too. The sound, the rhythm, it's pretty awesome. But don't tell the Tango, Rumba or Waltz I said that because they all think they're my favorite."

A few them made notes and Abbey fused the smile on her face.

"How old were you when you started dancing?" a man in the middle asked. His stern tone and expression reminded her of Simon Cowell.

"Four. My mom enrolled my big sister and me into a neighborhood ballet class. It didn't go over well at first though." She paused to dangle the hook a little. "There was one older boy in the class who got to kind of stand in the middle just to walk a girl around or dip her over his arm. I wanted that job. The teacher finally told me I could once I learned everything they had to teach me." She nodded at the people watching her. "Turns out it was a good deal, because I really liked the dancing part."

After that, she ad-libbed her brains out, answering more questions for another ten minutes.

When they thanked her and she walked down the hallway, she thought she might burst with excitement. She saw Blake at the door and couldn't help herself. She leaped into his arms and hugged him tight before pulling away.

"Good news, I take it?" he asked. The surprise on his face overrode the concern in his eyes.

"I don't know yet," she said, following him outside. The warmth of the sun felt good after the cold audition room. She didn't even let the fact that he scanned the street in both directions get her down. "It went really great." She grabbed his arm and stopped him. "Like, really, really, fantastically great. I've never spent that much time in an audition. They really wanted to hear more about me. They laughed and we talked and it was awesome."

"Good. I'm glad." His blue eyes sparkled in genuine happiness.

They piled back into his SUV and Abbey squealed after closing her door. "We have to celebrate," she said.

The open-mouth surprise on Blake's face made her laugh. "What's your definition of the word *celebrate?*"

She pointed ahead. "Ice cream. There's a little shop about a mile down. C'mon. It's on me."

He looked through the rearview mirror then at her. "You're on." He found a parking spot in the lot and together they walked into the empty store with pink-and-purple dots on the walls, amid pictures of ice cream, floats and shakes. A few minutes later, they emerged with double scoops of ice cream on cones. Gold medal ribbon for her. Mint chocolate chip for him.

The sun blazed down as people walked by and cars cruised down the busy street.

"Let's walk across to the park," Abbey suggested. Blake took another look around and Abbey wasn't sure if he'd agree. "C'mon. Troy didn't see anything when we left the house and he followed us too. We're fine." Although she hated the bruises on his face and couldn't help feeling guilty. If he hadn't been at that audition, he wouldn't have gotten hurt. Of course, she'd probably be dead so grateful probably out-weighed guilt. After waiting for the light to change, they walked across the street as they enjoyed their cones.

Abbey found a secluded spot near a small grove of magnolia trees. She sat down on a bench then faced Blake, kicking one leg under the other. The smell of fresh cut grass filled her head.

"How does your face feel?" she asked. His eyes were on her mouth and she wiped her lips with a napkin.

"It's fine. A little tender like my ribs, but okay."

"Good. I'm glad you're feeling better." The whole world seemed to be looking better at the moment. Blake was healing and she had a great audition. Life was good. She grinned and took a long lick of her cone.

"This job means that much, huh?"

She nodded. "Yeah, this job could be it for me. Make or break. This is high profile. The real deal." A wasp flew by her head. She yelped and crouched forward then shoved closer to Blake as it made another pass.

Blake swatted it away, but when Abbey sat up, their faces were inches apart. Blake reached up a hand to her face, but Abbey shied back. "You just have some ice cream," he said. He tapped the spot on his own lip to show her and she wiped her mouth again.

This close, she smelled the heady, woodsy clean scent of him. The sparkle in his blue eyes faded as he watched her and something serious took over. He leaned in a fraction and, terrified that he might try to kiss her, Abbey stood up and walked toward a nearby tree.

Blake looked around the mostly empty park as he joined her. "Can I ask you something without you getting mad at me?" He took a bite out of his sugar cone.

"I don't know. I guess it depends on the question." His lead-in scared her.

He glanced up at the branches above her head before leveling her with his beautiful eyes. "Are you gay?" He rushed on before she could answer. "I mean, it's fine if you are, don't get me wrong. People should be free to live their lives the way they want as long as they aren't hurting anyone else or..." He closed his eyes, shook his head and exhaled a long breath. "Look, I'm not usually this big of an idiot, but..." He opened his eyes. "I don't know how to... I don't know...about you. And I want to."

Abbey stood frozen. He thought she was gay. It shouldn't surprise her really, but it had never crossed her mind. She could lie and tell him she was, and it would solve her Blake dilemma, but it wasn't like her to lie. Keeping herself private didn't make her a liar. "No," she finally said, cocking her head a little. "I'm not gay."

"In all the time I've known you," Blake went on, "I've never seen or heard about you going on a date."

"Julie keeps me pretty busy," she said, hoping that sounded plausible.

He watched her like a hawk eyeing his next meal, gauging her face and her words. After a few seconds, he shook his head. "Nope. I don't believe it. Especially since she married Troy. He does half the stuff you used to do, simply because they live in the same house. Try again."

She should've seen this coming. The man was training to become a PI. As she well knew, Troy was a good mentor to Blake. "It's really none of your business if I go out on a date or not," she told him. She tried to keep her voice even.

"I thought you said you wouldn't get mad at me." He gave her a small, chastised grin.

"I'm not mad at you."

"Then tell me why you don't go out."

Abbey looked over his shoulder. Maybe she should just tell him. There existed a good chance that he figured it out or at least considered the possibility.

He shrugged at her silence. "There are a few reasons it could be." He ticked off one finger. "Maybe some bastard hurt you somewhere along the line. Maybe he cheated on you or lied to you. Or maybe your parents might've had a rocky relationship and it's tainted the way you see men."

She waited for his next reason, but he just watched her. Maybe he *hadn't* figured it out. Or maybe he just didn't want to go there. "Nope, my parents are solid. Very solid. They're actually kind of disgusting with all the hand holding and touching."

Blake nodded. "Yeah, my folks are the same. I can see how two people in love is really gross." He lifted an amused eyebrow at her.

Abbey playfully smacked his arm then had to shake the sting out of her hand. God, he was hard bodied.

"That leaves the 'some bastard hurt you' choice," Blake

continued. It was true, but maybe not quite the way he imagined. "If you don't give a guy a chance, how can he prove he'll be good to you?" he whispered, but his steely-eyed gaze meant serious business. He had a valid point, but it went beyond giving a guy a chance. It was about her fears. Her phobias. It was about her ability—more like inability—to be close to a man.

"I'm not good with touching," Abbey said softly, her eyes downcast, she couldn't look at him. "It's kind of hard to have a relationship with someone if you can't stand to be touched."

"But I touched you in the elevator the first time we ever met." A breeze blew through his hair and she remembered the softness of it from the other night.

"Because I thought we were going to die and it just seemed like I needed to hold on to something, someone. You were there, so..."

"How long have you been like this?" he asked.

Abbey finished off her ice cream and wiped her mouth. "A long time."

Chapter Ten

Blake looked up to the cloudless blue sky and tried to tamp down the rage building under his skin. To think that someone had hurt her, that someone might have violated her made him crazy inside, but he didn't want to leap to a conclusion. "Why?"

"I think you might know the answer," she told him. "But trust me, you don't want to go there. *I* don't like going there either." She looked around the park and Blake followed her gaze, made sure the coast was still clear. No one seemed suspicious. A guy throwing a Frisbee for his dog, two women with babies in strollers. It was pretty quiet. Except for his insides. His insides boiled with anger because everything she said took him to a dark place.

"Someone hurt you. Physically," he said.

She nodded.

Blake had to wrap his brain around that. How could anyone hurt this woman or the girl she used to be? "How old were you?"

"I'd just turned fifteen."

He ran a hand over his jaw as his rage multiplied. He turned and looked up at the tree line. "Fuck," he said under his breath. He searched for calm so he wouldn't go off like a fucking lunatic and demand answers so he could track the son of a bitch down and kill him. Turning back to her, he shoved his hands into his back pockets to keep from reaching out to her. "So was this like a first boyfriend situation?" Fifteen was young, but about the age of sexual exploration. Maybe some asshole took things too far.

"No, I've never had a boyfriend."

She was twenty-four years old and never had a boyfriend.

He must have looked skeptical because she continued.

"You heard me right." She folded her arms across her chest and watched him. "I've never done a lot of things. I'm pretty useless when it comes to any type of relationship knowledge, so you're better off knowing that now and...you know...moving on."

Her body language said hands off, but her eyes looked wistful, like a woman who knew she was missing out on something, but didn't know how to get it. She looked over his shoulder and the longing on her face had him following her gaze. A young couple had set out a blanket beneath a nearby tree and the kiss they currently shared might've gotten them arrested if a cop walked by.

"Has anyone ever kissed you, Ab?" he whispered the question.

She looked at his lips as she shook her head. She'd started breathing harder and he hadn't touched her.

"You look scared and interested at the same time," Blake said, reading her expression.

"I guess I am." She met his gaze and struggled with something. "If I'm being honest, I'm afraid I won't ever share a first kiss with someone." She uttered the words so softly that Blake barely heard her.

"We could fix that right now, if you want to." He didn't dare get his hopes up. "You know I won't ever hurt you, right?"

Her eyes widened. "I didn't mean now. Here. God, how embarrassing. Blake..." She trailed off, but the look in her eyes changed to something closer to optimism.

"We can start small. An Eskimo kiss," he blurted.

Her brows pulled together. "What?"

His confidence spiked. "An Eskimo kiss. You know what an Eskimo kiss is. No lips."

She looked suspicious and he smiled.

"It'll be completely painless. I promise. Want to try?" It took her a few seconds to think about it, but when she gave him a slight nod, an instant bolt of heat shot through his gut. "Keep your eyes open, okay. Watch me." He leaned in slowly, clued in to her uncertainty by the rising of her chest. "Eyes on mine," he whispered as he closed the distance. He grazed the side of her nose with his as they stared at each other. Their lips so close together, he felt the warmth of her breath across his cheek. He continued to softly nuzzle her nose. First one side, then the other. His skin tingled all over with electric energy. It took every ounce of will power he possessed to keep his hands stuffed in his pockets, to keep his lips from joining the party. Just his nose, brushing against hers in a playful little two-step. God, she smelled like fresh lemons. Finally, he pulled away but not too far. He had something else planned. "Not bad, right?" he asked.

She swallowed again and shook her head. "No."

"I've got another one for you," he said.

"Another Eskimo kiss?"

"A butterfly kiss," he told her. Before she said no, he leaned in again, his nose grazing hers before he fluttered his lashes against her cheek. He felt her smile, felt the warmth of her lips a fraction of an inch from his skin. After a few seconds, he pulled back. "Not so bad, right?" She lowered her gaze and shook her head. "How about we go for a small one. If you don't like it, you can bail and I won't mention it again. Deal?"

She looked skeptical. "I don't know."

"Have I steered you wrong yet?" he asked.

"No, but..."

"Are my hands still stuffed in my back pockets?" he asked. Touching her would only send her running.

She smiled at that. "Yes."

"Then...? What do you say? Totally up to you."

Her tension ratcheted up about ten notches before she said, "Okay."

All he wanted to do was take away the fear. "It's all right," he whispered. Blake moved in slowly and nuzzled her nose again with another Eskimo kiss. He wanted to wrap her up tight in his arms, put his lips on hers and kiss her forever, but if he did that he'd lose her. Slowly, he let his lips brush against hers in a barely there kiss. She was as soft as he imagined. Hell, softer. Her plush lips begged for more, but he kept it simple, kept it sweet. Back and forth, so slowly. Her breath washed over his mouth in short gasps and Blake pulled back a fraction.

She opened her eyes and he saw a mix of surprise and panic. He wanted to touch the smooth skin of her cheek, wanted to run his hands through the softness of her hair. "That wasn't so bad," she said.

His heart lodged in his throat and he nodded, tried to find his voice. He gave her reassuring grin. "See? Your first kiss and you survived fine." He let her process that. "Wanna try another one?"

Shyly, she nodded and swallowed again as her gaze fastened on his lips. She looked more ready to do battle than kiss.

Blake moved in again. The same speed, the same movement. Setting his lips on hers he just brushed across back and forth, let his nose nuzzle hers as he moved over her mouth and let her feel his breath. His heart beat loud between his ears as he savored her softness and fought the same demons demanding he take her in his arms and make her his. Show her exactly what they could do together with a little encouragement. He was about to pull away, when she got closer and deepened the kiss. She molded her lips against his and actively participated. Blake had managed to keep his dick from calling the shots, but now it perked up with an immediate need for attention. Blood flooded south and pressure built behind his jean's zipper.

Abbey's mouth parted a fraction as they kissed and Blake lightly grazed the tip of his tongue across her bottom lip.

Sucking a quick burst of air, Abbey froze as Blake took the kiss to another level. She might've pulled away, but he continued to be so gentle, so patient that she just didn't want to end the contact. His warm breath mingled with hers as his lips continued to graze across her mouth, taking little nibbles along the way. She drowned in his scent, the way it blanketed her. An overwhelming sense of safety enveloped her. Once again, his tongue teased across her lips, this time along the slightly parted seam and Abbey's heart galloped faster. Heat crept up from her stomach all the way to her chest, neck and face. He didn't storm her mouth, but simply waited for her to join him.

What if she did? Would he think it meant she was on board for more? Would he take matters further and lock her in an embrace? Would she panic and bolt? Her heart raced with fresh panic, but Blake didn't seem to notice. He just kept brushing his lips across hers in the sweetest, gentlest of kisses. Every few passes over her lips, his tongue darted across her mouth, just a hello, a little reminder that more waited the second she wanted to experience it.

God, she wanted to be brave. Wanted to find out what it felt like to really kiss him, to taste him fully. What if this was her only chance? What if no other guy wanted to be as patient as Blake was being now? He was giving her an opportunity and she had to take it.

Tentatively, she reached out and touched the tip of his tongue with her own. He tasted like mint chocolate chip ice cream. He tasted like Blake. Like heat and sex appeal and patience. He didn't take her action as a cue to pounce, he simply took it in stride and kept up his sweet assault. Just the tips of their tongues danced together in a little game of *you're it* as they met, retreated and met again.

Blake slanted his mouth more fully against hers and Abbey opened wider for his kiss. His groan vibrated into her mouth and after another, longer taste of his tongue against hers, he pulled away, breathing hard. He rested his forehead against hers. "You have no idea what this is doing to me," he murmured.

To him? What about her? Her heart pounded so hard, she felt seconds away from a coronary. "We should probably get back. Julie and Troy might be worried about us." She needed to regroup.

The old fashioned *brrrng* of a telephone sounded in the quiet moment and Abbey reached for the small pack slung around her shoulder as she backed up from Blake. "Speak of the devil. It's Julie," she said, after retrieving her phone. She punched the screen. "Hi." She leaned against the tree as she scanned the park with its big green magnolias and manicured lawn.

"Hi. Everything okay? I thought you'd be back by now," Julie said.

"Yeah. The audition went great and Blake and I stopped to celebrate with some ice cream. We're headed back in a couple of minutes. Be there soon. Did you need something?"

"Nope. Just checking that you're okay. I can't wait to hear about the audition," Julie added.

"I'll tell you all about it. See you in a few." She disconnected the call and Blake stepped in front of her.

"One more for the road?" he asked, leaning in, his breath already fanning across her mouth. His panty-melting grin had always affected her, she'd just been good at not letting it show. But now, she couldn't help but smile back at him.

"One more ice cream?" she teased, her face just a fraction of an inch from his.

His mouth hovered over hers. "Uh…no. Not ice cream," he whispered. Heat bubbled from her stomach once again and crept all the way up to her cheeks. "One more of these." His lips touched hers and everything else disappeared. Nothing registered but the pressure on her mouth, the slight rasp of his stubble against her skin, the clean scent of him and taste that was uniquely Blake. When he finally pulled away, Abbey's skin tingled as if she'd been lit from within.

Blake did that to her.

She'd known from the beginning that he liked her. He'd never been quiet or shy about that fact. She'd known him for over a year and had never heard about or seen him with another girl. She couldn't assume that he'd been waiting for her all that time, but just the amount of patience he'd shown her from day one had her softening to his teasing nature.

The best part about this whole situation so far was that he'd quit asking questions.

Chapter Eleven

"Thank you." Kim hung up the phone in Leo's kitchen as the stainless steel appliances and deep cherry cabinets blurred and swayed in front of her.

"You okay?" Leo asked as he poured them both cups of coffee.

"I don't know." That was a lie. She wasn't okay. The last two days had been the most surreal of her life. The first twenty-four hours of that time had been spent crying on a famous movie star's shoulder. Talk about bizarre...

And now bizarre just took a left turn. Carl told her that investigators had found no sign of Stephanie's body. On top of that, the limo driver, Phillip, had disappeared too. A full investigation had started. Kim would've suspected Carl if his house hadn't burned down. But did that fact sway the detectives?

With nothing but the clothes on her back, Kim's options had been limited. Carl had called yesterday and offered to pay for a hotel room. Kim had hesitated. She'd only come in the first place because Stephanie had requested it. Carl had been a giant pain in the ass from minute one and not someone she wanted to owe anything to. Besides, he gave her the willies. And losing all her money and starting from scratch had taught her to watch every dollar, so the combination of everything with the added problem of affording a hotel room plus transportation... Kim had instead taken Leo up on his offer to stay a night or two.

"That was Carl," Kim said. "The fire investigation team went over the property again and found no sign of Stephanie." A ray of hope streaked through Kim's broken heart. She hadn't believed them the first time they'd told her no body had been recovered. Despite Carl's grumbling that Stephanie had run off and left him, he'd ordered the second pass through the rubble.

The idea that Stephanie might have burned to death had been devastating.

"I thought all of the cars except for The Asshole's were still in the garage. If she wasn't in there, where is she now?" Leo's question put a dark cloud over her hope.

"That's what I want to know." Kim picked up the phone again and called Carl. She got rolled over to voice mail. "Carl, it's Kim. I just thought of something. Do you remember the limo driver mentioning if Stephanie planned to go anywhere once he dropped her off? Call me, please." If she hadn't been in the house, then where was she? Carl must have been thinking these same things. Kim disconnected and the screen faded to black. "This doesn't make any sense." She tapped her nails on the one-of-kind mosaic tile table. "Where is she? What happened?" She picked up the phone again.

"Now who are you calling?" Leo asked. He set the coffee in front of her and sipped his own as he sat next to her.

"My best friend and business partner." She got rolled over to another voice mail. "Chels, it's Kim. Can you call me back or text me with the name and number of that PI you used to find Trace? It's Mills, right? I forget his first name. Tom or Tim? Let me know as soon you can, okay? Thanks. Bye. Tell Matthew hi for me." Kim disconnected the call and set the phone on the table. "She better not be having that baby or I'm dead meat for not being there."

"Got a bun in the oven, huh?" Leo asked.

"A giant bun," Kim confirmed. "But she's still three weeks away, so I thought I had time to do this for Stephanie before I wanted to be back for Chelsea."

Just thinking about Stephanie sent a fresh knot of emotion in her throat.

"Look, I know this is a rotten time," Leo began, "but—"

"But you probably didn't expect me to stay any longer." Kim stood up. "Look, you were very nice to let me crash here, but I should shove off. I can find a hotel. I really appreciate you putting me up. I don't think I could've handled being alone the last couple of days." It had been so weird to make friends with a man she had no respect for. She'd let the media make up her mind for her and so far, their perception of him had been completely wrong. Being in advertising—even if was the accounting end—she wondered about the two very different sides of Leo Frost. So far she'd seen no sign of the spoiled, egomaniac playboy he'd been billed as. He'd been an understanding ear, a shoulder to cry on and he'd made absolutely zero moves on her. She might've been a little insulted, but her eyes were still puffy, her hair was a wreck and she'd been wearing a pair of his old sweats for two days already.

Time to get her act together.

"Actually, I was going to ask if you'd mind helping me sort through those files I got from Nathan's office. I'll pay you whatever Carl is paying you. I don't expect your time for free."

Kim froze halfway out of her chair before sitting down again. "You don't even know me. Why would you want me to go over your books?"

His steady gaze met hers. "If Wyncott trusts you, I don't see why I can't. You seem decent...honest. I'm down with that." The sunlight hit his chiseled features and a little tingle tickled the base of her neck.

Sipping her coffee, Kim took a second to process his request. Granted, Leo hadn't done one thing to set off any alarms with her, but his request still came from out of the blue. "Wouldn't you rather have someone who works in this town? I mean, I don't even live here."

Leo shrugged. "The simple fact is I don't know anyone else here. Sure, I could call a few friends and get recs, but I've got you here now and you seem pretty sincere. I wouldn't ask if I wasn't sure about you."

Working for Leo would give her a good reason to stay in town while the police tracked down Stephanie. It wasn't as if she could get on a plane while one of her best friends from college was missing. Plus, there was a possibility that Chelsea might have the baby later than her due date, and Chelsea had Matthew with her, whereas Stephanie didn't have anyone but Kim. And the Asshole.

"Okay. Deal." She extended her hand and Leo shook it. His warmth and strength gave her a much needed shot of focus. As long as she kept those little tingles buried and kept it business, she'd be fine. "First things first. I really need to get out of your clothes and find something of my own to wear. Where's the nearest mall?"

Leo gave her his multi-watt smile. "I can do way better than a mall."

Leo opened Stella's door and Kim slid in, all long legs and styled blond hair. He'd had her red outfit cleaned from the night of the explosion and the repairs would see her through this shopping trip before she'd have to toss it. Now, she'd borrowed one of his blazers, rolled up the sleeves and looked like a sex kitten. Something had snapped her out of her daze. He wasn't sure if it was the prospect of actual work, the idea of shopping or just the fact that her friend hadn't burned to death in a house fire.

Along with the initial tears and shock, she'd been pretty quiet and Leo hadn't pushed her. She had a lot to absorb. He'd had a plate of his own shit to deal with because on top of Megan's care, now he had first degree burns on his back. He was glad he had Kim to smooth on the aloe vera cream. He wouldn't have been able to apply it without help. The days of having a female in his house at any given time were long gone. He didn't count his assistant, Vivienne, who barely worked a handful of hours a week and only popped in when he needed her. The fifty-something grandmother he'd hired years ago was no-nonsense, efficient and blunt. So blunt that he actually often found himself avoiding her all-knowing stares. He had to admit her looks had leaned more toward worry than condescending in the last year, but he didn't want to deal with that either so it was easier to keep their relationship strictly business.

"If we're not going to the mall, where are we going?" Kim asked after he settled in Stella's driver's seat.

"It's a surprise."

When Kim had gone to shower, Leo had called an old friend of his who had just launched his own clothing line. Kim had the body to pull off any one of the outfits Cesar designed. Leo cruised out of his driveway and headed into Beverly Hills and Cesar's shop. A few minutes later, he pulled into a back alley behind the store and killed Stella's engine. He glanced at Kim, looking at him with a very serious face.

"We're one street away from Rodeo Drive. What makes you think I can afford clothes near Rodeo Drive?" She didn't make any move to exit the car.

"No worries. Cesar's a good guy. He'll make you an offer you won't be able to refuse." Her narrowed eyes said she didn't trust him or his friend. "Look," he said, unbuckling his seat belt. "If the price is too steep, we walk out and go someplace else. No harm, no foul."

"I don't want to insult the guy if he's a friend of yours."

"You won't. Trust me." Leo pulled out his phone, sent a quick text then unfolded himself out of Stella and opened Kim's door. He knocked on the back door of Cesar's shop and a few seconds later, it opened with a whoosh. His bald-headed friend beamed from the interior.

"Leo!" Cesar pulled him into a big hug and Leo winced as his back burned at the contact. "Where have you been? I haven't seen you in months?" He looked behind him and spotted Kim, his dark eyes assessing her. "And this must be Kim." He abandoned Leo and took Kim's hands in his, pulled her closer as he inspected her. "Leo, how could you let this poor girl out of the house wearing *this*?" He fingered the blazer with a truckload of distaste. He opened the front and examined Kim with a critical gaze. Her wide eyes said she was about to go ballistic on Cesar's butt.

"Kim," Leo said, "don't let Cesar throw you off. He's a magician when it comes to fashion."

"I didn't know I needed a magician," she said evenly. Then she looked down at her stained and slightly torn outfit. "Okay, maybe I need a magician, but it's because of extenuating circumstances." She eyed Leo before settling her gaze on Cesar.

"I like you," Cesar said with a crafty grin. He looked at Leo. "There's something different about her. I like her."

"So I heard," Leo muttered. He gave Cesar a small headshake but it was too late. Kim's lifted eyebrow spoke volumes. Not that it should matter. His past had no bearing on now or his future. Hell, it wasn't like he and Kim had done anything. In that aspect alone she was definitely *different*.

Cesar folded Kim's arm under his and led her into the customer-empty store. He'd closed up shop for their visit. Leo planned to make it worth Cesar's while.

The next two hours passed in a blur of changes. Kim tried on everything Cesar brought her from skirts to dresses to slacks to shoes and every accessory known to man. Leo sat outside the dressing room and watched as Cesar worked his artistry. Kim made Cesar look like the genius designer he was.

Kim came out of the dressing room in black slacks that hugged the curves of her hips and thighs and flared out slightly at the bottom. The matching black stilettos put her in the stratosphere. A low cut black blouse with muted designs in maroon and teal brought out the sharp green of her eyes.

Cesar smiled and nodded as he looked her up and down. "She is the reason I do this." He adjusted the shoulders of her slinky top, which bared more cleavage. "You make my clothes look the way I imagine them in my head." To Leo he said, "She is beautiful."

"She is," Leo murmured. Very beautiful. And strong as hell. He liked her backbone. Liked the way she stood up to Carl even when she'd been heartbroken. Liked the way he had to coax her to stay with him on that long scary night.

A blush stained her cheeks and Leo held back a grin. He liked what the color did for her face. She'd been way too pale the last couple of days. It was the first indication that Kim had some vulnerability. He didn't count her sadness when she thought she'd lost a friend. That was grief.

A few minutes later, with all the choices in front her, and much to Cesar's dismay, Kim cut the choices in half. "I don't need all of this," she explained. "I can mix and match most of it."

So that's what she'd been doing. No wonder she'd kept to the same color scheme. He'd caught her looking for tags, but Cesar didn't put prices on his clothes. He figured anyone shopping in his store could afford what he put on his racks.

Leo handed over his credit card at the register.

"What are you doing?" Kim said, pulling her wallet out of her purse. "I don't expect you to pay for my clothes."

He exchanged a look with Cesar. "It's not a problem," Leo assured her. "Let's call it a down payment for the work you're going to do for me."

She considered that. "It depends how much this comes to. You're not paying for my clothes."

When had he ever had a woman insist on paying for herself? Uh...*never*.

"What's the damage?" she asked Cesar.

Leo gave him his card. "Here. Take it. We'll call this a retainer," he told Kim.

She scowled, but showed a little give. "I don't like it."

Cesar, smart businessman that he was, had already run Leo's card. His smile dimmed as he blinked at his computer screen. "Um..." he glanced at Leo and regained his smile. "I'm sure it was just a mistake, eh? Let me try again." He slid the card through the machine and the same surprised look came over his face. He leaned in close to Leo. "Your card was declined," he whispered.

Leo felt a rush of heat to his cheeks. Kim closed her eyes and bit her bottom lip.

"Couldn't be," he told Cesar. He whipped out another card. Platinum. "Use this. Someone must have stolen the number somehow. I'll call the card company when I get home." Goddammit. Not what he needed right now, but credit card fraud ran rampant everywhere. He paid for card insurance so he'd be fine.

Cesar ran the new card and his eyes widened as he read the information on his screen.

What the hell? Leo felt his heart thumping harder behind his ribs. Cesar shook his head.

Kim opened the wallet she never replaced in her purse and whipped out a card. "Here. I've got this. No need for him to pay," she told Cesar. "What's the damage?"

Leo gave Cesar a very clear look. "Didn't you tell me you've got a seventy-five percent off sale happening on last season's line?" There was at least ten thousand dollars of merchandise sitting on the counter. Probably more. Even a fraction of that was going to cause Kim to balk.

Cesar read Leo's deliberate stare. Leo had told him when he'd called that if Kim wouldn't let him pay for the whole thing, he'd at least cover what she couldn't afford. He was a longtime customer and good for the money. Not to mention the advertising of his clothes when Kim wore them while on Leo's arm. Cesar knew what good business entailed. "Yes," he said, beaming at Leo then Kim. "Seventy-five percent off. You came at the perfect time." He started punching numbers on the register. "It's your lucky day. Your total is two thousand five-hundred, twenty-seven dollars and sixty-four cents.

"Two thousand five-hundred and..." Kim swallowed. "twenty-seven dollars."

"And sixty-four cents," Cesar added.

"Can't forget that," she murmured. She started going through the pile again, clearly looking for pieces to discard.

"What about your first time shoppers discount?" Leo asked, giving Cesar another pointed look that said, *you know I'll pay you every dime, just get us the hell out of here.*

"Right!" Cesar jumped on the excuse. "How could I forget?" He punched more buttons on his register and brought the total down another five hundred dollars and change. He nearly whimpered and Leo coughed to cover the sound.

Kim tilted and shook her head at the same time. Didn't look as if she was buying any of it. She separated two more items before requesting another tally. The bill came to just under eighteen hundred dollars. "Well, bottom line is I love your beautiful clothes and I need them so I'm in." She handed over a credit card. After a hesitant glance from Cesar, Leo nodded slightly and Cesar finished the transaction. The card went through without a problem and Leo felt another wave of heat against his neck. Cesar carefully folded the clothes between tissue paper and lovingly eased them into handled shopping bags with the store logo on the side.

He came around the counter and gave Kim a massive hug before holding her shoulders and pulling back to look at her. "You will do my clothes justice." He kissed each cheek then turned to Leo. "She is special. I like this lady. You will bring her in again, yes?"

"Cesar, you are a wonder with fabric, and I thank you for your *sale*." The tone of her voice very clearly indicated she smelled the bullshit. "But I won't be in town long. I just had a clothes emergency and Leo was nice enough to help me out. I can guarantee the next time I'm in town, I'll be back for a visit. I have a feeling it might a take a couple of trips to make up for the favor you did me today."

Cesar beamed.

Two minutes later, they climbed into Stella. Leo had no clue what to say and Kim gave him a sidelong glance.

"Thank you," she said.

"For what?" Embarrassing himself? Giving her something to go to the tabloids with? He could see the headlines now. *Leo Frost Destitute and Living on His Last Dime*. Great. He started the engine and Stella purred.

"For talking Cesar down about twelve thousand dollars' worth of clothes. I'm not stupid, you know. Just out of my league. There's a difference." She adjusted the delicate silver watch on her wrist. "I should've rented a damn car and gone to the mall, but you hit my weakness. Beautiful clothes. I'm just treating this as next year's vacation budget."

Leo felt like shit. He hadn't planned on her paying anything. Add to the fact she couldn't really afford it when he could. He intended to make this up to her.

Back at Leo's house, Kim put away her new clothes. After Cesar's place, they'd stopped at a luggage shop, a pharmacy to pick up essentials and Sephora for more essentials. A girl needed her makeup. And if she planned to stick around town another week, she needed to look halfway decent instead of her current zombie state.

Time to put on her big girl panties—thank God Cesar had sold underwear too—and help figure out what happened to Stephanie, not to mention looking over Leo's finances.

She went downstairs, wearing one of the newly purchased outfits. A short, flowing black skirt, with a cream-colored sleeveless top. The three-inch black and cream wedges tied it all together and along with a little bit of height, the shoes were surprisingly comfortable. As she neared the kitchen, she heard Leo in his office.

"I don't give a shit what your computer is saying. It's wrong. I'm not even close to maxing out any of my cards." He paused and Kim heard rustling. "What?" She barely caught his whisper. "That's not possible," he said. "I would've known, I would've—" He stopped or got cut off and Kim continued toward the kitchen. It seemed almost impossible to spend as much money as he made per movie, but if this house and his cars were any indication, then the man had expensive tastes. She'd heard he had homes in New York, Hawaii, Paris and London.

Talk about excessive.

Not to mention that he used Carl's crooked accountant. It all added up to trouble.

Kim poured herself a glass of ice water and stared out the French doors that overlooked the massive backyard. A tennis court and pool surrounded parklike grounds. Two wicker sofas with green cushy pads bookended a large fire pit. A perfect place for entertaining.

Leo stormed into the kitchen and stopped short when he saw her. He quickly covered his scowl, but she watched his color deepen. He was still embarrassed about the shopping trip.

"You know, I didn't plan or expect for you to pay for my clothes. I don't know why you have such a bug up your butt about it."

"I don't have a bug up my butt," he insisted. He opened the fridge door and pulled out a beer. It was still early afternoon. "You want one?" He held out the Stella Artois. The man had a fascination for all things Stella.

"No, thanks." She crossed her arms over her chest. "Look, I couldn't help but overhear and it seems too coincidental to me. Maybe I should just start on your stuff now. The faster I begin, the sooner I get out of your hair so you can..." she gestured to the bottle in his hand and lifted an eyebrow, "...do whatever it is you do when you get upset."

Leo looked at the beer in his hand and glanced back at her. He shoved the thing back in the fridge and slammed the door shut. He paced the massive kitchen, a tiger on the prowl, his hands running over his head with nervous energy. Finally he stopped and faced her.

"Look, apparently, I'm in a deep hole of shit and I had no idea."

"You picked up your files a few days ago when we got Carl's. Didn't you go through them?"

Leo leaned back as if she'd spoken something taboo. "Go through them? It's like reading another language." He shook his head. "Numbers are not my friend. The more of them on a page the more my brain shuts off. I was waiting for a couple of references before I just took the files to someone else to figure out."

"That's why I'm here, remember?" She gestured toward the office. "Lead the way. Let's get this party started."

But Leo didn't move.

"Something wrong?" she asked.

"The bank said..." He couldn't finish. "Look, today. I need to apologize." He faced her. "You're right. I did want to buy you those things because you've had a tough couple of days. Your friend is gone. You lost everything you came here with besides the clothes on your back and even those were basically ruined because I tackled you."

"I'd rather have ruined clothes than be dead, and that's what I would've been if I'd gotten closer to the house. I can handle that as a price to pay. You're the one who got burned."

He closed his eyes, shook his head and waved her off.

"As far as the clothes..." She waited for him to look at her. When his cobalt blue eyes landed on her, she got an unwanted blast of tingles across her arms. "It was a nice thought on your part and I appreciate it, but I take care of myself. No one buys me stuff other than me."

His lips curved upward in a barely there smile. "Even for your birthday and Christmas?"

"Those are two exceptions. The other is Valentine's Day. I'm a sucker for chocolates and flowers, but don't tell anyone."

He studied her and a wave of heat followed the tingles. "Why can't people buy you things?"

"That's a topic for a different day." No way did she plan to unload her garbage on Leo Frost. He might've been acting like a decent guy, but he was in a crap load of trouble for one reason or another, and not only was he paying her to find out what it was, but she wanted to know for herself.

Chapter Twelve

Though Blake had slept in his own apartment the night before, he was happy to be back at his boss's house the next day, working on a new missing person's case. The woman in question had last been seen at her husband's nightclub and Blake had been checking her recent credit history to see if any leads arose from out of the ordinary purchases. Usually, he'd be working from the office in Century City, but shadowing Abbey made it necessary to work from Troy's home office.

Julie had called Troy away from the computer to ask him a question about the upcoming remodel of the guesthouse, so when a scream came from the kitchen, Blake dropped the file in his hand and ran full out across the house, his heart slamming against his ribs. He slid into the kitchen in time to see Abbey dancing happily around the center island with the phone to her ear. He nearly dropped to his knees in relief.

"Got it. Bye." She hung up and let loose another sound, this one closer to a squeal.

Julie and Troy ran in from the backyard.

"What?" Julie asked. "What happened?"

"I've got a callback!" Abbey flawlessly moonwalked across the floor then turned in a perfect Michael Jackson spin. "This afternoon." She looked up at the three faces watching her. "I have to go back to my apartment for some stuff."

Julie hugged her fast and hard. "Wonderful!"

Blake looked at Troy. They'd discussed this already. Any time Abbey left the estate, she became a target. Though no one could definitively say that the speeding car had been intended strictly for Abbey, neither Troy nor Blake believed in coincidence.

"You guys!" Abbey said, her aggravated reprimand clear in her tone. "Showing up to this screen test without the right clothes and makeup is just as bad as not showing up at all. Julie, will you please tell them that I have to do this."

Julie looked from Troy to Blake then back to Abbey. "You have to do it, but you also have to be really careful. Troy knows his stuff. If he's concerned, then there's something to worry about."

Abbey looked at Blake and gave him her best sad face.

Shit, she played him like a fucking maestro and like any instrument, he just sat there and took it. Blake rolled his eyes as much from his own lack of backbone as her puppy-dog pout. "Yes, I'll take you. Quit with the face."

Abbey clapped her hands and squeaked again, as excited as a toddler, and Blake couldn't help but smile at her happiness. This was the Abbey he loved to see, the free-spirited lady who'd stolen his heart a year ago.

An hour later, she sat shotgun next to him as they headed for Abbey's apartment with Troy following to watch for any tails. Troy peeled off after twenty minutes and went back home.

At her place, Abbey changed and came out of her bedroom a vision in black and green. The form fitting black leggings outlined the outrageous curve of her perfect ass, and calf-high black boots with a three-inch heel gave her even more height than usual. A green flowing top draped seductively over her figure inspired imagination. The sheer material over her collarbone and shoulders had him itching to touch the soft skin beneath. She rummaged around a pile of papers on the small desk in the corner of the room and pulled out a headshot before they left her apartment. Walking back to his SUV, the light breeze plastered the fabric against her chest and made Blake long to feel those curves for himself.

The screen test took place in a different building than the dance auditions. People moved in and out of a single wood door. A small sign with an arrow pointing upstairs read Casting Office, and they made their way up the narrow staircase. The stairs turned right and another flight opened into a giant waiting area filled with people. Four numbered doors indicated different studios and they were all closed.

"I'm good. I need to sign in," Abbey said, pointing to the small desk with paperwork in the corner of the room. She gave him a finger wave before walking away.

Satisfied she was safe, he went back downstairs and waited. Down the hallway, Blake saw a man moving boxes into an office, before he stepped outside. After waiting thirty minutes, he got fidgety. He opened the door as it was pushed open from inside and came face-to-face with Abbey. Her green eyes were lit with excitement.

"Oh my God, that was so awesome, you have no idea."

"Awesome enough for another celebratory ice cream and walk through the park?"

She gave him her *Julie* face. One eyebrow lifted while the other eye narrowed. "I think you're looking to score another kiss."

Didn't he wish. He gave her his best smile. "You say that like it's a bad thing."

She swatted his bicep.

Rubbing the spot, he laughed. "Seriously, you have to admit, that was a great first lesson. I don't see why you wouldn't benefit from another one."

"I just see *you* benefiting from another one."

"Why can't it be both?"

She shook her head and snorted. "I need to call my agent. I told her I'd give her the scoop as soon as I left."

Abbey made the call from the SUV, and Blake heard about every second of the audition as Abbey relayed it to her agent and then hung up.

They got halfway back to Troy and Julie's place when Abbey's phone rang.

"It's my agent again," she said, glancing at the screen. "Hi, what's up?" She listened. "No way. Now? Seriously?" She patted his arm and motioned the other direction with her thumb. "I'm on my way. I can be there in twenty minutes."

Shit. He didn't want to know.

Abbey disconnected the call. "You need to go back. They want to talk to me again."

"That's crazy. They just saw you." But Blake turned the Explorer around and headed back anyway.

By the time he returned to the building, there was no street parking because of traffic. Blake drove to the lot in the back and waited for a truck to move so he could park.

Abbey's leg bounced with nervous tension as she glanced at her watch. "I'm gonna run in," she said, checking her makeup in the pull down mirror.

"No." Blake saw a spot on the other row and tried to move around the truck, but it started moving…albeit very slowly.

"I can't wait," Abbey said, unbuckling her belt. "Don't worry. I'm just going to run in. It'll take me a few seconds."

"Abbey, no!" But she was already out the door and sprinting to the building. "Wait, Ab!" Blake slammed the SUV in reverse and burned rubber, pulling into the parking spot in the next row. He didn't want her out of his sight for a minute.

Abbey bounded into the building, her jitters as plentiful as the hope busting in her chest. This whole process had felt right from the very beginning. These people liked her and she felt her luck shifting for the first time in years. Granted, working for Julie was awesome and the lady treated her like gold, but Abbey's dream was to dance for a living, not be Julie's assistant.

The best move she'd made was to take the choreographer position with her dance troupe when Stacy had moved. Choreographers had more clout, were taken more seriously. This credit on her resume said she could not only handle the dancing, but she could create as well. She'd been dying to prove herself. Dancing was the one place she could let go and just be. She had no worries, no cares, only the music and her body to express the emotion harbored in her chest.

This job could mean the life change she'd worked so hard for. She'd miss Julie and Julie's mom, Elena, and the excitement of the movie sets, but she'd get to trade it in for the love of her life. Dancing.

She started up the stairs, looking forward to this next interview. Had someone come late and wanted to meet her or did they want to mix and match her with another choreographer or the host of the show?

"Abbey?"

She almost didn't hear her name and backtracked down the few steps. A man leaned out of a doorway from down the hall. He had shaggy brown hair and looked vaguely familiar as he smiled and waved at her. "We're in here this time," he said.

"Oh. Okay." Had she seen him earlier? She definitely remembered him from somewhere, but something was different. She moved down the hall toward him and he gestured into the room and followed her in. A pine desk occupied the right side of the small room and two gray filing cabinets sat along the back wall. No sign of any camera equipment or producers.

This didn't feel right at all. The hair on her neck prickled as she felt his presence behind her. Her heart rate soared as his beefy arm wrapped around her from behind, but Abbey was already moving, twisting, spinning out of his reach. He lunged before she formulated more of a plan than just *get the fuck away from him*. His weight bore her into a stack of boxes that toppled over. She followed them down to the carpet and struck out with long fingernails against his cheek.

He trapped her hands in his large one. "Fucking bitch," he swore. "Don't fight me, little girl. You won't win." His hot breath panted over her face and his dark eyes glared into hers.

Fresh fear sent adrenaline shooting through her veins. Her pulse raced and her lungs threatened to seize. She couldn't lose it now. Time, she needed to buy a little time. "I have forty bucks in my wallet, it's all yours. Just take it." She only wished that was what he wanted. It suddenly dawned on her why he looked familiar. It was the man from the Sports Center. He'd not only shaved off his mustache, but without the hat and sunglasses, she hadn't recognized him. "You," she whispered.

His eyes narrowed. *Shit on a stick!* Why did she have such a big mouth? Fresh panic had her squirming until his grip tightened painfully on her wrists.

"Stop fucking fighting," he growled.

"Okay, okay!" She gave up, her heart racing frantically as he stared down at her. He got to his feet and pulled her up roughly by her bicep. Abbey grabbed her stomach and bent over. "Ah!" she moaned. "Wait a sec. I think you cracked my rib." He bent toward her and she clasped her hands together and lifted up hard. Using her momentum and the strength of both fisted hands, she slammed him in the cheek. The force snapped his head and Abbey followed up with a kick. She'd aimed for his groin, but he swiveled and she caught his thigh instead. She bolted for the door, but he caught her before she made it. "Hel—"

A sharp fist to her kidney cut off her air. Pain exploded in her back and ricocheted in her torso as Abbey dropped like a rock. "I'm not supposed to damage the merchandise. Don't fucking get me in trouble," he growled. Abbey struggled to get air in her lungs and he wrapped a huge arm beneath her stomach and yanked her up like a rag doll. Despite her renewed fighting, he trapped her arms against her midsection and placed a white handkerchief over her mouth. Abbey struggled not to breathe. She wiggled in his grip and finally slammed her head back against his chest over and over until she was dizzy. One, two, three. The guy wasn't budging. The exertion was too much. Her lungs burned. She had to take in air. Instead she took in the rank chemicals in the handkerchief. Her vision blurred and her strength ebbed until even the pressure of his arm around her disappeared as everything faded to nothing.

Blake heard the tussle and his heart nearly beat out of his chest as he bolted in the room. Seeing Abbey hanging limp in the big man's arms sent every caveman instinct roaring for vengeance. The guy's bloody cheek told him she'd put up a hell of a fight.

"Set her down nice and easy," he growled. Sweat prickled his spine.

Nodding slowly, the guy assessed Blake with narrowed eyes as he set Abbey down. Before he stood up, he launched himself at Blake and they slammed into the back wall. Blake had expected the attack and shifted just enough to get leverage after impact. He landed on top and planted a fist in the guy's face, exactly where Abbey had scratched him. He got in another shot before something slammed into his arm. Pain ripped up his shoulder as the blow knocked him over. He scrambled to get his footing and looked up just in time to see a massive fist make contact with his face. A lightning rod of agony exploded in his head before he fell back.

When he opened his lids, a twenty-something redhead with wide frightened eyes kneeled next to him. "Are you okay?" she asked.

His head hurt like a bitch. Blake shook off the cobwebs and wished he hadn't when the room got fuzzy. What the hell had hit him? He'd had the first guy pinned so someone else must have joined the fight. How long ago—

Abbey!

He scrambled to his feet. "My friend. Did you see where they took her?" He checked his watch and headed toward the door. He'd only been out a couple of minutes. He looked up and down the hallway. "Two guys just took her out of here. Did you see anything?"

She shook her head no. "I was upstairs in the casting office. I heard a commotion, but I didn't see anything. I heard tires squeal out back—"

Blake ran for the back parking lot. Nothing. Then he bolted through the hallway to the street side of the building. Nothing again. His heart pounded and his stomach rolled with nausea. He ran back into the building where the redhead waited by the stairway.

"Maybe you should sit down. You look a little pale." She motioned to her cheek. "You're bleeding."

Wiping at the throbbing knot under his eye, Blake came away with blood on his knuckles. "You must have seen something," he pressed.

"I'm sorry. I wish I could help. I called 911. Police are on the way."

A sick bubbling of apprehension made Blake's pulse beat faster. "Maybe someone else in your office saw something."

"There's no one left. We finished all the auditions over an hour ago. I was wrapping up."

"But you called my friend back for another audition. Abbey Washington. I was with her when she got the call."

"Oh, Abbey. I remember her. We saw her last today. The guys loved her."

Blake swallowed back his panic. "So you didn't call her back for a second interview after the original one today?"

She shook her head. "No. Sorry. The guys still need to look at everyone's tapes and make decisions."

He needed reinforcements besides the police. "Can you hang on one second?" Blake pulled out his cell phone and called Troy.

"Hey, everythi—"

"She's gone! She's fucking gone!" He ran a hand through his hair as every muscle tensed. "She jumped out of the fucking truck before I parked. She couldn't wait for me." Blake quickly told him what he saw and what happened. "It was a setup! She's fucking gone right under my nose!"

"Blake," Troy said sharply. "Pull it together. Call the police. Find people in the building. Ask questions. You're no help to her if you can't think straight. The fact that they took her instead of leaving her body is a good sign." The idea that he might've walked in to see her dead body made his stomach clench and Blake took a deep breath. "She installed that cell phone tracker app on her phone, right? We'll find her. I'll get working on that while you talk to the police." Troy paused. "We'll get her back. We'll get her back."

Blake disconnected the call, shut his eyes and exhaled hard. *Get your shit straight, St. John.* Desperation made his chest ache as he went back to the redhead. He had a few minutes to ask questions before the cops arrived. "You said she was the last interview you saw for the day."

She nodded. "Yes, that's right."

"But her agent called and told her to come back. She said they wanted to see her again."

"Nope." She started up the stairs and Blake followed. "I'm the one who would've called the agent and I didn't. Who's her agent? I can't imagine how this happened."

"I don't know." He'd have to find out though.

She went into the far studio and started rifling through headshots on the table. "Here she is. Her agent's name is at the bottom if you want to call." She checked her watch. "Although they're probably gone for the day by now."

Maybe Troy could find her.

Blake took the headshot. A label at the bottom gave her agent's name, agency, address and telephone number. Something like this could very easily be on the Internet. What if the guy had somehow got her audition information from her agent? All he had to do was pick up a phone in the building and the caller ID would give the building location. He could pretend to be the casting agency and her agent would send Abbey back to the place in hopes of bagging the job. Then they pull off the snatch and grab. "Fuck," Blake muttered again. "Look, if there's anything you can remember that might help us find her, it would be great."

She shrugged. "I'm sorry I didn't see anything."

Blake paced the front of the building, his nausea growing worse as time ticked by. Every second that passed was another second Abbey got farther away from him. He should've walked in with her. Should've been by her side every second. How could he let this happen?

His cell phone rang and Troy's name blazed across the screen. "Find anything through the tracker?" he asked by way of a greeting.

"Yes."

Relief sent a rush of air from Blake's lungs.

"She's moving north on the 101 freeway. CHP is putting three units in pursuit."

"I'm headed in that direction," Blake said, moving through the building and toward the back parking lot.

"Stay and talk to the cops. Tell them anything and everything you can about what happened. They need descriptions, times and anything else you can think of."

Blake wanted to roar.

"The cops will get her back. They're closing in as we speak. As soon as I know anything I'll get back to you."

Twenty of the longest minutes of his life passed by in a blur. The police arrived and he told them everything he knew, which wasn't much. Though he got a good look at the guy holding Abbey, he hadn't seen the man who'd knocked his lights out.

A pounding headache continued to remind him of the blow.

When his cell rang and Troy's name appeared, he snapped it up, his pulse hammering hard. "Did they get her?"

The brief silence nearly crushed him.

"No," Troy said. "She wasn't there. They found her phone in a minivan belonging to a family of four. They'd stopped for gas in Los Angeles and opened the hatch to get something from the back. Abbey's kidnappers must have tossed her phone back there to buy some time. No one in the family noticed it."

"Jesus, Jesus," Blake whispered. His gut swirled with fresh nausea as he stepped outside. "She could be anywhere."

"This isn't over. Check her apartment. See if you can find anything. I'll be in touch."

Blake ended the call. Leaning his head back, he shut his eyes before staring at the darkening sky. He'd only felt this helpless one other time in his life and he hated the crippling feeling. Hated the turmoil in his stomach that made him want to puke.

Ten seconds later, he cranked the engine of his Explorer and peeled out of the parking lot.

Chapter Thirteen

Abbey woke to a steady hum beneath her body. The instant awareness of dry mouth coincided with the sick taste of a gag and made her stiffen. Restraints burned her wrists and ankles, and fire shot to her brain along with the ache of sore muscles. The odor of smelly old sneakers assaulted her senses. She opened her eyes to complete darkness.

Her heart nearly shot into her throat and her lungs seized in a familiar tightening. She closed her eyes. *Breathe. Through your nose. Breathe.* She imagined Blake with her just like the first time they met in that crazy elevator ride from hell.

Oh, God, Blake. Did he even know what happened? Was he okay?

Trembling with paralyzing fear, Abbey felt the thump of each rapid heartbeat in her head. She could easily die right here, right now. A full body flop sweat broke across every inch of her skin.

Breathe with me. In and out. C'mon now. Breathe with me. Slow and easy. You're okay. You're going to be okay. Big breath. Exhale slow. Do it again. Blake's blue eyes had locked onto hers. She concentrated on his words and the way he'd held her hand against his chest as he'd breathed with her.

Get a grip, Abbey. It's all on you this time.

Tamping down the urge to vomit, she willed her body to stop shaking. *Get tough. Get tough.* Julie would expect it. Blake would want it. She owed it to herself. She'd let fear dictate her actions nine years ago and she wouldn't do it again.

The guy that grabbed her...the one from the Sports Center. His words rang in her head.

I'm not supposed to damage the merchandise. What did that

mean? God, did they plan to sell her? Was that the reason he'd kept her alive? Fresh chills streaked across her damp skin. She'd die before she let that happen.

Okay, time to think, to breathe evenly and find a way out. She felt behind her, tried to find something sharp, but came up with nothing. She moved her legs and shifted, attempted to cover more space in the cramped quarters. There had to be something here. A crowbar? A tool of some type. Something she could stow in her jeans or up the sleeve of her shirt.

Some type of blanket had been tossed in behind her and she searched under it.

Wait. What was that? Long, slim, plastic...a pen? Yes. She'd take it. At this point, she'd take just about anything she could get her hands on.

The car went over a bump and the movement sent a shockwave of pain through her ankles and wrists. God, she was so sore and her mouth was so dry. She needed water. Needed to get this filthy rag out of her mouth.

Breathe, breathe. She couldn't work herself into another fit.

How long had she been out? Where were they? The air was hot and stuffy and it had been late afternoon verging on evening when he'd snatched her. She might have a better idea once they let her out. Which brought to mind another problem.

What did she do when the trunk door opened? Did she play possum? Did she acknowledge her abductor? Did she pretend she wasn't scared spitless and stare daggers at him or anyone else she might see?

Or maybe she should play the weakling. Maybe she should convince them she wasn't a threat. Make them think she'd comply as long as they didn't hurt her. But how long would that go over before they did try to hurt her? Not very long she suspected. Still, she had to buy time. Had to make them think she wouldn't try to escape.

All of her self-defense lessons came back at her. What could she have done to the big guy before he'd dropped her with a kidney punch? She'd clawed, kicked and tried to scream. The fact was he was too fast and too big. Next time, she had to be smarter. Had to think faster.

The car slowed and took a right turn. A minute later, it stopped and her pulse picked up as two car doors opened and closed. More sweat popped out on her skin and she felt clammy and sick. Right before the trunk opened, she shut her eyes and willed her breathing to even out.

The lock snicked, the door lifted and fresh warm air invaded her nostrils. The relief was temporary as someone covered her with the blanket that had been behind her and roughly scooped her out and over his shoulder before he started walking. As she bobbed over his shoulder, she tried to see something, anything that might give her a clue, but the blanket was in her way. She caught sight of a neatly manicured lawn against a cement walkway, but that didn't help her much.

He finally stopped at a door, unlocked it and strode in. He tossed her on a bed, yanked the blanket off her and walked out. A lock snapped into place.

Abbey waited a few minutes before opening her eyes. She peeked through her lashes first to see if someone was there, but the tiny room was blissfully empty. How much time before that changed? No windows meant no escape. The deadbolt locked from the outside. Not fire safe of course, but these people weren't interested in that. She craned her head and spotted a small bathroom to the right. Maybe a window in there led out of this place.

Easing her legs off the bed, Abbey sat up. The room swam in front of her and she closed her eyes to get her bearings. Shit, she wasn't going anywhere with her ankles bound. And if she didn't get this gag off, she was going to throw up. Her stomach rumbled in a warning.

Male voices got louder outside and a new surge of panic whistled through her. The men stopped at the door, a key wrestled in the lock and Abbey froze, twisted toward the door as it opened.

"See, told ya she was up." The big guy who had snatched her said over his shoulder. One side of his face was bloody and bruised along with her scratches.

"When you're right, you're right. I should know not to doubt you," the second man replied. He came in then, and a fresh round of panic whistled through Abbey. It was him, the big black guy who'd been the guard at the Sports Center, the man who'd hurt Blake's brother and had helped kidnap his family.

The first guy had a bottle of water in his hand and Abbey

nearly wept at the thought of a taste. He waved it as he moved toward her. "You want some of this?"

She nodded and realized a whimper had come from her own throat.

"And you're not going to scream or make a sound, are you?" His tone threatened a punishment otherwise.

Abbey shook her head. *Please, please, take this vile thing out of my mouth.*

He grabbed a fist full of her hair and yanked her head up as he watched her with a cold grin. "This is probably gonna sting." He ripped the tape off her mouth and the instant screaming burn forced a yelp from her throat and made her eyes sting. She choked out the gag with a couple of dry heaves as he released her and she bent forward. A couple seconds later, he grabbed her hair again and yanked her head back. He must have opened the bottle because now he poured it over her mouth, letting it run over her cheeks, across her face, down her shirt. She swallowed as much as she could catch as the men laughed. He emptied the bottle, but not before dousing the front of her shirt, plastering the silky fabric to her breasts.

"Yo man, you just wasted a perfectly good bottle of water. California's in a drought, you know."

"She asked for it? Didn't you see her nod?" He pulled her head up and down, enjoying the whole thing as his friend looked on stone-faced. He bent his head next to her ear and took a long sniff of her. "I might have to give you a taste," he murmured. "Especially since you caused me nothing but grief. Besides, you're all wet for me."

Revulsion ran through her, thick and hot, but Abbey held back a shudder. She refused to look at him, refused to acknowledge her fear. He was a sick, miserable man. They both were. But she was going to make sure they knew they picked the wrong woman to fuck with. She'd been a victim already in her life. She wasn't going to be one again.

Blake paced Abbey's apartment in West Hollywood, nearly out of his mind with worry. Abbey had been gone for hours. She could be anywhere by now. She could be dead by now. Running both hands over his head, Blake banished the thought. He couldn't even go there. She was too young, too sweet, too damn beautiful to be dealing with this kind of shit. Her life had been tough enough, dealing with whatever ghosts she had in her past to have to face this.

Blake had tried calling Abbey's agent, but only got voice mail. No way to find out what she knew until Troy worked his magic or the police contacted her.

His phone rang from the kitchen table and he pounced on it. Brendan. Fuck. Not who he needed to hear from. "Hey, what's up?"

Brendan was out of town with his boss, Seger Hughes. Although he loved his twin, Blake would've given just about anything for Brendan to have a different boss. Had Bren not offered the Seger Hughes tickets in the first place, none of this would be happening right now. They never would've been at the concert and Abbey would've never been a witness to an assault and potential murder.

"Are you by any chance at the apartment? It's not important, but Seger asked me which cruise line Mom and Dad took and I don't remember. Mom wrote the information down and I put it on the desk."

"No. I'm at Abbey's."

"No shit?" The grin on Brendan's face came through loud and clear. "She finally cave?"

"She's missing."

"Missing?" Brendan's playful tone disappeared. "As in playing hooky or—"

"As in kidnapped," Blake clarified.

"Oh, fuck." Brendan swore softly. "How long ago?"

"It's been a couple of hours now."

"You've got no clues? What's your boss doing about this?"

"He's at his office making phone calls doing what he can from there. The cops are on it. I came here to see if I could come up anything from this end."

"You need me to come back?" Brendan asked.

The last thing Blake wanted was to tell Brendan about Kwami. He'd probably not only quit his job to come find the bastard, but he'd do something illegal and get himself thrown into prison. "I'll let you know if it comes to that. Thanks. I'd better go. I'm waiting for Troy to call with any news."

"Got it. Hang tight and call if you need me."

Blake disconnected. What he needed was to find Abbey alive and safe.

"We should just get rid of her." The black guy looked aggravated as he spoke to his friend, who still had Abbey's hair in his meaty fist. "The boss doesn't know about her yet. He can't get mad at losing stock he doesn't know about."

"C'mon. We've never seen a piece of ass this fine run through these doors. I'm taking advantage of this, you better believe it." He stroked the side of her cheek with his thumb, and cold chills streaked along her neck and back. "When we finish with her, we present her to Michael and bam! We get a bonus. He's always looking for fresh meat."

"We're not supposed to fuck 'em. We just deliver 'em."

The Neanderthal let go of her hair with a jerk and she lurched forward. "Who's gonna know? You gonna say anything?"

"No, man. No. But if she's bruised, he's going to tell."

"Fuck that. How's he going to know it was us?" He looked down at Abbey and grabbed hold of her hair again. "You're not going to tell, are you, pretty? Because then you'd have to have a little talk with my knife." He gave his buddy a cold stare. "Look, you can either participate or take a hike for fifteen minutes. The choice is yours."

"Hey, it's one thing to mess with her a little, but we should just shut her up permanently now. If she starts saying the wrong thing to the wrong person, it's going to come back on us and, he's going to cut off our fucking balls."

"Not if she's too doped up to know what's happening." He gave his friend a slow nod, suggesting something that made her skin crawl even more. "You know where Michael keeps his shit. Go get some. Let's get this going on." He pulled his dirty, blue T-shirt out of his pants. "She's going to bring in a shitload of money. I'm telling you, once she's flying on Michael's shit, she's going to be like all the others." His fist tightened in her hair.

"I still don't like it. A witness is a witness. I want to get rid of her."

"Let's talk about it afterward, man. Seriously, where you

going to find an easier ten grand? Just for handing her over? She's easily worth that to Michael." He licked his lips. "I need to have me some of this sweet piece." He looked down at her, his eyes cold and evil. "You better be really good if you want to survive through the night. Hear that?" He yanked her head for emphasis and Abbey's eyes burned from the sting. Fear pounded through her bloodstream like hot lava and she broke out in a cold sweat. Tears pricked her eyes.

His partner thought about it and nodded. "Fine, but I don't plan to change my mind."

"So go get the shit already." He moved behind her, but kept his fist in her hair with her head all the way back. "You ready to get a taste of your new life?" A new sick wave of fear crashed in on her. He looked at his buddy. "What are you waiting for?" he asked, his dispassionate gaze cold. "Go get Michael's stash."

Without saying a word, his buddy left.

"We're gonna get dirty now, bitch." He circled to the front.

Dirty. The word took her back nine years to a nightmare she couldn't get rid of.

He bent like he might kiss her, but instead he slipped his hands under her armpits, lifted her and tossed her back on the bed. He took out the knife he'd talked about and shoved it toward her. "Remember what I said about this. If I were you, I'd keep quiet." He sliced the restraints on her ankles. The initial tightening had her gasping at the burn. "Although it's not like anyone on the grounds will give a shit. They all know what's happening here." He leaned close to her ear. "And they aren't going to give a fuck."

Her stomach knotted and swirled. "My hands?" she croaked in a rough whisper. "I need my hands free." She hoped the pen stayed buried in the waistband of her jeans.

"Oh, yeah?" He grabbed her shirtfront and yanked her up. "What do you plan to do with those hands?"

"Whatever you want. Just please don't hurt me. Don't cut me. I'll do whatever you want."

"Yes, you will." He stroked her jaw. "Yes you will," he repeated softly. He sliced her restraints and her wrists burned as the plastic slid off. He leaned back, a smug smile across his lips. "Take off your top, real slow," he told her.

Abbey swallowed hard. She eased her shirt up and over her

head and watched his nostrils flare. A sinister grin made her stomach roil. "Please put the knife down. You're scaring me."

"I know, pretty. I like you scared." The blade inched toward her face and he slid the steel along her cheek.

Abbey's skin prickled with fear. If she didn't strike now and strike fast, she'd lose her chance. She had to do this before the other guy came back. She rose up on her knees and unbuttoned her jeans. His smile got wider as she eased her hands around back like she meant to push her jeans down.

He turned just a fraction to set the knife on the end table and Abbey reached for the pen in her waistband. She moved as he shifted. She grabbed for his crotch at the same time she plunged the pen in his face. His instant howl and the warm, slippery wetness against her fist gave her fresh confidence. He backhanded her and pain exploded in her head as it snapped to the side, but she cranked harder on his man parts and delivered another blow to his face. This one connected with his eye and he yanked back, ripping the pen from her slippery grip. Scrambling from the bed, she hauled the lamp from the nearby table and swung it like a Louisville slugger. The second before she made contact she saw the damage of her attack. Her pen lodged in his eye and blood covered his face and hands. The lampshade broke apart on contact and took him to the floor. With another precise strike, Abbey hit him again, slamming the hard metal of the lamp against his head. This time he didn't move.

Breathing hard, Abbey dropped the lamp, her hands shaking violently, her face throbbing. *Run*. The word screamed in her head with a roar. She snatched her shirt from the bed and whipped it on, then hiked her jeans back in place and buttoned up. Hysteria lurked right on the edge and Abbey battled it back. If she didn't do this now, she might never get the chance. She didn't see his knife, but she spotted her purse and phone on a scratched dresser near the door and snagged them as she sped by. It took one second to slip her mobile inside her bag and settle it over her head so the strap bisected her chest.

Easing the door open, she checked outside. She was in some kind of outbuilding, but maybe people were too far away to hear anything. A crystal clear pool winked at her in the moonlight. A Jacuzzi sat off the far side of the mammoth property, an estate of some kind. Palm trees swayed in the hot stale air. Several heart-stopping moments later, she stepped out, closed the door softly and ran to the left.

"Hey!" A voice yelled from behind her.

Abbey didn't look back, she simply ran for her life.

A pop sounded and a bullet slammed into the building wall. Abbey ducked from flying pieces of stucco as more bullets whistled by. A hot sting zipped across her thigh a second before she turned the corner. She bolted catty corner to the row of free-standing buildings like the one she'd come out of and hurdled the low fence that enclosed a small yard. Her lungs burned as she ran. Her arms and legs pumped with everything she had as she tried to negotiate her way in the dark. She scrambled left and then right around another larger guesthouse. She heard men behind her, heard them calling out orders. At least two, maybe three. She turned another corner to a large cement path between two long one-story buildings. The place was more of a compound than an estate. It was enormous. Her panic tripled at the lack of any place to hide. She ran to the nearest door. *Please, let it be open!* It wasn't. She heard the running footfalls and tried the next door six feet away, tears stinging the backs of her eyes as she yanked on the knob. She stumbled back as the door opened effortlessly, then she jumped in and closed it quickly and quietly behind her.

Complete darkness closed in on her. The hot, pungent smell of fertilizer invaded her nostrils. Arms outstretched, she found a metal shelf to her right. Within two steps something blocked her way and she reached down to find two large bags. Probably the fertilizer. Her hand brushed against something rough on the shelves and she reached for it. Burlap. Taking the material off the shelf, she eased out the two large bags and slipped behind them. She covered herself with the burlap piece, pulled her knees to her chest and made herself as small as humanly possible.

Several sets of hard footsteps rounded the corner and Abbey bit her lip. *Control your breathing, control your breathing. Please, please, please, let them keep going.* She concentrated on how Blake taught her to breathe. If she got out of this, she'd give him the chance he wanted. She just needed to get out of this. She needed to call for help. So far, with the exception of her kidnappers, the place seemed deserted.

"She couldn't have gotten far." She recognized the black

man's voice. The door burst open and she quit breathing, her eyes squeezed tightly shut. Her heart nearly burst out of her chest. Then the door closed. "Benz, take left. Call Herrera. Get him on it. Spread out. Find her."

"How could you fucking let this happen?" a new voice demanded.

"I didn't let anything happen."

"Did you see Damon? Jesus, she took out his fucking eye then clubbed him."

"I told that asshole we should've just taken her out."

Abbey squeezed her legs tighter to quit from shaking. Her thigh burned like hot coal. Her pounding heart seemed as loud as a concert drumming in her ears. Sweat broke out on every inch of skin. The smell threatened to close in on her just like the dark.

"Fuck," the man swore again and started firing. She jumped at the sound. She held back a shriek and bit her lip harder.

"Cut it out!" the first guy said. "You're gonna bring the neighbors down on us, jackass."

The other man roared, something slammed into the door and Abbey jumped again as she buried her head under her arms.

"Let's go. Firing off these rounds isn't going to find her. And we don't want people asking questions."

"I don't fucking care," the man groused. "She fucking mutilated my brother and she's going to pay."

"We aren't going to find her standing here. Let's go." The two men strode off and Abbey didn't move. She didn't breathe. She listened as they checked every door along the path. She needed a plan. Needed to find a way to get out of this hot box and get help. Troy and Blake had to know she was gone. It had been hours. They had to be looking for her.

Her purse vibrated against her stomach and scared the crap out of her.

Her phone!

Except when she pulled it out of her purse, she discovered it wasn't her phone.

Blake had talked to the police, he'd talked to Troy and he'd talked to Abbey's agent. When his phone buzzed with a notice of a text from a number he didn't know, he nearly ignored it. But the first words of the text showed up on his screen—*It's Abbey! Need help!*—and fresh adrenaline pounded through him. He blinked to make sure his mind wasn't playing tricks on him. "Abbey?" He only got the first few words of the text before he unlocked his phone and got into his messages. She'd sent a group text to both him and Troy.

It's Abbey! Need help! Got away! Hiding n storage room. Some sort of estate/compound. Satellite says Palm Springs. She texted an address next. *Can't talk. Afraid they'll hear. Can't text cops. Can't call. At least 3 men looking 4 me. Maybe more. Same guys from the concert! What do I do!!*

"Holy fucking Christ," Blake breathed as he scrambled to text back. His relief ran a race with his panic. *Sit tight. On my way.* He calculated Palm Springs from his location now... *Gonna take at least 75 min to get there.* He'd be driving ninety miles an hour to make that time. *Troy will find your cell signal from the # you're using. I'll find u. Will call cops from here.* The phone rang as he sent the text, and Troy's number came up on the screen. He answered. "You got her text?"

"Yeah."

Blake hustled out of her apartment and ran for his SUV. "I'm headed in that direction now. Can you call the cops and find her cell signal for the mobile she's using?"

"Already working on it. Be careful."

"You know it." He reached his Explorer, climbed in and cranked the engine. A new text came through from Abbey.

Scared. Can't breathe.

Blake's heart lurched. She'd sent this one strictly to him. Remembering her in the elevator, the way she'd hyperventilated with an anxiety attack the first time they met, he got sick inside.

In n out. U can do it. Breathe. N the car. Need to hit road. God, he didn't want to let her go. *U hurt?* He needed to know she was healthy like he needed air to breathe.

Think he shot me. Not bad, but 2 dark 2 see. Can't risk the flashlight app.

Rage exploded in his chest. "Fuck!" He slammed his fist on the steering wheel then took a deep breath. He needed to keep his shit together or he wouldn't be any help to her. He wanted to know what happened, but had to keep this quick. *Where?*

`Thigh. Keeping pressure on it. Glad it's`
`dark. 2 afraid to look. Chicken.`

"Not even close, sweetheart. You are anything but chicken," he murmured. Blake wanted to howl. He wanted to kill the men who hurt her and break them into tiny bits. He was dying. Couldn't get to her fast enough. *U=brave. Can't text going 90. Hang tight. On my way. Not stopping for anything. Remember/breathe. Stay where u r. Coming for u. Plm Sprngs cops will find u. SWEAR TO GOD. Will take u out of there. Have 2 trust me.*

Ok. Thx. I...just hurry. Pls hurry.

Blake was about to peel out, but hit the brake instead. One more text. *Know u can't talk. Want me 2 call so I'm in your ear? U don't have to say anything.* Her dots indicated her typing.

Yes pls. Phone on vibrate.

Euphoria he didn't expect filled his chest. She wanted him to talk to her. She needed him. He punched in the number before he screamed out of his spot, burning rubber on the road.

The phone only rang once before the call went through and the open line of her phone filled his car from the Bluetooth.

"Ab? Can you hear me?" He spoke quietly. "Press one of the numbers on the keypad if you can." A quick beep indicated she was listening.

"I'm coming. I'm on the road. Troy's calling the cops. We'll get you out, I promise." God, he'd already said this in his text. He didn't know what the hell to say. "Ab. I was so scared. I'm still scared and I know you are, too, but it's going to be all right." He heard an intake of air. "Don't cry, baby. I'm coming." He reached the freeway and floored the Explorer. It gave him an idea. "I'll bet I'd beat mighty Trace Bradshaw on the road even in my piece of shit old SUV." He heard another sound. Might've been another muffled sob or muffled laugh. "I've always wondered how fast this old thing can go. Looks like I get to find out." He searched for something else to say. He sucked at ad-libbing. That was Julie's profession, not his.

"I don't think I ever told you about what my brothers and I used to do to our big sis. She used to boss us around when our mom was gone or when she was outside in the yard so we'd gang up on Jess and tie her up." He didn't expect to hear anything, but he hoped he got a smile out of Abbey. "But Jess was so small and wily, she could get out of just about any knot. I think the girl is double jointed or something, I don't know. But she never told our mom. Of course, one time, Mom came in before Jess got out of the knot. Man, did we get in trouble that day. I think the four of us were grounded for a month. I don't think we tied her up after that. At least, not as often," he amended.

"Punch a key if I made you smile." He heard the beep of a key and swallowed back emotion of his own. Another call rang in and Blake checked the screen. "Ab, it's Troy. I should take it. Hold on." Blake switched over. "What's up?"

"Tell Abbey to leave the phone and get out. If we can track that number, so can the guys on the property. Do it fast."

Blake's palms sweat as he switched back. "Abbey, listen carefully. Leave the phone where you are and get out now. If we can track you so can they. Whatever you do, ditch the phone." He didn't have to see her to know she was wide-eyed with panic. "Breathe, Abbey. We know your general vicinity and cops are on the way. You can do this. Go."

It nearly killed him, but Blake disconnected the call and it hurt as much as any sucker punch.

Chapter Fourteen

Darkness threatened to suffocate her as the call disconnected. "Blake? Blake?" she whispered. God, no. She checked the screen. Nothing. Help was on the way, but maybe not soon enough if she didn't get out on her own first.

Despair strangled her chest and she fought to keep from shaking. She wanted his voice in her ear. Needed his reassurance that she was going to get out of this. His story made her smile. He was the real deal. A good guy with a tight family that loved him. He deserved way more than she could ever give him.

She stood from her spot in the corner and her leg burned. A wet spot grew on her thigh. Using the phone light, she found a pair of cotton gardening gloves and some rope on a nearby shelf and made a makeshift bandage. After securing it across her thigh, she peeked out the door. A dark moonless night made the stars shine brighter.

She hated that she had no view of anything, no idea where to go for her freedom. But Blake said get out and she trusted him. At least she had the cover of darkness. She needed to get the hell off the property. Maybe the men were still looking for her or maybe they'd extended their search outside the estate walls. Either way, she wouldn't risk having this phone lead them to her.

"C'mon, Washington," she told herself quietly. "Suck it up. Get the hell out." After stuffing the phone under a heavy bag of soil, Abbey cracked the door and peeked out again. All clear. She edged along the building, Her leg burned, but she barely favored it. It sure as hell wasn't going to keep her from running her ass as far and fast away from this place as possible.

Creeping toward the end of the building, she peeked around

the corner and drew back immediately when she spotted a man with a very big gun head down a long pathway toward the front of the property. After another check in that direction and one behind her, she scampered across the open area to the cover of hedges along the walkway. A minute later, she dashed across the remaining ten yards until she reached the edge of the property and hid behind a row of large plastic garbage bins.

Sweat coated her skin and her thigh burned like a fire. Running footsteps disturbed the eerie silence.

At the end of the line and on her own, she had to make a choice. Follow the path along the property or try to scale the giant wall against her back.

A no-brainer. Walls never bothered her before. She'd do just about anything to get out.

The cans reeked of trash and a handful of stacked empty boxes of different sizes leaned against the wall. If she stood on the trash cans, she'd be able to reach the top of the wall. Then it was a matter of heaving herself over and dropping to the next property...

Where guard dogs or a steep drop or any number of things might be waiting for her.

"No choice. Do it, Washington," Abbey told herself quietly. Staying here wasn't an option.

Voices got louder and Abbey's heart rate spiked as she eased farther behind the trash cans and crouched low.

"I haven't seen her."

"But we know you winged her. We found blood on the pavement."

Oh God! What if she'd left a trail of blood to this exact spot? Another shot of fear made her veins icy.

He spoke louder, anger lacing every word. "I don't give a fuck what you find unless it's actually her. She can't get away. I already made the fucking call. A girl who looks like this is going to go for fifty grand. Probably more. Depends on who gets involved in the bidding. I'm not about to lose my take of that."

Chills prickled Abbey's skin as the burn in her thigh got worse. More blood seeped through the cotton gloves the longer she stayed crouched.

"Take another pass. When we find her, she's going to wish she'd never tried to run. And we'd better cover our asses, so have two of the guys move the merchandise to the other location. I'm not going over the border with half a load."

Abbey bit her bottom lip to keep it from trembling. She couldn't afford to move anywhere. *Breathe. Breathe.* She kept Blake in her mind's eye, kept seeing his concerned face as he helped her by breathing with her. In and out. Slow and steady. She concentrated on the sound of his voice, his gentle tone.

New footsteps pounded forward. "I've looked everywhere and I can't find his phone. If she's called for help, then we're busted."

"Move, now!" the first guy ordered. "Take one last pass where we lost her, then meet up front."

Footsteps faded and Abbey checked through the crack in the trash cans to see the men had moved out of sight. She slowly eased up and bit back a groan as fresh pain streaked through her leg. She tightened the knot again before hopping up to the top of the closed plastic bin. She quickly stood on the lid and jumped for the top of the wall. After hauling herself up, she threw her good leg over the top and edged over the other side. She didn't have anything to break her fall on this end. It was a good eight feet from the top of the wall to the hard packed earth below.

It was going to hurt.

"Do it, Washington," she gritted between clenched teeth.

Abbey let go.

She tried to roll as she landed, but her right leg crumpled and the pain ripping through her seemed to come from everywhere. She lay on the ground, her breathing ragged as she tried to get her bearings. "Get up, get up," she told herself, her jaw clenched tight. *Run.* She wasn't anywhere close to being in the clear.

Abbey rolled and got to all fours, taking another few deep breaths before she tried getting to her feet. Looking up, she saw a massive hedge that outlined something on the other side. Maybe a road or a building, she couldn't tell from her angle. If she got on the other side of the hedge she'd at least be hidden from searching eyes from this direction.

Using her good leg and the wall for support, Abbey stood up and held back a groan of agony. She couldn't risk being seen so she had to go through the hedge.

"Just some branches," she whispered aloud. "Big deal." But she soon discovered, it *was* a big deal. The hedges were packed tightly together. She was just too big to get through them without some type of cutter to open a hole. Tears pricked her eyes and she wiped them away furiously.

Limping, she made her way along the hedge until she came to a weak spot. The leaves were dry and brittle and Abbey broke apart the dry branches and forced her way through. Twigs tore at her skin and clothes, but she kept going. It was only a couple of feet. Not even twenty-four inches.

The beam of a flashlight hit the spot next to her and she froze. Her black jeans and green shirt were perfect camouflage, but they'd catch her if they found her now. With her ass nearly hanging out the back of the hedge, she had no clue if they'd seen her or not.

The bushes shook a few feet away and her adrenaline soared. *Something* was next to her in these bushes!

"Hey, I hear something," one of the men shouted from the behind her.

"Shoot it!"

A bullet slammed into the space a few feet away and the creature living in that part of the hedge scrambled for safety. Abbey did the same. She lurched forward and took the brunt of the branches on her head and shoulders as she powered through. Hair ripped out of her skull as it caught on larger twigs. More shots were fired and the animal near her raced for freedom.

"It was only a fucking possum," the guy said. "A fucking family of possums." His voice faded as he moved away from the wall.

Abbey let three silent sobs escape before she wiped her eyes and got to her feet again. Stinging pain arched up her leg. She wanted a phone. Wanted to hear Blake, needed his voice in her ear. Needed it like the air pushing in and out of her lungs.

Looking around the property, she made out an unfinished house and giant palm trees lining the street fifty yards away. With renewed hope, she limped toward the street. The chain link lock on the gate had just enough length for Abbey to slide through. After one more look to the house of horrors next door, Abbey took off in the other direction. Screw the pain. She got about a hundred yards before two police cars came screaming around the corner with their lights flashing. Abbey nearly passed out with the relief burning through her. She slowed and waved both hands flagging them down with the last of her energy.

Blake took the exit leading to Bob Hope Drive and floored the SUV. The fact that a haze of smoke wafted from his engine just added to the list of shit he had on his plate tonight.

Troy had already called with the address of the hospital Abbey had been taken to. Knowing she was safe hadn't made his foot any lighter on the pedal. Having to hang up on her earlier had just about killed him, but now a whole lot of hope raced through his system.

Blake pulled to the E.R., cut the engine and headed in. Troy had used his considerable weight with the Los Angeles police to clear the red tape on this end, so getting in to see Abbey wasn't a problem after Blake showed his ID. One of several cops loitering in the waiting area took him back to a treatment room.

He gestured toward the last curtain on the left. "She's okay," he said. "Scared and a little beat up, but okay."

"Abbey?" Blake eased back the curtain and peaked in.

Abbey.

His chest tightened up at the sight of her. God she was a mess. Florescent lights illuminated scratches and welts marring her smooth skin and a particular bruise on her cheekbone came from a hand. A new surge of anger pummeled Blake. A hospital gown and thin white blanket covered most of her with the exception of a bloody bandage over her exposed thigh. Her shredded clothes lay in a heap in the corner of the room.

Her face crinkled up and tears welled in her eyes as he moved closer. She wrapped her arms around his waist, crying into his shirt, her body shaking in his arms. Bits of dried leaves stuck in her wrecked hair.

Blake held her tight. Didn't give a shit about the residual soreness in his ribs. He'd never been happier in his life to feel a little pain. Kicking a stool closer, he sat down and tucked his head next to hers, breathing in the scent of her. Finally, he leaned back to look at her.

It took a minute but she pulled herself together. "I'm okay. I'm okay." Her eyes looked anything but okay as she dabbed them with a crumpled tissue. Blake wanted to kill the men responsible for putting that fear there. He brought her close again just to feel her warmth.

"Thank God," he whispered, stroking her back and willing his pulse to slow down for the first time in hours.

Finally he moved away and gestured to the bandage. "Did the doctor fix you up yet?"

She shook her head. "Not yet. I just asked and the nurse said I'm next on the list. The EMTs thought I need two or three sutures to be safe. It's really not bad. They thought a few stitches would keep it from being a nasty scar."

That news just burned Blake up more.

Her gaze softened as she reached up and stroked her thumb under his cheekbone. "What happened here?"

"I was ambushed by a second guy before they took you out of the casting building. I'm okay." He took Abbey's hand and linked their fingers, needing to know what happened after the phone call.

"What did you do after we hung up?" he asked.

She told him about scaling the wall and running down the street. "I got a few houses away when the police showed up. I flagged them down. They called the ambulance." She gestured toward the officer at the door. "They're still searching the place as far as I know. I think the guys must have cleared out right before I reached the street because they were there when I first got over the wall. They must've been worried that I'd called for help with their friend's phone. I thought it was mine when I ran, because it was next to my purse."

"They tossed your phone into a van headed in the other direction. The diversion worked for a while. If you hadn't texted us, we wouldn't have found you." Blake swallowed back the lump in his throat.

"You just missed the officer in charge. He was really nice. He rode with me in the ambulance and said he didn't want me to have to come into the station if he could avoid it."

"I think we have Troy to thank for that. I'll have to send the guy a thank you note." That got a whisper of a smile and Blake squeezed her hand. "Are you going to be okay telling me what happened? Because Troy and I need to know too."

She nodded. "I know. Can it wait until we get out of here?"

Blake nodded. "Sure. Not a problem." He didn't want to rush her.

The doctor entered the room and Blake stayed as Abbey got

three stitches to close the gap from a bullet. Blake didn't think he could ever be as angry as when he'd seen his brother get cut in front of him, but he'd been wrong. Because he was pissed. Really pissed. He wanted these guys to pay for what they did to her. He wanted them behind bars for a good long time.

Abbey left the hospital in a set of green scrubs that made her eyes pop like dark gems.

Blake helped her into the Explorer then checked his watch. Way past midnight. He cranked the engine and started out. A mile down the road, he spotted a motel with a vacancy and pulled into the lot.

"Why are you stopping?" Abbey asked, concern evident in her voice.

"The Explorer was about to overheat when I pulled up to the E.R." That was bound to happen after pushing the seventeen-year-old truck so hard. "The engine's got to cool down if we plan on going anywhere. I'm afraid it's not going to get us home tonight." At least they'd both had food at the hospital when a nurse brought them sandwiches.

"Oh." She nodded, but he saw her reluctance.

"It's okay. C'mon," he whispered. "Let's crash for the night. I promise I'll keep you safe, Ab. I'm not letting anything else happen to you."

Swallowing, Abbey nodded and Blake hustled to open her door. She eased out of the Explorer, grimaced when her feet hit the ground and grabbed his arm for support.

Blake snatched his athletic bag from the back seat and tossed it over his shoulder, then took Abbey's hand and led her inside. He checked them in while Abbey stopped in the ladies room. Five minutes later, he ushered her in their room and flipped on a light. No frills, two double beds, navy and maroon, but it was clean.

Abbey stood at the end of one of the beds as if she didn't know what to do first. Blake set his bag down, moved in front of her and took her in his arms. Under the sweat and fear he caught the faint citrus scent of her. Her arms came around him tight and her shoulders trembled.

"Can you tell me what happened back at the audition?"

She pulled away, inhaled and exhaled, her forehead creased with the memory. "He was waiting for me at the callback. I never even made it up the stairs. He told me we were in a different room downstairs and when I walked in he...he—" She took in a shaky breath. "He grabbed me. It was the guy with the knife from the Sports Center, but I didn't recognize him at first. He'd shaved off his mustache and he didn't have the cap on. I tried to fight him, but he put something over my mouth and I couldn't breathe. I don't remember what happened after that. I woke up in the trunk of a car. We were moving. He tossed me in a room when we got there and a few minutes later he came back with the other guy from the Sports Center. The guard."

Kwami.

"Did you get names? Anything that might help us identify them?

"Y-yes," she said. "Damon. He was the one who knifed the man at the Sports Center." Her chin trembled, she took another deep breath and his fucking heart broke at the catch in her voice. "The guy who tried to... The guy I hurt." She closed her eyes tight. "There were three more..." She pressed her lips together as she thought harder. "Benz, Herrera and one other guy that no one named. He's Damon's brother. I told the police officer."

A fresh round of rage sizzled through Blake and close on its heels was that same pulse pounding fear. "Ab?"

Her green eyes met his gaze.

"Did he, did one of them...?" He couldn't even put it in words.

"Not the way you think," she said softly. "It was close, but, no. I got out."

Blake's relief came out in a rough exhale. He wanted to help her, comfort her, do something and he felt so impotent, because this was Abbey who never let him in, never let him get close.

She finished telling him everything and the story tore him to pieces. The fact that he hadn't been able to prevent it, that she'd had to go through it... He wrapped her in his arms again and held her close. That she let him meant more to him than anything else in the world.

Blake fought back his own emotion, but his unsteady breaths were a dead giveaway. "I was so fucking scared," he admitted quietly. He ran his hand down her hair, cupped her head against his shoulder.

She hiccupped a breath and nodded. "Me too."

He barely heard her. She was so fucking brave and he was so proud of her. "You did good, you know?" She needed to know. Needed to realize that no matter how she got out, she'd been justified. "I'm so proud of you," he said quietly. "I mean, I'm pissed that you didn't wait for me, but I'm so fucking proud that you got away." His answer came in a sniff and subtle nod. "Let's get you to bed okay?"

Pulling away from him, she wiped her eyes. "I need to take a shower and get this—" she shuddered, "—off me." She wasn't referring to the clothes and his anger boiled hot again. Moving around him, she headed for the bathroom.

"I brought my bag in," Blake said. "I've got a T-shirt and sweats in there. You can wear them if you want. They'll be big, but they're clean."

She gave him a shy smile and it was like a rainbow after a hurricane. "Troy is rubbing off on you."

That made him grin. "Really? You think so?"

She nodded. "Yeah. I think so." Her smile faded and she moved into the bathroom as Blake got fresh clothes from his bag.

Chapter Fifteen

Abbey had wanted to take a shower and scrub off the grime from that filthy man's hands, but the spray was too hard on her skin so she'd settled for a shallow bath since she couldn't get her stitches wet. After eating an apple that Blake had snagged from the front desk, she felt marginally better. Nearly every inch of her hurt. The livid bruise on her cheek made the scratches look like nothing. The welts had gone down and Blake had made two trips to the ice machine so she had ice packs on the worst of her bruises and her ankle.

Blake's sweats sat on the counter, but she'd thought long and hard while cleaning up in the tub and she'd come to a decision. If she didn't make the choice to move on with her life and overcome her fears, she faced the terrifying prospect of losing the choice completely.

How could she have thought that being a victim once already meant she was free of it happening again? She'd been living in a bubble of her own creation, tiptoeing through life in the hope that if she didn't acknowledge other people, they wouldn't notice her.

Dancing gave her the freedom she craved. Music lifted her spirit, and letting the music flow through her kept her sane. When she danced, she was no longer a victim. When she danced she was free of the fear and shame she always battled. She was the music. She was in control.

She never pictured this moment. Never imagined reaching the day when she'd let someone inside of her. Sure, she'd been attracted to Blake from the first day she'd met him, but attraction never had her thinking about sex. Very little had her thinking about sex.

Abbey brushed her teeth and combed out her hair with new purchases from the front desk. Her face was a lost cause. Blake might not even want what she had planned for him tonight, but maybe he'd do it—her—as a favor. She'd rather lose her virginity to a friend and someone she liked than face the alternative. With these men after her, she couldn't waste time wondering if they'd catch her again. Because if they did, they wouldn't let her go a second time. She knew that deep in her soul.

Coming out of the bathroom, Abbey spotted Blake in the far bed, holding one of those emergency kit ice bags to his cheek. He sat up against the headboard wearing his same T-shirt with the sheet pulled up to his waist. His folded jeans took a spot on the chair in the corner of the room. He'd turned down the blankets on the second bed. The gesture put her heart in a vise. He knew her well enough to know she liked her space, needed it. She wasn't good at being touched unless she instigated it. Extreme highs and lows prompted those times and he knew it.

"Did you call Troy?" she asked, placing his sweat bottoms on the bed.

His gaze lifted from her legs to her eyes. "Yeah. He said the police are searching the estate now. I told him we were crashing here for the night." He set the ice pack on the end table. There was something else he wasn't telling her, but at the moment she didn't care. Walking past the readied bed, she slid into the sheets next to him. He tried to hide the surprise on his face as he scooted toward the other side of the bed, but she saw the question in his eyes.

What the hell is she doing?

Abbey turned on her side, on her good leg and faced him, tucking her hands under the pillow as she watched him. "Can I sleep with you tonight?"

He nodded, his eyes full of emotion she couldn't name. Worry, compassion, all the things she'd seen already, but something else too. He didn't seem to get what she meant though, so maybe she'd have to show him. If she only knew how. Or where to start...

Kissing. Yes, they'd kissed already. Amazing, heart-stopping kisses that not only stole her breath, they nearly stole her sanity. Granted, having nothing to compare to, she couldn't be sure, but just from their little interlude in the park, Abbey realized she was dealing with an expert when it came to kissing.

"How many women have you kissed?"

He leaned back, his eyes widened. "What kind of question is that? I don't know. I've never kept a tally."

"I was just curious. You're really good at it and I figure practice makes perfect so..."

"If you've never kissed before, how would you know I'm good at it?" The half curve of his lips screamed sex appeal as he shifted lower, crooked his elbow and leaned on his hand.

"Call it woman's intuition. I have a feeling."

He watched her for a second then nodded. "Okay," he admitted. "Maybe I've kissed a few girls. But it's been a long time."

She waited for more and when he didn't elaborate, she pressed. "Why?"

His gaze didn't waver. "I think it's wrong to kiss one person when I'm thinking about another."

Did he mean her? She blinked and her heart stumbled along unevenly. But this was a good thing if he meant what he said. She crooked her elbow the same way so they faced each other more evenly. "Maybe we could do it again. The kissing," she clarified.

They were in a bed. She might be a virgin, but she wasn't stupid. Bed plus kissing equaled sex, or it should anyway. Of course, the fact that she'd been beaten up might still seriously damage her chances.

His brows quirked again and that look of concern clouded his eyes. "Maybe that's not such a good idea right now?"

"Because my face looks like hamburger or because—"

"Jesus. No!" he said, cutting her off. "Because you went through hell today and I think you should probably rest, that's all."

Life was too short for that. "What if I don't want to rest?" She glided her thumb across the dark stubble on his jaw. He was so damn cute and sexy. And young. Two full years younger than her. No, it wasn't a lot, but the age difference had always bothered her a little until tonight, when she figured out it's not the age that matters, but the person.

"Ab," he warned her. It was very similar to the way she'd said his name a few days ago and she smiled.

"Blake," she repeated in the same tone. Then she went for it. She leaned in and brushed her lips across his. Heat sizzled up her center just like the last time she kissed him. She had been a little panicked before, but now she felt a certain amount of power, a certain knowledge that she affected him whether she intended to or not.

Her courage multiplied and she eased her tongue across the fullness of his bottom lip. He groaned and leaned in farther, took more possession of her mouth as his tongue stroked out and met hers. Her pulse revved faster and her breathing turned erratic.

He pulled back, his own breathing unsteady, his eyes electric blue and wide open as he watched her.

"What's wrong?"

"I... I... Jesus." He moved away, landed on his back and stared at the ceiling.

"Talk to me," she whispered.

He swallowed and met her gaze. "Talk to you?" he asked. The question almost sounded like a warning, but he nodded and never looked away. "Okay. I want to touch you so bad, I can barely think straight and all I do is worry that if I reach out, if I try and lay a finger on you, you'll run. That would kill me, Ab. I want you so much. I want to show you how it feels to be touched the right way." He rubbed a hand down his face. "How's that for a conversation starter?"

Not what she expected, that was for sure. She copied his move and lay on her back next to him. She owed him the truth. After everything he'd gone through for her, it didn't seem like a lot to ask.

"I'm sorry." She bit her bottom lip. "I didn't mean to make you feel that way. You're always so good about giving me space and I just figured..." That he looked at every woman the way he looked at her? That he teased other women the way he teased her? "I don't know what I figured."

"You went through something traumatic. I understand that. God, I understand it better than anyone, but I need to know what happened to you, so I don't mess up. I don't want to touch you a certain way that's going make you run." He leaned up on his elbow again, head in hand. "But I also don't want you to remember a time that's going to hurt you either. So you see I'm torn."

He looked it too. So confused and worried about her. Maybe if she told him, he'd give her what she needed tonight.

"It's not a fun story," she said softly.

He nodded. "I didn't think it would be."

She exhaled slowly. "I've never told anyone before."

He nodded again and the resignation in his eyes said he didn't think she'd tell him now.

"I had just turned fifteen the week before," she said and understanding dawned across his face. "We were visiting my cousin's new apartment in downtown L.A." She stared up at the ceiling as the memories clicked in like a movie, frame by frame. "We'd forgotten the house warming gift in the trunk, and Bernie and I were racing to the street to get it. She took the elevator and I took the stairs." Abbey swallowed as sweat pricked her skin. "I saw a man, but I didn't think much about it. I was just going to run by him, not disturb him, but he heard me coming and probably got a glimpse of me the closer I got. He'd been sitting on the landing and he stood as I turned the corner and started down the stairs. I was concentrating on the steps, you know. I could beat the elevator if I ran fast enough. It was nine flights, but the elevator took so long on the way up and I just wanted to beat Bernie." She'd always wanted to be as good as her big sis. "I was always trying to beat Bernie."

The ceiling blurred and Abbey took a deep breath. "He grabbed me as I passed him. Just wrapped his arm around my waist and took me off my feet." She'd never forget the surprise of it, the shock of a stranger grabbing her so quickly and efficiently. "At first I didn't know what he was doing. Maybe he thought I was going to fall, or maybe... I don't know. But then he had his hands on me." Big, rough hands that haunted her dreams for years. "When I finally found my voice, I screamed bloody murder. I fought him. I fought as hard as I could, but he was bigger than me and stronger than me." Her heart had already been beating fast because of her pace, but it had gone into hyper speed when she realized the danger. Abbey wiped away a tear that streaked past her temple. "I was wearing shorts and he didn't even take them down. He just shoved his hand..." She waited until she got her voice under control. "He shoved his hand inside me. Told me I was a dirty girl. Told me dirty girls liked what he was doing to me. What he was going to do to me." Those terrifying minutes had replayed in her head hundreds, maybe thousands of times. "The whole time he just kept shoving into me. Hurting me."

For the first time since she began, Abbey glanced at Blake. His red-rimmed eyes brimmed with tears and his jaw clenched tight. She took his hand and he held on tight.

"Luckily, Bernie knew exactly where I was and when I didn't show up in the lobby, she came into the stairwell and yelled for me. I screamed for all I was worth. I screamed my head off until he muzzled me with his hand and hauled me out of the stairwell. We were on the fifth floor. I didn't realize it at the time and Bernie couldn't tell from where she was. She just knew I was in trouble. She ran all the way back up, hoping to find a clue and by the time she got to my cousin's apartment to tell everyone, she was screaming and crying herself. They called 911 and the cops showed up in minutes." Too bad they hadn't found her in minutes. Her skin prickled remembering the dark closet.

"The guy that took me…he was visiting his brother. He was a registered sex offender and just released from prison. He got scared knowing Bernie had heard me scream. He wrapped duct tape across my mouth and taped my hands and ankles together. He told me not to fight him. Said if I fought him, he'd find Bernie and hurt her too. Then he was going to kill my whole family. He told me in graphic detail how he was going to do all of it." She exhaled an unsteady breath. "He told me to shut up and not make a sound, not to move or he'd make good on his promise. Then he shoved me in a closet in the back bedroom and shut the door.

"I heard the sirens outside. I heard the police knock on the door. I waited and waited and waited." Her hope had died when they'd moved on to another apartment. "I waited three hours until they came back. That's when they found me. The manager didn't know the guy—his name is Earl—and the police contacted his brother and looked up is priors. That's when they had probable cause and searched the apartment. My clothes were still on, and he hadn't…he hadn't…" She never knew how to finish this sentence.

"Yes, he did," Blake said softly. "On the staircase." He sat up against the headboard and wiped his eyes with the heel of his hand. "Please tell me this guy is still in prison."

"He is." Abbey nodded, crossed her legs Indian style as she sat up and faced him. "Bernie totally saved me that day. If she hadn't come looking for me the second she got off the elevator, I don't know what would've happened. Actually, I guess I do know. He would've done much worse." She ran her finger along one of the many scratches on her hand. "I just remember his hands all over me, hurting me. Over and over, and I've never been..." Never been the same since. "I want to get past it, you know?" She gave him a shaky smile. "I don't want to think about him or that day, but someone will reach out and I shy away because...because..." She shook her head. "I don't know why. I mean my head knows it's not him and my eyes see it's not him, but my body goes into this fight or flight thing and I panic." She wiped her nose with the back of her hand. "Stupid, right?"

He shot up, faced her. "No," he said adamantly, his breath warm on her skin. "Not even close to stupid." He ran a hand through his hair. "Sorry. Didn't mean to get in your face like that." He took a few deep breaths and let them out slowly. "I seriously want to find this pervert and kill him."

"You'd have to get in line behind my dad," Abbey said. "Then my mom. Then my sister. I think by the time you get him there probably won't be much left."

Blake didn't care. He'd never wanted to hurt someone more. Well, besides the men who'd hurt Abbey today. He would've gotten out of the bed to pace, but he'd stripped off his jeans and the last thing he wanted to do was scare Abbey while he strode around in his underwear. That would go over well after the story she just told him.

"Don't forget *me*. I get a crack at him before you." She continued to trace the scratch on her hand, her eyes downcast. "But then I think I really don't ever want to see him again. Ever. Not even to get some type of revenge. I just want to be done with it." Looking up at him, she gave him a forlorn smile. "I wish someone had a wand that could erase the bad memories."

Blake nodded. "I'd buy it." He knew exactly what he'd get rid of with it too.

Abbey took his hand for the second time and floored Blake.

He'd never seen her like this. Add to the fact she was wearing just his T-shirt with her spectacular bare legs glowing from moisturizer and she smelled like clean lavender soap in the bathroom, his hormones walked a very thin line. "I don't have a wand tonight," she said. "But I know how you can help get my mind off my rotten day."

She couldn't possibly be thinking...her original words hit him like a two-ton trailer. *Can I sleep with you tonight?* Had she meant in the literal sense and not just in the same bed?

He was suddenly thinking in a language he didn't understand, trying to grasp the meaning of Abbey's words.

Smiling at him, she lifted one eyebrow. "I believe this is the first time I've ever seen you speechless."

It might've been the first time he'd ever *been* speechless.

Then Abbey leaned in closer and closed her moss green eyes right before setting her lips on his. The girl was a quick learner. She smoothed her mouth across his slowly, taking her time, taking little nibbles along the way until Blake had to taste more of her. Struggling to keep his palms flat on the bed as he leaned into her, he met her tongue with his and wanted to groan at the contact at the soft plush feel of her lips.

The beast in him roared for more and Blake refused to listen. He let Abbey lead the way. Let her fingers stroke into his hair as she leaned closer until she was fucking straddling his lap with her arms around his neck and her tongue deep in his mouth.

God, he wanted to lay her down so bad he itched with the need. To finally sink inside of her and lose himself in her heat, in her softness. So when she pressed on his shoulders, eased him back to the pillows, he let her. He let her touch him, let her drive him insane with her soft hands and long fingernails. It felt like every drop of blood in his body resided in his throbbing erection. She had to feel it too. She was right there, the heat of her right on top of him, sending clear messages to his baser instincts.

When she came up for air after the longest make-out session of his life, his lips were chapped. Not that he gave a shit. By some miracle of the universe, he'd managed to keep his palms flat on the bed. Well, more like fisting the sheets, but still a huge trick to not have touched her when he was beyond desperate to do exactly that.

"When are you going to take over?" she asked as she spread

light kisses across his jaw. God, what he wouldn't give for a razor. He'd have to add whisker burn to her injuries after this.

Wait a minute. "Take over?" His warped brain tried to catch on.

"Yes, take over. When are you going to make a move? Make love to me? I want you to make love to me." She looked dead serious. He'd seen that look before. It was her tackle-an-obstacle face. If and when she saw a problem, she didn't stop until she figured it out.

The static in his head crackled like feedback on a bad speaker.

"I've been totally improvising this and I have no clue what I'm doing, so it would good if you…you know…took over."

"Took over?" Jesus, when had he become such a moron?

"Blake," She gave another seductive rub over his straining dick. "Make love to me. Please." She set her mouth on his again and Blake couldn't help but kiss her back. His brain didn't and couldn't say no to that. Neither could his mouth or his tongue. But when she started yanking his T-shirt up and her warm hands started caressing his chest, he about went out of his mind. And he couldn't afford to lose his mind. One of them needed to keep a sane thought.

The next time she came up for air, he gasped her name. "Ab. Abbey." But she was back on him again in a flash and his blood revved so hot he felt like his Explorer a couple of hours ago, nearly ready to combust. "Abbey." This time he cupped her face in his hands. "Listen to me."

"No." Her fear shone clear in her eyes. "I don't want to listen. I want to get this over with. I just want to do it so they can't take it from me or kill me before I get the chance."

Another tidbit of information that landed like a bomb. She didn't want him to make love to her because she wanted him. He was just the better of two evils. *Fuck, fuck, fuck.* He shook his head. This was not how he wanted his first time to be with Abbey. Not even close. Especially not after waiting for this moment for over a year.

Blake lifted up on his elbows and scooted back to the headboard, making sure to keep some distance between them before he chucked his abstinence plan. As if.

"What's wrong? Where are you going? Did I do something wrong?"

"No. Yes. *No*. I just..." He put a hand over his eyes and tried like hell to do the right thing. "Abbey, I can't—" He had no idea how to finish his sentence. "I don't think this is a good idea. To do this tonight," he explained.

Her bottom lip trembled and Blake felt like scum. Worse than scum. Scum on scum.

She moved back to her spot on the bed and slid between the sheets, her silence like a club to his head. She rolled over and gave him her back. *Fuck*.

Blake moved up behind her, nearly spooned her. "Ab. You have no idea how much I want to. But I want you to do it for the right reasons. I want you to want me as much as I want you. I want you to need me. To care about me the way I care about you."

She rolled over and faced him, her brows a straight almost angry line. "It's my choice," she told him quietly. "I should be able to decide who I lose my virginity to and when it happens." Her eyes brightened with moisture and the sight put a knife through his heart. "You have a choice too and you've made it clear." She started to roll over and Blake stopped her with a hand on her shoulder.

"Whoa. Wait. I understand where you're coming from."

She shook her head. "You can't possibly understand. I don't want something I've protected my whole life to be violently taken from me. But if you won't—"

"It's not that I won't. C'mon Abbey. Give me a break." God, he didn't want to tell her this way. Didn't want to bear his soul when it was the last thing she needed on her plate. "Is it wrong for me to want you to feel something for me before we do it? Is it wrong for me to want the same level of emotion? You mean more to me than just a *let's get it over with* fuck." There had to be a way to make this right...or at least make it better. "Okay, so maybe we don't make love tonight." That didn't mean he couldn't give her something she'd never had before. "But maybe we do something else."

"What's the point of something else if it doesn't get rid of my virginity?"

How did he explain this? "I still want you, Ab. More than anything. More than the air I'm breathing. More than my PI license. Above all else, I want you and I think you know that."

Her gaze skittered away.

He wasn't about to stop now. "Can I ask you a personal question?"

She snorted, but without one bit of humor. "I can't see how we could get any more personal than where we're at."

"You told me in the park that you've never done a lot of things. Since then, you've kissed." He traced a light finger over the round corner of her shoulder and let her get used the feel of him. "You've actually become fairly proficient at it in a very short period of time." Understatement. She fucking knocked the lid off his fantasies with just her mouth on his. "I'm thinking there's another lesson I can give you tonight. Something you might like as much as making love for the first time." Especially since he knew the first time was going to hurt her. Knew it with a certainty that made his stomach cramp.

Her skeptical eyes indicated she had no clue what he meant.

"Have you had an orgasm, Ab?"

She closed her eyes before glancing up at him again and shaking her head.

"You've never touched yourself?"

"No," she snapped a little too quickly. "What did you not understand about my first answer?"

"You're embarrassed and you shouldn't be." He slid the palm of his hand slowly down her arm and she inhaled. A good sign or a bad one? He didn't know.

"I'm going to make love to you tonight, Ab, but not the way you think. I am definitely going to make you come. I'm going to show you how good it feels to be touched the right way, by the right person." He kept his caress all the way down her arm and to her hand, which rested on her thigh, then he let his fingers trace circles on her soft skin below his T-shirt.

She was a work of art. Every smooth inch of her gleamed in the shallow light of the room. Didn't matter that she was scratched and bruised, she was the most gorgeous woman in the world.

"Remember that Eskimo kiss?" he asked. He read the doubt in her eyes and couldn't wait to do the things he planned on doing to her. "I'm going to give you Eskimo kisses everywhere." To show her, he bent his head and nuzzled her ear, around the shell and back the other way. He let his breath fan over her, let his lips barely graze her skin. She sucked in a small, sharp breath.

"I'm going to make love to you when you want me to do it because you need me, because you're dying to have me inside you. Not because you have to get rid of your virginity."

"You know it's not about that." She stilled his hand and looked into his eyes. She wanted understanding.

"I know what it's about for you. You need to know what it's about for me." Fuck it. He had to come clean. "I love you, Abbey. Ever since the first day I met you in that elevator from hell. I love you. You walked into that car and my whole life shifted."

"You can't love someone at first sight," she argued quietly, her eyes soft and soulful.

"Bullshit," he whispered back. He grinned. "You know when I knew for sure?"

Her lips curled the slightest bit as she shook her head.

"When the car took that first jolt and you said, and I quote, 'Shit on a stick.'"

"I think you said something just as eloquent."

He nodded. "I'm sure you're right." They seemed to come to a truce. She didn't care for him the same way he did for her, but he'd known that. If she wanted him, she was going to get every last bit of him. Not only his body, but his heart and soul. If he had to drag her love out of her, then he'd do it one orgasm at a time, starting right now.

He caught her gaze, started his fingers moving again over her skin. "Are you ready for me? Because I'm going to take you on one hell of a ride. In fact, it's going to be so good, you're going to beg me for more."

She grabbed his hand and stopped him again. *Fuck.*

Chapter Sixteen

Abbey was still in shock. Still didn't believe that Blake really loved her. Maybe he thought he did, but he was young after all. Besides, maybe he was right. What if she'd gotten ahead of herself? It wasn't fair of her to ask this of him. He deserved more. Someone not broken. She was—after all—very, very broken. As much as she wanted him, she still had a hard time letting him draw those tiny circles on her thigh.

Leaning over her, Blake kept his hands on the bed. "If anything I do makes you uncomfortable, then you stop me. Deal?"

She nodded. How bad could it get? It wasn't like he was going to make love to her, he'd already told her that.

His lips came down softly on hers and since this territory had been well covered, Abbey relaxed into the warmth, into the heat he generated as he moved over her. Sweet man that he was, he kept most of his body on the bed. She'd felt the size of his erection, had even briefly worried about it, but ultimately, she needed her virginity gone and Blake was the prime candidate.

The warmth of his lips eased along her jaw and toward her ear where he nuzzled her with his nose and dragged the tip of his tongue along the outside shell. She gasped as a wave of heat and tingles spread along her back. He was so good at making her feel, at making her want things she didn't even know she wanted.

He continued his descent. His lips stroking over her collarbone and back toward her neck before heading south. She still wore his T-shirt and her self-confidence sputtered.

"Don't you want my shirt off?" she asked through a gasp as he gently bit the side of her breast through the fabric.

"Not yet," he mumbled as if nothing fazed him. He continued to graze his mouth over her chest until he got to her nipple where it prodded the soft cotton. Blake took the peak in his mouth and laved it with his tongue. Over and over and over until the T-shirt plastered to her breast and she craved his mouth on her skin. The unfamiliar feel of moisture pooled between her legs and Abbey rubbed her thighs together.

"You are feeling it in the exact right spot," he growled as he moved his mouth to the other breast and gave it the same treatment. By the time he left, she was a panting mass of goo and her—his—T-shirt was soaked and molded to her breasts.

He continued to move down, his mouth the only part of him at work. She wanted to feel more of him, wanted to feel his hard muscled body against hers. He shifted as he got lower so that he eased between her legs. He nuzzled the dip of her hip and gently bit her hipbone. The pressure sent an erotic bolt of lust through her that had more heat building from her stomach and climbing up her chest. A thin film of sweat coated her skin as he got his shoulders between her thighs.

A needy moan whispered from her throat as he hovered over her.

He moved even lower and Abbey's heart pumped faster. When he set his hands on her thighs and spread them wider, her lungs seized. Air refused to go in or out. Remembering rough hands and pain, she grabbed his head. "Blake!" His name came out on a wheeze and he moved off her in an instant.

"It's okay. You're okay." The concern in his eyes killed her. She didn't want this between them. "Breathe, Ab. You're okay. It's just me." He placed soft kisses along her jaw and down her neck. "Just me," he repeated. "I swear I won't hurt you. I'm not even going to touch you with my hands the rest of the night."

"If you don't touch me, then I won't—"

"Shh. I said I wouldn't use my hands." His sweet gaze conveyed all that love he talked about. "But I'm definitely going to touch you." He brushed his lips across her cheek. "Ready to try again or should I go back to my corner?"

Abbey shoved back the fear. She wanted this. She needed this. "I'm...I'm ready."

"Trust me," Blake whispered. "Trust me." He started kissing her again. Covering the same path he'd already taken, making her crazy for more of that elusive thing he'd tapped into before she'd put on the brakes. He lifted the T-shirt with his teeth, bared her middle, and drove her insane with his beautiful mouth.

"What are you doing?" she finally panted, when it seemed as if he had no plans to do anything but torture her skin with his lips and tongue.

He chuckled, his breath hot on her stomach. "Living out a fantasy." Then he leveled her with his gorgeous eyes. "Trust me, Ab. I'm gonna make this really good for you." Then with slow deliberation he eased down and nuzzled her right *there*. Abbey nearly shot off the bed as she gasped her surprise.

"Shh," Blake whispered. "Easy does it." He continued to use his nose along her bikini line on both sides between the vee of her legs, edging her legs farther apart as his hot breath followed the path. Every so often he hit that same spot and Abbey gasped. It was like getting hit with a pleasure stick. The shock, the sizzle, stoked her blood pressure higher, sent her pulse hammering wildly.

"Blake," she whimpered. She had no idea what she wanted to tell him. Her brain wasn't functioning on its usual level. All sane thoughts had vanished many minutes ago.

"Should I stop?" His question was muffled since his mouth was right on her. The heat of his words penetrated the fabric of her thong and seemed to seep straight inside of her.

"God, no. It's just so..." What? Intense? Erotic? Intimate. All those things. And it was wildly, wildly stimulating. What would it be like without any barrier? Just the thought had another surge of moisture dampening her underwear.

Somehow Blake knew. Or he guessed because he stuck his tongue right there, right over the fresh wet spot and sucked.

Abbey cried out. The warm, wet flat of his tongue pressed right between the crease of her thigh where her thong covered a very thin private line. Abbey legs trembled. Every inch of her shook with need, with want, with a rising hunger she'd never expected or experienced.

"Blake." She moaned his name this time. Couldn't help it.

"You okay?" he asked, still nuzzling with his nose and licking with his tongue, alternating between hard strokes and feather light kisses and each touch took her a little closer to insanity.

"I'm going to die," she breathed. "It's too..."

"Too what?" he asked when she didn't finish.

"Too everything." God, she had to know what it felt like without the material in the way. "Will you keep doing that if we take off the thong?"

He froze in midnuzzle and his gaze locked onto hers. The gleam, the sparkle was impossible to ignore. His slow nod spoke volumes and as he stared at her, he lifted up enough to grab the elastic band in his teeth and pull it down.

Her legs shook more and she slammed her head back on the pillow. She wasn't brave enough to watch him. "People do this a lot?" she asked.

"If they're lucky," he muttered, his mouth full of her underwear. He inched the thong down evenly with his teeth until they got low enough to kick off, then Blake moved back into place.

Abbey chanced a glance, shocked at the expression on his face as he looked at her. He watched her like he might be watching something he'd never seen before. Something he very much appreciated.

He hadn't touched her again with his hands. Only his beautiful mouth. His fabulous lips. His erotic tongue. He started over with his soft nuzzling and sweet small kisses. Off to the side, over the top and on her thighs, but he dodged the spot where she needed him. The sweet spot where all the pleasure came from.

"Blaaake." She felt his smile against the inside of her thigh.

"Change your mind? Should I find your thong?"

A burst of laughter erupted from her chest and shocked her. She hadn't thought anything could make her laugh, not after the day she'd had and not when she was so on the edge of...something. God, she couldn't even name it. She needed, wanted...it was elusive, it was beyond her grasp. "You do and you'll suffer."

"In that case, we'll skip the thong." He licked her fully for the first time, his tongue stroking right along the slick line of her and ending in that spot so sensitive it felt as if an electrical shock buzzed through her. Before she came down from the high, his tongue repeated the same path.

Abbey gasped and moaned. She fisted the sheets and arched her back as each new bolt of energy shimmied through her.

Blake kept up his assault. Kept his mouth and tongue moving around and around, up and down, everywhere at the same time, driving her higher and higher until such a pressure built that Abbey thought she might explode.

"I don't...I can't..." She could barely breathe. Sweat soaked the T-shirt to her skin. He'd put her in this state with only his mouth. It was unbearable. It was fabulous. She rode an edge so sharp, so sweet, she didn't see how it could end.

"Just let it happen," he urged softly and gave her a series of lashes right where it did the most good.

Abbey arched into his mouth. She had no control as the urge consumed her. The urge to get closer, to move into the caress.

With one final hard lick, something inside her broke free. Euphoria exploded between her legs and shimmied into a hot ball of delicious fire that tunneled up and out to every cell. Blake kept moving, kept those waves cresting over her until finally they eased to soft pulses of sweet aftershocks.

Holy fucking hell. She didn't even have the energy to lift her head.

"Oh my God," she breathed. "Oh my God." Then she must have said about a hundred more times. She said it as Blake kissed the inside of each thigh. She said it as he found her thong and eased it up her legs. She said it as he moved next to her and took her hand in his.

"Really, you can call me Blake," he teased. "God is so formal." The smile on his face was pure satisfaction.

She caught a glimpse of the straining erection in his black boxer briefs before he yanked the sheet up. "I guess now I know what all the fuss is about." And how.

"I guess so. At least I hope so."

God, he was gorgeous when he stared at her like that. "What happens now?" she asked.

He shrugged. "Whatever you want. Sleep is probably the smart thing." He watched her. "Why the face? You should rest."

"Because." She didn't know how to say it. "What about you? I mean, I got this whole firecracker and light show and you just have to lay there and watch? It can't work like that usually. I mean, there has to be something in it for you."

"Oh, I'm doing fine," he said around a chuckle while nodding his head. "Trust me. I am so far beyond fine it's not even funny."

She turned more fully into him. "I want to make you finer."

"I don't think that's a word."

"I'm serious. I want you to get some...you know...relief. It's only fair."

Blake sighed then shook his head. "I don't want to overload you. That's *not* fair."

"What's not fair is you doing what you just did and not letting me help you get the same satisfaction. I mean, I know I have issues, but it's not like *you* have a problem with someone touching *you*." She paused, unsure how to continue. "You could let me touch you."

If she touched him, he'd go off like a rocket. Blake doubted he'd last thirty seconds if she put even one finger on him. He was that hard. That primed. That stoked to have her. Hell, she could probably blow on his dick from across the room and he'd come like a cannon.

"I don't think that's a great idea," he said. He licked his lips and still tasted her there. His dick twitched with need.

"Why?" Persistent, she was. But he'd always known that about her.

Still, he should be honest. "Because boys are messy. I don't want you to freak out, you know, when I come." He also didn't want her to see him. She might decide to never let him touch her again.

"That's lame." She didn't bat an eyelash.

"Yeah. Maybe." He nodded. "I just don't want to push you."

"You're not." She snaked her hand under the covers and her gentle touch landed on the flat of his stomach and slowly moved down. She watched him. Watched as his eyes glazed over as she found him and stroked her hand over him and his underwear. "Can we lose these, so I can feel you?" She asked so softly that Blake—like everything else where Abbey was concerned—couldn't say no.

"If it's really what you want." He took a fortifying breath. "Yes."

She leaned in and her soft lips connected with his. She just kissed him, deeper, harder, longer than she had before, with different quality. With a sense of freedom, maybe. She inched her fingers under his waistband and he helped her get his underwear over his hips and over his massive erection looking for relief.

He would've loved to lose his T-shirt, but he didn't want to overwhelm her with skin. He understood her sense of fair play and it only made him love her that much more. This was the Abbey he'd watched over the last year, the girl who took care of everyone around her. How much had he always wanted to be in her inner circle, one of the people who got her smiles and her laughs? One of the people she wanted to please.

And Holy God Almighty was she pleasing him. He let her take complete control. Let her tongue explore his mouth as her hand moved down his thigh, testing the waters, up and down. The soft glide of her fingers drove him to the brink of begging.

Breathing got tougher as her crafty fingers curved around the upper inside of his thigh. He clenched his abs before he fucked things up, rolled her onto her back and made love to her for real.

That sly hand of hers stroked up over his hip and low across his stomach then grazed underneath his erection. She froze and Blake's heart pumped a river of blood that all seemed to converge at his dick.

As much as he wanted her hand on him, he wouldn't push her. "No pressure, you know," he told her, but it came out between clenched teeth.

"Blake." She pulled back and looked into his eyes. "Shut up." Then she kissed him again and her hand reached around and hovered over his dick. It was the most incredible torture, feeling the heat of her palm, waiting for the second she touched him. "I'm just nervous," she whispered. "I don't want to hurt you."

He nearly choked out a laugh. "I don't see that happening." Of course, at this point if she *didn't* touch him his head might explode.

"I'm serious," she continued. "Any contact I've had with this particular area of a man has been about protecting myself. It's been about delivering pain." Concern filled her green eyes. "Tonight...earlier...I really hurt the man that...that..."

"The man that hurt you?" he asked.

She nodded.

"Good. He deserved it." Blake wanted to touch her so bad, he ached with the need. To slip some hair behind her ear or trace her jaw with his thumb, or kiss the bruise on her cheek. "Abbey, you won't hurt me and no matter what you think, you don't have to do anything right this minute except maybe close your eyes and get some rest."

One finger touched the swollen head of his penis and he jerked. "It's okay," he assured her when she yanked her hand away. "That was a good thing." He clenched his jaw and held his breath as she slowly followed the thick line of his ridged flesh all the way to the base before moving up again, this time with two fingers and more pressure.

Blake closed his eyes and tried to control his rough breathing. That Abbey was touching him like this almost made every one of his dreams come true. He'd been practically convinced it would never happen.

After a few passes up and down where she got more used to the feel of him, she wrapped her hand around his length, careful to be gentle. Eventually he'd show her she could handle him with a much firmer hand, but right now was all about Abbey and her comfort level.

"You're not normal, are you?" she asked. It was such an honest question that Blake found himself laughing again.

"I thought I was pretty normal. Why do you ask?"

She squeezed him then. Hard enough for him to suck in a rush of air. "*This* can't be normal. You're giant. I mean, I have seen a picture or two so..." She studied his face seriously. "Not normal, right?"

Exhaling slowly, Blake focused on her words and not the urge to thrust in her hand. His fog-filled head only had one thought in it. Abbey stroking him to completion. "I'm normal for my family," he managed to say. "I'm a twin, remember?" Sweat broke out on his skin. Everywhere.

"Brendan has the same equipment?" she asked.

He laughed again. "Don't tell him I told you. He'd probably not like having that advertised."

"So the guys in the locker room must be really self-conscious around you." She kept up the dialogue as she began stroking him in earnest, and the will to hold onto any bit of self-control eroded away with each pass. Her brows quirked together. "So when do you come? What do I have to do to make you come?"

That. "Aw, shit." Apparently, all she had to do was say the word because her touch was too new, too intense after everything he'd done to her tonight, and the immediate coiling of heat and desire shot him to the finish. His come jetted out in thick spurts across his stomach as Abbey held him.

"Are you..." Her eyes widened as she watched him...as she felt his dick throb in her palm. When he finished, a bone deep shudder shook him from head to toe. Abbey gently released her grip. "I'll get a towel," she said, and slid out from under the covers.

A few minutes later, after they'd cleaned up, they lay facing each other, several inches separating them. Abbey didn't look freaked out at all. In fact, she watched him with something different in her eyes. He didn't know if it was confidence or knowledge or what, but he liked the look.

"How about we go to bed?" He'd set his watch alarm for eight in the morning. They still wouldn't get close to six hours of sleep, but at least it was something.

Her eyes were already closing and she nodded and sighed. "Thanks," she whispered. She took his hand, held it snugly between them and fell asleep. Blake had never been more at peace.

Chapter Seventeen

Kim closed the large black binder in front of her, rested her elbows on the giant espresso-colored desk and rubbed her temples. How was she going to break the news to Leo? He clearly had no clue. Not even an inkling of the trouble he was in. And this was just another reason why she was glad she'd quit looking for a sugar daddy. Seriously, what happened when you married someone for money, then something happened and they lost all that money? Then what were you left with?

A truckload of unhappiness, that's what. And possibly an asshole like Carl.

Rolling the chair back over the spotless bamboo floor in Leo's opulent office, Kim stood. Every room in this mansion screamed money. He ate it, drove it, lived it and breathed it. At least he used to.

This room alone said a lot about the man. Although she hadn't figured out if all the memorabilia stemmed from conceit or pride. Framed movie posters signed by cast members covered the walls, along with pictures of his time in Africa calling attention to starving children. His Oscar, Emmy, Golden Globe and two People's Choice awards sat on a floor-to-ceiling bookshelf across the room. Deep tan paint gave the room a masculine feel, along with the dark leather sofa and chairs in front of the fireplace to her right.

She sighed. Needed to tell him. She needed to walk across the house, find him, sit down and break the news to him.

It wasn't as if she could call someone else to do it. It was his business who he chose to tell, not hers. He never talked about anyone else. No family members and he hadn't mentioned any good buddies. It seemed as though he had a lot of *friends*, but not a lot of friends, at least not the kind that stuck with you through thick and thin.

As easy as it was to sit here and admire Leo's career, Kim forced herself to move, then paced back to the desk for the binder. She'd need proof because he wouldn't believe her. She almost didn't believe it herself. How could a person be so oblivious about their own life? She watched every dime like a hawk. Of course she had to. She was alone and in charge of her own destiny so if she didn't look out for herself, no one else was going to do it. Poor Leo had let someone else be in charge and now he'd suffer the consequences.

Leo was about to learn one nasty lesson a very hard way.

Kim stopped at the signed movie poster of *Dangerous Race*. Unlike the others, the extravagant frame of this one matched the colors in the poster. The whole cast had signed it along with Trace Bradshaw and her husband Mac Reynolds, the couple on whose life the movie was based. Kim shook her head as she moved away. The circularity of the universe always amazed her.

"What's got you so serious?" Leo asked as she entered the massive den. Muted green walls set off the pristine hardwood floors and big comfortable leather sofas and chairs faced the giant TV.

Watching a baseball game on his seventy-inch flat screen, relaxed in his faded jeans, bare feet and plain black T-shirt that molded to his sculpted muscles, Leo was about to fall from the top of the world. His tan came from hard workouts in the sun with every sport imaginable. In the few days she'd been at his house, she'd seen him bicycle, surf, run, lift weights and swim. He loved cracking a sweat every day.

She stopped next to the coffee table. "I like your Dangerous Race poster," she said, buying a few more seconds before she sprang the news. "Did I tell you that Trace Bradshaw was one of my clients in Indiana?"

"No." His genuine grin socked her like a punch to the gut. She was about to wipe it off his face. "You told me you knew her sister, right?"

"Yeah. Her sister is my partner. We have an ad agency and we help Trace promote her race school."

"Sounds lucrative. Doesn't she make millions in endorsements?"

Kim nodded, her forced smile fading at the thought of the millions that Leo assumed he had in the bank and actually didn't.

"It's about time you took a break. Feels like you've been locked in there for days. I was coming to see what you wanted to do for dinner tonight. Want a drink?" He got up and headed for the bar in the corner. A thick multicolored area rug covered a large chunk of the hardwood floor.

Up until now, they'd either gone out or defrosted one of the frozen meals Leo had delivered by a personal chef at the beginning of each week. Not a bad deal if you could afford it. Which he no longer could.

He'd asked if she wanted a drink. God, yes. "Sure. You might want to get something for yourself." They'd struck up the oddest friendship. She kept waiting to dislike the guy and it never happened. He gave her his full attention when they talked and he laughed at her bad jokes. He opened doors for her like a gentleman and not once had he put the moves on her.

"What's it gonna be?" he asked, perusing his selection. "I've got beer, wine..." He lifted a dark eyebrow along with a bottle of Jack Daniels. "Your favorite, the good stuff."

This news definitely required fortification. "I'll take the good stuff."

"You got it." He poured her a Jack and water on the rocks.

"You remembered." She hadn't thought he'd been paying much attention the other night, but she'd learned that he always paid attention. It dawned on her that all the garbage she'd read about him might have been just that. Garbage. In a nutshell, he was a hard man to dislike. If this was how he acted with every female, it made sense why he had so many women in his life. Who wouldn't want to be around a gorgeous guy who treated you well?

"Trust me. A man doesn't forget a woman who drinks Jack and water." He poured their drinks as she came forward, slapped the binder on the bar and sat on a leather stool. "Why so glum?" He handed her the drink. "Here's to a decent tax return," he said, knocking their glasses together then taking a sip.

If she could only drink to that. "Leo, come over here and sit down." There was no easy way to do this and she'd never hesitated telling someone bad news before. Like years ago when she told her business partner they were out of money and couldn't afford to stay in their building anymore. They'd gone from rags to riches and back to rags in under two years. What a ride.

Leo took the stool next to her, the playfulness gone from his blue eyes. "Nathan screwed me, didn't he? I'll bet I owe a truckload of taxes this year." He eyed the binder. "No wonder he wouldn't return my calls. I should've guessed. He mentioned putting in for an extension. How bad is it?"

Kim took the first long swallow from her drink, using the bite to push through. "I'm not going to sugar coat it. It's bad, Leo, but not the way you think."

He took another sip of his drink, his gaze never leaving hers. "Go on. I'm listening."

God, how did she start? "Nathan paid all your bills." She worked hard to say it as a statement and not a question. And though she knew it was fact, it still seemed so ridiculously obscene that she just had to make sure she got it right.

"Yeah. He's been paying my bills for years. It frees me. I'm out of the state half the time on location and I need him to do that stuff. Do I need to fire him? Once I find him?" he added with a surly growl.

"More like you need to have him arrested," Kim mumbled. "Look," she said, before Leo could comment. "He stole from you, Leo. A lot."

Leo laughed. "No he didn't. Hey, I know he invested my money. He told me he takes out chunks at a time to invest, but he always puts it back with more. It's what he does. I'm not worried about it."

"You should be." Kim took another long drink and told Leo to do the same. He did. "Here's the deal," she said. "Nathan liquidated every dime he could get his hands on. You've got foreclosure notices on four different properties and back taxes due from three years ago."

Leo's face drained of color and Kim's stomach swirled with Jack Daniels. "But I've got money in the bank to cover all that," he said. The panic in his eyes had her chest heavy with empathy. She'd been there. Lived it. It wasn't fun. Watching everything you worked for disappear was one thing, but being sandbagged by something so shocking was bound to make anyone sick with fear and helplessness. At least she'd had a warning. She'd known when to call it quits when they had just enough money to scrape by on. But Leo had some fancy footwork ahead of him if he planned to stay above water.

Kim shook her head. "I'm sorry, Leo. You don't have anything. It looks like Nathan wiped you out then disappeared off the planet. You need to contact your lawyer because you're in some serious trouble. Real serious trouble."

The seven and seven Leo had ingested threatened to come back at him so he moved away from Kim. "This has to be a mistake," he said, even though his gut told him otherwise. Despite the queasiness, he grabbed more whiskey behind the bar and reloaded his drink. He kept the bottle out.

"I know it's hard to hear and I'm so sorry I'm the one to break it to you." She followed him, her new heels clicking on his hardwood floors. She seemed genuinely upset for him. "The notices from the IRS are filed in the binder. Doesn't even look like Nathan tried to hide them."

Because the bastard knew Leo trusted him. Knew he wouldn't ever glance at it. Dammit. What the hell had he been thinking to trust his whole life to one man? "Look, there has to be something left," he said, scrambling to find a tiny silver lining. Especially since he'd have to pay his high price attorney over four hundred dollars an hour to deal with this mess. Tom Cox had joked that since Leo had been staying out of trouble the last year, his vacations had been cut in half. Yeah. Haha.

The pity in Kim's eyes held very little hope. "I'm assuming your other houses are filled with furniture and art. You could bring in Sotheby's or Christie's for an estate sale and auction off everything. That will help. I noticed you have a lot of collector's items and movie memorabilia. All that should probably sell well. If we can get to the banks before they actually start foreclosure proceedings, you can possibly sell the properties yourself to help pay off your tax debt."

Leo grabbed his glass and the bottle and paced in front of the comfortable sofa. A sofa he'd probably have to sell if everything Kim said was true. He stopped, took a long swallow of his drink and the whiskey burned as it went down. He'd worked like a dog for almost twenty years to build his fortune and he'd practically given it away to a man he'd considered a friend. His chest tightened to unbearable proportions and he sat down.

"I'm so pissed and mad for you that I can't even imagine how *you* feel," Kim said, moving closer, the anger in her voice giving truth to her words. She sat on the chair nearest him and her cinnamon scent filled his head. "Especially since this guy was supposed to be your *friend*." Her eyebrows shot together in an angry line. "How long have you known him?"

"A long fucking time," Leo murmured. "Since junior high. We were the odd couple at school. I played sports and he was the short, smart nerd. I needed a tutor for some of my classes and Nathan offered his help. You can't spend all those hours with someone and not build a friendship. Then I needed help with a few advanced placement classes so we stayed connected through high school then college and into adulthood. Nathan went on to be a CPA and finance manager, and handling my money seemed like the natural progression of things. Nathan's investments made me millions."

Until now.

His dismay started a slow burn in his gut, which the liquor fueled very nicely. "What the hell happened?" he asked, needing another hit of whiskey.

"As far as I can tell, he was pulling a Bernie Madoff. He told you he was investing your money, but he wasn't. Maybe he was doing this with all of his clients and one of them found out. Maybe that's why he's missing. He either took what he could and ran...or someone found him and..." She yanked her thumb across her throat.

Leo took another drink. He hadn't eaten and the alcohol was already going straight to his head. So was the panic. His palms broke out in a cold sweat. If he didn't have money, how the hell was he supposed to take care of Megan? He couldn't afford the institution without money. A lot of money. He swallowed more alcohol.

"Maybe we should get something to eat before you have any more of that," Kim said. But she took another hit of her own drink.

Leo leaned forward, set the bottle and his glass on the coffee table and rested his head in his hands. "I am so fucked." Emotion welled up in his chest like a geyser ready to spew and he didn't want Kim around. Didn't want anyone around to see him crack.

He shot off the sofa, grabbed the bottle and headed outside into the breezy summer night. He looked out at the sparkling pool with its underwater lights illuminating the blue and green tile on the edges and the fountain that ran into the Jacuzzi. He'd helped design all of it. It was his heaven from the crap the outside world dished on him on a regular basis. It was the place he'd banished himself to after he'd hit his own personal low last year.

Welcome to new lows, asshole.

Ditching a co-star who'd been an on-set fling had been his usual M.O. after a film, but he'd never driven anyone to kill until last year when Carrie Ann had gone off the deep end. That his radar hadn't caught her serious personality disorder had shaken him up. Now he was left with an unfinished film because he couldn't see releasing it and causing the woman, who had been institutionalized even more stress. She'd be bound to hear about it and if her reviews were as tough as they'd been in the past, it might affect her in a negative way. He didn't want to be responsible for that. He knew casting her was a risk, but her audition had been so perfect, he'd had to go with his heart. He'd blown millions of his own money on that film and unless he did something with it...

Kim placed her hand on his arm. "I'm so sorry."

He appreciated her sentiment, but she had no clue what any of this meant. He pulled away from her grip and took a long painful pull of whiskey straight from the bottle. That shit burned going down. He needed space. Needed to think. Needed to figure out how the hell he was going to pull his life together.

Leo set the bottle on a nearby table, took two steps, a deep breath and dove into the pool, jeans and all. The cold hit him like a punch and shocked his system. He swam to the bottom of the deep end and let the silence of the water surround him. Just the loud beat of his heart thundered in his head. It kept saying, *you're fucked, you're fucked.* Many long seconds later, his lungs began to burn and he heard the rush of a splash behind him, but didn't care. In the next instant, a feminine arm reached around his shoulders and started pulling him back and up.

Kim must have thought he meant to commit suicide. Bubbles inadvertently escaped as he let out a harsh laugh. He couldn't kill himself. He had to think about Megan first and foremost, but Kim didn't know that. Instead of fighting her, he let her drag him to the surface for air then to the shallow end.

"Are you okay?" she asked. He hadn't intended to put panic in her pretty green eyes. "What were you thinking?" Her brows slanted in a pissed-off line. He didn't blame her. She'd just doused her new clothes with pool water. New clothes that now plastered to the soft, perfect curves of her body. It wasn't that he'd overlooked this detail, but having all that bounty right in his face reminded him of what he'd been missing. So did the way her nipples poked out of the thin wet material clinging to her chest. She smacked his chest and his gaze returned to her face. "I'm serious! You can't just give up because life gets tough. You have to stick it out and get to the other side." She was serious with this. Almost yelling at him. "You are a very lucky man. Yes, you're in some trouble, but you'll pull out of it. You'll keep working, you'll pay off your debt and you'll be fine. So what if you have to downsize or relocate or sell your car. So what if—"

"My car?" Had she lost her mind? "Stella? There's no way in hell I'm selling Stella."

After a tiny shake of her head, droplets fell from her lashes. A cool breeze whispered through the trees and she crossed her arms over her chest. "You're not going to have a choice, Leo." She pulled her shoulders in, her anger evaporating along with her body heat. "I'm sorry." That look of pity crept back into her eyes. "But it's no time to throw in the towel. It's time to pick yourself up and fight."

"You really thought I meant to kill myself?" True, they didn't know each other well at all, but did he really strike her as a coward or someone with mental instability? He'd have to work on changing that.

She gestured to the deep end, her exasperation clear in her wide eyes. "You dove in with your clothes on and went straight to the bottom. And you *stayed* there! For almost a minute. You totally freaked me out!" She shook in earnest now and guilt grabbed a hold of Leo's balls and hung on tight. Or maybe that was his jeans plastered to his legs. He took Kim's arm and helped her out of the pool. At least she'd taken off her shoes before diving in. Smart lady.

The night breeze chilled their clothes to uncomfortably wet degrees. Leo grabbed two fresh towels from the small storage space under the outside ottoman and wrapped the first one around her shoulders. He smoothed some wet strands off her cheek and stared down at her. "Sorry. I didn't mean to freak you out. I'm a bit freaked out myself."

"I know." Her voice softened. "It's a lot to take in."

"I'm just so fucking mad. I just..." He wanted Nathan to explain, to look him in the eye and tell him why. He wanted the douche bag to come back and make it right, but he had a feeling that wasn't going to happen. "I need to figure this out."

"Maybe I can help you with that."

"Why?" No reason to dance around the subject. "If I'm in the hole for as much as you say, then I don't even have enough money to pay you for what you've done much less for what you might do in the future."

She started rubbing the towel over her arms. "Maybe because I know how it feels. How's that? Maybe because if I can help you, I'll, I'll—"

"Get your wings when you get into heaven?"

That got a smile out of her and he liked the smiling Kim better than the panicked or angry Kim. She rolled her eyes and that made *him* smile.

He liked her. Genuinely. How could he not? The woman just jumped in the pool to save his sorry broke ass without thinking about herself. That was another thing...how many women would've hung around after learning he'd lost everything?

Christ. He'd lost everything.

The weight of it hit hard, like a double whammy to the nuts.

"It's going to be okay," she told him softly.

"I'll be honest." He met her gaze. "I seriously doubt it." He rubbed the towel over her arms. "You should get out of those wet clothes before you get sick."

"Fine, we'll both get on dry clothes and we'll have dinner. Then we come up with a game plan."

Sixty minutes later, they were back poolside, relaxing on their individual chaise lounges with their drinks of choice next to them. Clouds covered the stars and the still air seemed freakishly quiet. Kim sipped her Jack and Leo gulped his whiskey. She'd changed into a pair of his sweat pants that engulfed her completely. She'd had to roll up the sleeves on a matching sweatshirt a few times to see her hands, but her sweet curves rounded out the soft lightweight cotton.

Kim chuckled and Leo glanced over at her.

"What?" he asked.

"I keep thinking about the pizza delivery guy. He's never delivered here before, has he?"

"No one's delivered here before. I'm not supposed to have pizza. It's a gut maker."

"A gut maker? Are you kidding me? It's the next best thing to an orgasm. Especially if you haven't had any in a long time."

"Any pizza or any orgasms?"

She laughed again and her shining eyes gave him a ray of hope that made no sense. "Pizza is good brain food," she explained.

"I'll let you duke it out with Hans, my trainer. He's got a different take on it. By the way, if you tell him I ate pizza, you're fired."

Another laugh sent a ribbon of warmth through Leo's chest. "Your trainer's name is Hans? That's priceless." The Jack was definitely loosening her up. "By the way, you can't fire me since I'm working pro bono now, but you will need to fire Hans."

Dammit. Hans had been with him for more than twelve years.

A loud rumble sounded and their chairs bounced. The water in the pool sloshed against the sides and Kim shot to her feet, every muscle tense, looking around as if she might find the culprit. "What was that?"

Leo's adrenaline slowed as he waited for more and after a few seconds he motioned her back to the chaise. "Just a little earthquake. We're fine. Relax."

"Relax?" Her freaked-out eyes were anything but relaxed. "Are you kidding me? The earth just moved."

"You're forgetting who you're with," Leo said. "I happen to be pretty good at making the earth move." When his joke didn't fly, he stood up and rubbed his hands down her arms. "That was just a little earthquake. We're fine. It was so little that I'm not even going to bother checking the house for damage."

"Will there be another one?" she asked, scanning his face. Probably gauging if he meant to lie to her or not.

"You never know, but I doubt it."

"You doubt it?"

He pulled her closer. "I have an earthquake kit to beat all

earthquake kits. You're as safe with me as you'd be with the fire department."

She relaxed in his arms and just stared up at him. "Okay," she said softly. The moment between them stretched out and the air seemed to crackle with new energy. Time to get down to business. He'd sworn off blondes over a year ago after Carrie Ann had gone postal.

"So..." He took his spot on his chaise and she did the same. "You think if I sell all my properties, I might be able to pay off the debt?"

She looked around, finished off her second Jack and water like she needed the fortification then faced him. "Once we connect with your lawyer and form a game plan, we can work out a deal with the IRS and the other creditors once they realize you've been swindled. I think you're going to be okay. It's just going to hurt a little."

"You mean hurt a lot."

She nodded, her face serious again.

Leo swallowed and that nauseous feeling returned. He rested his head in his hands again and heard Kim shift over to his chaise, felt her hip resting against his. She put her arms around him and just held him. Goddammit. He felt the sting behind his eyes and would not go there. He was fucking Leo Frost. He didn't fucking cry. He took an unsteady breath to get control and she ducked her head near his.

"It's going to be okay. It really is. I was in a very similar situation with my business partner when we lost our main account. Do you remember years ago when Timothy Sandstrom died?"

"Sure. It was big news." The CEO of Battle Sportswear had made his mark as a world famous philanthropist. Among his many accomplishments, he'd set up scholarship funds for underprivileged kids and fed starving people in third world nations. "He had a massive coronary, right?"

Kim nodded. "Yeah. Well, you probably aren't aware of this, but it was my partner, Chelsea, who came up with the Break the Rules in Battle slogan. Problem was, when Tim died, the new CEO decided to go back to the old ad agency. Once we lost the Battle account, most of our other clients bailed. By that time, we had a huge space in a high price building in Chicago and a whole staff who expected paychecks. I had just purchased a gorgeous new condo and I was spending money like a fool. Then, because the PI Chelsea had hired finally found her sister—"

"Trace," Leo supplied.

"Yes. Once he found Trace, we spent the last of what we had on the trip to the Arrow 500 to meet her. When we got home, I had to sell my new condo and we moved to Indiana to be near Trace. FYI, I lost my shirt in the sale."

Leo had a quick vision of Kim without a shirt and nodded. Not a bad thing to envision. Okay, so maybe she did have a clue how he felt when it came to losing everything. But she hadn't been betrayed by a lifelong friend. That kind of pain hurt from the inside out.

"I'll be here if you need me," Kim continued. "I know I have to go back to Indiana, but we'll keep in touch and you can call me day or night."

Leo lifted his head, met her gaze. Her eyes softened because she saw his pain, saw what this was doing to him. She stroked her fingers over his ear in a gentle caress. Her hair fell in pretty waves after the unexpected dip in the pool. She smelled like chlorine and summertime. He nodded subtly as he watched her, as his gaze drifted to her full lips...lips given to her by Mother Nature and not a doctor with a needle full of collagen in Beverly Hills.

Her eyes moved to his mouth and she shook her head the slightest bit. "I'm not going to kiss you," she whispered. "I really have no desire to kiss you at all."

Neither one of them budged.

"Good. Me either." The words barely came out and somehow they got a fraction closer to each other. Leo smelled the faint scent of her cinnamon perfume under the chlorine in her hair. He slanted his head a fraction, just to take in another whiff of her as the breeze picked up, and now they were barely an inch apart, her breath warm on his lips.

"I'm serious." Her lips almost moved against his mouth. "We're not kissing."

"Right," he agreed a hundred percent. "This is us...not kissing."

Then she had to go and lick her lips. Just the tip of her tongue, a quick sweep across the seam.

Screw it. What the hell. His life had gone to shit today. He may as well kiss her. He leaned in that whisper of an inch and their mouths connected in the softest of caresses. Only a brush back and forth, barely a touch. Her breath caught and the sound did something to Leo. He pulled back, waiting for her to get angry or stomp inside, but she didn't move.

"That was kind of sexy," she murmured. "You know, considering we didn't kiss."

Leo agreed. So did the body part that suddenly had all his blood pumping in it. "I think we shouldn't kiss again."

"I think it would be a big mistake. Seriously Leo. You are a man I intend to steer clear of. Like a thousand feet clear."

Because he was broke, or because she believed everything she'd ever read about him?

"And yet, you haven't moved," he whispered.

"I know." Her brows angled down in a perplexed slant. "You're like a piece of forbidden candy. You're not good for me, but I know how great you'll taste if I have you."

His dick responded to her words with a full on salute. "Speaking of taste, I want some of your Jack." Before she pulled away, he took her lips again in another kiss. This one a little more involved than the last. This kiss had his hand moving through her hair to cup her head. It had her opening to his questing tongue. It had her moaning her approval.

Chapter Eighteen

Kim hadn't been kidding. The last thing she needed was Leo Frost. The only person with a worse track record for love than her was this guy. The gorgeous movie star with personality issues, woman issues and not a dime to his name.

So why couldn't she separate her lips from his? Why did she keep running her fingers through the thick softness of his dark hair and why had she practically climbed in his lap?

Jack. That's why. This was the reason she'd quit drinking. Jack always made her want things. Solace. Comfort. Companionship. Jack made her loose and foggy and unable to think straight.

Stupid Jack Daniels. Stupid earthquake too. She couldn't forget that. Nothing like the earth moving to make a girl reach out and grab life. Or the gorgeous man at her fingertips.

Leo's hands stroked down her back and she pressed harder into his chest. Sank into his kiss a little bit more. Their tongues dueled in a wicked game of slide and seek. She detected the sharp bite of his whiskey and went in for another taste.

He pulled away, his breathing as ragged as hers. "Okay. We really need to stop. I don't want this to happen right now. We've been drinking and God knows it's not a smart move. Especially after the day I had."

She held him tight, her head pressed into his neck, and she breathed in the spicy scent of him. "Exactly. I agree. I'm glad we're on the same page." She kissed the spot just under his ear that had his dick pulsing against her hot spot. When had she straddled him? Didn't matter. What mattered was the sexy stubble along his jaw, so she kissed that spot too. And the spot that led to the corner of his mouth, because it was right there when he turned toward her.

His hand stroked through her hair again and his eyes searched hers. "Screw it. I like this page," he murmured. This time when their lips met, the kiss exploded into something hot and fiery. As out of control as kisses got.

God, the man knew how to kiss. Knew how to set her senses on fire as his hands snuck under the sweatshirt and glided over her skin. Of course, he would know how to kiss since he'd allegedly fucked nearly every starlet in Hollywood. That reminder alone should have her pulling away from him, but she couldn't seem to do it.

She blamed Jack for that too. For her inability to say no when someone as fabulously sexy as Leo Frost came her way and showed interest.

Another one night stand. Even as she went in for another long, deep kiss, she recognized what this meant. She wasn't looking for a lifetime commitment. She would've laughed at the thought but her mouth was otherwise engaged—and oh so perfectly—with Leo's.

Besides, Leo was also not on the market for a long-term commitment. Every interview he'd ever done had warned the female population of that fact. It all seemed very adult. Very clear-cut. For lack of a better term, this was simply a fuck and run.

Kim rubbed herself against the straining erection in Leo's loose cotton sweats. The growl deep in his throat gave her fulfillment on so many levels, it was as if her heart took flight.

It had been five long years since she'd had sex and she'd picked a hell of man to break her streak with. But as long as she was going down, she'd go big. Leo Frost big.

Making this very seasoned man growl satisfied her immensely. She loved the sound so much she wanted to hear it again, so she wrapped her legs tighter around his hips and moved against him again.

"That did it," he panted, breaking away for air. But he returned in a flash with a mind-altering kiss as he shifted and stood with her still wrapped around him. One hand dove into her hair and cruised down her back as the other cupped her ass and kept her against him. He touched her everywhere and sent electric streaks of tingles racing across her skin. She had no clue where they were going, didn't care. All that mattered was Leo's mouth on hers. His tongue stroking along hers, his hard body pressing against her.

The world got tipsy as he bent her backward. She landed on something very cushy and soft, the outside sofa in his little cabana off the pool. They took a few seconds and slowed things down. Really looked at each other. Recklessness made her horny and giddy. So did Jack. But she sensed his hesitation.

"This is crazy. I can't do this," he said, touching his forehead to hers. He had her pinned beneath him with her legs wrapped snuggly around his hips and her arms draped over his shoulders.

"I know. I know. You're right." This was crazy. Beyond crazy. She hugged him, fit her face into the curve of his neck and breathed him in. He smelled like his pool and like Leo. *Sex on a stick*. Not the first time she'd had that thought when it came to him.

That low rumble in his throat vibrated as he took a small nip from her ear lobe. A fiery bolt of heat blazed to her hoo-ha and she fought fire with fire when she rubbed against him one more time.

"You're making this really hard for me," he warned her.

She looked at his crotch then slapped a muzzle on her unintentional giggle. "I see that."

"I'm just trying to do the right thing." He looked so serious. And so damn sexy.

She stroked a finger along his jaw and stared into his striking blue eyes. "I know you are." This man had one of the worst reputations in Hollywood. He'd been plastered on as many tabloids as the Kennedys or Kardashians. He'd been center court on some gnarly lawsuits. And he was doing his damnedest to keep from screwing her because they were tipsy. "Get up and I'll go away." She smiled and tried to soften the harshness of her words.

He didn't move. He just brushed his thumb across her lower lip, his eyes taking in the movement. Then he leaned in slowly and pressed her lip down as he opened her mouth for his kiss.

His crazy panty-melting, hot open-mouth kiss. A kiss that penetrated unlike the others. A slow, deep kiss that shot heat and energy through her chest to her middle and through her arms and legs. He consumed her. Took everything she was in that kiss.

"I'm not going to fuck you on my cabana sofa," he told her, but it sounded as if he meant the words more for himself.

"Good," she told him, encouraging his willpower without showing any of her own as she came back for more. "Don't."

He snuck his hands into her waistband and discovered she'd gone commando. Her underwear was still drying over the shower rod. "Goddammit," he swore, taking her mouth harder, driving his tongue deep and sure. "I can't. Goddammit. I...can't..."

Can't stop was what she assumed since he worked the sweats off one of her legs before guiding his hand back in place around her hip. His sweats slid down his thighs after she pulled at the knot on his waistband. His erection sprang free of his boxer briefs with a little shimmy and tug.

This time she growled as she slid herself along his ridged erection.

Leo pulled back, his eyes wide and almost wild. "Tell me to stop or I'm going to be inside you in about three seconds."

She should absolutely tell him to stop. Instead she stared at him, her eyelids heavy, her heart slamming against her ribs, every burning inch of her needing every hard inch of him inside her.

"Kim." The warning tone only made her smile. "Tell me, Goddammit."

She shook her head and glanced at his lips, her heart pounding at a primitive beat, before she leaned up and captured his mouth. His fingers pushed inside her first and Kim moaned with the pleasure of the invasion. He pumped a few times, worked the cream he discovered all around to ease his entrance.

"Jesus, you're so ready," he murmured between kisses. He teased her clit with his thumb and she jerked at the shock of it. In the next instant, the fat head of his penis crowded her tight entrance. Leo pushed in a fraction at a time. Let her feel every hard inch as he moved inside her. He stared down at her, watching her so intently, and she watched him.

God, she'd never been like this during sex. Never kept her eyes open and watched a man's face as he filled her. She saw his pleasure, his need. The way he looked at her, searching for any signs of...what? Tension? Pain? Fear? She didn't know. She just wanted to comfort him. That's how this whole thing started out, wasn't it? To comfort him.

"God, you feel so...so..." His eyes widened and he suddenly pulled out. "Jesus! A condom. I forgot a fucking condom." Before she said anything, he reached into the bottom drawer of the little end table next to the sofa. He came back with a condom. That he probably had condoms stashed everywhere throughout his house shouldn't surprise her. She really did know what this was about. It was sex for comfort's sake. He suited up in seconds and his weight came back over her a second time. "Sorry about that."

"Not a problem." At least it wouldn't be now that he had protection. Where had her common sense gone?

Everything faded away as Leo started moving. She'd never been a huge fan of missionary, but Leo knew his way around a woman. In only a few minutes, he had her figured out. He found her sweet spot and worked it with precision, angling her exactly the right way for the most effect.

The rope lights on the interior of the cabana spun as Leo took her higher. She arched her back with every hard thrust and Leo got deeper each time. God, it was so good, so unbelievably good and she didn't want it to end. Digging her nails into his back she adjusted the slightest bit to ease him off her hot spot. She just wanted to soak in his weight, his warmth, feel his slick skin beneath her hands as he slid over her.

"Oh no you don't," he huffed as he angled her hips where they'd been before. "You're going to come if I have to wring it out of you." He pushed in again, over and over, dragging her back under with every perfect stroke. The point of no return loomed just around the corner. Another few seconds and she'd be—yes—right on the edge, right there, hovering, ready to fall. God, so good, so perfect.

"Now goddammit," he growled in her ear. "I feel you. Fucking come now." With one last thrust, he hit the spot that took her over the edge. Everything blurred as the internal wave hit her, pummeled her senseless with shock after shock of unadulterated bliss. She was still coming, he was still moving as his climax hit. He groaned in her ear, his breathing harsh, ragged. His muscles stiffened and she felt the hard throbbing of his release inside her. His fingers flexed in her hair and the slight hint of pain had her arching into him. God, it triggered another orgasm that shimmied through her in tiny aftershocks.

His grip finally loosened, but his weight kept her pressed into the cushion. She wouldn't regret this. Not for a minute. Well, at least not right *this* minute. She meant to comfort him. No, she hadn't planned on this, but she could've said no. She just hadn't wanted to.

Finally, he lifted on his elbows and looked down at her. "Holy, Jesus. That was unfuckingbelievable."

She laughed at the surprise on his face, the roundness of his eyes. "Don't go all melodramatic on me. It was good sex and I know you've had a lot of good sex."

His brows slanted down and nearly met in the middle. "Not in a long fucking time. Trust me, that was unfuckingbelievable."

His comment brought back that sense of satisfaction, which made her marginally happy considering the circumstances. It also made her curious. "How long?"

He paused. Either he needed to figure out the time or he debated telling her completely. "Over a year."

That floored her. "That can't be. I saw a picture of you with..." Wait. When was the last time she saw him on a tabloid cover? Maybe it had been over a year.

"Just because I show up on the cover of a rag magazine with a female doesn't mean I'm fucking her." He pulled out and Kim inhaled at the sudden emptiness. He got to his feet and turned his back to her as he reached for a discarded towel and cleaned himself up. He lifted his underwear and sweats and covered his sculpted ass.

She didn't want to add to the crap of his day. "I'm sorry," she said quietly. "That was a shitty thing to say."

He looked over his shoulder, his blue eyes like lasers in the dark night and feeling hugely self-conscious with no bottoms, she reached for the sweats he'd stripped off her and put them on. He sighed and came back to her, lifted her legs and sat down before settling them back over his lap and leaning his head against the back of the sofa. "You didn't make me mad. I'm just an idiot. Every time I think I've got a handle on the idiocy, I do something else and I'm right back to square one. Idiot."

Did that include their little session just now? Maybe she didn't want the answer to that. Though it would've been smart to create some distance between them, Kim didn't. She liked this quiet, almost domestic, few minutes. It made Leo more human and less the bad boy sex symbol she'd always read about.

Kim hadn't moved from her spot on the sofa, aside from adjusting her—his—sweats back into place. "So you're not an idiot because of this. Or maybe we're both idiots so it cancels itself out."

That made no sense to Leo. "Why are you an idiot?" He was the one who couldn't keep his dick in his pants. At least not tonight. Although it was a hell of a way to break a drought. Kim had a unique ability to make him feel like a...a normal guy.

"Because I drink and I fuck and I feel like trash afterward."

He knew the feeling. All too well. "Sounds like we have more in common than I originally thought."

She met his gaze. "Is that why you've taken a fuck break?"

He chuckled. "Fuck break?" Nodding, he sobered. "Yeah. I guess so."

"There's nothing worse than facing yourself in the mirror when you feel like shit."

He didn't want her to feel that way after what just happened. He leaned his head back against the sofa and stared at the cabana's flat ceiling. "I tried to stop. Sex always screws things up. You don't deserve to feel like shit."

"Cut yourself some slack. You would've stopped if I'd helped you any."

"True that," he teased, stroking his hand down her leg. "So let's make a pact that neither one of us feels like shit after this. Fair?"

"Yeah. I like that. We don't have to tell anyone and it'll be our little secret. I won't let a few orgasmic minutes keep me from what I promised you earlier or change our relationship. If you need me, I'll be here for you. Financially speaking. From here on out."

He caught her meaning loud and clear. From now on they were strictly about business. They shouldn't have fucked around in the first place, but she was a reprieve from the absolute collapse of his life. He still couldn't think about it. Couldn't go to all the dark places his rampant thoughts took him. Like...

How much longer could he stay in his home? He looked

around the pool area, at the guesthouse on the other side of the manicured lawn and the tennis court on the far left side of the property. This place had been his haven for the last decade and there was every chance he was going to lose it. Megan came first. He had to keep her at the Marion Institute. She had the best doctors and the best care. She wouldn't survive a move to another facility. She needed the stability and familiarity of her routine.

He needed to sit down with Kim and talk finances.

A certain freedom came with the knowledge that she didn't want him again. So did a certain sorrow. Something about her struck him differently than other women.

"Leo," she whispered his name and he caught her troubled gaze.

"I'm sorry I didn't stop you." Her big green eyes held a mountain of remorse. "Not because it wasn't a great few minutes, don't get me wrong. I just didn't mean to let you down."

"How is it letting me down?" Didn't he do that just fine all by himself?

"Because I know you're trying to be different. I see it. I feel it. And I don't want to be the reason you backslide somehow."

He could get pissed at that. Or he could bite his tongue and treat the words as Kim meant them. "How could you know I'm trying to be different? You hardly know me." Which was a lie, since she sure as shit knew his finances and those told a whole story on their own.

She sat up, stuck her chin on her knees and wrapped her arms around her legs. "You are nothing like the tabloids make you out to be. That means either you never were or you've changed." She studied him, her eyes growing heavy. "I think you've changed."

Leo looked away from her penetrating gaze. Maybe he *had* changed. Maybe all the lonely years had caught up to him and he was ready for something else. If Kim saw through him, would anyone else? Hell, maybe he didn't care anymore. At least not for himself. He still had Megan to protect though and he couldn't forget that.

The last thing he needed was for people to think he'd changed. Of course this whole mess would give the press a whole new angle to crucify him, so it probably didn't matter. The point was to keep giving them stories so they didn't dig into his private life any more than what he gave them. Leo didn't plan to comment on Kim's statement. "I think you're drunk," he finally said, changing the subject as he eased some hair behind her ear, surprised at the fresh jolt of desire that coursed through him at the touch.

She nodded. "I think I am a little." She didn't or couldn't look at him and despite what she'd said earlier, he got the feeling that he'd completely fucked everything up between them.

Chapter Nineteen

Two days after her kidnapping, Abbey sat in the backyard of Troy and Julie's place staring at a bubbling fountain and not seeing a damn thing except a non-stop internal video she couldn't shut down. The trunk of the car, the bite of the tape on her mouth, the taste of the gag, the heart-pounding fear as she fought then ran for her life... The same horrible scenes kept replaying in her head.

She should be happy. Relieved. She was alive after all. But they were back to square one when it came to her safety. As the cops located the owner of the property, who happened to be Michael Facinetti, the cousin of the man who'd been behind Blake's family's abduction, Abbey and Blake had gone back to Los Angeles. If Blake had been surprised to hear the Facinetti name again, he didn't show it.

The slider door whooshed open and closed and Abbey exhaled hard at her lack of privacy.

Julie sat next to her on the bench. "How's the ankle feeling?"

"Fine," Abbey assured her. "It was just a little twist. The ice did the trick the other night."

Nodding, Julie exhaled a soft breath. "I really wish you'd consider coming with me," she said. "I could use your help while I'm there."

"You know I can't." Yesterday she'd discovered she was moving on to the next level of auditions for the reality show. Thankfully, the auditions would take place on a secure studio lot. She had another four days for the bruise on her cheek to heal. Makeup should cover what was left by then. "And you hardly ever need me when you travel," she continued, stating what they both knew.

Julie shoved Abbey's shoulder with her own. "Sometimes I do."

This went beyond work. "If I leave now, I kill any chance I have at this show. You know how hard I've worked for something like this. I can't just bail." If anyone understood, it was Julie.

"I know." The reluctance in her voice came through loud and clear. "If I could cancel on this thing, I would in a second," she added. Julie was speaking to Congress on behalf of a coalition devoted to worldwide women's rights.

"I know, but it's too important. You have to go. It's not every day a girl goes to Washington and gets to have dinner with the president and first lady."

"Now, *them* I would cancel on," she teased. She'd been waiting for this appointment for months.

Abbey chuckled. "Liar," she coughed and Julie grinned at her.

It was times like these with her boss, where their friendship mattered most to Abbey. She could go to Julie with anything and have her ready support. It was one of the reasons she worked so hard for this lady.

The smile on Julie's face dimmed as she looked out to the slate fountain. "You'll stay here, right? It's safer."

"I'll stay here." She'd already brought enough clothes to last a week and Troy's home gym made working out even easier. "But I can't live here forever. You know that, right?" Abbey needed her space.

"Yes, I know." Julie patted her thigh and stood up. "Troy's waiting for me."

"Don't want to keep the man waiting," Abbey said with a lopsided smile.

Julie crooked her index finger and Abbey obediently stood up. Julie gave her a sisterly hug. They didn't hug often, but Abbey let her because Julie was a worrier. "Don't go anywhere."

Abbey just nodded, because as soon as she got a time and location for her callback, she was out the door.

No sooner had Troy and Julie left for the airport that Abbey's phone rang. The detectives on the case had discovered a body. A body they were hoping she could identify as the man who'd been knifed at the Sports Center.

Blake hated the idea of leaving the house, but he took Abbey to the police station anyway. She got queasy thinking about identifying a dead man. Would it be like television or movies where they pulled him out of a cold cubby in the wall and unzipped a bag? Would his eyes be open and sightless? Would he have more wounds than what she remembered on that horrible day?

"The body we recovered matched the description you gave us, otherwise we wouldn't be asking you to verify," Detective Patrick said.

"I understand." Abbey felt Blake's hand brush across hers, but she wouldn't take it. She'd had to take a step back after their night in Palm Springs. The whole thing had embarrassed her beyond belief. Her request, his denial. His actions after that... God. Her cheeks got hot from the memory. So, no, she wouldn't take his hand.

The detective pulled out a picture from a file on his desk. "Here it is."

The relief washing through Abbey was enough to weaken her knees. She'd pictured a walk through a cold morgue. Still, her stomach rolled over again anyway because she had to identify the man.

A second before the detective lifted the picture, Abbey changed her mind, took Blake's hand and squeezed tight. He squeezed back.

"He was buried within a plastic tarp, but it wasn't sealed tightly. Meaning the body was open to certain elements." He waited for her nod before revealing the picture.

Abbey braced herself for something gruesome, but not quite enough. His sheer white face had the same look on it as when he'd been knifed. His brown eyes sunken in his skull held the same fear. It was the slice on his cheek that sealed the ID. She turned away. "It's him."

"You're sure?" Detective Patrick asked. "Maybe you can take another look just to be positive."

"If she said it's him, then it's him," Blake said, giving her hand a squeeze before wrapping his arm around her shoulder.

Abbey took another quick look anyway even though it made her stomach flip. "Yes. I'm sure. I'll never forget his face." She met the detective's gaze. "He was so scared when we ran into each other. Did he have any identification?"

"We didn't find anything on him, but we do have a missing person's report and he matches the description. We're waiting for someone to confirm the ID."

"Will you let us know who he is?" Blake asked.

The detective nodded. "Sure." He showed them out and Abbey practically ran to Blake's Explorer.

"You okay?" Blake asked as he slipped on his sunglasses and started the SUV. The shades almost hid his latest bruise, but not quite.

"I think so." She nodded and took a deep breath. "I just a need a minute to chill." Then she needed a time travel machine to go back to the day this whole thing happened so she could avoid the Sports Center. Abbey glanced over at Blake. His jaw was set and his mouth a grim line. He could've been upset for a few different reasons. There were plenty to choose from. "Are you okay?"

"I guess." He didn't sound too sure as he pulled toward the exit, then he shook his head. "I hate that you had to ID that guy. You've been through enough."

"You've been through a lot too...because of me."

He glanced at her, his expression unreadable behind those dark shades. "That's not an issue."

"It should be. I don't get why you have any desire to be around me. All of a sudden I'm like a trouble magnet."

"That's BS." He checked the rearview mirror and made a right turn onto the street. "You saw something you weren't supposed to see and now you're a target. It's not your fault."

No. But it made her a victim. Again. "You know..." she stared out the window as the city buildings blurred by. "I told myself I wouldn't be a victim again. I've taken so many self-defense classes, I think I could be an instructor." She took a deep breath. "And it didn't matter."

"Bullshit. You better believe it mattered. You got yourself out of that place in Palm Springs. You saved yourself, Ab. How many people, men included, could've done what you did and get free?" He glanced at her again. "Not many. I guarantee it. I'm so proud of you for that." He shook his head. "God, I can't tell you how much I wish I'd been able to get free during..." He trailed off and Abbey's heart sank at the helplessness in his voice. The one time they'd talked about this, he'd been exhausted after nearly being run over by a Hummer. But her curiosity still burned.

Yes, she'd seen the movie, but movies only told one story and Blake had his own.

"Will you tell me what happened?" she asked. The movie had shown the aftermath of the actual kidnapping with only short flashbacks of everyone's individual struggle. It left the majority of the actual kidnapping to the viewer's mind. Sometimes that was more powerful than images.

Blake swallowed and nodded as he made a left hand turn. "It was Saturday, late afternoon. Brendan and I were coming home from a movie." He shook his head. "I don't even remember what it was. I just remember we were laughing and fucking around. We came in through the kitchen like always. Bren was ahead of me. His phone had died and he wanted to call his friend, Dave, about a computer sale." Blake took another right turn and kept checking his rearview mirror. "The house was really quiet. I should've felt the difference in the air, but I didn't. I stopped at the fridge to get something to drink and I heard Bren in the hallway. Then I heard this giant thump. At first I laughed. I thought he slipped or something taking the stairs, but then I heard more." He swallowed again. "I dropped the Gatorade in my hand and bolted for the hallway. As soon as I came out of the kitchen, I got nailed in the face. The son of a bitch was just waiting for me to turn that corner. Two guys were beating the shit out of Bren." He got a faraway look in his eyes and Abbey's heart rolled over. "We had this little table in the entry hall and when I bounced off it, I grabbed at it and swung hard. I got the guy who nailed me, but another one jumped me from the other side. There were four of them." He shook his head. "I remember the weight of them pressing me to the floor. I remember the fists and the boots. Mostly I remember hearing Bren grunting every time they hit him. But he wouldn't quit. He just..." His voice cracked and he swiped beneath his glasses. "I remember screaming for him to stop. We were outnumbered. I figured we walked in on a robbery. Let 'em have whatever they want. It wasn't worth it. But..." He checked his mirror again and ran an agitated hand through his hair. "They weren't there to rob us.

They cuffed and gagged us both so we wouldn't make noise when everyone else got home. They picked everyone off one at a time. My mom was last." His jaw clenched tight. "I didn't see it, but I heard it. She took the first guy out with one well-placed hit to his temple."

"With her fist?" Abbey asked.

Blake shook his head. "Her purse. Dad's always joked that she carries bricks in that thing. Her wallet alone weighs a ton. The house was destroyed by the time she got in. They couldn't let her get as far inside as we did because she'd have known something was wrong. They pounced on her as soon as she walked in the kitchen door. I heard someone drop and I got so sick to my stomach. I knew she'd hit the deck. But then I heard her voice and I thought, man, my mom is so fucking tough. Then the big guy who'd beat the shit out of Bren went in and..."

He paused, took a deep breath. "He hit her so hard, all the blood vessels popped in her eye. She was unconscious for hours. I thought my dad was going to puke. By that point, he was tied and gagged like the rest of us." He took another unsteady breath. "But my mom..." Blake shook his head. "Man, she's so strong, she never quits. Never lets anything get her down. She was the one who nearly got us out of that house. She managed to get the key from the guy guarding us, then she lured him back in and I slammed him in the head with a wooden chair leg. We got out the back door, and Eric and I made it over the fence." He shook his head. "We just weren't quick enough. They discovered we were gone and caught us." He rubbed his chest. "That was when I learned the difference between a bruised rib and a broken rib."

Abbey didn't know what to say.

A few seconds later, he shook his head and rolled his shoulders. "Sometimes I wake up in the middle of the night and my shoulders hurt because of being in those cuffs so long. I can't even stand to have blankets tucked around me anymore. I need to be able to move, to have my hands and legs free."

He finished the drive to Troy and Julie's place in silence.

It was as bad as her experience, maybe worse on another level because not only had he been beaten, but he'd had to watch his family as they were beaten as well. Abbey might have been violated and thrown into a dark space for a few hours, but her issues dealt solely with herself. Blake had to deal with hearing the ones he loved being brutalized repeatedly.

Once the gate closed on the property and Blake cut the engine, he looked at her. "So for the most part, I do understand what you went through. I mean, obviously I'll never be a woman and know what it's like to be..." he had a tough time saying it, "...violated. But I understand being bound and gagged. I understand the helplessness."

Abbey nodded and felt a kinship with him that she hadn't experienced before. He'd gotten past his trauma and lived his life.

Something she still needed to do. Something she would do.

As they got out of the SUV, a sudden realization hit Abbey head on. All this time she'd been keeping Blake at a distance when he was the one man who understood her better than anyone. Everything he did, all his words, said what she'd been hoping to hear her whole adult life. She'd been too focused on her inability to have a relationship instead of opening her eyes and seeing what this man had to offer.

Why run from the emotions he stirred in her? He made her feel normal, wanted and loved.

Another realization smacked her like a punch. Blake was like this dance show. She wanted him and she'd do whatever it took to get him.

She loved him. Her heart raced as the word swam around in her head. She loved him.

It was time she took the first step in her journey to get better. Time she let Blake know how much he meant to her. And there was no better way to do that than to show him.

Blake walked into the house, tossed his sunglasses on the entry table and rubbed his eyes. He'd only shared that story twice before. First to his family when they'd been held hostage by a whacked out Vegas casino owner and then to the police when they'd been rescued. He'd never planned to talk about it again. It brought up too many feelings he couldn't deal with. Being helpless was his biggest fear. Being tied up and watching the ones he loved as they suffered was more devastating than any beating.

So though he could relate to Abbey's trauma, there remained

that one element of difference. She'd been a young girl and she'd been violated. What kind of sick bastard got off on hurting innocent girls? Blake shook his head to get that picture out of his mind. If he thought about it for too long, he'd drive himself crazy.

The other thing driving him crazy was discovering that the owner of the Palm Springs estate was none other than Paul Facinetti's cousin, Michael. Like Troy, Blake didn't believe in coincidence. Kwami was the one factor that the Facinettis had in common. He got a whole new bad feeling about the entire situation.

He needed to burn off the frustration. Not only because of this last conversation, but because of his quasi-relationship with Abbey. He had no clue where he stood with her. He'd spewed his heart and soul, and though she'd nodded and related to his experience, he wasn't sure if sharing the ordeal had helped her in any way.

"I need a shower after that meeting," Abbey said, walking down the hallway toward the guest room. "I'll be out quick."

"I'll be in the gym." Pounding his aggression out on the heavy bag. Thinking about those days being a victim always keyed him up. Blake watched her walk away, unable to tear his gaze off the perfection of her ass.

Whipped much?

Shit, he was toast when it came to her. So far gone he'd need a guide dog to find his way back from Abbey.

Blake didn't bother changing clothes, he went straight to the gym. The faster he hit something or lifted something heavy, the faster he'd clear his head. His phone rang just as he walked over to the free weights and he checked the screen. Brendan.

His brother almost always called when Blake was about to blow his top. Somehow they shared a connection like that. Blake had grown almost used to it. He punched the screen. "Hey," he said. "What's up? You home yet?"

"Not yet. Seger agreed to add another couple of nights to the schedule since it's the last stop for a while. What's up with you? How's Abbey doing?"

They'd talked the day after Blake had found her in Palm Springs, but Bren would want to know how she was handling the aftermath. They all knew about aftermath.

"She's okay. We just came from the police station. She had to identify a body. It was the guy she saw at the Sports Center, but they don't have a name for him yet. They think they will soon though since he matches the description of a missing person."

"Okay. Now tell me how you're doing." Brendan could always read between the lines.

"I'm fine."

"Right. And I'm a Bieber fan. What's up?"

Blake snorted a laugh. Bren always knew how to get a smile out of him. "I thought Abbey and I crossed a threshold and I was wrong."

"I know you're into her, but if she hurts you...bro, I am going to be pissed off."

"Down boy. I can handle whatever happens Abbey-wise. I've waited this long."

"Yeah I know. I'm not a fan of the wait either. You deserve better than a chick who dicks with your feelings." Bren had hardened after his ordeal, but Blake couldn't blame him. It had changed them all. "Shit, Seger's calling. I need to go. You're okay right? I just got a weird feeling and thought I should call."

"Yeah. I'm good bro. I'll see you when you get back."

"Sounds good. Later."

Blake punched End and set the phone on the stack of mats piled along the wall. He kicked off his boots and habitually checked the blade tucked in the sheath sewn into the inside as he removed his socks. Getting kidnapped taught a guy a few things about self-preservation. Bren had a similar one in his boot too. They'd both worn boots instead of cross trainers since the kidnapping. Easier to hide a knife that way.

He grabbed two forty-pound dumbbells and curled them alternately. At the ten count he felt the burn in his forearms and sweat prickled under his arms. He pushed it to twenty-five then took a break to slam the punching bag in the corner a few times. He should wrap his hands since the road rash was finally healing, but he was too wired from reliving the incident to take the time.

Something had to give with Abbey or he was going to back off for good no matter what his fucking heart wanted. A guy could only take so much rejection from one girl. After a few minutes on the bag, he went back to his dumbbells.

He heard—or maybe he sensed—someone behind him

because he turned. Abbey stood in the doorway, shower fresh, her skin dewy smooth, her hair soft and straight to her gleaming shoulders. A pair of black yoga shorts showcased her mile-long legs and the white button-up top draped seductively to her curves. A slice of heaven marred by the fresh white bandage covering the stitches on her thigh.

"I've been thinking about something," she said. She set her phone on the small entry table and looked so serious, so absolutely Abbey, that the undercurrent of bad news screamed off her.

Blake put the dumbbells away on the stand, snagged a towel from the cabinet next to it and wiped off the sweat. He braced himself for the *just friends* speech. Maybe if she cut him off completely, he'd get over her. But he doubted it. "I'm all ears."

Chapter Twenty

Leo's phone rang and Kim checked the caller ID from the desk in his office. His lawyer, Tom, had called back and they'd been strategizing his survival—and lawsuit against Nathan—for the better part of forty-eight hours. "It's your accountant's office. Do you want to get it or should I?" she asked. Considering she wasn't an actress, she'd done an amazing job acting as if the sex had never happened.

"Fucking Nathan." He hopped off the sofa and snagged the phone. "Where the hell have you been and where's my money, asshole?" he said into the receiver.

Kim cringed at the tone and rage in his voice. She understood it, but it still sounded harsh.

"Oh, sorry, Bonnie."

She stood up from behind Leo's mammoth desk and stretched her legs. She'd been working for hours, going over his finances and the flash drive from Nathan's office. It had been a long day and she was about ready to punch out. Dinner sounded good right about now. With a tall glass of...soda. No more Jack for her. Not the rest of this trip anyway.

Leo's tone had gone deathly quiet as he sat on the sofa and ran a hand through his hair. This did not look good. "What? Can't be," he murmured. "You're sure?" He squinted his eyes shut. "Yeah, yeah. Okay, okay. I believe you." He blew out a rush of air. "Thanks for calling, Bonnie. Good luck." Leo disconnected and tossed the phone on the sofa next to him. He leaned against the cushion and rested his head all the way back, thoroughly defeated.

She waited, let him process whatever news he'd just heard.

He finally sat up, blew out another gust of air and met her gaze. "Nathan is dead."

What? "Did you just say he's dead? As in never coming back?"

He nodded. "I did."

This was bad.

"This is bad," Leo said.

"What did Bonnie say?"

"She'd turned in a missing person's report not long after we picked up our files," he said, referring to the day they'd met in Nathan's office. "The cops found a body and it matched her description. They sent two cops over with a picture and she identified him a little while ago."

"Wow. That sucks." *On so many levels.*

"On so many levels."

"Stop doing that."

"Doing what?"

"Nothing." She paced the room. "I can't believe this. How did he die?" Stopping, she faced Leo.

"She said he was stabbed." Kim grimaced and Leo continued. "They asked her if Nathan had any enemies that she knew of."

With a snort, Kim started pacing again. "Apparently a few."

"Yeah, like every client on his roster, I imagine."

"Maybe so, but not every client knew he was stealing." She stopped and faced Leo again. "And it's possible he didn't steal from every client."

"Just the rich ones," Leo groused.

"Lucky you," Kim murmured.

"Now what do we do?" he asked. "Do I have any recourse where he's concerned?"

"Absolutely. We just need to call Tom back so he knows what he's up against. Although we don't know if Nathan's estate has any money in it. That's the million dollar question. For now, we continue on with the plan of selling everything we can and digging you out of the hole. I should hear back from the IRS tomorrow and we'll see if we can't get a payment plan going. Things might be tight for a while, but you'll be okay eventually. The good news is you shouldn't be going to jail."

His eyes rounded. *"Shouldn't be?* That's not at all reassuring." He looked adorably concerned, his blue eyes wide and his hair tousled from running his hand through it so much. Still sitting forward, Leo dropped his head in his hands. "I can't believe he's gone. Jesus, I've known him more than half my life. I can't believe..." He trailed off as his friend's death sank in.

She had the giant urge to comfort him, but that would only lead to stupid foolish things. Like the things she did when drinking Jack and she wasn't drinking Jack. Maybe not ever again.

Shouldn't be going to jail. The words circled in Leo's head as Kim leaned against the front of his desk. He took a deep breath and tamped down his rising panic.

She smelled as good as she did that morning when he'd come into the office and found her working. "As much as I'd like to guarantee you everything is going to be super-fantastic, I can't do it. I need to talk to the powers that be. I would think when they hear the extenuating circumstances, they'll cut you some slack," she said.

"You *would think?* More reassuring words. Thanks," Leo grumbled, not at all placated by her attempt to make him feel better.

Her brows tilted in a worried pucker. "C'mon. I'm hungry. Part of this deal is that you feed me. What's in the fridge?" She walked out of the room without a backward glance.

The woman mystified him. She didn't act or react to him the way most women did. He could categorize most of the females he'd run across. First, the die-hard fans that wanted any piece of him. Second, the ones who took all the shit in the press seriously and wanted nothing to do with him—which is actually how Kim had started out—and third, the ones that didn't care about either of those points and just wanted to get lucky. He did have a reputation after all.

Thinking about his reputation brought to mind the evening on his cabana sofa. He'd tried not to put too much stock in the blistering great sex with Kim. There were a few reasons it could've been so good. Namely the fact that he hadn't had sex in a long time. Or just the surprise of her playful attitude before and during.

Kim stuck her head in the doorway. "Are you coming? I thought you were behind me. I've been talking this whole time to nobody." Her exasperation made him smile and he hadn't expected anything to make him smile after hearing the news about Nathan.

Leo followed Kim into the kitchen where she pulled a couple of meals out of the freezer as she talked about all the steps he had to take for his financial freedom.

She'd dressed for business in one of her new skirts, tops and wedges that gave her more height. Her tone calves reminded him of her strength as she'd wrapped those legs around his hips the other night.

His blood started pumping, taking a familiar path to his crotch, and Leo forced his gaze out the window as she yammered on about money. He should be paying attention, but he couldn't concentrate. Couldn't focus on anything but the fact that it was all going to go away.

He'd come to terms with it last night, but the one thing he couldn't let happen was Megan losing her spot at The Marion Institute. It was the one place he'd seen her thrive and the one place he couldn't afford to lose.

Kim closed the oven with their food inside and adjusted the temperature. "You didn't hear a word I just said, did you?" She faced him with her arms crossed.

He shook his head. He owed her a little honesty. "No. Sorry. My head's somewhere else. I keep thinking about Nathan getting stabbed. That's the kind of shit I deal with while I'm playing a part in a movie. Not real life."

She nibbled her lower lip and Leo remembered doing the same thing. God, she'd been at his place for days and he had very few indecent thoughts. He'd let the other night get away from him and now all he could think about was touching her soft skin and sinking into her welcoming wet heat.

"It's going to be okay." Her cell phone rang and she snagged it from the counter. "It's the PI that I hired," she said, before taking the call. She headed toward the French doors that led out to the backyard and Leo looked around his place, knowing it wouldn't be his for much longer and feeling the loss in the pit of his stomach like an unbearable weight.

Before Abbey could tell him what she'd been thinking about, her phone rang. "They identified the body," she said after disconnecting with Detective Patrick. "His name is—was—Nathan Berman. He was a CPA." She set her mobile on the small table by the door and stepped farther into the room.

Blake studied her face. "You okay?" It was one thing to have seen the man get stabbed, but it was another now that he had a name and occupation.

She nodded. "Yeah. I guess. It just makes it more real somehow, I can't explain it." She shook it off. "Look, before the phone call..." She hesitated. "You sounded mad," Abbey said, her eyes narrowing. "Is that because of me?"

"I don't know." Blake's frustration was eating at him. If he didn't spill it all now, he never would. "I guess I thought after the other night, we'd made a breakthrough. I thought things had changed between us, but I'm not sure." He watched her for any sign of agreement and when she didn't say anything, heaviness hit his chest. One step forward and three steps back. *Shit.*

He walked away from her, couldn't stand to see the pain in her eyes. The fact that she knew she hurt him, but couldn't help herself. Couldn't help the way she felt. Or didn't feel. That destroyed him as much as anything. That she somehow felt he'd give up and leave. That maybe she'd be alone her whole life because no man took the time to give her the space, and at the same time, attention she needed. He wanted to be that guy more than anything.

So what could he do? How could he help her...help them both? He couldn't touch her, so what was the alternative? He looked up, needing some guidance. Something.

He glanced at the chin-up bar mounted on the ceiling. In the corner of the room, he spotted several blue and green elastic bands used for stretching. Maybe... If he... Christ, he swore he'd never be tied up again. Just remembering the pain of having his hands cuffed behind his back for four days was enough to make his shoulders burn with pain. What were his other choices?

He didn't see any.

"Ab?" He caught her gaze from across the room. "What were you going to say when you walked in?" She looked broken and he hated it. Wanted to get that look off her face and replace it with the glow she'd had the other night. Wanted her to be relaxed and happy, not stressed and uncomfortable.

"Do you think I like being this way?" she said, answering his question with her own. She sounded resigned. Done. With him...maybe with everything. "Do you think I don't realize that I'm different? That people look at me funny when I shy away from them? I want to be different than this. I want to..."

So maybe he could help her with that. Maybe... God, he'd been looking at this all backward. She'd already come up with the answer the other night. "I get that I can't touch you... But there's nothing stopping you from touching me." Blake snagged the industrial sized rubber bands from the floor and wrapped and knotted an end around his wrist.

"What are you doing?" Abbey asked, taking a few steps closer.

"Just like the other night in the hotel room. You touched me, got more comfortable with me. So we'll do it again, only you don't have to worry about me touching you." Blake tossed the free end over the chin-up bar then tied it to his other wrist, effectively tying and locking his hands in the air and out of commission. A phantom ache throbbed in his shoulders. He could do this. This didn't involve any threats with guns or knives. No one had his mother at knifepoint or a gun trained on his father. This was voluntary and strictly for Abbey, so she could feel the freedom to explore. To get comfortable with his body. With her own body. He didn't need to have sex with her now to know he'd love her forever. As long as he had hope, he'd stick it out. If she agreed to this, then he had hope.

"I'm giving you free rein to touch, knowing I won't—can't—even by accident—touch you back. Have at me. I'm all yours."

She stepped closer, her green eyes wide as understanding dawned. "I can't let you do this. I know how you feel about being tied up. It's not fair."

"This has nothing to do with fair. It's about trust, Abbey. I trust you to touch me anywhere. I trust that you won't hurt me or do something to make me or you uncomfortable. I trust that we can be really good together, but you have to trust too. You have to want it, Ab." He looked up at the ceiling again. He had no clue how to explain this to her. "If you don't want me, Ab, that's okay. I'll walk out the door in the next ten seconds. But if you want me and you're scared to want me, then I want to try and fix that."

Abbey licked her lips and swallowed. "Blake..."

"Just take your time and feel what it's like to touch someone. Me." He should've thought of this earlier. Not only did she rarely let people touch her, but she hardly ever touched anyone either. Clearly the other night in Palm Springs hadn't been enough to give her the breakthrough she needed. "Unless you don't want to do it." None of this worked if she felt any pressure. "Totally your call."

She came forward and stopped right in front of him. He smelled her, let all that sweet citrus fog his brain. Cupping his cheek in her hand, she tilted her head. Blake leaned into her warm palm, loving the gentle touch because it meant his answer. A shot of triumph and joy blazed through his heart and he grinned down at her.

"Does this still hurt?" she asked, stroking beneath the bruise on his cheek.

He shook his head. "No." He didn't want anything in the way of her decision.

She exhaled a long breath. "You're just going to stay right like that?"

"Right like this. I'm not going to move. Promise."

She stood just inches away and his pulse picked up. A couple of light fingers traced down his right side and the other hand joined in on the left side. She reached the hem of his T-shirt and grabbed the edges. "May I?" she whispered, her voice barely there.

"Absolutely, you may." His own voice sounded husky and not his norm.

She eased the material up high and over his head. He grabbed it where it stayed bunched in his hands.

That's when the game got going.

First with small strokes, just a finger or two. Then more. Abbey's hands danced over his skin. She set her palms on his abs and stroked slowly up to his pecs. He held his breath as all the blood rushed to his dick. Her hands eased over his shoulders, up his biceps and arms as high as she could reach before smoothing down again to his chest, down his sides and back to his stomach. Blake met her gaze as she eased behind him.

She trailed her fingers, her palms, over the expanse of his back and sides. He clenched his jaw as her touch set him on fire. She left nothing undiscovered. Each fresh contact of her skin on his sent every nerve ending sizzling. Then she moved.

"You're so hard," she murmured, landing in front of him again. "But your skin is so soft. It's like satin over steel." Blake sucked in oxygen as she leaned closer and set her lips against his chest. He bent his head, to get a stronger whiff of her hair and the movement pulled at his wrists. Every nerve tensed as her kisses continued across his chest. Her lips landed on the hard bud of his nipple and her pink tongue darted out for a taste. His hard-on strained against his jean's zipper and desire coiled low and tight in his gut. Abbey moved in even closer, until her breasts connected with his bare chest. She eased her hands around and cupped his ass as her plush lips continued grazing over his nipple.

Too good. It was too fucking good. Just feeling her touch, her breath against his skin was almost enough to make him come. He wanted her so bad he might die from it.

He waited for her to stop. Waited for her to understand how he felt when it came to touching her. How much joy he got from it. How much pleasure. He wanted to ask if she understood, but he couldn't pull enough oxygen into his lungs and his brain couldn't form the words. The only thing on his mind was the need for more. More of her touch. More of her heat against his skin.

She never stopped. Her warm hands explored and tested every bit of his chest and back. Her hesitant touches grew bolder with every second. She took another pass around him and hugged him from behind, pressing the softness of her breasts against his back as her hands moved up and down his ridged abs.

"You're so sexy," she whispered against his skin.

He felt her smile and his first taste of victory brought a burst of euphoria he hadn't expected. A tortured laugh erupted from his mouth. "Not half as sexy as you, Ab. Not even half."

She moved to the front of him again, her eyebrows lifted high. "You're going to argue with me while you're tied up?"

"Not arguing," he said with more confidence. "Just stating a fact."

The gleam in her eyes hinted that she had a plan, and Blake narrowed his gaze. What was she thinking?

He discovered a few seconds later when she unbuttoned his jeans. Though he'd known the possibility was there that she'd take this as far as she could, he hadn't really expected her to. Closing his eyes, he reveled in the feel of her taking down his zipper one small fraction of an inch at a time.

"Breathe," she told him quietly in the same tone he'd used on her a number of times. "In and out," she teased. She hooked her thumbs under the waistband of his jeans and proceeded to inch them over his hips.

"Ab." His heart rate jacked up as his breathing faltered even more. He didn't know if he meant to warn her or urge her on.

She looked up at him, her gaze full of emotion, full of appreciation. She stood on her tiptoes and Blake leaned his head down. Their lips met in a soft kiss, a small taste, a promise of something more. Her full lips brushed across his in the barest of touches as her hands worked his jeans down his thighs. Her eyes widened as she came across his security blanket. "Is this a knife?" she asked, easing his blade from his back pocket.

He nodded. "And one of my best friends," he added, though it came out on a breath. Her hands moved up sensuously to cup his neck as she opened her mouth, deepened the kiss and urged him to do the same.

Yeah, like that was a problem.

His knife hit the floor, momentarily forgotten.

Blake wanted to dive in for more. Wanted to take her mouth in a furious kiss of possession and need. Needed to. Iron will kept him from breaking. This show belonged to Abbey. If he had any shot in hell at making her trust him—them—he had to let her lead this whole seduction. And that's what it was. How far did she plan to go?

He had no clue, but he'd set himself up for this, so he'd take whatever she dished out. God, he wanted her so bad. Every pulse-pounding second with her mouth on his and her hands on his skin had his dick straining for attention.

After long minutes kissing, she pulled away. The sight of her lips, swollen from his kiss, had the caveman inside him beating his chest with possession. She was all his.

Her gaze flicked down to the massive erection breaking free from the waistband of his boxer briefs. With a determined stare into his eyes, she eased his jeans down the rest of the way to his legs, crouching in front of him. "Out," she commanded. She looked up at him from her spot and impossibly his dick got harder. Blake tipped his head back and watched the ceiling to keep from climaxing just because of her eyes watching him. But like the obedient fool he was, he stepped out of his jeans and let her shove them away.

She rose in front of him completely dressed as he stood in his underwear. Then she began touching him all over again. Walking around him, letting her hands graze him everywhere. On a pass in front, she stroked her palm up the hard ridge of his erection and he clenched his teeth.

"That really is very impressive," she said. "A little daunting if we're being honest with each other."

He didn't want her worried. "Don't be scared," he whispered. "I told you there's no pressure."

She stepped back and his heart plummeted. She was done. Not willing to take the time to touch and explore him further.

Her hands went to the first button of her top. "Do you mind if I...?"

Was she freaking asking for his permission to strip? "Hell no, I don't mind."

One by one, she slipped the buttons through their holes then very deliberately eased the shirt off her smooth shoulders. Jesus, she was so amazingly beautiful. He loved her shoulders. Had never known anyone with such perfect posture, and her shoulders turned him on like a switch. Her breasts weren't big but they were full and her nipples pebbled beneath the lace of her black bra. The low waistband of her shorts accentuated her flat stomach and hard abs.

"Ah, ah, ah," she reprimanded. "Eyes, here." She pointed to her own eyes and Blake had no problem with the new scenery. He loved her green eyes as much as every other body part.

She took another pass around him, touching him in all the erotic places that set his blood to boiling.

He needed mercy.

She had none to give.

Her hands roamed to the backs of his thighs and stroked down and back up on the insides. He spread his legs and gritted his teeth harder as her light touch nearly incinerated him.

She eased around him again, letting her skin slide along his before she stood in front of him, her thumbs inside the soft material at her hips. With their gazes locked, she slowly pushed her shorts down her long toned legs before kicking them aside.

Eyes riveted to her hers, Blake's mouth watered at the sight of her in just a bra and matching black thong. His chest rose with deep breaths as she watched what she did to him.

"I think it's time for another taste. What about you?"

Words wouldn't come so he nodded like a fool.

This time when she stepped forward he stretched to reach her mouth. He meant to own her, to drive her to the brink of insanity where she'd brought him. Waiting, wanting, needing her touch so desperately that his skin tingled with it.

She kissed him back just as thoroughly, her tongue dueling with his in a wet tangle. She pulled back, breathing hard, her hands around his neck as she looked up at him. "I think this was a good idea," she said, catching his mouth in another hot connection before stepping back. Without breaking eye contact, she hooked her thumbs into his underwear and pulled them down his thighs. She stepped between his legs and took them the rest of the way off with her foot. "Out."

He followed her simple command and stepped out of them. His raging dick wanted inside her heat desperately. Although this touching party had plenty of benefits, it didn't include penetration of any kind.

When her gaze moved to his dick, it was as lethal as a touch. He twitched and a drop pearled at the tip. His chest rose and fell with harsh breaths and heat burned him up from inside.

Abbey's gaze moved back to his as she slowly unclasped the front hook of her lacey bra.

His eyes riveted on her hands, to her slender fingers and short neat nails. He wanted to feel them dig into his skin as she held him tight.

The bra separated and she let it slip down her arms to the floor. Her erect nipples begged for his mouth, his hands. She moved around him again, gliding her hand over his sensitive skin. He wallowed in her touch and the picture of her bare ass with just that strip of black material parting it and curving around her hips.

She stopped in front of him, her arms around his neck, her lips on his jaw. Her pebbled nipples prodded his chest and Blake fought back the urge to release the knot and take her in his arms.

"You won't move from this spot, right?" she breathed into his ear.

"God, no," he promised. He wouldn't jeopardize these minutes with her for anything.

Abbey brought his head down and the lip-lock was pure fire, intense need. The instant hot connection of their tongues set Blake on a ride straight to heaven. Feeling her bare chest along his made him itch for more. Her hands stayed busy doing something else and it took him a second to realize she'd rid herself of the thong. She stepped back and the loss of her lips had him groaning his frustration. The sound of something tearing took his attention from her mouth to her hands.

A condom?

"Where the hell were you hiding that? And what are you doing?" But even as he asked, she tossed the wrapper aside and began rolling the condom over his erection. He clenched his jaw at the pressure of her hand, at the warmth of her palm on his flesh. They only needed a condom if they had intercourse and that's not what this was about. "Abbey," he ground out, a definite warning in his tone.

"Hush," she whispered then set her hands around his neck and brought him close for a mind-altering kiss. A few seconds later, she wrapped her arms around his neck, then hopped up and hooked her legs around his waist. Blake's mind went blank as he took her weight and steadied himself before all sorts of warning lights went off his head.

He smelled her heat as she kissed him deeper. Every muscle strained to be closer to her, a part of her. Inside her. She shifted and her heat slid along every inch of his throbbing dick. Blake moaned at the rub, at the feel of her silky skin against his. She kept it up and with each stroke she made a little sound of pure need that ramped up his desire.

They were both breathing hard, both sweating. The hot open-mouth kisses spread over her jaw, along his neck. They couldn't get enough of each other. Abbey tasted like the chocolate kisses Julie kept on the kitchen counter.

But when she rose up and tried to ease down on his straining erection, Blake froze, his heart pounding in his head like a fucking drum and those warning lights flashed brighter. "Abbey, don't." Jesus, he was too much for her like this. He needed time to get her ready, time to ease the way. But she didn't listen to him. She just sank a little bit farther down. Blake's eyes stung with heat and moisture. "Abbey, God, please. Don't do it this way," he begged. He'd promised her he wouldn't move and he didn't want to go back on it.

"How does it feel?" she asked.

"Jesus, Abbey." Like heaven only better. She was so tight, so wet. She was everything he wanted, needed and hoped for. "Please, let's do this together. Let's find a bed, let's do it right." She only had the very tip of his head inside and the pressure was killing him. So good and not nearly enough. Blake dug his head in the crook of her neck. "Let me out and we'll do it right."

"I have to do this now while I'm ready," she whispered. "Psyched up ready," she clarified. She pushed a little farther down and a catch sounded in her throat.

Blake's chest felt tight, like couldn't-breathe tight. Or maybe that was because his heart was in his throat. "Ab." He was about to cry like a fucking baby. "I wanted you to touch me and get comfortable, but if you're serious about doing this here and now, let me go."

She set her mouth on his and her kiss was pure sweet seduction. She worked herself on him, up and down, just the first couple of inches. "It's not so bad," she said before her mouth slanted across his. But the second she tried to go deeper, she made that little sound of pain and Blake thought he'd go out of his mind. He'd never felt anything as good as the tight sheath of her body. Never wanted to plunge into anything as sweet as the hot clasp of heat between her legs. She tried working herself on him again, taking it slowly, but it wasn't getting her anywhere.

"Tell me I can hold you," he pleaded. "Tell me I can let go or fucking untie me. You have to do it. You have to trust me."

She shook her head, made that little gasp again. "I have to do this. Doesn't it feel good for you?" she asked.

"It's not me I'm worried about. It doesn't feel good for you. It's going to hurt unless we do this right." He wanted to hold her so bad he shook with it. She had to untie him because he promised her he wouldn't. Abbey reached up and Blake felt the tension of the knot before it loosened around his wrists. Then he had Abbey in his arms, her head buried in his neck, her arms tightly around his shoulders. Gently, he eased her off him as he carried her across the room. "I am so mad at you," he said softly in her ear.

Chapter Twenty-One

Abbey held tight as Blake broke their connection while he carried her to the thick cushy floor mat on the edge of the room and laid her down. Still rock hard against her thigh, he spread soft kisses along her jaw and her cheek. His fingers stroked through her hair, but he didn't try to push inside her.

"I'm so mad at you," he said again. But his lips kept grazing across hers so softly and sweetly. "Why, why are you so damn stubborn? Forget it. I don't want to know." He looked into her eyes, solemn and serious. "I need to touch you, Ab. With my hand, okay?" He looked so worried and she didn't want that.

She nodded because he wouldn't hurt her. She knew that bone deep, despite the mix of fear and curiosity that swirled together in her head.

His lips came down on hers again as his hand eased over her thigh, his thumb teasing her bikini line before landing on that button that was so sensitive. Abbey gasped and moaned, the contact sharp and sweet. This was nothing like the pain she felt at trying to take all of him.

Blake spread the moisture between her legs, until he slipped a finger inside of her. Abbey sucked in a rush of air. "You okay?" he asked between kisses.

"Yes. God, yes. Very okay."

He moved his finger in and out, slow and steady until he added another one Her body adjusted to the pressure, to the invasion. Through it all he kept kissing her. He kept her wanting more, wanting him. Wanting that same release he gave her the other night. Their tongues played a game of chase, back and forth, her mouth, then his mouth.

"Do it," she said breathlessly, many long minutes later when they came up for air and he had her on the edge.

"Patience," he murmured as he settled himself over her. He took a nibble from her neck and she gasped again. She felt his hard length against her thigh, the heat of him at her entrance, then the pressure of him as he pushed in. He only got so far before the same intense pain seared its way up her middle.

"Breathe," he whispered. "Just breathe." His thumb returned to stroke her clit and all of sudden she didn't care what else he did. He hit her sensitive spot with unerring precision. He circled and circled and she arched up into his touch, forcing him in a fraction farther. He pressed harder on her clit and the swell got bigger, took Abbey over the edge in a blissful free-fall, her inner walls throbbing in sweet release.

Blake pushed inside her, his heat and hardness like hot iron. The pleasure and pain had Abbey gasping for air, holding Blake tightly against her as she processed the sensation of full penetration. As her orgasm faded, she concentrated on Blake's strong arms wrapped around her tightly. On the steady beat of his heart against her chest, the way his lips cruised over her ear, her neck and her jaw. The pain between her legs slowly ebbed as Blake continued kissing her. Her tense muscles eased as her body stretched to accommodate his width.

"You okay?" He stroked his thumb across her temple as she nodded. "I wasn't kidding when I said I love you. I don't ever want to see you hurt or in pain." His lips brushed hers softly, sweetly as he slowly pulled out of her and just as slowly moved back in. She inhaled as he filled her. The long, slow glide kissed internal nerves she didn't know existed. Every part of her focused on their connection. "You're not running from me anymore, Ab. I'm done with that." He withdrew and pushed in again and this time he moved over the tight bud of her clit. An immediate shock of pleasure arced through her.

"I swear to God, I'm going to make this so good, you're not going to think about anyone but me for the rest of time. You're not going to look at anybody or want anybody. Just me." His rhythm stayed slow and even and every time he made that slide in, he had her gasping for air.

"I already don't want anybody else," she told him. Why would she?

He froze and stared down at her. "What did you just say?"

"You heard me." She brushed her thumb along his jaw. "Do you think I'd let just anyone in? Did you think I'd do this without realizing what it meant to both of us?" A mixture of joy and hope clashed in his eyes and made her smile. "No one's ever cared enough to figure me out. No one's ever had the patience. You're this amazing man. You're confident and caring. Strong and patient." She shifted beneath him, took him a little deeper. "And you're so beautiful." His lopsided grin melted her. "Don't get me wrong, I'm still a wreck, okay. I'm still the same girl with the same issues, but I'm getting better. Getting stronger. Because of you."

"I love you." He followed the whispered words with a slow kiss and deep penetration.

Abbey's heart filled with emotion. With deep, gratifying waves of appreciation, satisfaction and most of all love. "I love you too."

The sound of Blake's moan vibrated from his chest as he pushed into her. Over and over he stroked inside and arrowed pleasure everywhere he touched. Where she'd hurt just a few minutes before, now she craved. She felt the same familiar build up, the climb to something breathless and wondrous.

"I could be inside you forever, Ab," he whispered roughly. "I can't get enough. I'll never get enough." His words just stoked her further, sent her faster to the peak. She lifted her hips to meet him, begged for more of his power, his strength as she clasped her legs around his waist and held on.

Blake moved over her with single-minded determination. His mouth took hers with a possessiveness that seared her, marked her as his. And she wanted that more than anything. With her head cupped in his hand, his tongue deep in her mouth and her body taking all of him, Abbey had never felt more wanted, more needed, more loved.

"Oh God," she panted. He had her there again. Right on the edge, hovering on that cliff before the fall—or the rise—or whatever it was when she tipped over the edge into oblivion. "Blake," she moaned his name, wanted him to take the plunge with her.

"You're so beautiful, Ab," he whispered in her ear. He circled and plunged deep again. Between the friction and his words she tumbled over.

She bit his shoulder to keep from screaming and his harsh groan rumbled from his chest into hers as he came. The power of his orgasm throbbed inside her and she held on as he rode it out.

Breathing hard, Blake collapsed on top of her, careful to keep his weight on his elbows. Slowly he pulled out and Abbey breathed with the loss. After dropping next to her, a rogue smile flashed across his mouth. "You doing okay?" he asked. He reached behind him and grabbed the towel he'd used earlier to wipe her thigh.

Her own grin faded and her heart pumped harder when she saw the red streaks on the towel. Blood. She yanked the towel from his hand, sat up and covered herself before he could get a closer look.

"It's okay. I think that's probably normal," he said, sitting up next to her. "Give me a sec to clean up and toss this," he said hopping to his feet and disappearing into the bathroom.

He was right. It was probably normal. Just embarrassing as hell. "Sounds like you've never done this before," she said as he returned. God, he was gorgeous, so sculpted. And still so hard. She nearly lost her train of thought. "I mean...have sex with a..." There it was. The V-word.

Shaking his head, he watched her carefully as he sat across from her. "No, I never have." He grinned again. "I'm feeling a little honored." That made her laugh and his smile widened. He was so beautiful when he flashed those straight white teeth. But his grin faded and fresh concern clouded his eyes. "How do you feel?" He gestured with a nod of his head toward her nether region.

"I'm good. Great. Maybe a little sore." A lot sore, but she didn't want to freak him out. "And very..." What was the word she wanted? "Very..."

He waited, watching her carefully. "Happy? Satisfied? Either of those things?"

"Both of those," she told him quietly. Her legs felt like noodles and her female parts all tingled. Little aftershocks still buzzed through her body. But there was something else too. Something more elemental. "I feel very loved."

His smile dropped completely as he moved to her, his lips taking hers in a gentle kiss that turned deep and soulful. "I do love you." He stroked her cheek with his thumb as he stared into her eyes. "I've loved you from day one in that freaking elevator. I just knew then. You were it for me. My dad told me that's how it was when he first met my mom. He just knew."

She stroked her finger along his jaw, envious that he could sit and talk to her without a stitch of clothing on, like it was the most natural thing in the world. "How old were they?" She never imagined falling for a guy. She'd have bet money she was going to die an old virgin.

"Sophomores in high school."

"Oh my, God. They were babies." She remembered the movie and how young the parents were, but she thought that had been a Hollywood trick to keep everyone young and beautiful.

"I don't think love has an age requirement," he told her, diving in for a quick soft kiss.

"Maybe not, but..." She paused, her curiosity getting the better of her. "Can I ask you something personal?"

He eased away from her and nodded. "You can ask me anything you want, anytime you want."

She fiddled with the tag on the towel. "How old were you when you lost your virginity?"

"Seventeen." He didn't seem annoyed at all.

"Was it a good experience?"

"Uh. Yeah." He nodded as a blush crept on his cheeks. "I'd have to say yes. Her name was Shawna. She was one of my big brother's friends. She was very persistent."

"Persistent? So you didn't want to lose it?"

"I definitely wanted to, but I didn't think I was reading the signs right. I didn't see how someone older would want to be with a kid who didn't know jack-shit." He leaned on his side, propped up with his elbow and looked like a sex god on vacation.

Abbey moved on her side, too, and faced him in the same position, keeping the towel over the important parts. "How much older was she?"

"Only three years, but back then it seemed like a lot. She was in college and I was still in high school."

"How long did it last?"

He snorted as he rolled his eyes and she smiled at his grin. "Not long. I was her winter break fling. She went back to school and forgot about me."

"Broke your heart?"

He nodded, lost some of the smile. "Maybe a little." He lifted his gaze and his solemn eyes spoke to her on an intimate level. "Yeah. I tend to fall hard." He gave her a very meaningful lifted eyebrow before kissing her again. "For some reason, I've always been attracted to women a little older than me."

She laughed. "I remember the first time we met and I thought you were a baby. You look so young."

Blake shrugged a shoulder. "It's a curse."

She laughed again. "We should all be so cursed."

His grin widened. "I'm only a couple years younger than you. You make it seem like a decade."

"I just never imagined myself with a younger man." She glanced away. "Honestly, I never imagined myself with anyone."

He tipped her chin to face him. "And now?"

She looked into the gorgeous blue of his eyes and couldn't imagine anything—or anyone—else. "Now, I only see you. I love you."

His eyes welled up as he took her hand, linked their fingers and smiled at her. "You know that's about the best news I've ever heard."

Blake wrapped Abbey in his arms and held her close. Finally, finally he had her, all of her, body, heart and soul. He had a little taste of what his dad went through when dealing with his mom over two decades ago. His dad's words echoed in his head. "All good things are worth waiting for."

She stroked her fingers along his back and his hungry dick responded by growing harder against her stomach. She eased back, her eyes wide. "No way? You know when you came out of the bathroom, I noticed that bad boy, but seriously, can you do it again already?"

He laughed and hugged her a second time. "I could. But I won't. I know you're a little tender and I don't want to hurt you."

Her eyes got that soft, doe-eyed expression he loved so much. "That's very considerate of you."

"Yeah, well. I have the only sister on the planet who made sure her brothers knew that if they took a girl's virginity to be aware of the after effects. I'm under orders to be 'considerate.'"

"I knew I liked your sister," Abbey teased.

Blake's phone rang from the stack of mats next to him. He swiped it up and checked the screen. Bren again. He nearly laughed. It figured. "Give me one sec to take this," he told Abbey. "What?" he said, after punching the screen.

"Are you in any position to save my ass?" Bren asked. He sounded breathless.

"Maybe. What do you need?" Blake sat up and reached for his clothes a few feet away where Abbey had tossed them.

"You're gonna kill me, but I need you to go to the apartment, open my desk and look for a packet of passes in the top drawer. I swore I packed the envelope, but I can't find it anywhere. Long story short, I need those passes ASAP for Seger's guests by the next show. If you don't overnight them now. I won't get them in time."

"What if I get Eric to do it?" Blake asked. He didn't want to leave Abbey alone.

"Eric and Danny split for Santa Barbara this morning for two days. I tried them first."

"Okay, okay. As soon as Troy gets back from the airport, I'll go. I just don't want to leave Abbey alone."

"Awesome! Thanks, bro. I owe you one."

"One? Are you serious? This is more like one hundred." He winked at Abbey and she grinned. His heart flopped over like a happy puppy wanting its tummy rubbed. After a little more ribbing of his brother, Blake disconnected the call.

"Family calls, huh?" Abbey asked, pushing her hair behind her ear.

"Yeah. Sorry about this." He checked his watch. "Troy should be here in a little while. After he dropped off Julie, he was stopping at the office to get some paperwork. As soon as he comes back, I'll take off. It'll give me a chance to bring some fresh clothes from the apartment while I'm there."

Abbey leaned forward and brushed her soft lips against his. "I'm going to miss you."

He released a puff of air and leaned his forehead against hers. "I have been waiting forever to hear you say those words." He slanted his lips over hers in a deeper, wetter, hotter kiss and she moaned into his mouth. Blake stroked a hand through her hair. "If I don't get up and shower real quick, Troy's going to walk in on us doing it on his gym mat."

"Surprise!" she whispered.

Blake pulled back. "You're like a comedy store these days. I love it."

Her smile slayed him. She was so fucking gorgeous. "I want you to think about something while you're out," she said and her tone turned very serious. "Think about me. Under the sheets. With no clothes on. And think about you in the same place with me. Also with no clothes on. Then think about what might happen once you get that picture in your head."

Blake's eyes nearly rolled to the back of his head and his dick got harder. He jumped up from the mat and ran to the shower. "The faster I get back, the faster I can make that happen."

Troy returned a little later and Blake left for his apartment. As he searched Bren's desk for the all-important envelope, Bren called to say he'd found it in the ripped lining of his suitcase. Crisis averted. Blake grabbed a bag of fresh clothes and headed out.

Taking the stairs at a fast clip toward the garage, he pounded through the doorway on a mission to get back to Abbey. He caught sight of a black sedan outside the iron gate of his apartment's secure garage and slowed his step. The hair on the back of his neck prickled at a presence behind him. Blake ducked and spun at the same time as a massive weight hit him full on and knocked him back. Air whooshed out of his lungs as he struggled to get to his feet and reach the blade in his back pocket. A fist plowed into his face and pain exploded in his head, but Blake came back with a hard punch of his own and knocked the guy off him. He got to his feet only to be slammed from behind by someone else.

Two against one, just like the last time. Anger and fear pounded through his gut as he fought, throwing punch after punch, but it didn't seem to matter. They came at him from every direction. He hit the pavement and someone yanked him up while the other one whaled on him with a series of blows to his face and his stomach. He barely got a look at the guy nailing him. Every fresh hit sent a new round of pain blossoming through his body until he was numb with it.

"Just end it," a voice behind him said. He knew that voice.

With one final massive blow, the last punch sent a rocket through his head then knocked all the lights out.

Chapter Twenty-Two

Kim sat forward in the big leather chair and tapped her thumb on the desk while she scrolled through a file on Leo's computer. She'd been scanning the screen for five minutes and the longer she stared, the more her eyes narrowed. With her glasses on and her hair back, she looked every inch the businesswoman. Leo wanted to take her in his arms, slip the glasses off and find the seductive blond knockout who'd dropped into his life like a mushroom bomb a week ago. He knew exactly how soft her hair would be if he took it down and ran his fingers through it. His dick sparked at the memory.

Sitting on the other side of her with his feet propped on the desk, Leo finally broke the silence. "Something wrong?"

"Oh, sorry." She glanced at the papers next to her. "I can't find how these numbers relate to you at all and there are some crazy big numbers here. Do you own property in Palm Springs?"

"Nope."

"I didn't think so. The other flash drive had all your information, so is it possible Nathan's secretary gave you this one by mistake?"

"Anything's possible."

"We should get this back to her. She might be looking for it." Kim picked up a pencil and rolled it between her fingers. "I wonder if she knew what her boss was doing? I know Tom plans to speak with her, but I'd really like to talk to her before I leave tomorrow."

Like he needed the reminder she was going. "Do you think she'd tell you anything even if she did know?"

"Probably not, but now that Nathan's dead, it's worth a shot."

She slid her glasses on top of her head and pegged him with her gorgeous green eyes. "I mean, what if she knows where your money is? Right? Maybe we can avoid the worst case scenario if we get some information." She lifted a blond eyebrow. "I think we should find her. I'll bet my PI can get her address."

"I can do better than that. She told me she's still at the office...giving Nathan's clients time to come by and pick up files while she closes up shop. I'll call and check, but she might still be there."

Kim's smile was luminous. "Wanna take Stella out for a spin?"

He grinned. "Baby, that's always one of my favorite things." He stood and gestured toward the door. "After you."

"Give me one minute to grab my purse. Meet you in the garage." Her smile did weird things to his chest and watching her ass as she clicked out of the room in her high heels did something else to his dick. Never in a million years did he see himself lusting after an accountant. And yet...

A quick call confirmed Bonnie was at the office so the plan was a go.

In the garage, Leo opened Stella's door and admired the way Kim slid into the low seat with her short skirt and stilettos. She was made for luxury, for the finer things in life. He wanted her to stay longer just to show her what this town had to offer. He closed her door and the sound snapped reality back into his brain. Didn't matter what he wanted to do because he couldn't afford it. Technically, he couldn't afford the gas to fill Stella. That made this trip to see Bonnie that much more important. Because if Kim was right and Bonnie had information maybe he could avoid this whole bankruptcy thing. God, what a colossal clusterfuck. A clusterfuck he was about to face on his own without the help of the pretty blond kick-ass female who'd worked her butt off most of the week helping him figure out his life. No easy feat. He owed her so much.

A few minutes later on the road, Kim cleared her throat. "Um... May I ask you a personal question?"

Leo nearly laughed. "You're seeing just about everything there is to see while you're going through my books. I didn't think there was anything too personal left to know." A big lie considering Megan was still under wraps, but just barely. When

Kim had asked about the monthly charge for The Marion, Leo had told her it was an estate in the Hamptons. She'd told him he'd have to sell it just as he'd have to sell his other property and Leo hadn't uttered a word.

"I'm really curious about something."

A wave of heat spread from Leo's center and worked its way through his veins. What if she found something about Megan after all? He didn't think she'd tell anyone, but then he never thought Nathan would take his money. "Curious about what?"

"That lawsuit with the cheerleader. For weeks it was headline news, then one day it disappeared. What happened?"

Relief swept through him like a cool breeze. Although this was his second least favorite topic. Still, better than Megan. "Roxanne wanted to keep her money. That meant she kept her mouth shut."

Kim faced him, her long legs crossed at the ankle in the leg well. "I don't buy it. Not after the time I've spent with you."

Leo kept his eyes on the road as he passed a chrome Fisker Karma. He'd take Stella any day of the week over that thing. "What's not to get? She dropped the charges because of the settlement."

"I don't get why you were with her in the first place. I just don't see you with teenyboppers."

Cringing at the word, Leo glanced at Kim. "Trust me, I don't either."

"You're really going to make me piece this together aren't you?"

Leo exhaled hard and caved. "I was on location and met Roxanne at a club. She was dressed to kill in fuck-me pumps and enough makeup for three women. We danced. We drank. She told me she was twenty-five. I took her back to my hotel room. We fucked. The next thing I know, my people are getting calls from her lawyer and I'm in hot water for statutory rape. She seduced me. She played me all night long and I let her. Hell, she insisted on buying the first two rounds." Thinking about that night still made his gut roll. "She knew exactly what she was doing from minute one. I coughed up five million to make her go away because there was no way to win that case in court. No one would be believe *that Sweet Girl* did something so premeditated." He shook his head and accelerated when the silver Lexus in front of him slid out of the lane. "I was the Hollywood Bad Boy taking advantage of young girls. When my lawyer showed me her deposition, I didn't even recognize her. No makeup, conservative clothes. She looked like a teenager. If that had been the girl I'd met that night, you can bet I wouldn't have touched her with a twenty-foot pole."

"You think she was out specifically to hurt you like that?"

"Me specifically? I don't know. Maybe she was out for any man who she thought she could scam and I happened to be the one that ended up in her trap. There were a lot of men with deep pockets at the club that night...directors, producers, managers. With her clothes and makeup, she easily passed for twenty-five and she knew it. She had an agenda."

"That's one hell of an expensive lesson." Kim tapped her chin. "Where is she now?"

Leo slowed down as he realized his foot had gotten heavier on the gas with the story. "Don't know. Don't care. But you better believe I check for ID now."

"You didn't check mine," she mused with a lifted eyebrow. "What if I'm seventeen?"

Leo glanced at her. "I've never met one single teenager with your kind of style." He slowed for a red light.

She cocked her head. "Leo. You dodge bullets better than anyone I've ever met. Instead of reminding me that seventeen was over a decade ago, you turned it around and gave me a compliment."

"A decade ago?" Leo glanced at her again. "Now you've surprised me. I thought you were going to say five years ago."

"And bam, he does it again." Her smile turned serious. "I still don't see why you never came forward to clear your name. Why let her get away with that?"

"No proof. Who's the public going to believe? The actor with the bad rep or the high school cheerleader without a blemish on her record? I had no way to win. Trying to defend myself was only going to make me come out looking worse. It was easier to give her the money to shut up. And she *does* have to keep quiet or she has to give the money back."

Kim growled, soft and low. "Nothing makes me angrier than conniving little bitches. I wouldn't mind meeting her one day in a dark alley." She'd had the same thought when Jennifer

Baumgarten had slipped ex-lax in Kim's smoothie on the day of cheerleader tryouts in high school. Kim had been stuck in the bathroom and never made the audition—much less the squad—and Jennifer had slipped into the open spot without any competition.

The light changed and Leo hit the gas. "I don't think I've been championed before." He liked the feeling.

"Well someone should've stood up for you when she came crawling out of the woodwork. Where's your family? You must have a support system that can come forward when stuff like this happens."

Dicey territory. "My parents died a long time ago." He shrugged and hoped that worked as an answer. "Now, it's my team. Agent, manager, publicist, assistant. They keep me moving. What about you? Still have your folks?" He edged into the left lane to pass a slow-moving bus.

"No." She paused for a few seconds before continuing. "I lost them in a car accident not long after I moved to Indiana."

"Wow. Sorry about that," he said, glancing at her. "That must have been rough."

She nodded. "It was. Especially since they were coming to visit me. I moved there from Chicago and they thought it would be fun to take a road trip and visit."

"What happened?" he asked.

"My dad fell asleep at the wheel and went off the side of the road. Wrapped the car around a telephone pole."

Ouch. "I'm sorry."

"Me too." She adjusted the watch on her wrist and pressed her lips together. "It threw me off for a while. Really got me thinking about my life and what I want…and don't want."

"Tragedy will do that." So would a crooked accountant. "So what *do* you want?"

"For starters, I wouldn't mind a bigger city." She smiled wistfully. "I loved Chicago, so moving to Indiana was an adjustment. Trust me, I'm not averse to someplace different."

"Why couldn't you sell your part of the business and move?" he asked.

"Honestly, I can't imagine leaving my partner high and dry. Doesn't seem fair."

"I thought she was 'living the dream.' Would she really

care?" Nathan's building loomed ahead to the right. "Seems like if she's really a friend, she'd understand your need to move on.

"Here we are," Leo said, turning into the parking lot. "Whoa!"

A black GTO slammed on its brakes as it tried to exit at the same driveway and nearly plowed into Stella. The driver, an African American with a harsh look on his face, took the turn anyway and hopped the curb to avoid Leo. The GTO burned rubber as he departed.

"Asshole," Leo muttered as he parked. Something about him seemed familiar.

"Did you notice his car didn't have license plates?"

"I didn't, but I'm not surprised if he drives like that on a normal basis," Leo said, parking and cutting the engine in the almost empty lot. The same beat up Honda sat in the corner spot, assuring Bonnie's presence.

Together they walked toward the building and Kim sniffed the air. "Do you smell something?" Leo took a whiff of the air as he opened the door. Black smoke trailed out and hit them simultaneously. "Oh my God," she said, squinting into the dark haze. "Fire!"

Not again. Kim's pulse doubled as she bolted into the building. "Bonnie!" she called, staying low.

"Kim! Goddammit!" Leo's voice sounded right behind her.

Fire crackled in the back office on the right, but hadn't engulfed the whole place. Black smoke filled the air and burned her throat.

Leo grabbed her shoulders and pulled her back. "Get out of here! Call 911!" He covered his mouth and nose with the bottom of his white T-shirt. "Bonnie!" he yelled as he ducked farther into the building.

Kim ran outside, sucked in clean air and made the call. The dispatcher kept her on the phone, asking questions and after a couple of very long minutes and no sign of Leo, she had enough. Tossing her bag and phone on the sidewalk she ran into the smoking entrance.

Hot air and black smoke hit her like a wall. "Leo!" she yelled and coughed up a lungful of smoke. Staying low, she squinted and tried to see through the dark haze. The fire had already moved out of the office and trailed along the sides of the walls almost as if it had a path to follow.

"Get out!" he yelled from the back office. "It's moving too fast! Get out!"

Kim followed his voice, dodging burning desks and open file cabinets along the way. A piece of the roof fell next to her and she scrambled faster. She found him trying to heave a filing cabinet and almost asked *What the hell are you doing?* until she saw legs sticking out from underneath it.

Bonnie!

"Goddammit, Kim!" Leo said when she landed at his side.

She ignored him, grabbed the edge next to him and heaved. Smoke filled her lungs when she inhaled, but together they lifted and rolled the heavy cabinet. Bonnie lay unconscious, blood pooled beneath her torso. Kim choked out smoke as Leo scooped Bonnie in his arms.

"Go!" he yelled and Kim went.

Gasoline. That was the odor she smelled. No wonder the fire moved so fast. A minute ago it was only the back office and now the whole place crackled with flames. The faint sound of sirens combined with the crackling fire.

Kim made it outside and turned to help Leo. They set Bonnie on the cement and coughed up more smoke. Covered in soot, Leo had blood all over his shirt.

"Are you hurt?" Kim asked him.

He shook his head. "It's Bonnie's blood." Even as he said it, a fresh stream of blood pooled next to her.

Kim pressed her hand over the wound but it didn't seem to do any good. Bonnie's eyes fluttered open and she spotted Leo. "You. The...ashdri—"

"Shh, Bonnie, help's coming," Leo said. He stroked her wild hair out of her face.

She shook her head. "Flashdri..." she choked out. "Wyncott's. He wanted...wanted—" Her voice trailed off and her eyes glazed over before they became fixed and dilated.

Kim's skin prickled and her chest got tight. "Oh my God," she whispered. "Oh my God."

Leo started CPR.

Sirens blared loud as a fire truck and police cars pulled into the parking lot. First responders moved them out of the way as they took control of the scene. Though they attempted CPR, they never revived Bonnie before loading her into the ambulance.

Looking down at the soot covering her from head to toe, Kim's stomach rolled in a nauseous somersault. Leo's arm wrapped around her shoulders and Kim turned into his chest, into his arms.

"It's okay," he whispered. "It's okay."

But it wasn't okay. Not for Bonnie.

"What do you think she was trying to tell you before..." Kim swallowed back the words. *Before she died.*

"I don't know. I barely heard her."

"She said something about Carl's flash drive. *Wyncott's flash drive.* I wonder if that's whose file we have."

Leo shook his head. "I have no clue. I mean we picked up our stuff on the same day. Do you think she got them confused?"

"I don't know. All your stuff seemed to be on the first one." Kim held tight, needing Leo's strength and the comfort of his voice. "I should probably call Carl, but I thought I'd had all his information when I started going through his books. It doesn't make sense." The steady beat of Leo's heart under her hand gave her much needed solace. It could've just as easily been him on the way to the hospital. If a piece of that ceiling had fallen on him or if he'd gotten trapped in that office trying to free Bonnie... Kim shuddered and Leo held her tighter.

"Excuse me, miss," someone said.

Kim wiped the moisture from her stinging eyes and pulled away from Leo. An officer and EMT stood waiting to talk to them and it was like the other night all over again.

But this time, they had a suspect because both of them had seen the man leaving the scene. Kim soon discovered that Leo recognized the guy from his first visit to Nathan's office when he'd collected his files.

It was hours later, after EMTs treated a few minor burns on both Kim and Leo and they had given a description of the suspect, that they returned to Leo's house. Kim showered off the soot and came downstairs to find Leo in the den, sitting in front of the muted flat screen TV. Shower fresh himself, he'd thrown on a pair of navy blue sweats and looked like every woman's fantasy. Clean shaven, hair still damp and eyes that could melt a pair of panties in the Artic.

"I like your outfit," he said a second after a prolonged once over. The heat in his eyes gave her a full body flush, which went against everything she stood for. Just because he flashed those amazing eyes at her didn't mean all her girl parts had to wake up and sing.

She looked down at the oversized black sweats—his again—and looked back at him. "Technically, I think it's your outfit." She ran her hand over the material on her thigh. "These are the softest things I've ever had against my skin. If I thought I could afford them, I'd buy a pair for myself."

Leo gave her his slow, sexy smile. "Take 'em. They look better on you anyway." He patted the sofa. "C'mere. I need t—" The doorbell interrupted him and he jumped off the sofa. "Gimme a sec. This won't take long." He jogged out of the room and Kim sat down on his spot on the sofa.

She snuggled against the cushions into the heat he left behind. She barely heard him at the front door as her lids closed over her eyes. Exhaustion blindsided her.

A few minutes later, Leo entered the room and the crinkle of paper piqued her curiosity. Kim cracked open an eye and spotted a couple of shopping bags from Cesar's store.

"What's that?" Nothing gave her a hard-on quite like a shopping bag.

"Just a little somethin' somethin'," Leo said, his smile sly and devastatingly handsome.

Somethin' somethin' looked very expensive. "Leo... What did you do?" Kim sat forward, the accountant battling the woman.

"I thought since you ruined another outfit today, you'd need a replacement." He handed out the bags and when she didn't take them, he set them on the coffee table in front of her.

She shook her head. "No. I'm not even looking in those bags." She bolted up to catch the delivery guy. Maybe it wasn't too late and the contents could go back now. But Leo anticipated her move and blocked her. She ran right into his hard chest and slowly looked up at him.

"Take the bags," he said softly.

"No," she repeated just as quietly. "You can't afford what's in those bags. If we don't send them back now, we take them tomorrow before my plane leaves. I refuse to be responsible for any unnecessary spending and I honestly can't afford any more of Cesar's clothes. They go back." Now she should *move* back, but being this close to Leo set her pulse hammering. She loved his aftershave or cologne or whatever he used to make himself smell so damn sexy.

He shook his head too. "What if I told you everything is bought and paid for without money. Would you keep it then?"

"You can't buy things without money." What had he done? She narrowed her eyes as she tried to figure it out.

"Don't look at me like I'm a criminal," he admonished quietly. "It's all legit. The bags don't go back." His lethal smile gave her a quick chill across her arms. "Open 'em up."

"Not until you tell me how you paid for them." She stepped back and crossed her arms.

Leo backed up a step to the bags. "Fine, then I'll open them." Before Kim got a word out, Leo removed the contents of the first bag. A skirt and top similar to the ones she'd lost in today's fire along with two more tops. The next bag contained a gorgeous dress and another skirt and top ensemble. The outfits were spectacular. Ones she'd already tried on and discarded days ago. They'd fit her perfectly.

Kim would've checked for price tags but knew none existed. She took the clothes out of Leo's hands and stood in front of him. "I don't know how you did it, but I will find out. What I want to know now is *why* you did it? It's totally not necessary since I'm leaving tomorrow."

Taking her hand, Leo looked down at her, his blue eyes serious. "Consider it a thank you or a going home gift. You ran into a burning building. I think that deserves some recognition."

A lump lodged in Kim's throat and her hard heart cracked. "I—" She had to clear the emotion from her throat. "Leo, I can't. Actually, you ran into the burning building so you're the hero. You're the one who deserves—"

Leo took the clothes from her other hand and set them on the sofa before pulling her closer. He tipped his head toward the bags on the table. "They're not my size." His grin made her chest heavy. "You have to take them. Cesar would be disappointed if you didn't. Besides, I want you to have it all." His thumb stroked little circles on the back of her hand and sent tiny currents of electricity streaking up her arm. "Don't say no."

They watched each other for the longest time as Kim debated what to do. She shouldn't keep the clothes and she couldn't afford them. How did Leo pay for them without money?

"You traded something, didn't you?" she asked. He had a ton of stuff. It could've been anything.

"Not telling." Words a ten-year old might say spoken by a very serious man. He stroked her cheek with his thumb. "Say yes."

Somehow in the next few seconds their lips were inches apart. "Leo," Kim whispered, still torn. Not only because of the cost, but because of the gesture. Because he made her feel special and no one had done that in a long, long time.

His lips brushed hers and Kim closed her eyes to take in the taste of him, the feel of his arms as they wrapped around her. The soft, slow minty kiss knocked down all her walls with astounding efficiency. "Say yes," he murmured against her mouth before kissing her again.

"What am I saying yes to?" she asked the next time they came up for air.

His gaze searched her eyes as his fingers sifted through her hair. "Anything? Everything? Whatever you want." His mouth connected with hers again, and Kim let him own her, let him work his magic with his sneaky tongue and hot lips.

"I thought we weren't going to do this again," she said when he pulled back to trace kisses along her jaw.

"I guess I wanted to celebrate the fact that we're alive." He closed his eyes, shook his head. "I keep seeing Bonnie...and all that blood."

So that was it. She nodded. Watching Bonnie die had been pretty devastating for both of them. "Me too. I kept thinking it could've been you if the roof caved in or...I don't know." She stroked her thumb along his cheek. "I'd..." She couldn't finish, didn't want to say anything that might give away just how much she liked him.

"You what?" he asked, watching her closely.

"I'd hate to lose a new friend."

His sharp blue gaze bore into hers. She saw his loneliness, his despair. The fact that he was going to lose so much, but that he'd—they'd—survived the day seemed like a great reason to celebrate life by living it to the fullest.

Kim reached up at the same time Leo leaned down. She lost the will to fight anymore. She'd take anything he wanted to give...the damn clothes, his body. The soft kiss didn't take long to heat up. She kissed him with a hunger she'd been holding back, with a passion she'd thought she'd lost.

No Jack Daniels to blame this time and she wouldn't regret being with Leo. Maybe he wanted to give her something, but she *needed* to give him this time, her body. She needed him to know he could get through whatever came his way in the upcoming months and if giving herself right now helped him do that, then he deserved it.

Leo pulled back, his lips wet from kissing her. "No cabana sofa tonight." He took her hand and started walking backward. Kim followed. She followed all the way to his bedroom. He stopped at the side of his enormous bed and kissed her again, his magnetism lethal. Easing the sweatshirt over her head, he barely lost a beat between kisses. He slid her bra straps over her shoulders and made a meal out of uncovering her breasts and dropping the bra to the floor. The sweetest torture as he kissed the sensitive skin at her cleavage and finally her ultra-sensitive nipple. She held his head as he cupped her and sucked the hard bud into his mouth. Streaks of fire zipped between her legs and made her wet and eager. His sneaky thumbs dipped into the waistband of her sweats and he brought them down, kneeling in front of her in the process. She loved his soft growl as he realized she'd gone commando again.

"Do you ever wear underwear?" he asked before circling his tongue around her belly button.

She smiled, slipped her fingers through his soft hair then gasped as he nibbled on her hip and sent a full-body chill across her skin. "I only bought a couple of pairs at Cesar's." Grabbing a fistful of his shirt, she lifted it up and over his head. Their eyes locked as he stood in front of her. He set his mouth on hers again as she divested him of his sweatpants and boxer briefs in one shot. His erection grazed her stomach and he groaned when she put her hand around his penis and squeezed. In the next second he had her off her feet and flat on her back. His weight pressed her into the cushy bed, his erection prodding her slick entrance.

"Two things I have to do," he said, trailing kisses across her jaw.

"God, I hope one of them entails pushing inside me soon."

He growled again. "Three things," he amended. "First…" He worked his way to her breast again and sucked hard on her nipple.

Kim arched into his mouth, whimpered at the zing of fresh sexual craving. "Leo," she begged. "Now."

"In a minute," he said. "Don't be so bossy." His mouth trailed farther down. "I'm hungry." He ended up between her legs, his breath hot right before he dove in with his tongue.

Crying out, Kim locked his head between her thighs as he went to work with hard delicious licks and soft sucking kisses. He drove her crazy with pressure on her clit only to back away when she got close to coming. Over and over he kept her on a tenuous line, just on the cusp of a free fall. "Leeeoooo," she pleaded, desperate to go over the edge.

"Little busy here," he mumbled, finally slipping a finger into the mix and forcing a sharp inhale at the invasion.

She grabbed his head as she arched into his touch, into his mouth, and with one last hard lick across her clit and the fullness of his fingers inside her, she hit that point of no return. Everything inside her tightened up a second before the pressure exploded into a massive euphoric release. Her muscles clenched, spasmed as Leo continued to pump and suck, drawing out the pleasure to unprecedented lengths.

Gasping for air, Kim finally let loose of Leo's hair and all her muscles went slack. Sweat coated her skin and Leo moved next to her. She heard a drawer open, heard the rip of a foil packet and smiled. She wanted to give him the same ride he gave her. She wanted him gasping and begging for mercy.

With new determination and before he had to chance to pounce, she turned and pinned his shoulders to the bed as she straddled him. "Suited up pretty quick there, I noticed," she said before kissing him. She tasted herself on his lips and rubbed her very sensitive clit against his thick erection. They both moaned.

He held her face in his hands. "I'm gonna go off like a rocket in about three seconds so you might want to climb on board before this ship sails."

"So romantic," she said, taking his mouth in a fiery hot kiss as she adjusted herself over him. "All aboard," she huffed out, and sank down on him as he lunged up. She bit back a moan and held on tight. The pressure surprised her. She didn't remember how tightly he filled her and she froze, breathing through the initial shock.

He froze too, his breathing harsh in her ear. "You okay?"

Kim nodded, keeping her face buried in his neck. She loved the way his hands glided down her sides, over her ass and back up along her spine. He made her tingle everywhere he touched. "You feel really good." She gently bit his collarbone and felt the instant twitch of his cock inside her. The low growl in his chest rumbled beneath her.

Spreading kisses across his jaw, she eventually sat up and admired his spectacular pecs and washboard abs. "Very nice," she murmured, lifting off him and sliding back down.

He grabbed her hips and adjusted her pace, moved up into her every time she came down. The friction took her on another ride, one she hadn't expected.

"Oh God, Leo..." It was so good. Too good. She wanted to do this forever. Be in same amazing moment where their bodies fit perfectly and nothing mattered but the way they moved together. He took her breasts in his hands as he arched into her again and after three strong thrusts he pinched her nipples. Crying out, Kim let her orgasm envelop her like a massive wave, crashing over her in the perfect storm. Leo's cock throbbed inside her as his own climax finally took him over.

Breathing hard, she collapsed on Leo's chest and his arms came around her, holding her close. She could let herself fall big time if she kept this up. Good thing she was finally on a plane tomorrow.

A hell of a way to end her stay in Los Angeles.

Chapter Twenty-Three

Abbey paced the front entryway and checked her watch. Blake should've been here by now. He'd told her an hour at the most. Twenty minutes to get over the hill, two to find the envelope in the desk, a few minutes to pack up some fresh clothes, send the envelope off in the mail and twenty to get back over the hill. It had been twice that amount of time.

Troy came out of his office. "No sign of him yet?" he asked.

"No." Abbey shook her hands in nervous energy. "I've called his apartment and his cell phone. I don't have a good feeling about this."

"Neither do I." Troy never sugarcoated. "Will you be okay here if I go to his apartment?"

"I want to go with you."

He shook his head. "You're safer here. I already called the detectives and they're going to have a car drive by and patrol the neighborhood. I want to go check things out. I'll call you if I find anything." He grabbed his jacket and headed for the garage. "Don't go anywhere no matter what," he warned over his shoulder. "Your ass stays grounded here." The door closed behind him.

Ten minutes after he left, Abbey's phone rang and she snatched it out of her back pocket. Blake's name blazed on the caller ID and relief hit her like a punch to the gut. "Finally," she said, into the phone. "I was worried about you."

"Aw. That's so sweet." The voice didn't belong to Blake and fear rose up from her center and lifted every hair on her body.

"Who is this? Where's Blake?" Her voice shook and she swallowed back heart wrenching fear.

"Your boyfriend is here. With me and my friends. We're just waiting for *you* to get this party started."

She didn't recognize the voice. *Think*. What would Troy do? What would he ask? What would he want?

Proof of life!

"Just because you have his phone doesn't mean you have him." She sounded way braver than she felt.

The man laughed. "That is true. Here, I'll let you talk to him." There was jostling and she heard breathing. "Say hello to your girlfriend, asshole," the man said. "You're on speaker phone." She waited and didn't hear anything. Just that same breathing then a rush of air. "I said, 'say hello,'" the man repeated and she heard a grunt of pain.

Was Blake keeping quiet so she wouldn't do what they said? He'd do that for her. She knew he would. He'd do anything to keep her away from the men who wanted her. But what if it was a trap? What if they really didn't have Blake?

"Blake?" she asked.

"Looks like your boyfriend doesn't want to talk to you, Abbey. But we're going to make him. I'm sure you know what happened to his brother a couple years ago. And they are twins. I think it's only fair that they be twins in everything."

His ear! "No!" she screamed. "No! I believe you. I believe you. Don't hurt him! I'll do whatever you want."

"NO! Abbey, no!" Blake yelled.

She heard him in the background, heard the sound of his struggles, and tears slid down her cheeks. "Don't! Whatever you want, I'll do whatever you want. Just don't hurt him."

"Don't call the cops, Abbey, or he dies. We've got eyes on you. We're listening. Just get in your car and come to the address I text to your phone. Tell someone and your boyfriend bites the dust."

"Okay, okay. Please. Just don't hurt him."

"We're texting you the address now. It should take you about thirty minutes to get here. Don't be late, Abbey. Or your boyfriend loses his ear and then maybe a finger or two." The call disconnected before Abbey could say anything else.

Fresh tears slid down her cheeks as she blindly raced for her purse and ran to the front door. "Shit, shit, shit." She couldn't call the police because they said they were monitoring the phones somehow. As far as watching her... Maybe they had someone on the street, but no one had eyes *inside* the estate. She could leave a message for Troy. After sprinting into the kitchen, she scribbled out a note with the Santa Monica address they'd texted to her. Short and sweet. *They have Blake.* She jotted the address. *Told me not to call police or they'd know. I* had *to go! Hurry. Abbey.* She ran for the door again and the walls started spinning. Her erratic breathing made it tough to get oxygen into her lungs. Falling against the door, she forced herself to slow down. She couldn't help Blake if she passed out or hyperventilated to death.

"Breathe, girl, breathe," she told herself as she took in and released measured breaths. *Think, think.* How could she help Blake? What could she do? Walking into certain death didn't sound like her best option, but how could she turn this around?

She needed protection. She needed a weapon. Abbey ran back toward the kitchen.

Pain roared through Blake with breath-stealing force. His shoulders burned in an ache he'd only dreamed about for almost two years, and his chest was on fire. Even his fingernails hurt. He cracked open his one good eye since the other was swollen shut.

Jesus. God. The same gray room. The same house in Santa Monica. Built below ground, there was only one window up high and it was boarded up. A lantern on the floor glowed dimly in the dark. He wouldn't be waking up from this nightmare and be able to shake it and go back to sleep. This was real. The burn in his chest got thicker as he struggled to keep the emotion buried. He would not let these fuckers win. God, what time was it?

Abbey!

Was she on her way? Already here?

He had to get away before she got anywhere near here. Had to get free. He wrestled with the rope binding his wrists. At least they weren't cuffs this time. He actually had a shot at freedom. He reached for his back pocket. Shit, it was too much to hope that they hadn't discovered his blade. But maybe... He rotated his right ankle and felt the six-inch blade still there. It had been worth every dollar to have a leathersmith sew the sheath into the lining.

Yes. The little victory gave him hope.

With his hands bound behind his back, Blake had to reach backward to get to his boots. Fresh pain arced through his chest and he gritted his teeth. His wrists burned as he fumbled to get his pant leg up to snag his blade. Carefully, he pulled it from its sheath. His hands were nearly numb with the loss of circulation. It took every ounce of strength and concentration he had to keep the knife in his fingers as he worked on the rope binding his wrists. Breathing hard, he felt fresh adrenaline power through his veins. He could do this. Almost there. Finally, he got his blade on it and the tight rope split like cake. Blake's shoulders throbbed with pain as he eased his arms forward. He lay there, breathing hard, sweat soaking his skin. *Focus, focus.* He had to get out of here. Next, he freed his ankles.

Footsteps warned of someone's approach. Quickly, he retied his ankles together and hid the loose knot between his legs. He sat up and hid his hands behind his back after tucking his knife in the back waistband of his jeans.

The door swung open and a man came in. Shit. This didn't bode well, especially if the guy picked him up now or found his knife. His heart thumped along and fresh sweat slicked his palms.

"How was your nap?" the man asked. His dirty blond hair hung in his eyes. When Blake didn't answer, he went on. "It's going to be permanent as soon as your girlfriend shows up. She's late. But don't worry, we're waiting for her. Got everything covered with the guys watching from the top floor. I'll snatch her when she comes in either entrance." The guy looked to be in pretty good shape, but Blake beat him in height and weight. He'd need every advantage about now.

A walkie-talkie—similar to one in his earthquake kit at home—squawked softly at the guy's belt. "Just got off the phone with the boss. He wants the merchandise out tonight even if it's not a full load. He's not happy with the heat coming down. As soon as she gets here, we move it all out."

"Copy that." The guy clicked off the walkie. "Your girlfriend totally fucked up the operation. The boss is never happy when we deliver less than promised."

"You don't need her. Just take your fucking drugs and go," Blake muttered.

"Drugs?" The guy shook his head. "We're not dealing in drugs, asshole." His dead stare said what his words didn't. If they waited for Abbey, then she was the merchandise they wanted. "You can be glad you're not her, fucker. Because if you were, you'd be wishing you were dead already. Damon's brother is here. Wade can't wait to meet your girlfriend. He's got some serious retribution in mind. Did she tell you what she did to Damon?" His cold stare shot daggers. "She fucking took his eye out then put him in a coma." The man grabbed Blake's collar and lifted him up. Pain ruptured in his chest, but Blake took the opportunity handed to him. "She used a fucking pe—"

Blake brought his blade up sharp and hard into the man's middle. He felt the give of flesh as the tip sank deep and the man's eyes widened in shock and pain. Blake swung across with his leg and took the man's legs from beneath him. He pounced and wrapped his hands around the guy's neck and squeezed. The man fought him, his face turning red as he struggled for air, then his lids fluttered closed and his muscles relaxed. Blake made sure the guy lost consciousness before letting go.

His stomach clenched. Heaving for air, he rolled off the guy as fresh pain squeezed his chest. His spit-dry mouth made him sick to his stomach and a new round of fear for Abbey snowballed. If she stepped foot in this place, they were both in deep shit.

With fumbling fingers, Blake tied the guy's ankles and wrists with the remnants of the rope. He yanked his knife from the man's gut. It bled, but not enough to kill him. Blake wanted this asshole behind bars. Wanted him to pay for everything he'd done. He stuffed a chunk of T-shirt in his mouth and gagged the asshole, securing it with rope. Then he flipped him over so his front faced the wall. It wouldn't buy him much time, but it might buy him a few seconds if someone came to check on him.

Slowly, Blake got to all fours then stood up. The room spun and he leaned against the wall for support until everything settled into place and the pain ebbed a fraction.

The word *merchandise* stuck in his head. So did the words *we move it all out*. Did they have women upstairs? Women who hadn't been as fortunate as Abbey to get away?

Blake looked around the room. He had to take this in phases. The last time he escaped this house, he'd gone out the back. That hadn't worked out too well and now he knew men were watching from above. Time to improvise. He reached down for the man's walkie-talkie and his gun. Both would come in handy.

Abbey's stomach tied in knots as she got closer to the Santa Monica home. *Mistake. Mistake.* The word flashed in her head like a neon sign warning her to turn back, but she couldn't. If she didn't show, they'd hurt Blake and she couldn't—wouldn't—let that happen.

Remembering the knife he kept on him, she'd grabbed two kitchen knives from Julie's place before rushing out to the car. She'd stuffed one in her purse and wrapped the other in a square potholder and slid it in the side of her boot. She'd seen the knife hidden in Blake's boot as he'd showered and it had given her the idea. Knowing he had the knife tucked away gave her a little bit of hope that he had something to defend himself with if the time came.

The time was definitely coming.

Abbey drove past the Santa Monica address, then stopped down the block. The stacked house had a view of the Pacific Ocean from the backend, but the windows in the front were boarded up. White paint peeled from the trim and the overgrown yard had more weeds than lawn. The house looked dark. Deserted.

The second she walked into the place, she was giving Blake a death sentence. And if she didn't, they'd torture him until he died. So what the hell was she supposed to do? She had to buy him time. Had to barter for his life...but with what? She didn't have money. She had her body, but they'd take that whether Blake was alive or dead. An involuntary shiver raced through her.

Knocking on the front door seemed completely ridiculous. Maybe a surprise attack would buy time somehow. What if she snuck in through the backyard? Blake's sister had done that in the movie based on their kidnapping. "It was just a movie," she berated herself aloud. Who knew what parts were real and which were fabricated? She hadn't thought to ask.

Taking a deep breath, Abbey grabbed her small purse and got out of the car. She put the strap over her head like she always did so she had both hands free, and she made her way to the house.

Using cars and bushes, she hid behind anything that would conceal her approach.

Quietly, she eased open the gate of the neighbor's yard and closed it behind her. Then she crept along the wall separating the houses. Unlike the estate in Palm Springs, she had no trash bin or boxes to help her scale the wall, so Abbey jumped and barely got her slick palms at the top of the wall. Sweat broke out along her neck and back as she lifted up to peek over the top. The yard was as dark as the front. She would've thought she had the wrong place if the address didn't match what they'd texted her.

With fresh determination, Abbey heaved herself over the wall, dropped quietly into the yard and ran for cover behind a large dried up hedge. *Hold on, Blake. I'm coming.*

The house looked dark everywhere. Not one light shone from the inside. What if she'd gotten the address wrong? What if she was too late? She took a ragged breath and forced herself to take it slow. *In and out.* Blake needed her. She couldn't crumble now.

Carefully making her way to the back door, Abbey took every available cover offered. Hedges, furniture, whatever the yard provided. Finally she made it next to the door and tried the knob. Unlocked.

Whoa. She hadn't expected that. Sweat broke out along her spine. Except they wanted her in there, didn't they? Had they expected her to try and sneak in? Had they thought she'd just knock on the front door and say, *"Hi, I'm here. Go ahead and kill my boyfriend now."*

Boyfriend. The word gave her pause for a few seconds. She had a boyfriend... But only if she managed to keep him alive.

Abbey stuck her head in the door to listen. Nothing. No lights either. She strained to see the small laundry room as she stepped into the house. Her eyes adjusted to the dark. To the left, a hallway led downstairs, to the right was a bathroom and in front of her were more stairs leading up. She nearly got to the first step when a giant hand closed over her mouth from behind. She sucked in air to scream.

"It's me," Blake whispered. "Abbey, it's me."

She sagged in relief against the heat of his chest then spun in his arms and hugged him tight.

He gasped and she pulled back. Oh God, they'd beaten the

hell out of him. One eye was nearly swollen shut. His lip was cut and swollen, his jaw and forehead bruised. "Shh," he pulled her close. "I'll be okay. It's okay. Shit, Abbey, you shouldn't have come."

"I had to. C'mon, let's get out of here." She tugged him toward the door, but he held her back.

"They're watching." Even as he spoke, she heard footsteps upstairs and he pulled her up the short flight of steps and farther into the house. "They'll catch you before you get out of the yard." Fear erupted in her chest as he shoved her in the first available room and toward a closet.

NO! "I can't," she whispered, fighting his hold.

"You have to." He opened the slatted double doors and tucked her inside. "I'm going to try and distract them both, but if they split up, then one of them is going to find you." She would've freaked out at his words, but he slipped the gun into her sweaty palm and gave her something else to worry about. "As soon as this door opens... Shoot. Don't hesitate." Footsteps pounded harder from upstairs. He kissed her quick and hard. "If you've got your phone, call 911. I love you." He closed the doors and disappeared, leaving her alone and terrified and completely out of her element.

She hadn't even told him she'd left the address for Troy. Still, the cops could get here quicker. Abbey fumbled for her phone and punched 911.

"911. What is your emergency?" The operator's voice sounded like a bullhorn in the quiet space.

Abbey relayed the address and urgency as quietly as she could, then buried her phone beneath a pile of blankets next to her without cutting the connection.

Memories from nine years ago seared their way into her brain. The gag, the rope around her wrists and ankles, the pain from the violation of her body, scratches from his jagged fingernails that cut into sensitive tissue. Abbey crouched low into the corner and wrapped her arms around her knees. The gun weighed a ton in her hands. Her muscles trembled out of control as she waited and listened.

Heavy footsteps sounded deeper in the house. The rumble of low voices frayed her nerves.

She held her breath and swallowed the urge to run, screaming for help. Blake must have had a plan. He wouldn't dump her in here and run without her.

Time to pull her head out of her ass and come up with a plan of her own. Abbey wiped the sweat off her palm and white-knuckled the gun handle. She'd been stashed in a closet before, but this time she had a gun. This time, she wasn't a child and this time, she wouldn't let her fears rule her decisions.

Chapter Twenty-Four

Blake had a plan. Keep the assholes away from Abbey.

Granted, it was kind of sketchy at the moment, but he had the element of surprise going for him. At least for a minute or two until they found their friend. He'd known for a fact he and Abbey wouldn't make it out the backyard, because he seriously doubted his ability to get over any wall in his current condition, and Abbey wouldn't leave him behind.

Rolling into a Hummer had given him bruised ribs, but the two-on-one go-round in his apartment garage had done more serious damage. His chest hurt too much to be anything less than a fractured rib or two. When Abbey had hugged him, he'd not only nearly wept in relief, but a boatload of pain as well.

Right before Abbey had entered through the back door, the walkie had squawked and the men from upstairs warned the downstairs dude where to grab her. Blake had bought an extra minute with a whispered, "Copy" into the mic. But now, as both men ran downstairs, their flashlights bobbing in the darkness, the tiny window of relief vanished in a thick fog of fear. What if they found Abbey and she didn't get a shot off quick enough? What if, what if? There were too many possibilities to consider.

Blake squinted into the darkness from his hiding spot behind the sofa. One thing in his favor. The place was mostly boarded up and clearly lacking electricity.

"What the fuck? Benz? Where are you? Check downstairs," a guy ordered.

Yeah, that voice definitely belonged to the man named Kwami. The man who'd sliced off Brendan's earlobe. He'd kept up a running conversation as he'd cut Bren. Kwami had talked about Bren's choice of studs and since they looked like shit on Bren, they should just come off. Then he'd laughed. Blake's stomach rolled as it always did when he thought about that night. It had been the worst night of his life. He'd actually felt the pain in his own ear at the same time. It had been a weird-ass feeling.

A flashlight beam briefly illuminated another man before he moved out of sight. He was a big-ass son of a bitch. Probably one of the guys he'd tangled with in the garage and most likely the brother of the man Abbey had hurt. He needed to keep this guy miles away from her.

He didn't have much time. Once they discovered he wasn't the one tied and gagged downstairs they'd start searching the house. If he didn't take them out one at time, he wouldn't win so he had to work fast.

Kwami's walkie squawked and the other man's voice came over the line. "The kid is gone. Benz is unconscious down here. He's bleeding."

"Find them. Work your way up. I'll start here. They won't get far. He's too fucked up to go anywhere fast."

True words and Blake hated them.

At least Abbey had a weapon and could protect herself. She had a good chance if she stayed put and kept the gun in position and ready to fire.

Kwami moved into the next room, it could've been an office or den, and Blake eased from behind the sofa, his knife in hand, and stood along the staircase ready for him to come back out.

A shot rang out from Abbey's end of the house and Blake's heart stuttered. Kwami burst through the doorway and Blake didn't have a chance to do anything other than react. He slammed into him from the side and they both hit the ground, a gun skittering on the hardwood floor. Fire sizzled in Blake's chest as he slashed up with his knife the same way he'd done with the man downstairs. He came away with the knife and they tussled as he tried to land a second blow.

Another shot rang out, but this one split the wood floor right next to him. "Don't move a fucking muscle or she dies," a voice said.

Kwami took the moment of Blake's hesitation to slam him with a fist, and Blake landed hard on his side. Fresh fire ate up his chest and he struggled for air. He still had the knife in his hand underneath him. The other guy had Abbey in front of him, his arm wrapped around her neck and her hands fighting his beefy arm so she could breathe. Kwami swayed as he stood and just then seemed to notice his wound. "What the fuck? I'm bleeding."

"Join the fucking club. Bitch shot me in the shoulder," the second guy said. He kept his gun aimed at Blake. "I won't miss this time."

"No!" Kwami said. "This prick is mine." A murderous look morphed his face into rage and Abbey screamed as he moved toward Blake. She dropped, dead weight in the guy's arms and that's all Blake saw before Kwami came at him. The man grabbed his collar and pulled his fist back and Blake struck out with his blade, nailing him on the same side, deep and hard. Kwami landed the punch and pain exploded in Blake's head as he hit the floor again, but as Kwami went to grab him a second time, the man teetered and looked down. Blake must have hit something vital because blood gushed out of the wound. Kwami swayed right before something slammed into his head and knocked him sideways. He fell hard, out cold and Blake looked up.

A woman staggered back, holding a fireplace poker in a death grip. He spotted Abbey next. She stood by the wall, a bloody knife locked in her hands as, wide-eyed, she waited for the man on the floor to attack. Holding his throat, he tried to stem the blood seeping through his fingers as he gasped for air.

Blake put his palm out to the woman, barefoot, brunette and filthy in a sequined top and black skirt. "It's okay," he croaked, rolling over gingerly to get to his knees.

She grabbed the banister for support as she looked around. "Where are they? There's more of them." She sounded on the verge of hysteria as she lifted the poker again, her gaze scanning the rooms surrounding the staircase.

"This is it. It's okay."

She took a ragged breath before easing down to the steps. "I want to go home now." She looked up at him with tortured eyes as if he could just whisk her away and grant her wish like some cosmic genie.

Where the hell had she come from?

"Help's coming," he told her as sirens stopped in front of the house. "Abbey." Blake barely got her name out as he crawled toward her just as cops burst into the room, their weapons drawn as they yelled out orders. None of which registered with Blake. All that mattered was seeing Abbey alive.

Abbey rushed to him, her eyes bright with panic and fear. "Lie down, lie down. Don't move!" She eased him down with his head in her lap and she stroked her fingers through his hair. God, it felt good. Every stinking inch of him was on fire, but her touch gave him a comfort that nothing else ever could.

"Hey." Troy crouched next to him. "Paramedics are on their way in. You doing okay?"

"Don't I look okay?" Blake mumbled, his jaw clenched tight against the pain.

"You look like shit, kid." He pinned Abbey with a hard gaze. "And you...you're in a boatload of crap. Just wait until I tell Julie what you did."

"Leave her alone," Blake said. "She saved my bacon." He glanced up to find her smiling down at him, her eyes bright with tears.

"I think we saved each other's bacon," she whispered. "It's a good thing I like bacon."

"Another joke..." Blake grinned through his swollen, split lip. "She should get her own show on Comedy Central." A tear slipped down Abbey's cheek and Blake squeezed her hand.

"Don't cry," he told her. "S'gonna be okay." The room started to spin too much for his liking.

Paramedics came in and Troy moved back as they crouched next to Blake. "How ya feeling?" one guy asked as he took his pulse. Another guy readied a needle for an IV.

"Prolly about as good as I look." Everyone's heads started moving with the room and Blake saw the writing on the wall. "Don't mind me. I think I might just pass out for a sec." His words got thick and slow on his dry tongue. "I'll catch...you all...lat—"

Stephanie's alive. Stephanie's alive. The words ran a continuous loop in Kim's head.

Leo pulled up to the emergency room and she hopped out while he found parking. She told the nurse behind the glass partition that she was Stephanie's sister and they let her in.

Kim found her sitting up on a bed in the last treatment room, a blanket covering her from the waist down. Her breath caught when she saw Stephanie's face. The fading bruise along her cheekbone and the dark circles under her bloodshot eyes said she'd been through hell. She wore the same clothes from the last night they spent together in Carl's club. Stephanie's face crinkled up as Kim moved toward her and pulled her close.

"You're safe now," Kim whispered. It was the only thing she could say. As much as she wanted to know what happened, she didn't want to push Stephanie into reliving whatever trauma she'd been through. "You're safe." She noticed the IV that fed into Stephanie's hand and could only imagine the antibiotics and any other medications she'd need to counteract disease.

Stephanie wiped her eyes and pulled back. "I think they're going to keep me tonight for observation. Then I can leave tomorrow with some preventative meds."

"That's good." Kim gave her a reassuring smile, trying her best to be positive.

"The police asked a lot of questions about Carl," Stephanie said.

"What kind of questions?"

"Like...did I know his VIP table at the club had several microphones placed in the booth?"

Kim's eyes widened as she rifled through memories of their conversation in the club. "So Carl heard you talk about his mistress and that you planned to divorce him?" The implication kicked in. "You're telling me the police think he was the one who arranged to have you kidnapped?" That seemed like a stretch.

"Apparently, my husband is involved in more than I thought. Since he wasn't sure what I knew besides his affair, they think he opted to just get rid of me. And make a profit while he was at it."

Stephanie wrapped her arms around Kim's waist and they held each other tight.

Kim couldn't believe Carl would go to those lengths. Actually...come to think of it, she could. It was just scary as hell. "Where is Carl?"

"He's on his way. You beat him here. I think the police plan to arrest him." Her bottom lip trembled. "I called my sister and she thinks I should stay with her for a while. She's making airline reservations for me tomorrow. She wants me as far away from him as possible."

"Wow. New York. Tomorrow." The surprises kept coming.

A few minutes later, the nurse came in with a rape kit and asked Kim to leave.

Kim found Leo outside the double doors of the E.R. leaning against the wall. She didn't think too much about it when she walked right into his arms and let him hold her. His solid warmth gave her security she hadn't realized she needed until right that moment.

Two days later, Leo drove Stella to LAX with Kim sitting shotgun. He buzzed into the lot nearest her terminal, parked, shut the car down then ran a nervous hand through his hair.

Kim had spent nearly every minute with Stephanie before taking her to the airport yesterday. Carl had been arrested not long after Kim and Leo turned in the flash drive. Incriminating evidence implicating him and his partner—a man named Michael Facinetti, who was part of a large crime family—in a human trafficking ring led the judge to deny his bond. Investigators had found hidden microphones at his private booth in the club and theorized that Carl heard Stephanie talking to Kim that last night before she disappeared. He worried that she'd not only discovered his mistress, but his illegal activity as well. Police were still searching for Facinetti.

With nothing left to keep Kim in town, this was the big goodbye. There'd been no melodramatic moments from their other night together. Kim acted like the sex never even happened. Like she hadn't blown his mind under the sheets. Or out of them.

"You're sure you can't stay longer? I'll double your salary," he said. It was possible he already tried this route, but he was willing to try again.

Kim canted her head to the side. "I don't think I had a salary to start with," she reminded him with a soft smile. She got that pitying look in her eyes and Leo looked out the window as he wiped his palms against his jeans to keep from reaching for her. A giant sinkhole began opening up in his chest and with it came a feeling of abandonment that Leo had never experienced. "Besides, I don't want to be around for another earthquake. You couldn't pay me to live in this city." She exhaled a short breath. "You're going to be fine," she told him quietly. "You can call me anytime you want. Day or night."

Sure, he could call her, but would he ever see again? "As long as I remember the time difference," Leo replied.

She grinned and her pretty green eyes sparkled. "It would be nice, but if you don't, I won't hold it against you. Not unless it becomes a habit." She patted his knee. "You're going to be all right. You've already got people interested in all the properties. You'll get those sold off and we'll take it one step at a time."

But she wouldn't be here to help him with it. He wasn't comfortable sharing this crap with anyone on his team and he didn't want pity from his few real friends. Kim had worked her butt off and methodically taken the steps to keep him out of financial hot water.

He had to downsize. Dramatically.

The one thing he couldn't budge on was the Marion Institute, but he still hadn't mentioned it to Kim. He was still in the hole for forty-one grand with them too. His stomach cramped.

She checked her watch. "I guess I should get going," she said, but she didn't make a move to leave.

"Yeah. Security can be a bitch sometimes." They'd left extra early in case of traffic and they'd breezed in with plenty of time to spare.

Kim unfastened her seat belt and turned toward him. "Maybe that movie offer you were telling me about will come through. That should help even you out a little more." She hesitated as if she meant to say something, but got out of the car instead. Leo pulled her bag from the backseat and turned to find her standing next to him. "Thank you," she said.

He didn't expect to hear that. "Why are you thanking *me?* All I did was put you to work—for no money I might add."

Her soft smile cut a path of something warm and unfamiliar through his heart. "You gave me a place to stay after..." She looked down. "You put me up and took me shopping—"

"Where I made you buy clothes that cost the equivalent of your next vacation."

"Shut up," she said, smacking his chest, but she was laughing and he liked that. She had a great laugh. Low and husky. It matched the rest of her very sexy self. She straightened his collar and her fingers lingered. Then her green-eyed gaze locked onto his.

Leo took her hand and held it against his chest. Usually, he couldn't get away from a woman fast enough after he slept with her. But he'd never run across a woman who wanted to get away from him.

"So I guess I should go," she whispered, but she glanced at his lips and heat simmered under his skin.

"Yeah," he said. Only he didn't mean it. Maybe he could keep her here, maybe if he... Leo bent his head and she leaned up and before he knew it, their lips brushed in a soft tantalizing taste. He still had her bag in one hand and couldn't—fuck it—he dropped the bag and wrapped an arm around her waist, bringing her flush against his chest as he took the kiss into hotter territory. Tonsil territory.

He let go of her hand just so he could wrap her up tight in his arms and feel her heat. One of her warm palms cupped his nape while the other fisted the collar she'd recently tried to fix. Everything faded away except the taste and softness of the woman in his arms. The way she kissed him back with the same amount of need, the same desire.

A couple of flashes and clicks brought Leo out of the moment and he looked up to see a guy with a camera. One more flash that nearly blinded Leo and the kid took off running.

"Great," he muttered.

"Who was that?" Kim asked. She cleared the husky out of her voice.

"Paparazzi, probably." He looked at her. "Sorry about that. Be prepared to be page one of a rag magazine."

She shrugged it off. "Whatever. I'm nobody. Doesn't matter. And I'm leaving," she reminded him. She started to pull away, but he wouldn't let her go.

"Wrong." He searched her eyes. "You aren't a nobody to me."

Her soft smile cut that same path deeper in his chest. "I better not be after the past week. I better be your best friend. Or at least a good friend."

That's what it was. She'd become his friend. He admittedly

didn't have too many of those. But Kim had forced him to sit down with her and she'd shown him everything he'd been too busy or bored or not interested enough to learn when it came to his money. She'd forced him to grow up.

He nodded. "A great friend," he said. A great friend he'd laughed with and made love to. "And to think you didn't like me," he said, teasing her as he nuzzled his nose against hers.

"Yeah, just goes to show you that I am occasionally wrong about things." She leaned up and gave him a soft kiss. He was a heartbeat away from diving in for another hot, slick tonsil tango when she stepped out of his arms and reached for her bag.

He snagged it out of her hands. "I've got it. C'mon, I'll walk you in."

"You told me you hate airports," she said, falling into step next to him. "You don't have to walk me in. I'm a big girl."

"Trust me. I know that. I want to."

The mile-long security line gave Leo a few more minutes with her. The people around them asked for pictures and autographs.

Kim grabbed his shirt and tugged him close after the last few left. "Go home. I know you don't want to be here."

Wrong. He wanted to be wherever she was even if he had to put up with strangers. "We're almost at the end. I'll take off when they send you through. Another ten yards." God, he was pathetic…and so fucking scared to face this mountain without her.

She looked torn. Maybe he had half a chance of her changing her mind. "You'll call those numbers I left on your desk and finalize the pick-ups for the auction items?" A subject he didn't want to talk about.

He caught her gaze and nodded. "Check. Numbers on the desk. Finalize the pick-ups. Anything else?"

"The list is in the file on the desk. You can't miss it."

They moved up in line and Kim reached up and kissed him softly. "Go," she said at his lips. "Go home."

The place that wouldn't be his home much longer. He hated the sympathy in her eyes.

Fuck that.

He slapped on the Leo smile that wooed millions of women around the world. "I'll see you around," he said with a casualness that implied they'd never made love or kissed or done anything else that two people who had been highly intimate would do. He sauntered out of the line and walked out of the sliding doors without a backward glance.

Just one more Oscar winning performance.

Chapter Twenty-Five

Ten days after the ordeal, Abbey slipped into Blake's old room at his parents' house. His bruises had almost all healed thanks to his mother's holistic cream. The royal blue paint brought out the color of his eyes as he eased up against the headboard of the double bed. Tons of trophies, pictures and sports books filled the giant oak bookcase on the sidewall.

After his five-day hospital stay, his mom had insisted he come home to recuperate. Blake hadn't argued. He'd told Abbey no one argued with his mother when she gave *the finger*. Her index finger. She didn't use it often, but Abbey had learned that when Terry St. John stuck that thing out and gave her famous narrow-eyed stare, it meant the recipient was in for a Battle Royale. Still Blake insisted this was his last night at home and wanted back in his apartment. Abbey suspected he wanted privacy so he could ease the ache he'd been talking about, an ache that only she could relieve.

"Your man parts can wait a few more days," she'd scolded last week. Besides, his two cracked ribs still made it tough for him to move, and she didn't see any chance in hell of being intimate with him for at least a week, and more like three.

His face lit up when he saw her. The cuts and bruises had faded. So had hers. The man she adored with all her heart patted the bed next to him. "Are you the evening shift? Because I am in dire need of some TLC."

Abbey bent low and kissed his lips lightly before sitting next to him. "Not only am I the evening shift, but your mother and father are going out for dinner and a movie. You're going to be stuck with only me for about the next four hours."

Blake's jaw nearly hit his chest. "What? Are you serious?"

She practically saw the word *sex* written across his eyeballs as he reached for her and she deftly batted his arms away. "They're still here. Your mom's getting ready, then she's coming in to tell you to behave while they're gone."

Blake scoffed. "She's not the boss of me."

"Yes, she is," his father said from the hallway as he walked past the room. "She's the boss of all of us," he called as he trudged downstairs.

Abbey could totally see how his mom ruled the kingdom. She'd watched how all of Blake's brothers had been on their best behavior in her presence and saved the brotherly trash talk for when she left the room. It wasn't that Terry was mean in any way, but she expected the best from her boys and the people they chose to bring into their lives. Abbey lifted an eyebrow. "I do not want to get on your mom's bad side."

"Pfft. She loves you. Are you kidding me? You're her favorite kind of person."

"Oh, yeah?" Abbey's hopes sparked. Though they'd both been fixtures at Blake's hospital bedside, their conversations had revolved more around Blake. "What kind of person is that?"

"The kick-ass kind." Blake grinned up at her. "Tell me again." The unmistakable pride in his eyes made her feel a hundred feet tall. She couldn't believe this gorgeous man belonged to her.

Glancing at the ceiling, Abbey shook her head. Her first retelling of the story had been scary, but the more she told it, the braver she became. "No. You've heard it a dozen times already, I'm not telling you again."

He stuck his bottom lip out in a little boy pout. "Please." He pulled her closer and kissed her softly. "One last time and I won't ask you ever again."

That was a new one. "Really? Not ever again?"

Blake tipped his head from side to side. "Well, I mean, you'll have to tell our grandkids."

What! Abbey leaned back, her eyes wide. "What are you talkin' about, boy?"

Laughing, Blake grabbed his chest. "No fair. You can't make me laugh. It hurts." He flustered her faster than anyone else on the planet.

She stood up next to the bed. "You can't throw out a bomb like that and not expect a big reaction. We're not even official yet," she added.

His smile vanished and his blue eyes softened. "We are most definitely official, Ab." He reached for her hand and brought her back down on the bed. "I am officially yours from now until the end of time."

Heat blazed into Abbey's cheeks. "Blaaake." He was the sweetest, most amazing man in the world.

"Abbeeeey," he said back. He stroked a lock of hair off her cheek. "Tell me," he whispered.

Goose bumps rose along her arms when he touched her like that. "Fine." He wanted to hear about that minute in the living room when she'd been in that dickwad's grasp and Kwami had gone after him. "I told you I had the knife in my purse, which was around my neck the whole time. He didn't even think about frisking me. He found me in the closet and I shot him, but not enough to do serious damage. His left arm wasn't working very well since I shot his shoulder. He not only had his gun in his right hand, but he had that same arm around my neck. I thought Kwami was going to kill you and I had to remind myself to be on the offensive, not the defensive, so I went limp. I thought if I could force him down then shoot back up again, I could knock his head back and throw him off balance long enough to reach for the knife in my purse."

"And where'd you get that brilliant idea?" Blake asked, the smile back on his face.

"I happened to see someone's boot that had a knife in it and it gave me the idea to carry one myself."

"Must be one smart person." He lifted a dark eyebrow twice and made her laugh.

"Anyway," she went on. "I reached for the knife. I don't even remember slicing him. I just remember yanking it out and up and spinning at the same time. The next thing I knew he was on the floor holding his neck." She shuddered and doubted she'd be able to retell this story so many times if the man hadn't survived. Somehow, she'd missed his jugular and because paramedics arrived at the scene so fast, he'd survived, just as Kwami had. "I'm just glad it's over." At least until the trial started. But that was many months away.

"I still can't believe Paul Facinetti's cousin was part of the whole ring. Makes me wonder if anyone in that family is on the up and up."

"It explains how they knew about the Santa Monica house," Abbey said. "It was the perfect place to hide out since it's all boarded up. I just wish they'd find that cousin already."

"That makes two of us."

"Did Troy ever say whether it was Wyncott or Facinetti who found out about their accountant's knack for stealing their money?" Abbey asked.

Blake shook his head. "Not yet. Wyncott hasn't said anything and Michael is still underground." He squeezed her hand. "I don't want to talk about them anymore. They give me heartburn." The look in his eyes as he watched her was pure pride. Pure love. "C'mere," he whispered and she leaned over and gave him a soft kiss.

"Blake," his mom said from the hallway before entering his room. Abbey pulled away quickly and stood next to the bed as Terry came in. Dressed in straight leg jeans with awesome black high-heeled boots and a black, flowing shirt that accentuated her beautiful figure, Blake's mom looked almost half her age. "Listen to Abbey while we're gone. We'll be home around eleven."

"Mom, I'm not ten." Blake rolled his eyes like a ten year old and Terry lifted her brows at Abbey as if to prove her point. A look only a mother could pull off. To which Blake rolled his eyes again. Abbey bit back the urge to smile. She not only loved Blake but she was growing to love his parents too.

"Abbey, can I talk to you for one minute?" Terry motioned her out to the hallway and Abbey's heart suddenly chugged faster.

Uh oh. What did she do? Was she in trouble with Terry?

In the hallway, Terry linked her arm with Abbey's. Even in those heels, Abbey had her by a couple of inches. "My son is completely in love with you, you know that right?"

Had Blake told her that? Or was it that obvious? Abbey swallowed. "Um…" No reason to lie. "Yes."

"And you feel the same way about him?"

She watched Terry's serious blue eyes for any sign of what might be in store, but had no clue where this was going. "Yes."

He'd helped her become the kind of woman she'd always wanted to be. Someone able to reach out and grab all life had to offer. "I love him very much."

Terry nodded and a smile broke over her face. She winked. "I kind of thought so, but I wanted to be sure. I love my kids more than anything Abbey and I'll do anything for them. And for the people they choose to love. So from now on, our home is your home. Your problems are our problems. We're a unit and even if the boys don't live here anymore, we stick together. Blake told me your parents moved to North Carolina a couple of years ago, so if you're ever feeling like you need a mother's shoulder to cry on or just some girl time, you can always call me."

A fresh sense of belonging hit Abbey straight in the heart. "Thank you," she replied. To be included so unconditionally in such a close family made her chest tight. She missed her parents and Bernie like crazy so this offer meant the world to her.

"Terry, let's go or we're going to miss the previews," Blake's father, Jay, yelled from downstairs.

Terry hugged her and whispered something in her ear before saying good night and rushing down the hallway.

Abbey watched her, her jaw nearly on the floor as her brain registered the message. The kitchen door slammed shut a minute later and she walked back to Blake's room, still in shock.

After a quick glance at her, his eyes narrowed. "Uh oh. What happened? You've got that look on your face."

She closed the door behind her and sat next to Blake. "They left."

"They left?" His eyebrows lifted and he reached for her so fast, Abbey shrieked as she landed on his chest. He grunted, but didn't stop from his objective, which—turned out—involved kissing her lips. Very thoroughly. Very, very thoroughly.

She didn't fight him since—number one—she didn't want to hurt him worse, and—number two—she'd missed kissing him like this. She felt his immediate response as his erection grew against her stomach. He groaned into her mouth as she rubbed herself along the hard ridge. His fingers tunneled through her hair as his tongue circled around hers in a happy yet frustrated dance.

"I want you so much, Ab. I've missed you like crazy." He brought her head down again and proved his point with another nuclear meltdown of a kiss as his tongue explored her mouth. He pulled back as if he remembered something. "Wait. What happened? Are you okay? What'd my mom say?"

The fact that he stopped because he thought something was wrong made her love him that much more. "Your mom loves you a lot, you know that?"

He nodded, his eyes narrow and suspicious. "Yeaahhh." He drew the word out. "Aaannd?"

Abbey felt her cheeks heat again. "She said you're probably not ready to have sex, but that won't stop you and no matter what you said that I need to be on top because your ribs aren't ready for you to be there."

Blake's face turned bright red and he closed his eyes. "She didn't."

Laughing for the first time, Abbey touched her forehead to his. "She did. I didn't think I was hearing her right and she just walked down the stairs like it was an everyday conversation." Abbey stroked her thumb across Blake's cheek, loving the way his hands moved along her shoulders and arms, loving the emotion she saw in his eyes. "She's pretty awesome."

"She's embarrassing," Blake grumbled.

Looked as if she needed to get his mind off his momma. Abbey buried her head in his neck and kissed the spot below his ear. "I like her. Don't worry about it." She traced the shell with her tongue and felt the renewed interest of his erection prodding her stomach. "I think you're just going to have to be patient with me since I have no clue what I'm doing."

"Ab, baby, you're doing just fine. Just fine."

She eased her hand across his hip and under his boxer briefs and took satisfaction in his sharp inhale when she wrapped her fingers around his hot flesh. "Do you have any condoms around?" she asked as she bit gently on his ear lobe.

He moaned. "God, yes. In the side pocket of my toilet kit in the bathroom."

Abbey was up and back in a flash, minus most of her clothes. She took the sheets down, took his underwear down and kneeled between his legs. His thick, hard penis could've pounded nails. "That really is very impressive," she said, glancing at his raging erection as she ripped open the foil packet. She studied the condom before slowly rolling it over him. Hand over hand she brought it down and sheathed him, and he leaned his head against the pillow in sheer ecstasy. She laughed when a short and simple "Gah" escaped his lips. She pulled away to strip off her underwear, but he caught her hand in his. "Straddle me. Legs apart." He beckoned her with an index finger. Must be hereditary. "Over here." He brought her over him until their mouths were a fraction of an inch apart. Abbey kept most of her weight on her arms.

That he would touch her everywhere was a given. The fact that she wanted him to was a new, happy, almost giddy expectation.

"I may be moving slow, but I'm still moving." He eased her bra off as his hands caressed her skin in a sensual exploration. He cupped her head and brought her lips against his in a slow wet kiss of need, a kiss of love. He palmed her ass and guided her so she rubbed against him in a blistering preamble of the real thing. Hooking her underwear in his thumbs he eased them down over her hips and ass. "Out of these," he murmured between kisses and Abbey felt a surge of moisture between her legs. A tiny shudder ran through her and Blake pulled back. "You okay?"

She saw the concern in his eyes. The worry that he was going too fast or touching her too much. That maybe her shudder had been about fear and not excitement. But she'd changed in the last few weeks. Not only had Blake and his love changed her, but her ability to fight and stand up for herself had changed her too. She was a stronger person because of the past few weeks and if any good thing had come from the horror of it all, that would be it.

"I'm doing great," she whispered at his mouth. She teased her lips across his. "I'll be doing better when I get the hang of this." A newly familiar ache throbbed between her legs and she rubbed against Blake to ease the pressure.

"Trust me, you will." His fingers tunneled between them and she gasped as he found her G-spot so effortlessly. The more he circled and rubbed the wetter she got. "I love those little sounds you make when I touch you here," he said, sliding a finger over her clit. She gasped and felt his smile against her lips.

"Blake, show me," she whispered. She wanted on him, wanted him in her.

"Are you sure?" He looked so serious, his brows slanted

down and his gaze searching her face. "I want you to be sure."

God, she loved him. "I'm sure." She shifted a fraction and took the tip of his finger inside her. She moaned at the rising hunger cresting inside her, the need to feel more of him deeper.

Watching her, he pushed his finger inside her slow and deep and Abbey moved her hips to meet his gentle thrust. "Feel how wet you are?" he asked quietly before a soft kiss. Blake added another finger and Abbey moaned into his mouth as he pushed her higher. His hand pushed her farther to the finish, made her crazy with desire. "Blake." She moaned his name. "I need... I want..."

"What? Tell me what you need, what you want."

"You. Please. Just all of you inside me. Please. Now."

Blake held her hips and Abbey positioned herself over the tip of his erection. She eased down on him slowly, letting the invasion stoke her senses, stretching the moment into forever. He gritted his teeth and she didn't know if he hurt or if he felt the same incredible sensations she did.

"You okay?" she barely got the words out as he pushed inside with a fresh thrust.

"Über-epic," he huffed. "You?"

An unexpected laugh gusted out and she froze with him halfway inside her. "I'm going down," she warned him. "All the way."

Sweat trickled down his hairline and told her exactly how much effort he was putting into the process. He nodded and grinned. "Three of my favorite words. 'I'm going down.' You can make a note of that if you—" He gasped because she pushed down and took him deep. "Easy, easy," he coaxed, but she laughed because he was too late.

She circled her hips and arched her back, loving the fullness between her legs, the way his hands stroked over her back and ass and her sides. He kept touching her, all of her and Abbey had never known anything as wonderful. Lifting up slowly, she relished the size of him, then she pushed down again and sighed. "Oh God, this is so good," she murmured. "I can't believe I've been missing out on this."

"Makes two of us," he panted and she laughed again. His smile melted her. "Sit up," he told her. "Hold my hands if you need the balance."

Abbey kissed him softly before adjusting on top of him. She sat up and felt him sink impossibly deeper. He linked their fingers as he pushed up a fraction and gritted his teeth.

"Don't move," she told him, worried about the pain she saw etched in his face. Before he could argue with her, she lifted up and sank down, sending them on a pleasure ride so sweet, she did it again. And again, and again, and again. She moved faster and harder as the sweet friction built to a breaking point. Her heart thumped hard and sweat slicked her skin.

"Ab, you gotta come. I can't wait. It's too good. You're too..." He didn't finish as he clenched his jaw, but he let go of her hand and pushed his thumb on her clit and the pressure that had been building, the urge to reach for that absolute perfect place, exploded into a giant bomb of euphoria. Wave after wave of bliss drenched her from within and as those waves crested, Blake groaned and his own climax had him squeezing her hips tighter as he pumped hard inside her.

The intimacy, the absolute power of her love for this man filled her with a feeling of peace she hadn't known in over a decade. With his patience, Blake brought her happiness. With his love, he made her whole.

Tears stung her eyes as Abbey looked down at him and seeing his eyes wet with moisture she eased over him and kissed him softly. Though she wanted to stay connected to him, stay on top of him, she knew he hurt, so she lifted off and curled into his side.

"I love you," he whispered softly before kissing her forehead. "I love you."

Abbey looked up and stroked her thumb over his jaw. The love in his eyes gave her a new starting place. With Blake next to her, she had a new life, a new reason to be, a chance to live and not be afraid. She leaned up on her elbow and gave him another gentle kiss. "Thank you."

His lips curled into a half grin. "For what?" his voice sounded husky and sexy and that spot between her thighs tingled with a little aftershock.

"For being patient with me. For waiting. For loving me even though..."

"Don't finish that sentence." He eased some hair behind her ear. "There's no 'even though.' It's you and me from now on.

Nothing we can't tackle as long as we're together. I mean it. This is it." He paused as he thought about something. "In fact, this is so it, that if I had a ring right now, I'd ask you to marry me."

Abbey's smile dropped off her face. "What?" She shifted away from him because that was more news than she was willing to process. First he mentioned grandkids and now he spouted marriage. The guy was—

"Don't freak out on me." Blake pulled her back. "Jeez. You say the M-word and everything goes for shit." Humor lurked behind his serious expression. "I'm not proposing. At least not this second. But I would if I had a ring. You deserve it the right way. Something big. Something special." He grinned with a definite devil sitting on his shoulder. "When you least expect it, I'm gonna go big."

Abbey's insides nearly burst out of her, but she played it calm. "So I'd better have the right answer then, I guess, huh?"

His humor disappeared in an instant. "Damn straight. There's only one answer. You know that, right? Only one I'm willing to accept."

She nodded, her heart full. "Yes."

He nodded, too, one short shake. "That's the one. C'mere."

Abbey held back. "You know I love you, too, right. For real."

"Yeah." He smiled, the love in his eyes mirroring that in her own. "I know." Blake set his mouth on hers and Abbey sunk into his kiss, knowing she'd found the one man who'd give her everything she'd need for the rest of her life.

Epilogue

Two weeks later

Blake sat in a room with a dozen actors, waiting for Abbey. Most of them seemed to be here for another audition in an adjoining studio. He'd been getting out more and more and this little excursion gave him an excuse to be with Abbey. She'd been juggling dance jobs and auditions, and Julie and he only saw her at night when she came home exhausted.

But she always had time for him. No matter how tired either one of them were, they collided in bed like supercharged magnets. He couldn't wait to set eyes on her or be inside her, couldn't wait to talk about her day or hear her call his name as she came.

Troy had called him whipped.

To which Blake replied, "It takes one to know one."

Abbey came out of the room twelve minutes later, the queen of poker faces. She snagged his hand as she bee-lined for the door, tugging him behind her.

"How'd it go?" he asked as he lengthened his stride to catch up to her.

She hit the door with a thud, but once they got outside, she jumped into his arms. Fire speared through his still-sore chest, but he laughed. Loved that this woman let him in, and that she trusted him. "It went great. Fine. As good as it could." She kissed him...the kind of kiss usually reserved for their nightly meetings in bed. "But now I'm going to be practical. I have no control, so I'm going to forget about it." With one last quick kiss, she jumped out of his arms.

His eyebrows lifted high his forehead. "I'm glad you can forget about it because I sure as hell can't." This was the last round. The final callback. Abbey had even had to sign all the contracts in case they chose her. It was as far as she'd ever gone for a job and a part.

She gave him a wicked dirty smile. "We'll see if I can't do something to take your mind off it later." One eyebrow arched up and his dick caught wind of the implication. Knowing him as well as she did, Abbey glanced down at his crotch and shook her head. "That bad boy needs to stay under wraps until tonight." She laughed at his pout.

It wasn't that funny.

Abbey punched the speed dial on her phone. "I'm out. Did you need anything before I come back?" It must have been Julie. "It went great." She grinned and listened. "Really? Are you sure?" Then she checked her watch. "Okay. See you tomorrow... Yeah, he's here." She listened again. "Really? Okay, I'll tell him." She pocketed her phone and turned to him. "I have the rest of the day off."

"Wow. Good for you. I guess some people are special." He took her hand as they strolled back to his SUV.

"You also have the rest of the day off."

That stopped him in his tracks and he turned to her. "What?"

"You heard me. We're free birds. What should we do? Go to a movie, go out to dinner, go—"

He yanked her forward and crushed his lips over hers. She sputtered and laughed before falling into his kiss like a wicked woman should. "We're going back to your place and we're fucking like bunnies all night long."

"The romance never ends with you," she said, settling another kiss on his lips.

"I try."

Two hours later, they were sweaty and happy on Abbey's wrecked bed. Her cell phone rang.

"Let voice mail get it," Blake said, barely able to move after the last orgasm.

Abbey laughed into her pillow before dragging the phone off the night table. "I can't. It might be—" She bolted up like a rocket. "My agent. Shit, it's my agent. Hello," she said.

Blake sat up, too, his ribs still brutally sore, but the pain was worth every minute he got to be with Abbey. Watching her face as she listened was killing him.

"They did?" she asked, untangling her legs from the sheet. "Oh." This time she wasn't as happy. "Really?" she said and Blake waved her to finish. "Okay. Yes. I'll talk to you tomorrow." She listened. "Yeah. I plan on it. Thanks. Bye." She ended the call and set her phone back on the table.

"Well, what happened?" He was afraid to ask. *Did you get it?*

Abbey covered her face in her hands. Her shoulders shook visibly.

Shit. Tears.

He put a hand on her shoulder, but had no idea what to say. "Aw, Ab."

But when she wiped her tear streaked cheeks and looked up at him, she had the biggest, brightest smile on her face. "I got it! Oh my God, I got it!" She hugged him before leaping off the bed and dancing around the room, a vision of the most beautiful body he'd ever seen. Her happiness burst out of her in waves of sunshine.

Blake stood up and watched her, the love of his life, the woman he'd die for. When she came into his arms, he held her tight.

"I knew you were going to get it," he told her. "It was only a matter of time before people recognized what you have to offer."

Abbey pulled away and looked into his eyes. "You recognized it."

He nodded and grinned. "Yeah. I'm smart that way." He eased some hair behind her ear. "Look, this is a rough town. You know I'm here for you no matter what. Every step of the way."

"I know." She nodded. "And I'm not letting you go."

"Nope." He gave her an Eskimo kiss and his dick perked up as her lips brushed across his. "You are definitely stuck with me."

"Good thing since it just so happens that I'm stuck on you too."

Blake squeezed her tight, his love and pride for this woman more profound as each day passed. "I'm going to make you the happiest woman in the world," he promised, grazing his lips over her ear.

"You already have." With that, she took him down to the bed and took him on a ride he wouldn't soon forget.

The End

About The Author

After graduating high school in Texas, Dee moved to Los Angeles to pursue acting. For twenty years, she acted in television and worked behind the scenes as an acting/dialogue coach for sitcoms. Writing happened accidentally after a vivid dream and the urging of her husband to "Just write it down." Three weeks, fourteen hours a day, and four hundred and fifty (long hand) pages later, she had her first novel. Dee loves writing books filled with action, mystery and love. (Not necessarily in that order.) Her experience in show business led to her narrating many of the books in the Adrenaline Highs series for Audible.com. She is the wife of a wonderful man and mother to a fabulous daughter. She's a dog lover all the way, with a fondness towards Boxers and Pit Bulls. She is a member of several organizations, including Romance Writers of America and SAG-AFTRA.

For more information on Dee's books please visit:

www.deejadams.com